Kingdom Hill

by

Lindsay Delagair

This book is a work of fiction, Names, characters, places, and incidents are the product of the author's imagination or are used fictitiously. Any resemblance to actual events, locals, or persons, living or dead, is coincidental.

ISBN-10: 147932678X
ISBN-13: 978-1479326785

DEDICATION

To Good Friends: May we always be exactly that!
Thanks for the inspiration and encouragement. Your kindness will remain etched in my heart forever – I love you!

"A life without love is a life without reason to live."

Sarai - Kingdom Hill

ACKNOWLEDGMENTS

Adam Pawlowski – Surfing Advisor,
Karen M. Young - Editor
Lynda Elkin – Editorial Assistance

Prepublication Readers: Adam Pawlowski,
Lori Frances, Dr. Crystal Herold,
Monica Delesline, and Julie Tillett

PROLOGUE

It was a place that didn't seem to fit into the surrounding landscape. There is a natural lay to land; certain features are expected to fall into place when you've studied it all your life. Cassandra Henley knew about land. She was raised to observe, with a keen eye, the way Mother Nature arranged herself. Her family had a long history in topography, cartography, and surveying. Seven generations could be traced back to some of the original men who helped map out the United States. She was the first woman in the family to become a Geomatics Engineer and eventually the co-owner of her father's international surveying company, Henley Global Geomatics.

She put together a team of eighty of her best employees to tackle the job of remapping a large swath down the center of the United Kingdom, and although she wasn't familiar with this foreign landscape, her father once told her, land is land. Not only had her company won the bid, but she had also been highly recommended for her expertise and the pace at which she could complete a job. She would do this with her usual speed and accuracy, but for the moment, curiosity had her paused.

Three years ago, this same curiosity stopped her in the mesa in Arizona and helped her team identify a lost city of the ancient mesa inhabitants. She wasn't an archeologist, but it didn't take long when wind of something unusual in the land brought them snooping. The city had been buried in a catastrophic sandstorm thousands of years ago, leaving nothing but an unusual ridge where her knowledge told her there should only be flat land. If she'd known how much money was to be made from such a discovery, she never would have opened her mouth before exploring for herself.

There was good reason to come back to this place when she could feel comfortable to look around. She didn't know what, if anything, she'd discover. Perhaps it was just a geological anomaly, but she'd find out on her own.

"What are you looking at?" her companion asked.

She glanced at Dirk. There was no way she was mentioning this to him, but she'd have a moment's fun, "Do you see anything around here worth looking at?"

He grinned, "Take those clothes off and ask me that question again."

She smacked him hard in the chest, "Landscape, idiot, do you see anything in the landscape worth looking at?"

His gaze panned the surroundings briefly, without interest, "A big paycheck at the end of six weeks? Come on, Cass, I don't like guessing games. You take forever to pick exactly where you want to start a job; is this it or not?"

"No, we'll start at the spot I showed you about fifteen or twenty kilometers back."

"Why don't you like starting out with everyone at a motel? Wouldn't that be simpler?"

"Was there a motel twenty kilometers back?"

"Shit, no. You pick the middle of frickin' nowhere every time."

"If I do it every time, then what did you expect, the middle of London?"

"After all the aggravation you went through getting your permits from the RICS, no. And if I know you, you'll take the northern route just to avoid London completely."

A faint smile tugged briefly at the corners of her lips. He wasn't quite as dumb as he looked. "Come on, I have a lot of things to finalize before the guys fly in tomorrow, and Charlie is flying in tonight."

"You didn't. Tell me you didn't bring him along for this?"

"I love Charlie. And besides, he hates it when I leave him behind."

"He's *not* keeping me out of your bed."

"Probably not, but you will have to share. If you try to throw him out, I'll throw you out." There was no teasing in her statement. She meant every word, and she made sure he understood.

CHAPTER ONE

Cassandra waited impatiently as the Land Cruiser came to a slow stop. The insignia of the Royal Institute of Chartered Surveyors was on the door. She clenched her teeth.

"Remember to be nice to the natives," Dirk whispered through a half-grin.

"I've jumped through every hoop, filled out mountains of paper..." she started to growl when the driver's door opened, causing her to pause. She promptly replaced her scowl with a forced smile. She recognized him as one of the young men she'd dealt with when she cleared all the permits through the Institute.

Name, name, name? She had an excellent memory, but for some reason she was struggling with his name. He had been the man who spent most of his time stealing glances at her then blushing when she returned eye contact—and he was still blushing as he looked at her now. "Mister Rose," she finally said, glad that his blushing cheeks triggered the mnemonic in her head.

His blush turned scarlet. It must have surprised and impressed him that, with all the people she met at the Institute, she remembered his name. At the same moment, the passenger door opened, and a second man emerged. Unconsciously, and quite accidently, her smile became genuine. She definitely hadn't met him before because a man who looked like *that* would have stuck in her memory like a knife. His hair was dark brown and wavy over a somewhat heart shaped face, his skin had a golden glow unlike the pale English, and he had muscular arms bulging under his long-sleeved dress shirt.

She sensed her reaction to the second man caused Dirk to straighten to his full height. She turned her head slightly and gave him a wink unseen by the two approaching men, "You did say be nice to the natives."

He sighed in annoyance.

She stepped forward to accept Mister Rose's extended hand, "You're a long way from home. Please don't tell me, Mister Rose, I missed a permit."

"Call me Bobby, and no, you didn't. Everything is in perfect order. I am actually here to ask a favor."

She fought against the frown that immediately bubbled up at his statement. She only met him twice and, although he was also a handsome man, she certainly didn't owe him any *favors*. Being nice to the natives often sucked. "Really? What kind of favor?"

"Miss Henley," he said and then motioned to the man standing beside him, "this is a good friend of mine, AJ Lisowski; he's with National Geographic."

She slipped her hand into Mister Lisowski's warm, firm grip. *Nice handshake*. "National Geographic—that's pretty impressive," she still held his hand as she turned to look at Bobby, "but what does this have to do with my company working in your country?"

"He's wondering if—"

"I'd like to," Mister Lisowski interrupted with a very American dialect, "tag along with your crew to see if I can find a story in what you're doing."

She felt her eyebrows rise as she started to answer, but he spoke before she could.

"If that's okay with you?" He flashed an impressive smile, "I'm actually vacationing between projects, and when Bobby told me what you guys were doing, I thought it sounded interesting."

Dirk chuckled as he turned to walk away, "Good luck, guys."

His remark pissed her off. Of course, there weren't too many things Dirk did that didn't piss her off. Unfortunately, he was right because she did not like anyone getting involved in or, more precisely, interfering with her job.

"I don't usually—"

"I won't get in the way. You won't even know I'm around."

"Mister Lisowski—"

"Call me AJ. Mister Lisowski sounds like you're talking to my dad," he said with a small laugh.

"I would really appreciate it if you—" Bobby started to interject, but she cut him off.

"Mister Rose," she flared, dropping all friendliness, "would denying your favor affect the status of my permits with the Institute?" She believed in cutting to the chase; she didn't like kissing ass unless it involved her business, and even then she did so reluctantly.

"Oh, no—of course not," his face reddened again, "this has nothing to do with the Institute."

"I set a hard pace for my crew; time really is money. I've never allowed outsiders to get involved on a job. Our equipment is expensive, our insurance is expensive, and," she added, looking at AJ's surprised expression with distain, "I'm a real bitch when I'm working. I don't like reporters."

"I'm not a reporter," he stated sounding as if the term offended him, "I'm a writer. And I promise this isn't an exposé on your company. Give me a couple of days and if I'm getting under your skin, I'll go."

"Really? How do I know some nasty little write-up isn't going to appear next month in your magazine, or anywhere else for that matter?"

"Whoa," AJ said, putting his hands up in defense, "somehow we've started on the wrong foot. I won't put anything about your business out there unless you approve it. National Geo doesn't like lawsuits anymore than the next guy. My boss might not even be interested in an angle about an American geomatics engineer who's remapping in the UK."

Her eyelids lowered slightly as she stared at him, "Then why waste the time?"

He smiled broadly, "I told you; I'm on vacation. Wasted time might turn into money with the right story. And who knows, maybe I won't be able to keep pace with your team, and I'll pack it up after a day anyway. But if I can turn this into a story, you could get some good, free press for your company."

She studied him for a silent moment. Unless his exquisite build was fluff and steroids, he would certainly keep pace. Why did he have to be so damn good looking? There were a million reasons screaming in her head for her to look into those stunning green eyes and tell him no, but if she said no and then needed more permissions or permits from the Institute... "Fine," she blurted, actually astounded that it came out of her mouth, "you get one day for me to see if this is going to create a problem. If you distract the crew or stumble over any equipment, you're out immediately—no rebuttals, no questions."

"Great, I'll just grab my gear."

She watched as he opened the door of the Land Cruiser and pulled out a large backpack, an even larger duffle, and a camera case. She already regretted her decision. Dirk would be angry when he found out she agreed, and he'd say she only did it to try out the eye-candy standing in front of her. She felt a small, sly grin creep to the corners of her lips. Very few men looked as good as AJ Lisowski.

Hell, she sighed to herself, *he probably has a girlfriend, or, with those impish looks, maybe a boyfriend*. She studied Bobby briefly and decided he might possibly be the boyfriend. Plus, she doubted AJ was uncivilized enough to get into the base, rough stuff she liked anyway.

"I was surprised when Bobby told me you were actually camping out."

"Do you see any Holiday Inns around here?" The growling, unfriendly snap didn't hesitate to come out. She could tell her tone startled him by the look on his face. "If you're going to be with my crew, don't expect me to be sociable. We're right where I want to start tomorrow morning. We only stay outdoors when it's convenient. If you last, I'm sure we'll be in a motel soon enough." That didn't come out exactly as she planned, and she noticed, even under his great tan, his cheeks pinked.

"Thanks, Bobby," he said, turning to face his friend and shaking his hand.

"Call me and let me know how it goes." Then Bobby turned to Cassandra, "Miss Henley, it was very good to see you again, and I really appreciate you doing this for me. I'm sure AJ won't cause any problems." With that, Bobby cranked the Cruiser and pulled away.

"Frank," she yelled, "we have a *guest*. Show Mister Lisowski where he can sleep tonight then fill him in on our schedule for tomorrow." She turned to leave when she felt a light touch on her arm.

"I—I was actually hoping, after I put my stuff away, I could ask you a few questions—get to know you a little bit—for my story."

"No," came her terse response. "Frank has been with me almost two years—ask him." She turned to the lanky man who approached, "This is AJ with National Geographic. Put him on my crew tomorrow so I can keep an eye on him. Oh, and Frank, he's going to be asking you a lot of questions; make sure *I'll* like your answers."

Frank smiled, "Sure thing, Miss Cass."

She walked to the Hummer to grab her jacket. Even though it was late May, a cool evening mist was starting to roll in.

"I can't believe you agreed," Dirk stated, leaning on the fender. "You're either losing your touch for being queen of the bitches, or else you're planning to hump his brains out."

She slipped into her leather jacket as she leveled her unnerving, blue-green eyes at him then flipped her thick, honey-blonde hair out from under her collar, "Does either one of those bother you?"

"You not being a bitch anymore? I don't think I could handle it," he said with a small chuckle, but then grew serious. "And, yeah, who you spread those legs for *should* bother me, don't you think?"

"Dirk, are we married?"

"No, but—"

"Engaged?"

"No, but that's not the—"

"No claims, no games, remember? You find some little twit with a need to be ridden hard, then go for it. It's not my business; what I do isn't yours."

"Maybe I need to start making it my business," he said with a threatening tone, as he pulled her against his chest.

Suddenly, his hot mouth covered hers and he forced the kiss. She wanted to bite his tongue, but it would only serve to push him over the edge—and she didn't want *that* kind of a fight tonight.

"You should be mine, Cassie," he whispered when their lips parted.

"Wrong thing to say!" she shouted, slugging him hard in the arm.

The crew turned their direction, and all went quiet.

"Damn it, Cass—that hurt!" he yelped, rubbing his shoulder.

"Don't call me that again, or the next time it'll be your face!" She turned and headed for her tent. When she looked at the crew, they immediately looked away—the only one still staring as she disappeared under the canvas was AJ.

Within an hour, twilight descended. She could hear the men bantering with AJ as they sat around a small campfire. He was telling them tales about all the places his job had taken him as they fired back with stories of their own. Frequently, she would hear him laugh. His laugh was easily discerned from everyone else's. She liked it. It was an honest, deep-throated laugh, immediately revealing he was truly enjoying himself. She'd never heard someone whose sincerity was apparent in something so insignificant, yet so telling. She found herself smiling and waiting for the next moment it would ring out.

Her tent flap opened; Dirk ducked inside.

Charlie, her Boston terrier, growled at the intruder.

"Shut up, Charlie," he growled back.

"This isn't a good idea tonight," she snapped, as she sat up on her cot and closed the book she hadn't been reading.

"I'm sorry I called you—"

"Don't!" she said, raising her hand, "You'd be repeating a mistake."

He sat down gingerly beside her, "Why are you so tense? I know it isn't pretty-boy out there because you've been acting this way ever since we got here days ago."

She was tense—and tired. It wasn't physical exhaustion; the hard work would begin tomorrow. It wasn't the mental exhaustion that came with preparing four crews of twenty men each to work in a foreign country; she'd done that plenty of times. It was something else draining her, and she couldn't unravel the mystery. Her dad had been on her mind lately; her relationship (or lack thereof) with Dirk nagged at her, but it was more than just those two things—it was something inside her. Her hard persona felt more brittle than usual; emotional explosions were barely kept under control, and all the while, she sensed something in her carefully arranged world was getting ready to shift like an earthquake under her feet.

Her gaze drifted to Charlie, who sat nervously shivering beside her cot. He felt it, too. She often thought of herself in closer similarity to animals in that respect; they knew when something was about to happen. Just like the elephants that headed for high ground during the devastating tsunami in Indonesia, or the horses she watched in Utah that grouped together with their heads down and tails into the wind as dust devils suddenly emerged from seemingly everywhere—instinct alerted them before the event. Something in her world was about to change, and she was scared, but she'd never admit it.

"This is a big job, and—"

"You've tackled bigger."

"Yeah, well, Dad hasn't been much help this time."

"Shit, Cass, when was he ever much help?" The spark in her eyes immediately ignited, but he apologized before it set off her emotional powder-keg, "I'm sorry; I didn't mean that. We're both tense. Why spend tonight separated?" He reached over and began to massage her tight shoulders. "You need me, baby," he breathed against her ear, "and I need you. I want you, Cass. You always leave me wanting." His warm breath turned into hot kisses as he exposed her elegant neck and began exploring lower.

She moaned and tipped her head to the side, giving him better access. He didn't need any other provocation as he pushed her to recline and settled himself between her legs.

"Oh, yes, baby, yes," he whispered, as he unbuttoned her top and unhooked her bra.

His hands were large, but her breasts, full and firm, filled them. He teased her nipples between his lips as the needful sensation started to pool somewhere low in her pelvis; her hips beginning to gyrate against his jeans. She knew she was slipping away. It felt like love; it always started this way but never ended this way. She pushed at his chest, trying to put some distance between them, but it only excited him.

"Stop, Dirk, I mean it."

"You always mean it, baby, but you still want it; you still like it." His grip tightened down on her arms as she struggled beneath him, "Show me how much you *don't* want it, Cass." He gave a soft, panting laugh and then reached over and turned out the lantern.

CHAPTER TWO

At four a.m., the camp came to life as everyone pitched in to breakdown the tents and pack the gear. The sun would be up in an hour, and as soon as it was light, the teams would disperse. Cass had been up since three. She liked it when everything was quiet; she could work and plan without distractions—except for Dirk. He was still a bit of a distraction. He was acting as if he was still horny, although she couldn't believe it after the workout she gave him last night. He pestered her while she dressed, bothered her as she set up her computer, and now he was attempting to cop a feel while she fixed a cup of coffee. She had enough. She slammed her elbow into his ribs with startling force, taking the wind right out of him.

He was still sucking for air when she turned toward him, "I'd really hate to have to fire you, but if you can't keep your days and nights separate, I may have to."

He grinned through the pain as he straightened himself, "Right, I keep forgetting: boss-bitch in the morning, my bitch at night."

"I definitely am a bitch, but you can scratch your last comment; I don't belong to any man."

He opened his mouth, but she cut him off.

"Get my team leaders over here, and wipe that stupid grin off your face."

"Yes, ma'am," came his patronizing reply, as he saluted and walked away.

"Good morning."

She turned quickly toward the intruding voice to find AJ standing a few feet away. She didn't respond to his greeting; she never responded to 'good morning' unless it was spoken by someone whom she had to win over for a contract or a government favor. He looked a little disheveled and sleepy faced. "Not a morning person, Mister Lisowski?"

"Please—AJ. And actually, I'm pretty flexible. I can be a morning person or a night-owl; sleep just interferes with my style."

She laughed unintentionally then quickly tucked the moment of humor away, "Did Frank explain everything last night?"

She wasn't positive in the predawn glow, but he appeared a little embarrassed.

"Pretty much. He just didn't know whether you wanted me to work or if I was going to be free to roam to take pictures, and—"

"You'll work," she stated matter-of-factly.

"I don't know much about—"

She grabbed a handful of fine electronic devices with nickel-sized heads and short two inch stems that looked similar to dollar-weeds, "My dad invented these. They're called DSTs for disposable satellite transponders. This device," she said pulling out what looked like a small GPS, "will indicate precisely where to put the transponder. Pull the little plastic tab, shove the transponder in the dirt, or pull off the stem to stick it to rock or whatever happens to be at ground level, and then walk away to the next location. It's pretty much fool-proof."

He took one of the slender devices and twirled it between his thumb and index finger, "Yay, idiot work."

She arched an eyebrow, "Do you have a problem?"

He smiled. "No, I'm kidding. Is that a GPS?" he asked, reaching for the device in her hand.

"It's a slight modification of a GPS, so it's similar. It coordinates between the last placed transponder, the satellite, and the next placement location depending on the grid pattern. I already have it set. Don't play with the buttons," she warned.

"Did your dad invent this, too?" his tone was humorous as if he wouldn't believe her if she said yes.

"No. I did."

His smile wilted, "Oh."

If the conversation hadn't stopped cold from the look she gave him, it was going to end anyway as Dirk brought the team leaders over to her SUV.

"Okay, gentleman, six weeks of hard work starts in half an hour." She grabbed one of a dozen slender briefcases from the hood and handed the first one to Frank. "Everything you need as far as permits, permissions, identification badges, credit cards, and a small cash fund is in your crew's case. Don't use the cash unless they absolutely won't accept credit. And if you don't have a receipt, it's coming out of your pay. Keep your cell phones and computers charged at all times, and I expect the usual check-in twice a day with your coordinates. Download your readings to me by 8 p.m. And, for pity's sake, Norton, make sure you actually backup your data *before* you transmit."

"One bloody mistake," the thick necked Australian quipped, "and she's never going to let me forget it."

"That's right," she said with a sardonic smile, "because every time I remind you of the extra work you caused me, it reminds everybody else they don't want to be in your shoes. Any questions before we plant our first transponder and get this show on the road?"

"Do we get a bonus if we finish early?" one of the men asked.

She actually smiled, "We have permits and approvals for six weeks. I'd be happy to be home in four. If we can wrap-up in four weeks, you'll get six weeks' pay and a two-thousand dollar bonus."

"And if we run over six weeks?" Dirk asked.

She knew he knew the answer; he just wanted her to remind them all how much she hated to be overextended. "You'll get six weeks pay and I'll dock you for every personal expense after those forty-two days are used up, including food and lodging. Hell, I might even make you pay for your plane ticket home."

"Let's get going," one of the other men said, grabbing a briefcase.

"And by the way," she added, "Rubio put your magnetic door decals in the driver's seat of each vehicle. Have them displayed during the day, but if you're at a motel at night, keep them locked in the truck. I don't want some yahoo out there posing as a survey company—especially when it's my company."

She received a unified, "Yes, ma'am," just in time to see the first streak of sunlight burst over the horizon.

She took a transponder from AJ's hand, pulled the plastic tab, and shoved it into the ground with her shoe, "Gentleman, you're burning daylight." That was what her dad always said to christen the start of a new project, and then he would go find a place to get drunk. Cassandra didn't drink, and she also didn't put quite as much faith into her teams as her father often did. He trusted them to get done what he trained them to do without intervention; Cass preferred to keep a tighter rein. That was probably why she always finished ahead of schedule. Of course, bonuses didn't hurt, either.

"I'll take Teddy, Riley, and AJ with me. Frank, you and Desmond—"

"Put AJ with Frank and I'll go with you," Dirk tossed out.

The steam rising from her ears was almost visible, "Excuse me?" Her 5'8" frame seemed to extend a couple of inches, "You're a crew chief. I'm a crew chief. Why in hell's name would we both ride in the same truck?"

"I just thought—"

"When you own your own company, you can think. Right now, you need to get your four team members and get your ass on the road. As I was saying," she continued, still giving Dirk a hard look, "Frank and Desmond, split the other ten and let's get going."

Dirk snatched his briefcase from the hood, motioned to four of the guys and stormed off. She thought about saying something to him about his attitude, but she'd already pushed his buttons pretty hard, and although he was known for pushing back, he sucked it up this time.

"I don't want to cause any problems," AJ quietly stated, as he placed his bags into the back of her Hummer.

"Trust me; I'll let you know if you do. Dirk's attitude is his own problem."

By noon, they were twenty-four kilometers due north from where their trip began. AJ seemed to be quite adept at reading the coordinates and finding where he needed to place his next transponder. Cass spent much of her time shooting elevations with Teddy and Riley—and watching AJ on the four-wheeler.

They were close to the unusual hill, and she wanted time to do a little private exploring. The countryside in this area was sparsely populated, which was one of the reasons she'd chosen the northern heading. She preferred wide-open spaces to towns and cities. She radioed the men and told them to return to the SUV for a lunch break. Lunch today wouldn't be more than energy bars and Gatorade, but by tomorrow evening, they would be in a small town, and the food would definitely improve.

AJ arrived first, with Riley on the back of the four-wheeler, carrying the Total Station and gear. He started to drive up onto the trailer when Cass put up her hand to stop him.

"Leave it off for now. I'm going to use it while you guys have something to eat and take a breather."

"Where's Teddy?"

"He's just beyond that rise. Why?"

Riley was climbing off the back as AJ cut the front wheels the direction she indicated, "I'll go get him."

Normally, she would be quick to point out she just said she needed to use it, but he seemed to be having such a good time; she simply shrugged her shoulders and watched him leave. Within a few minutes, he returned with Teddy, and both of them climbed off.

She tucked an energy bar in her jacket pocket and was about to swing her leg over the seat when AJ asked if he could join her. The word no popped out without thought.

"I'd really love to get some pictures, but we've been too busy to—"

"Fine," she relented. He wouldn't have a clue what she was up to anyway. "But I'm driving."

"Hey, Boss," Teddy began in his deep Cajun accent, "you want me and Riley to wait on you two, or keep shooting when were done?"

"We'll be back in a little bit, so just wait for us. Teddy, throw the leash on Charlie so he doesn't try to follow me."

AJ settled in behind her, and she gunned the engine. His hands moved instinctively to her hips. The faster she went, the firmer his grip. She started to smile, and was glad he couldn't see her face. Actually, she doubted he could see anything as her hair blew backward. Suddenly, she felt one hand leave her hip and scoop her tangled blonde mane aside; then his chin came to rest on her right shoulder. She didn't expect that, and for a moment, she veered slightly off course.

His deep-throated laugh rolled up from his chest, "Sorry," he said above the roar of the engine, "I like to see where I'm going."

Damn it! Now he could see she was smiling—and for some stupid reason, she couldn't quit.

Once over the rise, the unusual hill came into full view. She circled it then parked under a large oak near a wide stream which ran from the west side. She didn't need to say anything to him; he dismounted immediately and opened his camera case.

She found a side that wasn't terribly overgrown and began her ascent. When she reached the top, she realized the hill was oddly shaped. From the bottom, it appeared rounded; however, it was actually more squared and rather steep with the exception of the uniquely shaped side from where the stream flowed. She could see for quite a distance. There was a lake to the south, and her SUV was visible to the southwest, but where was AJ? She turned and found him; he had come up the opposite side and was taking a picture—*of her!*

"I didn't agree to any photos," she growled. "Erase it."

"But if this becomes a story, I'll..."

When she was really pissed, she had been told, her expression was sharp enough to slice a throat, and by the look on his face, it was true.

He sighed and looked down at his camera, "It's a great pic. You're very photogenic." He looked up and met an even angrier intense stare, "Okay, I'm erasing it."

Her temper cooled slightly, "You already marked this area, right?"

"Yup. Strange place for a hill, though."

She couldn't believe what came out of his mouth. "Oh, really? And how long have you been a professional topographer?"

His slight remnant of a smile dissolved when she snapped at him. "Why are you so defensive? I just find it strange that, with the exception of the rises that practically make a fence around this hill, there aren't any others."

He was right. She'd been so fixated on a singular hill which didn't fit into the landscape, she hadn't noticed the peculiar features of the rises which were only apparent when viewed from the hilltop. Natural geography didn't have a habit of forming ninety degree angles—and certainly not four times. How could she have stared across the landscape moments ago and not noticed? She suddenly realized just how deep this strange new funk settling over her had become.

"I'm—I'm sorry, AJ, I didn't mean to be so sarcastic." Now she knew she was in deep shit; she actually apologized for something!

"Are you okay?"

She nodded, afraid to open her mouth at this point. Her emotions were off the charts, and she'd just apologized for something she wouldn't normally have given a second thought. *Crap, what's next? Tears?* She'd throw herself off this hill before she'd cry in front of a man. She began walking away, but he quickly caught up with her.

"I'd like to talk with you for a little bit. Frank was helpful but—"

"No."

"I was just going to ask some questions about the survey. I thought the process would be a little slower."

She sighed slightly and turned to face him, "This isn't a cadastral or boundary survey—I don't need to identify individual pieces of property and ownership—it would take friggin' years to map the whole UK."

"Then what are we surveying?"

"This is a geodetic survey. Well, it's also going to include the classic topographical survey elements, too." She sensed his confusion and knew he needed a better understanding, and (for once) she actually felt like being a little bit helpful, "We're going to make an exact mapping of contours and exact spatial positions of points on the land. It's like the base model for all other types of surveys."

"Can't you do this from a plane with sonar or radar?"

"Sure we can," she said, as she began to carefully navigate her way down the side of the hill. "My dad just finished working on one of those in South America for the Brazilian Government. And those can be accurate from a few millimeters to half a meter, but what I do is exact. TNR World Wide Communications wanted the best—and that would be me. They managed to talk Rand McNally into splitting the cost with them, so here we are." Her foot hit a loose stone, and she felt herself starting to slide when his firm grip latched onto her upper arm.

"I can manage," she said, pulling away.

"It's okay to let someone help you once in a while."

"I don't need any help," she huffed, regaining her balance.

"So, now that you've answered my survey question, how about you? Why the tough act?"

"I think you've asked enough questions," she stated, as she finally reached the bottom and started making her way around to the stream.

"I don't believe you're like this all the time. I mean, I saw a different glimpse of you at the top of the hill."

"How about today being your last day?"

"Come on Cass; let me in your head a little."

"Is being a shrink also a sideline of yours?"

"It wasn't one of my majors, but I bartend between jobs; you'd be amazed at how much psychology that employs."

She made it to the stream, and, though the stream was what she originally wanted to look at, she turned around to face him, "You're a—a bartender?"

"Did I just lower my social status?" he quipped.

"Doesn't your National Geographic gig pay enough?" Her shoe started to sink into the soft, water-soaked earth, and she could feel the cold seeping through her sock. The immediate thought distracting her from the question she just asked was that it wasn't a geo-thermal spring. This was cold water from either a natural spring or perhaps a very old artesian-type well.

"I make my living by writing and taking pictures for the magazine, but I like to keep busy."

"Yeah," she chuckled, "like working for a survey company on your vacation."

"See! That's the person I want to get to know; you dropped your shield for a minute."

The shield went immediately back in place. She turned, hands on her hips, and stared across the expanse to observe where the head of the stream roiled the surface of the water. She studied the dark source which appeared to be about eight to ten feet across. A furrow etched her brow. "This isn't right," she blurted, "it has to be man-made, but it must be really old."

"I'm not into geology, but doesn't it seem weird that the hill—"

"Seems to end on the edge of the spring?"

"Yeah."

She considered giving him a load of geological bullshit about how it was perfectly natural—just to throw him off—but she found it simply amazing that he recognized all the oddities that ninety-nine percent of the population would never notice, "It's getting late, and we're wasting time; I'll be damned if my team will have the least amount of ground covered today." She pulled her soaked foot from the edge and headed toward the four-wheeler.

"Well, you do have the smallest team—and a rookie."

She shot him a look that clearly indicated having the smallest team was no excuse, in her mind, for lack of performance.

"Can I drive?" he asked before she mounted the seat, "I hate to say it, but I think I ate a couple mouthfuls of your hair before I pulled it out of my face."

Damn asshole! He has me smiling—again! She let a little growl of frustration escape; she was going to give in to his request—and it really pissed her off. "Whatever," she said, motioning him to get on. She slid behind him and considered where she wanted to place her hands. She didn't want to be clinging to him when they pulled up to the Hummer; Teddy and Riley would be surprised enough to know she agreed to be a passenger; however, it was a great opportunity to demonstrate the kind of thighs she possessed. She fit perfectly against his rock-solid ass. She reached back, grabbed the gear rack, and then tightened down on him with her legs as if she had mounted a horse.

His head turned slightly, enabling him to see her in his peripheral vision. He had a light smile, "Ready?"

"What do you think?" It came out a little sultrier than she intended, and she was certain she saw him blush as he faced forward and hit the start button.

She set a brutal pace for the remainder of the day. The grid was set in two kilometer squares which meant a lot of driving. She decided against shooting elevations and left that to Teddy and Riley. She left AJ on the four-wheeler as she took the SUV and started placing DSTs, although it meant a lot of backtracking to help them keep up with her. By evening, they were still out in the middle of nowhere. She set up her equipment and satellite receivers and began compiling data while the guys erected the camp. She was frowning when AJ brought her a drink and settled beside her.

"Are those all the places we've been today or is that everyone?" he asked as he stared at the glowing pin-points on the screen.

She preferred to wallow in silence, but she was just too tired to argue, "That's just us. I won't get their data for another forty-five minutes."

"It looks like we did pretty well for the first day."

"Do you see me smiling?"

"Okay, I guess this means we didn't do so well."

"I have four teams of twenty men each. There are three trucks and three four-wheelers per team, except for ours. I should have four trucks and eight four-wheelers per team for better balance. If this job is going to be finished in six weeks, I'm going to end up wasting a day to get more equipment."

"Can you work more equipment into your project budget?"

"Don't tell me, please. Let me guess. You've worked in construction before, right?"

"I took a hiatus from writing about five years ago and, yeah, I had an uncle who ran a big construction company, and he needed some help. They put me in management."

"You didn't like it, did you?" she said with a light laugh.

"At first it was okay," he admitted, "but then it became just a nine-to-five job like everyone else in the world. I like a little more freedom."

"Like bartending and surveying?"

"We only go around once; I'm not afraid to try different things. What's your budget?"

"You realize most people wouldn't have the nerve to ask me that, right?" She was actually starting to like the way he could make her laugh when anyone else would have had his head bitten off. "And you honestly have a look on your face like you're expecting an answer."

"Sorry, I guess I don't know everything that's taboo about you."

"My true projections ran 3.75 million, but I padded it up to 4.5 in case I needed extras."

"Those are your costs, right? Not what you bid for the job."

"Tell me something, AJ: is any of this going to figure into your possible story?"

"Absolutely not."

"Then why ask?"

He shrugged his shoulders and smiled, "Insatiable curiosity, I guess."

"Most companies will triple their budget to arrive at a bid. When it's international or government work, those numbers go even higher. I like what I do, and I'm happy with doubling—I win most of my jobs that way—well that, and we have a hell of a reputation."

"And you're co-owner with your dad? I mean, I think it's pretty cool what you do, but you seem—ah, well, kinda young for so much responsibility."

She could feel herself retracting and regretting opening up to him—however miniscule it had been. The hard expression she normally wore returned, "I grew up fast." There was no way to disguise the bitterness those words were steeped in. "I have a lot of work to do and you're distracting me from my job—that's a no-no, remember? Why don't you see if Teddy and Riley need any help."

He took the hint and left her alone. She spent the next thirty minutes online ordering additional trucks, trailers, and four-wheelers. She emailed the confirmations to her crew chiefs, told them to take tomorrow off to go to Newcastle Upon Tyne, pick up the extras, and then re-distribute the crews. The only good thing in this entire mess was knowing the trailers she originally rented were large enough to hold two four-wheelers so she wouldn't have to trade them in. But her small glimmer of happiness faded when she downloaded the data from each group and discovered she had, indeed, covered the smallest area today of any crew—that never happened. Her cell phone rang as the last bit of information filled the screen. Without looking, she knew it'd be Dirk. She would never trust crucial job information to one hard drive—Dirk was her backup before she transferred the files to her dad in Texas.

"What?" came her surly greeting.

He was laughing—which really infuriated her; she hung up on him. Three seconds later, he called back. This time she didn't say anything when she opened the phone, but he wasn't laughing.

"I hope you're planning on sending him packing tonight."

"Now why would I do that, asshole?"

"Well, he evidently put a kink in your style, unless you were busy doing other things with him and left the work to Teddy and Riley?"

"Actually," she replied with a smile that could only be described as completely wicked, "he did so well today I'm thinking about hiring him—for your job."

"I know that's bullshit."

"He's learning quickly, but I do have the smallest crew," she relented.

"That never put you on the bottom before."

"Do you have a point, or did you just call to annoy *the wrong person*?"

"Actually, I was going to say it was a good idea to add an extra truck and additional four-wheelers; we felt kind of bogged down today."

His compliment took her off guard and left her speechless.

He continued, "I see you've rearranged the crews; that should help. How about you and I have lunch together tomorrow before we leave town? Cass?"

"I—I have something I want to check out tomorrow—on my own. I probably won't go into town."

There was a two second pause.

"Really? All by yourself? Or is AJ staying with you?"

"He can do what he wants, but I can tell you this: your newfound oh-my-god-I'm-gonna-behave-like-some-kind-of-jealous-high-school-boyfriend act isn't doing anything to impress me; we aren't a couple."

"Maybe I want to change that," came the surprising reply.

"I don't. And *what* brought all this on?"

"I've been doing a lot of thinking about us lately. Cass, you know I've always been crazy about you, and—"

"I have to go," she snapped the phone shut before he could say anything else. "And I thought I was in a weird funk, huh, Charlie?" she said, reaching down to scratch the indent between his bulgy eyes. She scooped him up onto her lap and nuzzled his little round head as he licked her face, "I've been ignoring you, haven't I, buddy? Sorry. We don't want a boyfriend, do we? You don't even like Dirk-the-Jerk; you growl at him." She laughed as he became frantically happy simply because she was finally paying some attention to him. For a few minutes, she relaxed and forgot everything that had been bothering her.

"Sounds like someone's in a better mood," AJ stated, as he sat down beside her.

She was prepared to shift back to bitch-mode when Charlie jumped into his lap and lunged for his face. For a split second, she feared his intent was to bite AJ, but to her utter shock, he licked him and acted as though they were old friends.

AJ laughed as he allowed the dog to lap the salt from his skin yet careful to avoid letting the dog lick him directly on the mouth, "Yeah, I do need a bath, Charlie."

"Yeah, you do," Cass laughed, and then feigned as if he actually did stink.

"You're no water-lily yourself," he reminded her.

She reached over and scratched Charlie behind the ears, "It's funny, but he doesn't normally like guys. I thought he was going to bite you."

Charlie settled into AJ's lap and looked up at Cassandra.

"Animals like me. I was actually adopted into a family of gorillas when I was writing a story on the Karisoke Research Center in Rwanda last year."

She burst out laughing, causing Charlie's head to cock sideways. Riley and Teddy both looked their direction.

"I'm sorry," she giggled, tears actually forming in the corners of her eyes, "but I can just picture you scrunched down between gorillas while they pick through your hair."

"That's exactly what they did! And then they tried to make me eat leaves."

She couldn't remember the last time she laughed so hard. He kept going on about how the gorillas treated him, and how he finally had to signal one of the researchers to get him out of there because a female gorilla was trying to put some 'amorous' moves on him.

She couldn't breathe, and her sides were aching, "Stop—please—stop!" she gasped.

Charlie seemed horribly concerned as to what was wrong with her and started whining and pawing at her hands as she covered her face.

"I'm okay, Charlie. Settle down, buddy." Her laughter slowly ebbed. She dried her cheeks with her sleeve and regained her composure.

"Hey Boss," Teddy called to her from across the camp, "it's good to hear you laugh."

She only smiled, "Thanks, AJ, I needed that."

"I heard part of your conversation, so I'm assuming it was Dirk on the phone. I guess we were last today, huh?"

"Normally, it would really bother me, but you know what? We worked hard, and I don't care."

"Can I see the data? How bad was it?"

She clicked her computer files open and brought up the multicolored map. "Our team is represented by the white dots, but it includes Dirk, Frank, and Desmond's crews. The other teams are the blue, yellow, and red." She hit a combination of keys, and the white dots suddenly contained either a 1, 2, 3, or 4. "We're the ones."

"We weren't *that* far behind."

"No, we weren't," she said closing the computer. "It's late. I'm gonna turn in for the night." She let her hand brush firmly against the inside of his thigh as she retrieved Charlie from his lap. She stood and then turned toward him with a wink, "I won't fall asleep for a while," she murmured.

His face wore an expression she couldn't decipher, but she had a strong inclination it meant he wasn't going to accept her invitation.

"Goodnight, Cassandra."

CHAPTER THREE

When she woke, only Charlie was beside her. Without much conversation, camp was broken down and everything was packed into the Hummer. By daybreak, they were headed south, back the way they traveled the day before. When they came to the place near the hill, Cass pulled off the road.

"I'm not going into town; you guys can handle it. Pick me up on the way back."

"Boss," Teddy spoke up, "we won't be back for at least t'ree or four hours, maybe more."

"I'll be fine."

"I'm coming with you," AJ stated.

"No. You go with them."

"I'd rather—"

"No—that's pretty simple. Come on, Charlie." The small, black-and-white dog jumped from the truck and ran to her feet

She unloaded the four-wheeler, grabbed a long coil of rope, a flashlight, and a few pieces of equipment. "See you guys in a few hours."

They stood there and watched as she drove away with Charlie precariously perched in front of her.

It was about two-and-a-half kilometers from the road to reach the rises. She drove slowly, so Charlie wouldn't slide off, but he'd ridden plenty of times on the four-wheeler at home back in Texas, so she wasn't too concerned. It only took a few minutes to reach the same oak she parked under yesterday. Charlie jumped down and began to explore. She brought her hand-held GPR and turned it on and started scanning as she moved up the hill. At first, it was uneventful; it was pretty much just dirt with very little rock, but when she reached the top of the hill, everything changed. “Holy shit,” she said out loud. She ran the radar back again to make sure she read it correctly. “Wow, I don’t believe it. It’s some kind of friggin’ wall.” As she started following the contours, she sensed she wasn’t alone. She looked up.

AJ was standing there, watching.

“What the hell are you doing here?! You scared the crap out of me, and why aren’t you headed into town like I told you!”

“You worried me when I saw you grab the coil of rope.”

“Why? Did you think I was gonna hang myself?” she snapped.

“No, but I thought you might do something crazy, like try to dive down into that spring.”

“Son-of-a-bitch! What do you do, read my mind?”

“No,” he laughed, “mind reading isn’t a profession I’ve tried.” A thoughtful expression crossed his face as he motioned to the equipment in her hands, “What did you find?”

She started to open her mouth but was undecided about sharing her discovery. It didn’t take more than a few seconds to realize he was someone she *wanted* to trust; it would be a true first for her, and she didn’t know if she could make herself do it. “I’m pretty sure I found a huge wall.”

His eyebrows rose, “Show me.”

They spent the next two hours discovering a massive structure had been buried under the hill.

“I think the spring is the entrance,” she finally admitted. “I’m diving.”

“Let me do that,” he cautioned.

“I have a diving certificate, do you?”

“No, but I surf every chance I get.”

“That’s not the same.”

“Maybe not but it’s physical. It’s going to take muscle to swim against the force of the water, and I’ll wager I can hold my breath longer than you.”

“I found this site when I first came to the UK. I know it’s something big, and there is no way you’re going to stop me. *I’m diving that hole*.” She faced him with a determined no-need-for-any-more-discussion attitude.

“You’ll wear the rope, and I’ll hold the end,” he conceded, “and I won't give you more than a minute before I pull you back."

"Two minutes."

"You'll pass out in a minute-and-a-half."

"Two minutes," she reiterated.

"Damn, you're stubborn."

"I finally agree with you."

When they reached the four-wheeler, he started uncoiling the rope, and she started undressing.

"What are you doing?" he asked, clearly surprised.

"I'm not going to soak my clothes. Don't look so worried; I'll keep my bra and underwear on; I'll need some way to hold my flashlight hands-free," she added with a smirk.

She found it humorous to note how he tried *not* to stare as she finished pulling off her shirt, but she definitely noticed his hint of a smile. It had been months since she last had any decent amount of sun, so her normal deep tan had faded to caramel. She pulled off her sneakers and socks, and began sliding her jeans down her long, slender legs. At the moment, she wished she'd worn a thong, but as a general rule, she found them uncomfortable. She'd just have to be happy she was wearing her string bikini underwear instead of a pair of hipsters.

"Let me free dive around the edges to get an idea how—"

"No, you're wearing the rope the whole time."

He reached around her as she raised her arms in apparent surrender. "If you insist on tying me up," she said with a sly turn to the corners of her lips. "Hand me my flashlight," she asked as he finished the knot. She took it from him and pulled the front of her bra forward and slipped the light between her breasts. "Don't get crazy on the end of the rope. I'll tug if I'm in trouble, but other than that, don't jerk me around."

"A minute-and-a-half—then I pull you out."

"You know you can be pretty stubborn yourself."

"You have no idea."

For the first time, she saw a different side of him; he was completely serious—all playfulness and humor had evaporated.

She made her way to the water's edge. *Damn, I hate cold water, but there's only one way to do this.* She jumped in; the chilly water momentarily took her breath away. The surface of the stream at the base of the hill was about twenty-five feet across, but it was the smaller, dark hole, deep below the surface, she wanted to investigate. He was right about swimming against the force of the water. On the surface, it didn't appear to move as rapidly, but underwater was a different story. She made her way around the edge near the base of the hill and dove toward the floor of the stream. The bottom was rocky, and she used the rocks to pull herself toward the dark abyss. She just reached the opening when she felt the tug of the rope.

She came spluttering to the surface, thoroughly angry, "Don't get cocky on that rope!" she yelled at him.

"It took you almost a minute to get to the opening. You're not going to be able to go in today."

"The hell you say!" she snapped. "I'm not stupid, and I don't plan on killing myself. I'll let you know if I get in trouble. Give me some rope, now!"

"Get out. We'll get some equipment and come back."

"I want another look. Loosen up or I'm untying myself."

"Don't do that." Once again, he became utterly serious.

He let the rope become slack as she made her way around to the opening once more. With her technique established of pulling herself along using the rocks, she made it to the opening slightly faster. She was amazed as the opening came into view; it wasn't a downward cavern as she expected, but it literally appeared to be coming from the side of the hill. She pulled herself into the darkness and illuminated what was above her, realizing it looked like a solid ceiling. She couldn't hold her breath much longer, but she wanted to see more before surfacing. She was looking up when the ceiling dissolved into nothing but water above her. The rope lost its slack and she was pulled from the hole—again.

"Damn it, AJ," she managed after her first big gulp of air, "I just got inside the hole!"

"Get out. You're trying to hold your breath too long. We'll get some tanks, fins, and masks."

She hadn't come this close only to be ordered out of the water like a child. She started untying the knot.

"What are you doing? Cass, don't you fucking dare!" he yelled.

It was too late. She was out of the rope and taking a big breath. She was determined to discover what was on the other side of the darkness. She dove, kicking hard for the bottom. She had no plans to end her life in a watery grave in the UK, but she had to know whether or not what she suspected was true. She pulled herself quickly along until she could tell she was, once again, under the ceiling. For an infinitesimal pause, she was scared to death. The force of the water seemed to lessen as she struggled upward into the inky unknown.

When her head surfaced, it was an eerie feeling; she felt disoriented, not quite knowing up from down. She pulled the Mag-Lite from her bra and then raised her arm out of the water, "Oh, shit! I don't believe it."

She was in a giant, ancient room. She'd been right; a castle was buried under the hill. The air was breathable but horribly stale and dank. She was treading water and about to start swimming for the edge when something grabbed her leg—and she let out a shockingly loud scream.

AJ surfaced beside her, and, for once, she was face-to-face with someone who was actually more pissed-off than she was.

"What the hell is wrong with you?! Are you out of your freakin' mind?"

"AJ," she simply said and then nervously laughed, "look."

He'd been intently staring into her face when his gaze shifted to where she was shining the flashlight. "Holy crap! It's a—it's a—"

"Castle," she finished with a giddy edge to her voice, "we found a buried castle!"

"I don't believe it. Damn, it stinks in here."

"Come on," she said, her hand moving to his bare waist when she felt the rope. "You put the rope on? What'd you tie it to?"

"If this wasn't such an awesome find, you'd be in a lot of trouble with me," he warned, but then answered her question, "I tied it to the four-wheeler. I thought I'd need it to drag your body out of here."

They were quiet for a moment, each aware of the skin-to-skin contact they made as they stayed afloat.

"Let's do some exploring," she whispered. She let go and moved toward the edge. He was right behind her.

The room was roughly fifteen-hundred square feet, not taking into account the small indoor lake which was the spring's actual origin and somehow ingeniously directed under an opening in the great wall. The ceiling height was about twenty-five feet above them and heavily fortified.

"Look at the architecture," she marveled, shining the light upward, "that took some good friggin' engineering to hold the load above us."

The wall farthest from the water was made of massive cut stones with a thick arch and an outsized door that appeared to be made of squared logs. Two large, horizontal beams had been placed in front of and against the door with their ends placed into cut notches in the stone.

"It's gonna take a chain saw to get through this," she said.

He was running his hand across a beam as he studied it, "I don't think it was meant to ever be opened, at least not after they sealed it this way."

"I want that door open," she said with a determined edge in her voice.

"Look over there," he motioned to her right.

She shined the light on what appeared to be a table and seats made from stone. "Wow," she stated in wonder, as she brushed what would surely be hundreds, if not a thousand years of decayed matter and dirt from the smooth stone top. Amongst the debris was a dark piece of pottery which held what appeared to be the remnants of a feathered quill, and it sat next to a dried and extremely shriveled piece of hide.

"A note?" she guessed.

AJ took the light from her hand and tried to see if anything left on the piece of leather was readable, but it was bug eaten and brittle to the point of crumbling as he touched it. "Too bad," he whispered, but then he looked up. "Cassandra," he breathed, sounding as if he suddenly lost all his air.

She tipped her head back to look up at the wall and, for the first time in her life, felt faint. The wall had a honeycombed appearance with six-inch-wide holes packed with what looked like wax. Carved in the stone next to each hole was a Roman numeral.

"What's that?" she barely whispered.

"I don't know, but we're going to find out, starting with number one." He tried to dig his fingers into the thick substance, but it was too hard.

"Here, use this, it was on the table."

It looked like a stone knife, and it worked perfectly to remove the thick coating. Once out, it contained a large map or roll of paper that had been pigeon-holed into the space. Very carefully, AJ pulled the item from its centuries-old resting place and moved it to the tabletop. It also had a coating of some kind of wax, but as soon as he found the end of the roll and started peeling it back, a beautiful scroll unfolded.

They were both dumbstruck as they stared.

It was several minutes before either one spoke; Cassandra was the first to break the silence.

"I have to find someone who can read this."

"It's Latin; I can read it."

"You've gotta be full of shit."

"I'm serious, Cassandra. My family is Catholic, and I was raised in a Catholic school. When I was in third grade, one of the Sisters taught us about the history of the Latin language and how it came to be considered dead, and I was hooked. As soon as she realized I really wanted to learn it, she started teaching me. My parents paid for private lessons until I was about sixteen, thinking I was going to become a priest."

"A priest?" she choked on the words. *Damn, no wonder he didn't take me up on my offer last night.*

"I had other plans for my life. Religion turned me off completely. I haven't been inside a church for years."

She ignored the last bit of conversation, "Well?"

"Well, what?"

"For crying-out-loud, what does it say?"

"In the year of our Lord," he paused and looked at her. "Septum octo tres can't be right. This would have to be—this is—this is almost thirteen-hundred years old."

"I think we just found early retirement," she stated with wide eyes. "Do you have any idea what these are worth?! Let's dig out the others and—"

"No. Not yet, anyway. Let's read at least the first one and find out what we have."

"So keep going," she urged.

In the year of our Lord, seven-eighty-three, I, Cynewulf, regrettably am left to write the final telling of our great king and friend, Othelleous Magnus, the first. Our colossal work being finished, we have spent our last years together recording and recounting the events which led to the fall of what should have been the greatest kingdom ever conceived. Woe unto one so great who fell into the hands of a woman so desperately wicked and ungodly. Had it not been for the one he made his queen, this destitution would have given way to glory.

He paused, and she felt goose bumps cover his skin as they huddled together and stared at the document in the limited light.

"Keep going," she begged.

"The next part is about us."

She felt her heartbeat increase as she considered every possible thing his statement could imply.

You have managed to find what he so desperately desired to keep removed from the world. He knew someday one would come into this place. Consider carefully the telling. Consider the cost he paid. Consider in your spirit what is wrong and what is right. Consider what honor and respect should be given in this, the place of his and his beloved's burial ground, Kingdom Hill.

"It's a tomb. The whole castle must be like a giant tomb." As she finished uttering the words, she noticed the flashlight seemed to dim, "We have to get out of here before it goes out."

"But how are we—"

"We'll come back with the right equipment. Don't worry," she added when she saw the apprehension in his eyes, "I'm not talking bulldozers and backhoes. We'll get some swim gear and florescent lanterns in here, so you can read a little more; then we'll decide what we should do."

"You keep saying 'we,' so I guess you're okay with doing this together?"

"If this is something we decide to let the world in on, not only are we both going to be rich, but I'll bet this will be the story of the century in National Geographic; a Pulitzer prize at the least. Let's go."

Exiting was much simpler than getting in because once in the outflow, it practically sucked them down and spit them out the other side.

They were both laughing when they surfaced in the sunlight. Charlie barked and paced nervously at the bank. He apparently wondered how the pair vanished, but now he happily vaulted into the water and met them as they neared the shoreline.

"Teddy and Riley should be back by... Whoa."

"What," he asked, as he offered his hand to her.

She couldn't take her eyes off what had caught her attention, "Major tattoo, AJ. I never would have guessed that was under your shirt."

He lifted and looked at his right arm. The intricate design ran from his shoulder down to a few inches above his wrist and had been part of his body for the last couple of years; he no longer gave it any thought, "Most people don't until I get in a warmer climate and shed the long sleeves."

"It's beautiful," she stated before catching herself. Complimenting people wasn't one of her traits, but it couldn't be contained this time. "Why is this part raised?" she asked, reaching up and feeling the design along the top of his shoulder.

"That was done with traditional Maori tools; I don't think I ever experienced anything so painful. The rest was done with standard tattoo equipment. It stung a little, but all-in-all a walk in the park compared to the bone chisel."

She was pulling on her jeans, glad the sun had warmed them in the cool sixty degree afternoon air as she continued to stare at the tattoo, "Let me guess; it was a story you were working on."

"Of course," he laughed. "They sent me down to New Zealand about two-and-a-half years ago to spend some time with the native Maori tribe. They're famous for their tattooing, but their preferred canvas is the human face. At least it was until several decades ago. Now they write their heritage on arms, legs, backs, and chests. It's a bit of a story, if you're interested."

She slipped her shirt over her head then pulled her wet hair out from under the neckline. "I would like to hear more about it, but at the moment, my brain is in overdrive about this," she said, motioning to the hillside. "This kind of changes every plan I had while here."

"Me, too."

He was giving her one of those not-quite readable stares, and she wondered why the unusual tone in his voice, but she couldn't let herself be distracted from the rush of thoughts entering her mind. She couldn't blow-off a nine million dollar contract, and any delay could rapidly devour her profits. She sighed as she watched him put on his shirt. His arms, chest, and abs were exquisite, which left her wondering why she didn't spend a little more time touching him when they had been shirtless and pressed together. *Not now, Cass, focus!*

She picked up her cell and noted she missed two calls. The last call was fifteen minutes ago from Teddy's phone. He left a message saying they were thirty minutes away. The other call was from Dirk's phone. She didn't honestly want to hear the message he left, but ignoring it couldn't possibly help things now.

His message was a bit of a shock. He simply said he wished she would have changed her mind and come to town, but, since it might be another day or two before they could meet up, he bought her lunch and gave it to Teddy to bring back. And then he paused and said he was having a hard time thinking about her being alone with AJ, and he hoped all the time they spent together over the last three years actually meant something to her because it *had* meant something to him.

She was shaking her head in disbelief as she shut the phone.

"Is something wrong?"

She stared at it for another second or so before looking up, "No; just Dirk getting a little weird on me."

"Is it about me? I understand if you and he are—"

"No," she quickly stopped him, "not at all. I hired him several years ago. We've..." What was she going to say? She didn't want to lay everything out and tell AJ they used each other to satisfy mutual needs, but in her mind (and she thought in Dirk's, too) that was all it had ever been. She struggled with what to say when he stopped her.

"It's not my business, so please don't feel like I'm asking for an explanation, but I've wanted to ask if you have a boyfriend or someone special in your life?"

She wasn't accustomed to blushing, but he took her by surprise, and she could feel the color warm her chilled cheeks, "I don't get into relationships."

"Me neither." His eyes squinted shut, and his hands went immediately to his temples. He appeared to be in genuine pain.

"Are you okay?"

"Migraine," he muttered, "coming on fast—must have been the cold water."

It only took her a few minutes to get everything back on the four-wheeler, but in the short span of time, he had become nearly incapacitated. She wasn't even sure if he was going to be able to hang on for the ride back to the road, but he managed to climb on and then slumped heavily against her back.

She was grateful to see the Hummer and another truck waiting for them when she made it to the road. Teddy and Riley helped lay him out on the back seat as he pled for someone to get his medication from his backpack.

Cass expected some over-the-counter migraine medicine but found a prescription bottle for Topamax instead. After confirming it was what he needed, she slipped the yellowish pill into his mouth and held a water bottle to his lips, so he could swallow.

"I'll sit back here with him. Turn around and head back toward Moffat."

"You gonna get a motel, boss?"

"Yeah. We have a change of plans."

Teddy didn't question her further. He'd been with her for more than a year, and she knew he believed it was a good idea to simply follow orders. She placed AJ's head on her lap and covered his eyes with her extra jacket. He couldn't do anything more than moan. She tried to gently massage his neck and shoulders, but he lifted his hand to grip hers and simply said, "No."

She found a small roadside inn and ordered three rooms. As soon as the guys helped AJ to bed, she darkened the room, slipped outside, and went to work. It was two in the afternoon and she had a lot to accomplish before tomorrow. Once again, she was re-arranging the teams, sending Riley to pull four members from the crews closest to their current location. Teddy drove her forty minutes away to get a Land Cruiser from a rental agency in Carlisle. She sent Teddy back to Moffat, but she wouldn't be returning for quite a while.

It was nine p.m. by the time she returned to the inn. She garnered a headache herself now, but she felt fortunate she had never been prone to migraines. Alice, one of her short-lived stepmoms, used to get them so severely she would stay in bed for days; Cass could only hope AJ's weren't as inexorable. She spoke with her newly formed crew and gave them their orders for the morning then tried to quietly check on AJ.

She cracked the door open to find the bed empty and the shower running. The bathroom door was ajar, and she decided to lean in to ask how he was feeling, but she discovered a huge surprise when she peeked inside. The bathroom was steamy, but she could clearly see him standing with his arm on the shower wall and his head resting on it as the water rained down. She'd seen him shirtless today, but he'd kept his jeans on; now, he was butt-naked. She could do nothing but stare; he was stunning in the nude. He had a golden tan, a muscled back that ended above the firmest looking round ass she'd ever seen, and all supported on a pair of sculpted legs. As she slowly savored the vision of 'oh-my-God' right in front of her, she realized he was smooth everywhere; the only hair on him was on his head. Well, actually, she couldn't see *all* of him; he was facing the wall. If he turned around, she'd be caught, yet she craved—with every fiber of her immoral thoughts—for him to catch her.

She sighed, knowing it was wrong to play voyeur, not that being wrong had ever stopped her before, but something was different when it came to AJ. She wanted to get dirty with a ferocity she'd never felt, but at the same time she sensed he'd turn her down if she tried.

She stepped out of the doorway and away from the great view, and called out to him. "Are you feeling better?"

"Cass?" came his surprised reply, "Ah, yeah, give me a minute, okay?"

"Sure. Do you need anything?"

"No—no, I'm good."

"I'll bet you are," she muttered then plopped down on the second bed.

When he emerged, all he had on was a thick, white towel around his waist. Cass was starting to think this was more temptation than any woman could handle. "Headache gone?" she innocently asked, while she considered snatching the towel away from him.

"Not completely, but it's bearable now."

"Have you eaten? I know a migraine can make a person nauseous, but—"

"You get migraines?"

"No. One of my stepmothers got them all the time."

He had a funny look on his face, "How many stepmoms have you had?"

"After my mom died when I was eight, Dad married three more times, but they never lasted. The money drew them in, and the booze drove them out. He gave up on finding the right woman when I was about fifteen."

"I'm sorry."

"Don't be," she suddenly shifted, her bitchy attitude resurfacing, "Look, I'm just trying to find out if you're hungry, but if you're feeling better, you can walk down to the restaurant yourself."

"Don't do that, please," he said softly, his hands starting to undo the top of the towel.

Bitchiness went right out the window as she gasped slightly and leaned forward in anticipation of watching it come off, "Don't do what?" Every thought in her head about their prior conversation dissolved.

The towel came off, and he headed for his duffle—in his boxer briefs.

She slumped back against the headboard.

"Don't put the shield back up. We're finally starting to get to know one another."

She wanted to tell him there was no way in heaven or hell she was honestly going to allow him, or anyone for that matter, to get to know her. She fought her anger as she considered what to say in response when he sat down on the bed beside her and pulled on a fresh pair of jeans.

"So where have you been all afternoon while I was curled up in misery?"

Unbelievable! She thought to herself. *I can't stay angry at him.* She smiled through her disbelief, "Well, let's see: I rented a Land Cruiser for us, picked up equipment for the hill, bought you a light wetsuit so you won't get a cold-water migraine tomorrow, gathered supplies, and rearranged the teams so for the next week or two, however long it takes us, we can spend all our time reading the scrolls."

"First of all, the wetsuit idea is perfect—thank you. And secondly, you are like an organizational maniac. Are you always this, ah—thorough?"

"Yeah, I am. I'm also a control freak, so this is going to be hard for me."

"What do you mean?"

"This is my dad's style; he starts a job and then steps back and let's it run. Me? I have to be in the thick of it, controlling every step, working, and watching the progress. Listen, AJ, the restaurant won't serve past ten, so we don't have much time. Can I bring you something to eat?" she had to switch topics; he was learning too much about her.

"Are *you* hungry?"

"I could use a bite," she admitted.

"Let's go down together."

A shiver ran through her; she liked the connotation of that idea.

They made it through the meal, and she was able to redirect the conversation every time he started digging into her personal life, but it wasn't easy. She would flip the questions back to gather information about him, but (even though she was certain he answered her honestly) she had the distinct feeling he, too, was keeping a big chunk of his personal side hidden.

"Ah, crap!" she suddenly interjected, as they paid the check.

"What's wrong?"

"Charlie. I can't get him under the hill, and he'll be miserable alone and tied out by the vehicle all day long. Damn it. I may have to waste another day shipping him back to the States."

"We don't know how long it's gonna take to read everything stored in that wall; couldn't he stay with Teddy and Riley?"

She knew Teddy liked her dog, and he would keep an eye on him as they worked. Charlie loved riding in the truck and on the four-wheelers, so he would be happy. He watched him all afternoon for her—to keep Charlie from pestering AJ. And, although she could order Teddy to do this for her, she'd much rather ask him, so it wouldn't seem like an imposition. They stopped at their room, hoping they were still awake, and knocked.

"Boss," Teddy said as he opened the door. Charlie uttered a small bark, but then ran to the door trying to wag his nub of a tail.

"Hey, buddy," she crooned, dropping to her knees and gathering him up, "have you been a good boy?"

"Sure he has. Me and he have become what we call pod nahs in the bayou—good friends, you know."

"Can we come in and talk for a minute?"

"Sure, boss-lady, you is paying for dis here room, so you know you welcome in."

"I told you earlier today I won't be working with you guys for at least a week or two, but I have a little problem where Charlie is concerned; he can't go with me. If I put a little something extra in your pay, do you think you could keep an eye on him until I finish this side-job I'm working on?"

He gave a strange look at AJ, and she wondered if he thought 'side-job' was a new American term for a-guy-I'm-doing-on-the-side.

"Sure, sure, boss—but, you don' need to pay me no extra."

"Thanks, Teddy. And I will pay you something extra; you too, Riley—because I expect you both to run this crew like I was right there with you. I'm going to take Charlie for tonight, but I'll bring him back before you leave in the morning."

They said good-night and then headed down the sidewalk while Charlie ran back and forth between their legs.

"So which room is yours?" AJ asked.

"This one," she said, opening the door to the room he'd slept in all afternoon.

"Then which one's mine?"

His entrancingly naïve expression made her want to throw him on the floor and rip every shred of clothing off his body. "This one," she said with a slow, seductive tone.

"Ah—Cassandra, I don't think—"

"I'm a big girl and you're a big boy." She honestly didn't know; she didn't get to see *that* part in the shower, but she was hoping he was. "There are two beds, AJ—if we need two."

He seemed to be truly nervous as he ran his hand through his hair and stood in the open doorway, not moving, "Give me the keys to the truck; I'll sleep in it."

She was crushed. She was fully aware of her looks and her figure. She'd never laid it out so plainly for a man before—*and been turned down*. "I don't want you to sleep in the truck," she stated slowly, fighting hard to keep her I'm-the-boss tone out of her voice, so it didn't actually sound like a demand. "You said you wanted to get to know me; this could be a great way to do that."

"I didn't mean *that* way."

"Are you afraid of me?"

He rolled his eyes and lightly shook his head, "No."

"Then stop standing in the doorway and come inside, at least so we can discuss it." She didn't want to discuss it. She was staring at his splendid, full lower lip and wondering just how good the kiss would be that she *would* eventually get from him.

He stepped inside, and she shut the door.

"I want you," tumbled out of her mouth before the latch barely slipped into the door frame.

"Cassandra, I like you. I *really* do, but I can't do this."

She hoped her thoughts on this subject would turn out to be wrong, so she went for the most honorable and noble possible excuse first, "You've got a girlfriend, right? Or maybe even a wife tucked away somewhere?"

"No. I'm single—no girlfriend but—"

"Damn it. I knew you were too good to be true. It's Bobby, isn't it?" The strangest look of astonishment came over his face, and she instantly knew she'd hit the nail on the head. "Am I right?"

"How did you know?"

"Your kind of perfection usually leads to... Never mind. I just knew—almost from the moment he dropped you off."

"And you're not mad?"

"God, this sucks," she grumbled, sitting down on the corner of the bed. Her headache that had vanished when she watched him in the shower was returning. "You're the kind of guy any girl would like to have for a friend, and then some, so I guess I can't be mad at you."

"I wouldn't have, but I've known him for years, and he was so insistent—"

She put her hand up to stop him. This wasn't the kind of confession she wanted to hear. "Forget it. I can't say I actually understand, but... Just forget it. I only have one question," she sighed as her eyes roamed up to his handsome face. She still wanted to kiss him so desperately, "Why couldn't you at least be bisexual?"

His response was as if she reached out and slapped his face as his jaw dropped, "Oh, no! No, that's not it. He and I aren't... No, we're friends. You know, really friends. He—he wanted me to check you out—for him."

Her expression froze; she didn't even blink. Her brain thawed, and her mouth opened, *"You're not gay?"*

"No."

Then what he'd just admitted hit her, and she instantly became angry—really furious, "You mean to tell me this whole bullshit about a possible story was—was bullshit?! You don't even work for National Geographic, do you?!"

"Yes, I do, honestly; you have to believe me."

"I don't have to believe anything you say!"

"I told him I would do him the favor, but it had to be story first and check you out second."

That tidbit didn't cool her temper at all.

"You asshole! I actually started to trust you!" she uttered in pure contempt. "I knew better than to trust a man! And now you know about the hill and—"

He grabbed her shoulders in a firm grip and told her to stop it, "Please, I'll beg forgiveness, but you have to know you *can* trust me. *Everything* I've said to you, *everything* we've talked about was the truth. The problem is my best friend is the shyest person on the planet, and he couldn't stop talking about you—and now, I—I can't tell him that I like you, too."

Brain freeze—again.

"What did you say?"

"Cass, I want to get to know you, but—but for myself now, not for him. I—"

Enough said. She laced her arms around his neck and pulled him on top of her as she reclined on the bed. "Then get to know me, *right now*," she panted.

"I can't do this and tell him afterward; 'Hey Bobby, she ain't the girl for you, but I hope you don't mind that I'm *banging* her now.'"

She liked the sound of that word. She wanted to feel the sound of that word. She wanted that word coursing through her veins like an out-of-control freight train. "Yes you can," came her fevered response.

"No, Cassandra, he really is my best friend."

"Then don't tell him about this."

"Do you want to get to know me? Really get to know me?"

"Ooh, yesss," she said with so much emotion that she was pretty certain if his body pressed any firmer against hers, she was going to have her first orgasm before they even got started.

"Then you have to understand I can't do this to a friend. Give me some time to talk to him so he doesn't get hurt. I have to know he's okay with the two of us. And there are things about me you don't know. You have to know certain things before this goes too far because I don't want to hurt you, either."

"Damn, you're like riding a freakin' roller coaster," she cried, going limp on the bed, "One second you have me on the peak, and the next second you're dropping me off the edge. AJ, I'm not into head games; I hate them with a passion."

"I promise no head games, but trust is essential. Can you trust me?"

"You're not going to sleep with me tonight, are you?"

"Nope."

"Are you going to at least kiss me?"

"Not now. Not until everything is out in the open."

Ouch. She suddenly prayed he didn't expect total openness from her. Trust? She could almost believe she could give it to him, but the truth about herself she could never expose to anyone.

"When?" she simply asked.

"You'll just have to wait and see. Agreed?"

She slowly let him out of her grip as he rose from the bed. She'd never had a need for anyone like this before. It was going to be a long night.

"Agreed."

CHAPTER FOUR

She woke without disturbing AJ then made her way down to where the crew was getting ready to pull out from the parking lot. Charlie was happy to be outside and eager to go for a morning walk. She picked him up before she got close to the crew and kissed the side of his head several times; he was her dog, and she loved him, but she didn't want them to see her moment of weakness. She took one last opportunity to hug his little frame before putting him back on the ground. She walked up and handed Teddy the leash.

"You should have plenty of dog food for him, but if he gets picky and doesn't want to eat, you may have to stop somewhere and buy him some canned."

"No problem, boss. We gonna get along just fine, ain't we, pod nah, eh?" With that, Charlie jumped up into the truck and sat in the center of the seat.

"See, no problems."

"Thanks, Teddy. I'll have my phone and computer on, so make sure you stick with the schedule and check-in twice a day—data by eight."

"Yes, ma'am. Will do."

She watched them leave the darkened lot and head north.

She was apprehensive as she wondered how the job would get done without her being right in the middle of it, pushing everyone to work harder, but she was more anxious to get back to the hill to spend time alone with AJ. She wondered what he meant last night when he said there were certain things she needed to know about him first. And why did he warn her about getting hurt?

He was still sleeping when she returned, but she couldn't blame him; it wasn't even daylight yet. She climbed into the shower and turned on the hot water. The climate in the UK always seemed cool with the average daytime high running from the mid fifties to the low sixties, so the hot shower felt wonderful. She filled the tub after she rinsed off, and soaked as she drifted in and out of consciousness. She could hear AJ was finally up, and it sounded as if he had turned on the television. Reluctantly, she sat up and drained half the tub, shaved her legs, rinsed again, and climbed out. She hadn't brought any clean clothes into the bathroom, and she seriously considered parading out in the buff, but why spoil the unveiling? If he was truly serious last night about being interested in her, she'd let him be the one to removed every last stitch of her clothing when the time came, and she hoped that time would come very soon.

She wrapped her hair in one towel and her body in the other, but making sure it was low enough to give him a taste of what her breasts looked like without a bra. She opened the door and stepped out—into utter shock. "Oh, shit!" she exclaimed, as two surprised faces turned her way.

Bobby was in their room!

Evidently, what she thought had been the television was actually the two of them in conversation. He turned a shade so red Cassandra wondered if he'd broken a blood vessel. She'd never been shy in her life, and since she was already standing there, she decided this was no time to start, "Hi, Bobby, didn't expect you here this morning."

He seemed to cower as he threw a pleading glance at AJ.

"And, AJ," she continued, "when you have mixed company in a room, it's a good idea to let the party in the bathroom know she has a visitor." She growled a little on the last part of her sentence but felt he deserved it.

"Sorry, I—I—didn't think—"

"You can stop right there; you're right," she grabbed her clothes and returned to the bathroom.

When she emerged for the second time, Bobby was still red-faced but smiling.

"I sent Bobby a text message last night and asked if he'd like to join us for breakfast, *so we can talk*," he hinted.

She wasn't sure she understood the gist of his statement, "Do you want me to come to breakfast with you, or is this male talk?"

"No, please," Bobby finally managed to speak up, "we'd love for you to join us."

Breakfast, although started under awkward circumstances, ended up being pleasant. Evidently, AJ already explained to him, while she was in the shower, how things hadn't gone quite according to plan, and that Cassandra knew the whole story.

"I apologize for putting AJ up to this. It really is quite embarrassing to not be able to speak with a woman. I didn't know, when you came to the office for your permits, if the big blonde fellow was your boyfriend or not and—"

"Dirk," she said with a roll to her eyes, "No. Lately he *thinks* he's my boyfriend, but it's just mutual convenience."

"You mean mutual acquaintance?"

"No," she smiled, "I mean—"

AJ kicked her under the table.

She glared at him and then turned back to Bobby and smiled, "I guess, yeah, that could be a good way to describe it. He works for me and my dad. I guess that's mutual enough."

She was getting the impression Bobby was still very interested in her, which could only mean either AJ didn't tell him that he also had a strong interest, or else Bobby felt like giving him a little competition. She looked Bobby over and realized he was the old-fashioned type of guy who would provide a strong and stable relationship; something she'd never experienced in her life, unless she counted Charlie. She guessed he was 6'2" (about an inch taller than AJ) and had medium-brown hair with an almost burnished copper sheen to it. His eyes were very light blue, and he was handsome and extremely sweet. Yup, big puppy-dog type. Nope, definitely not her type. AJ was fumbling with his explanation as to why they needed to talk in the first place when she decided it was time to scare sweet, little Bobby away, so he would look at AJ and say, "Take her! Please!"

"All right," she sighed, laying cash on the table to cover breakfast, "let's go back to the room and get both you boys naked."

Bobby had been saying something to AJ when he turned and looked at her with wide eyes, "Beg pardon?"

"I'm woman enough for both of you."

The kick came hard and fast under the table. She almost yelped, but anger got the better of her, and she kicked AJ back—hard.

"American humor," AJ said with a shocked, pain-racked smile, "she's teasing."

She started to open her mouth when he reached under and

gripped her hand with excessive firmness, "Cass, would you stop being a comedienne. I really need to speak to Bobby *alone* before he has to leave."

"Fine," she snapped, "I'll go pack our stuff and check us out."

She actually waited in their room and watched out the window as the two of them talked near Bobby's car. Their expressions were so serious that she worried how things were going. She knew how important it was to AJ not to hurt his friend. At one point, Bobby looked away and wiped at his eyes. A few minutes later they embraced, and Bobby got in his car and left. When AJ turned and started back toward their room she could see his eyes were reddened and misty.

Crap! What had they been talking about? She felt certain, even though she was co-owner of a corporation, she wasn't that great of a prize. In fact, she knew in all honesty, it would be AJ who would be hurt in the end. She would take what she wanted from him and then walk away; she always walked away. She refused to have a relationship with anyone. As he neared the door, a thought entered her mind that had never occurred to her before: if she didn't take what she wanted from him, then she couldn't hurt him. For once in her life, she determined to care more about someone else than herself.

She was quiet on the drive back to the hill. AJ asked several times if something was wrong. She placated him by saying she had a lot on her mind about the job and the hill. He finally gave up and joined her in the silence.

The morning turned rainy, which suited her new mood. She was completely depressed by her revelation concerning the most tempting man she'd ever met. And it wasn't just the physical attraction tempting her; she was finding an emotional temptation as well. It was like there was a new space inside her chest that hadn't existed before, and the only thing that would fill it was now off limits, and it hurt like hell.

"Stay in the truck," she ordered as she parked, habitually, yet unintentionally, returning to boss mode, "I'm going to see if I can tie off an underwater line, so we can—"

"Why? You bought me a wetsuit. I'll just—"

"AJ, it's about fifty degrees outside, drizzling rain, and the wind is picking up. You'll be cold and damp before you even get in the water."

"I'm not going to let you do all the work."

"I won't. I'll just do most of it."

"Did you bring a tent?"

"No, I figured we'd stay under the hill, if the air in there is okay to breathe. I talked with a guy at the dive shop in Carlisle, and he told me the odor might be a buildup of carbon dioxide. If it is, we'll either need to bring the scrolls out to read them or get a piece of equipment that will put some oxygen in that room. I'd personally like to stay under the hill."

"How do we test it?"

"He gave me two options: a Drager Aerotest kit for about twelve-hundred dollars, or this for about a buck-and-a-half, American." She pulled a Bic lighter from her pocket, "I've never been a cheapskate, but he proved to me the lighter is pretty accurate."

"How are you going to get all this stuff under the hill without getting it wet?"

"Ah, now we come to a high-tech, totally American invention which will allow us to keep everything dry." She reached behind the seat and brought out a box of Ziploc bags, "I have them from quart size, up to super-jumbo for the big stuff."

He started to laugh, "You actually do have a good sense of humor." Then the smile fell from his face, "Why did you say that to Bobby?"

"Oh, that," she frowned, recalling her threesome comment. She didn't want to get into a conversation about Bobby, but she felt he needed an answer. "I wanted to scare him off."

"That would have certainly done it—probably for both of us."

"I've been thinking about that. Listen, AJ, we honestly don't know each other. I'm—I'm sorry I came on to you last night, and I don't want to give you the wrong impression; I'm not looking to get into a relationship. I was just horny. I'm not right for Bobby, and I know I'm not right for you, either," she said the words hoping they sounded truthful, but the whole time the space inside her chest was starting to ache. The way he was staring at her made it hurt to a greater degree. "But you *are* the only person I want to share this find with, so if you're okay with that then..."

He reached over and cupped the side of her face in his hand, letting his thumb stroke her cheek. One touch and she was ready to fall apart, but he surprised her.

"I've been thinking the same thing. Not about you being wrong for me, but it might be best, for both of us, if we didn't take that step."

She had never experienced such a sharp pain in her whole life. If this was how a broken heart felt, she never wanted to feel it again. She smiled weakly, and pulled his hand away from her face, "Let me work on the underwater line. You can sit in here and put on your wetsuit." She opened the door before he could answer and headed to the back hatch to grab some gear. She was glad for the rain running down her cheeks; he'd never know she was crying.

She donned a mask, grabbed a Pony bottle of air with a regulator, a pair of fins, her rope, and a dive light that fit around her head. She knew they wouldn't need full-size air tanks because it wasn't a long swim to get to the other side, but going against the flow and pulling themselves along using the rocks was just too slow, especially if they were ferrying items under the hill. She hoped she could find a large enough rock on both ends to tie a taut line they could use to quickly pull themselves in through the opening. She removed her shoes and jeans and threw them into the back but left her shirt on.

The view under water was much better with the mask, and it didn't take her long to find a suitable rock. Once tied securely, she turned on her dive light and propelled herself hard into the current with her fins; within seconds she was out of the flow and scanning the bottom of the dark indoor lake, it was silted and on the creepy side, but she did find one of the large, rectangular building stones resting underwater not too far from the inner bank. The whole exercise took her about ten minutes; the pony bottle was nearly exhausted, but with the line in place, she shouldn't need it anymore. She tested the air with her lighter and was pretty sure the oxygen content was hovering between nineteen-and-a-half and twenty percent which was adequate. How long it would stay adequate with them breathing in there was another matter.

When she returned, AJ had wiggled, squirmed, and struggled his way into the wetsuit. It would have been a whole lot simpler if he'd been able to stand up, but there was no way to do that in the Land Cruiser. She gave him an extra large Ziploc bag containing a big florescent lantern, a towel, and a dry change of clothes to take under the hill. She also gave him strict orders to dry off and change immediately once he got inside. She was being bossy again, and he didn't argue.

She made at least a dozen trips bringing items under the hill. She was starting to feel exhausted and a bit hypothermic, so she knew it was time to drag her butt out of the water, dry off, and learn what AJ had uncovered with the scrolls. There was no private place, so she simply turned her back to him, stripped, dried, and dressed. She was cold enough for her teeth to start chattering.

He motioned her to sit on the sleeping bag. "You're freezing," he noted, pulling her to his side to offer a little warmth.

She was too cold to worry about sexual excitement, so she cuddled against him and tried to relax.

"I finished the first scroll we started yesterday, and it explained the last two scrolls were ones the king himself made, diagramming the whole kingdom. Take a look; the man was an absolute genius as far as architecture and building is concerned. The last drawing is of this room; he built it once everything else had been buried."

"Airshafts," she said, as she looked at the sketches. "He had an opening for them to walk in and out of before they sealed this, but he built in airshafts anyway."

"Where? I didn't—"

She pointed them out on the drawing, "They are pretty unique. I'm sure they're under dirt and grass, after all this time but if we can dig to them, this place will have plenty of ventilation. His coordinates are a little primitive, but I bet I can find them."

"You aren't going back into the water today."

"Oh, yes I am. I have to."

"You'll make yourself sick if you get chilled for too long."

"Yeah, well, we might make ourselves dead if we nod off and breathe all the oxygen out of here." She flicked the lighter and studied the flame, "We're still good. I just don't know how long it will last."

"What time is it?"

She removed her cell phone from one of the bags and opened it, "Almost one in the afternoon. Why?"

"Why don't you warm up in the sleeping bag and take a nap? Then we can both look for those airshafts."

"Sleeping before we know if—"

"I'll stay awake. You have to be tired."

She tried her best to suppress a huge yawn that appeared simply at the mention of being tired, but it was no use; he'd seen it.

"Come on, get inside the sleeping bag," he said, sliding off and unzipping the edge.

"I can't. The guys are supposed to check in."

"You don't have any signal under here. They—"

"What!" she was suddenly alert as she grabbed her cell and flipped it open again. She never looked at the signal bars when she checked the time. "I'll warm up in the truck," she sighed, trying to rise off the sleeping bag, but AJ wouldn't let her.

"They'll leave voice mails. You can check them later."

"No! I'm going—"

"Later!" he snapped back, becoming forceful enough to make her lie down. He had no clue he had just crossed a dangerous line—a line that ensnared her when a little girl lost her innocence. The look in her eyes was enough to make him let go, "I'm sorry. I didn't mean—"

"Yes, you did," she whimpered, staying down on the sleeping bag, "it's okay, you can hurt me—I can take it." She swallowed hard, "Do it." If she was going to stop feeling this foreign sensation, she needed to know he was the same as all the rest.

"Oh, Cass, I couldn't. I don't ever want to hurt you."

"Yes, you do. Every man I've ever known..." she swallowed again, but this time there were tears distorting her vision. "You're no different, AJ." The accusatory sound in her voice couldn't be masked.

"Maybe those are the only kind of men you've known," he said softly, "but I'm *not* that kind of man." He pulled his hands back as if her accusation had been a gun pointed at his chest, "I won't touch you. I won't take advantage of you, and I *will not* do anything to hurt you. You can trust me, Cass."

She sat up, shaking uncontrollably as she moved away from him, "I'll never trust anyone—and that includes you."

She grabbed up the bag with her cell phone and dove in—fully clothed and without a light—she didn't search for the rope; she swam to the outflow until it caught her and sucked her under.

It didn't take long for him to come up out of the spring. She was on the phone, but he didn't approach her. Instead, she watched as he grabbed a hatchet from the vehicle and began chopping a long, thin birch sapling. He cut away a few stray limbs from the top, ending up with a straight pole. He jumped back into the spring, and, with a bit of obvious difficulty, he disappeared under the hill with the pole in tow.

She spoke with all the crew chiefs—except one—she put off talking with Dirk. She wasn't sure how he found out she wasn't with the crew, but he'd left her a message earlier in the day asking her what was going on and to please call him. Please wasn't a normal word in his vocabulary. She finally decided against returning his call. She'd talk to him tonight when she downloaded everyone's data, but what she'd tell him about what she had been doing was another story entirely.

She wasn't ready to face AJ again, but there were things she wanted to do on the computer anyway. She was sitting in the Cruiser with the heat running and her computer on her lap when she saw him emerge again. She was getting that little angry rumble inside her chest as she wondered if he was trying to purposely piss her off by spending so much time in the water. She knew, even in this chilly weather, the wetsuit would keep his body temperature pretty stable, but his hands, feet, and more importantly, his head were exposed. "Why do I even care?" she stated aloud as he approached the vehicle. He opened the hatch and reached inside for the small shovel.

"What are you doing?" she was sounding like his boss once more. Before he answered, she snapped at him again, "You know, if you keep going in and out from under the hill, you'll eventually have another headache."

"I don't get them all the time," he argued. "I found one of the lower airshafts and I'm digging it out."

Curiosity had the better of her; she closed the laptop, slipped into her shoes, and got out. "How'd you do it?"

He finally smiled.

She missed his smile.

"When you pointed them out on the drawing, I realized the lower shafts should only be eight to ten feet from the interior to the outside. I found the opening inside and shoved the pole I cut through until I was pretty sure it should be sticking out somewhere. It's right over there."

She grabbed a hooded rain jacket and draped it over his shoulders, "At least put the hood up to keep your head warm." The anger and bossiness in her voice had faded and what was left merely sounded like someone who was concerned about him.

"Only if you do the same," he said, reaching in and grabbing the second jacket.

He held it for her to slip on and then pull the hood over her half-dried, blonde tangle. "Your hair is a wreck," he softly added, continuing with a gentle smile.

She reached behind his head and pulled up his hood, but, for the first time, she paused and allowed her hands to stroke his face. She'd wanted to touch his face since she first met him, and it felt wonderful—and cold. She frowned, "Your face is freezing."

He reached up to stop her from pulling away, "Your hands feel good."

They were so close, but she wanted him closer. She wanted to know if he was as decent and good as her heart was trying to tell her. Fear welled up inside; what if she discovered he wasn't? Or, even more terrifying, what if he was?

She tilted her face to his as she drew him against her. Instead of accepting what she offered, he kissed her forehead several times and wrapped his arms around her.

"When you trust me," he whispered, "then I'll kiss you."

She didn't answer; she just nodded and extended one arm around his waist, "Let's go find that pole."

The rest of the afternoon was good. The rain stopped, the mist burned off, and it was comfortable outside. They dug back several feet to expose the original opening for the vents and then carefully dispersed the soil and laid the sod over the fresh area so it wouldn't be immediately obvious that someone had been digging. There was a shaft on the opposite end at floor level and it was easy to expose, but it was the shaft through the ceiling that would pull the fresh air in from the bottom and allow the carbon dioxide buildup to escape that they really needed to find. It was almost seven-thirty by the time they discovered a strong possibility with the GPR.

AJ had just removed the sod when a three foot snake emerged, seemingly very unhappy to have been disturbed. Cass jumped, but didn't scream. She had more than a few run-ins with snakes back home, several of them poisonous, but she wasn't afraid of them.

"It's okay," AJ said as the snake suddenly twisted belly-up and became motionless, "it's just a grass snake. They play dead when you scare them." He scooped the snake onto the end of the shovel and gave it a good toss. "I wonder if she's been making her home in the shaft?" He dug a little deeper and the end of the shaft appeared, but it was full of dirt.

"We need another pole," she began.

"Nah. On this angle, I bet the dirt isn't packed very far at all in there." He flipped the shovel around pushing the handle into the soil. At first it didn't look like he was going to make any progress, but with a little more muscle, the dirt crumbled away and a burst of warm, smelly air hit their faces.

"Ah! You did it!"

"We did it," he corrected, "I didn't realize what these were in the drawings."

"Good. Now we can sleep in there tonight without worrying about running out of air." She glanced up at the sky and then pulled her cell out, "Almost eight. I'm gonna go back to the truck and get my computer ready."

"Mind if I sit and watch?"

"Not at all." And, for once, she meant it.

She smiled as the information filled the screen. Teddy and Riley definitely pushed the new crew; they had covered the most ground. And, as a whole, she finally had a couple days worth of data, so she could run her projection program.

AJ watched as the dots suddenly expanded and a mapped-out strip down the center of the UK was covered in points of colored light, "What's that?"

"Once I have a good base of data, I can project a more accurate completion date." She pointed to the number on the lower right, "Thirty-eight days is longer than I thought. I was hoping to shave at least ten days, maybe fourteen, but it doesn't look like that's gonna happen. But they may pick up more speed tomorrow, now that things aren't shifting around. I'll re-run the projection in a couple days."

"Is something bothering you?"

She sighed and then lifted her eyebrows for a second, "They had a good day today—without me."

"It just proves you've done a great job training them and organizing everything. They need you, just not necessarily cracking a whip over their heads."

"I can be a little overbearing, huh?" She could tell he didn't want to answer. "It's okay," she laughed, "I was the original person to term myself as a bitch."

Her phone rang; it was Dirk.

"I'll wait outside," he offered, grabbing the door release.

"No, you don't have to. Sit tight." She pushed the button, but Dirk was talking before she could speak.

"Where are you, Cass? I find out this morning you're telling your crew you're gonna be doing something else *for a week or two?* This isn't like you. Don't tell me that guy turned into a gold-digging Romeo and you're actually falling for it?"

"This has nothing to do with him."

"Really? Is he with you?"

"Yes, but—"

"How was it, baby? I could tell you wanted to try him out the minute you laid your pretty little eyes on him. *Does he like it when you try to get away?"*

"Shut up, asshole!" she snapped. She knew AJ could hear every word Dirk uttered, "I haven't slept with him. He's—"

"You? Come on, Cass, I know you better than that. You probably invited him into your tent the first night you were away from me."

It made her angry because he was right. She did extend the

invitation, but he turned her down, and Dirk wouldn't understand that part. "Whether you believe me or not, I'm not sleeping with him, but he is helping me with something."

He was quiet for several seconds. When he did respond, all the anger had drained, "Thank you, baby. I needed to hear that. Where are you? If you're not sleeping with him, then I want to see you tonight. I've got to talk to you about something that's been bugging me for a while about us."

"I—I can't. We'll talk in a few weeks."

"A few weeks?" he replied, his temper flared again. "This can't wait a few weeks!"

"Please, Dirk, I can't deal with anything else right now."

"What about the job? What about your crew?"

"What about them?" she fired back. "They're doing what they're trained to do. I guess Dad was right."

"You're taking lessons from the old man now? What's next? Do I find you curled up with a quart of scotch, passed out somewhere?" He must have realized what her reaction would be because he quickly added, "I'm sorry; don't hang up. All right, I'll be a good boy and get off your back, but I'm worried about you. Promise me you'll be safe, whatever it is you're doing, okay?"

"I have to go. Bye," she hung up before it could get any more bizarre.

"Cass, he sounds like he thinks of you a little differently from—"

"AJ, I don't know what the hell has gotten into him, but I swear to you there isn't a relationship between me and him. He's never, and I mean never, acted like this. I don't love Dirk. And I hate to say it, but I barely even like him."

"Then why—"

"It's all I know." Her eyes filled with tears for what seemed like the umpteenth time today as shame filled her, "Please, don't ask."

He pulled her against his chest and kissed her forehead once more, "If you ever feel like talking about it, I'll listen. Let's get under the hill before it gets dark out here. Tomorrow, we'll start the story of how all this happened."

The room smelled much better now that there was some fresh air in circulation. They were both tired and decided a good night's sleep was what they needed. Cass cracked a couple glow sticks and turned off the lantern to save battery power. She'd purchased several extra lithium batteries, but there was no need to waste them when their eyes would be closed anyway.

The room was slightly warmer than outside, but it was still chilly as they settled into their sleeping bags. After fifteen or twenty restless minutes, AJ asked if she was warm yet.

"No. I think the water dropped my temp a couple of degrees. It's gonna take all night to build up some heat." She heard his bag unzip and turned to see him kneeling beside hers.

He unzipped hers, spread it out flat then placed his bag over her. "Scoot over."

Her heart was pounding a mile-a-minute, and all she could think about was how his nice guy routine was getting ready to be shot to hell. She slid over as he linked the two bags together, zipped them almost closed, and then crawled inside. He stretched his tattooed arm out and motioned for her to rest her head on it as his other came around her waist and pulled her back against his chest. He wasn't cold. The wetsuit had done its job for the day; he was like an oven burning against her skin.

"Good night, Cass."

"AJ?"

"Yeah?"

"The tattoo—you told me it was a bit of a story."

She listened quietly as he told her about his month-and-a-half long adventure. How the Maori actually find it an insult if an outsider uses their family symbols in a tattoo. How he made the decision to use the beautiful swirls and geometric patterns that were not insulting to them, but, before the tattooing began, his host family said they had come to think of him as a son; they asked if he would like to bear their heritage. Part of the design would be done using the centuries old method with the uhi, or bone chisel, it would be painful, and the risk would be high.

"They have a sacred meeting place, the marae, where they believe the living must come together and offer support to each other. They invited me there to meet the other members of their family, but they said it was so I could become aware of my place in life. They wanted me to understand where I 'fit' into the world and to learn about the role deceased loved ones play as they continue to influence the tribe after death.

"Once they indoctrinated me, they basically put me through hell to carve the design in my shoulder. I ended up staying two extra weeks while they used all their herbs and concoctions to fight off infection, which is normal for this kind of scarred design, but it was rough, and I was so sick."

"Why did you have to learn about the role of deceased loved ones? Did they think they were going to kill you?"

"I felt like I was dying after all that, but... Cassandra, I told you there are things about me you don't know, and I'm honest-to-God afraid to tell you."

"Why?"

"Because—because I'm starting to feel something for you I've never... I mean, I thought I loved someone once. I asked her to marry me. Hell, we were both practically kids, fresh out of college. She was a swimsuit model, and I was interning with National Geographic. We thought we owned the world. Then I had a surfing accident in Baja while I was down there working on a story. Nothing real severe—just took a good hit to the head and needed a few stitches, but when the doctor looked at my x-rays, I knew something was wrong."

She became incredibly still, almost to the point of not breathing. Her heart was starting to pick up speed as she worried what he was about to tell her.

"When I told her what the doctor found, she broke off the engagement. She told me she was sorry, but she just couldn't handle it. I didn't blame her, but it changed my whole perspective. There have been other women in my life, but as soon as they know, they back off and say they just want to be friends."

"What's wrong with you?"

"I have a rare type of brain aneurysm." He paused and took a deep breath, "It's deep in the lobes, and they can't operate on it."

"Is that why the migraines?"

"They usually don't have any symptoms, but as mine enlarged, I developed the headaches."

"Can't they do anything for it? Even if they can't operate, isn't there something they can do?"

"I've been to USC several times. I think I've kind of become their lab rat. They went through the artery in my leg and inserted a platinum coil inside the weak spot, which is supposed to help, but mine just got bigger. Four coils over two years and they've told me they can't do it again; it's still growing."

"And if it bursts?"

"The kind I have is fatal about eighty-five percent of the time, twelve percent become vegetables, and a lucky three percent survive it—with complications."

"You're telling me you're gonna die? Did they say whether you can live a long time with one of those or—"

"Mine was discovered six years ago; I've already out lived ninety percent of the people who have the same thing."

A huge knot rose up and stuck in her throat, making it impossible to speak, but she had to ask him one thing. "Did they—did they tell you how long?" she choked.

His hand rose to gently smooth her hair away from her face; then he stroked the side of her cheek with his fingers, "Yeah...my time was up last year."

"Damn, you picked the wrong girl for this," she said, pulling away and sitting up on the sleeping bag. Her head rested on her knees when she felt his hand on her back.

"It's okay. I understand. I'm not—"

"No, AJ, you don't. It's not you—it's me. I think you're perfect—aneurysm and all. But why God brought you to someone as messed up as me just blows my mind."

"You're not freaked that I might stroke-out and die at any minute?"

"None of us have a guarantee on life. I could smack my head on that wall tomorrow when I leave the hill and die before you. But you don't know who I am. You don't know what I'm really like. You don't know—you just don't know—and I really think you'll be getting the worst end of all of this."

"Then let me know, Cass. Tell me about yourself. Trust me, please."

"I can't."

He suddenly appeared to be summoning his courage. "Why did Frank tell me to *never* call you Cassie?"

"Stop it!" she shouted, smacking him in the chest with both her hands, "You don't need to know, and I don't have to tell you!" She burst into tears, "Don't ever say that again. You can call me whatever you want, but that's off limits!" She was trying to stand when he reached out for her wrist.

"Whoa, slow down, Cass. I won't do it again. Please, don't pull away from me. I don't know how this is ever going to work out, but I do know I want you to stay with me."

"On one condition," she said with a quiver in her voice.

"What?"

"We don't discuss you and me anymore—not your past, and definitely not mine. We read the scrolls and see what happens."

"Okay, but I want to hold you, Cass. I want you to sleep in my arms.

I only understand a little bit when it comes to you, but can you trust me this much tonight?"

She'd never simply been held by a man. She nodded and crawled back to where warmth and comfort waited for her. She faced away from him as he pulled her close once more, kissing her neck, and telling her goodnight. It would be a while before she fell asleep as she listened to his breathing. As long as it didn't stop, this new world she was stepping into would keep turning.

CHAPTER FIVE

Time under the hill was motionless. There was no way to tell whether it was midnight or noon; with the exception of a slight glow coming from the underwater opening, it was always the same inside. She never slept late, but when she reached for her phone in the pale glow from the light sticks, she discovered it was after eight a.m. Her night in his arms had been some of the best sleep she ever had.

He didn't move when she grabbed her phone, sending a little spike of fear through her. He had rolled onto his stomach sometime during the night with his back exposed. Gently, she reached out to rub his shoulders. His skin was cool to the touch, and she panicked. "AJ?" she said as she gave him a shake.

"Hmm? What is it, Cass? What's wrong?"

Now she had a better understanding of why the women in his life backed away; no one wanted to be the one who failed to get a response. But there was no way she'd let it drag her from him. The only thing that could pull her away now would be her past.

She leaned over before he could roll onto his back and kissed his ear, "It's after eight. We kinda slept in." She kept her voice smooth and even so he'd never know she had been afraid, "Are you hungry?"

"Starving. Granola doesn't go very far," he said, referring to what they had eaten last night.

"Protein lasts longer. It's not eggs and bacon, but how about some beef jerky and cheese?"

"Mmm," he moaned, rubbing his bare stomach, "sounds like a feast."

She turned on the lantern and squinted in its brightness as she studied him, "I have to ask something."

"Nothing about our pasts, right?"

She laughed, "No, not at all. You don't—umm—you don't have any hair on your body. Do you wax?"

His throaty laugh rolled out of his chest, "I shave."

"Everywhere?"

He rolled his eyes, "I'll just say everywhere you can see right now. It's a habit more than anything else, and a lot of surfers do it. I also wrestled in high school, and it's pretty hard to hold on to someone who's, well, slick."

"Okay, slick, do you realize that was right out of your past?" She watched the sheepish expression hit him, but she smiled to let him know it was okay, "Let's eat."

The hardest part of their morning was deciding the most comfortable way they could sit for a long period to read. Once that was established, he carved out the wax from the next hole and pulled out the contents. They were both surprised by how it was written.

It read like a novel.

I still recall the moment I saw Emiline. My father, King Osric of Northumbria, invited the nobles from all parts of the country to celebrate my seventeenth year. At the time, I wondered why he celebrated me at all; we were always at odds with each other and often he stated he would have been better off without an heir. My mother died during my birth, and I believe he never overcame the tragedy. I became the reason and the focus for his loss.

I stood in the great hall of the palace, watching the lords and ladies as they brought their young daughters into my presence. At the time, a wife was not the substance of my thoughts. Rather, I thirsted for conquest and adventure, for battle and victory, but for the passions of a frail female, I had not given thought. Until I saw her.

I had not seen a maiden with hair of such utter blackness. It shimmered against the torch light, but her eyes reached out and seized my heart. They were the color of the morning sky, clear and bright. Her skin was white as cream, so much so, I had to fight my temptation to reach out and stroke it. She gazed at me from under long, thick, black lashes and removed the very breath from my lungs with her beauty.

Her father accompanied her and, when he presented her to me, I could tell it was not of her choosing. I smiled at her as I took her hand.

Her acknowledgement of respect was simply perfunctory, but her heart was far from it. There was no other I wanted from that moment forward. When it came time for dancing, she refused all requestors, until I begged her presence onto the floor. I remember every word.

She looked up at me with those shimmering blue orbs, "If I refuse you, will I be asked to leave?"

"If you refuse to dance, I shall be forced to simply stand here and stare at you like some court idiot."

She smiled slightly, "If you stand here and stare, people may think you mad."

"And if you continue to refuse me, I may actually go mad."

Her hand slipped into mine as I bowed to her and led her out among the revelers. She was like dancing with air, light and lithe, nubile and full of grace. "Your name is Emiline, correct?"

"My Lord impresses me that, with all the lovely young maidens presented to him tonight, my name is remembered."

"What lovely young maidens?" I asked, glancing around the room, "I only see one." I watched her cheeks fill with a pale blush of color, and I sensed I had done well to say such to her. I had no experience with the female kind, but I was a quick study. "You are the most beautiful creature in the palace tonight, dear Emiline."

"Thank you, my Lord."

"I would prefer you to call me by my given name, Magnus. Lord sounds as one who should rule over you. I would think any man would be happy to simply rule with you." The look on her face was a mystery to me, but in retrospect perhaps I was the one who first put the notion in her mind that, one day, she could rule over others.

"Do you not wish for me to call you Orthellous Magnus?"

My facial cast soured, "No—Magnus only, please."

"And someday when you shall be king of Northumbria," she said with a small smile, "will you still be merely Magnus to me?"

I grew angry without hesitation, catching her off guard.

"Forgive me, my Lord. I did not mean to be forward or disrespect—"

"Not at all, Emiline. I merely do not wish to be king of Northumbria."

"But—but your father is king. You are the natural heir to—"

"I did not say I do not desire to be king; I do. I will be king someday, but in a kingdom far greater than my father's. I long to depart from what is offered to me on a golden tray. I long to conquer and to build. I long to create a legacy marked in history well after my father is far

forgotten." Once again, I realized I said something to her that struck a chord deep within. I watched her eyes cut to where her father stood, as he observed us with careful scrutiny.

"Yes, dear Magnus, I can see that someday you will be a great king, one who understands the deepest needs of his people."

At the time I thought she was speaking of my future subjects, but would learn far too late she spoke of her own need.

I felt a touch on my arm and turned to see my best and greatest friend and fellow nobleman, Earland.

"Although this is your party, Magnus, one does not expect you to be so greedy as to keep the best dancer in the room to yourself."

I smiled and stepped back, placing Emiline's hand in his, "I should have known that your keen eye would discover such a thing." I bowed to her, "Enjoy the dance, my lady, you are in safe hands. Although you might need to guard your feet," I said, as I laughed and stepped away. Oh, for a moment, would God allow me now to turn time back, I would do so no matter the price; I had sealed his fate.

AJ reached the end of the scroll. It had taken him about two hours to decipher it. The Latin was a variant of what he learned growing up, so when he was stuck, he would read a portion before and after until he understood the meaning. He reached over and gently squeezed her arm, "I know we're going to find out, but I wonder what he meant by that?"

Cass spoke quietly as she stared at her feet, "Sounds like Emiline is going to be trouble for—for both of them."

"Uh-huh," he responded, seemingly deep in wonder, but then he shook his head, "I can't get over the way this story is told; it's exceptional for an ancient work. He was far beyond his years, literally centuries, because it's written like an elegant memoir."

"Do you think Magnus was the one who actually wrote it?"

"No. Cynewulf was his stenographer. I read that on the first scroll. The king told the story in exacting detail to Cynewulf, and he meticulously recorded it as it was spoken—that's incredible for something from the eighth century. How about we stretch our legs before we start the next one?"

"Yeah, I have to take a bathroom break anyway," she sighed, reaching for the clothes draped across the table, still wet from last night.

"Is something bothering you?"

She shook her head slowly then frowned, "We know he buries the kingdom; it doesn't have a happy ending, but I just get the feeling I'm not going to like what Emiline puts him through. Cynewulf called her wicked and ungodly, so why would the first scroll say he is buried here with his beloved? How could a man love a woman who is..." Her frown deepened to melancholy.

"What? You can say what you're thinking, Cass. Try to have a little trust in me. I won't let you down."

"Some people just aren't worth loving." She stared for a moment into his eyes, "Some people are ugly inside, too ugly to deserve something good in their lives."

He didn't need a neon sign; he caught the drift, "*Some people* are too hard on themselves." He leaned over and wrapped her in his arms, placing a kiss on the top of her head. "Don't deny yourself the good in life; you deserve to be happy," he whispered.

She pulled away, took her damp clothes, and walked into the shadows to change. She grabbed the bag containing her cell phone and stepped into the water, then turned to face him, "The guys should be calling in about thirty minutes so I'm going to stay outside for a little while."

He nodded as he finished rolling up the scroll.

"AJ," she gave him a faint smile when he looked up at her, "It's been almost twenty years since I've been happy, but being with you these last couple of days made me remember what it's like. Thanks," she added, and then dove for the opening.

She decided to pass the time as she waited for the crews to check-in by doing a little research on her computer, but this had nothing to do with her job. She researched the ancient kings of Northumbria. She found King Osric, but there was no mention of Orthellous Magnus, or simply Magnus. The successor to Osric's throne was a distant cousin he adopted as his heir, Ceolwulf.

The first King Magnus mentioned in history didn't appear until the thirteenth century. It puzzled her, but she didn't have long to think about it; her phone started ringing. Everyone checked in, including Dirk. Surprisingly, he didn't ask anything about what she was doing this time. He gave her his coordinates, told her how the job was progressing, and then said goodbye. She found this stranger than being grilled by him, but she certainly wasn't going to question him about it.

Just before closing her computer, she decided to check out one other person: Cynewulf. It was exciting to see his name recorded in history, but his life was listed as a 'veritable mystery' to scholars, calling him the 'shadow of a name.'

It fascinated her to be investigating a man who was a mystery to the world, yet one she was becoming intimately familiar with. History couldn't even put a correct date to his existence and gave several different time periods and possible backgrounds. She immediately knew which one was correct: Cynewulf, Bishop of Lindisfarne from the 780's. Evidently, when Magnus died, Cynewulf moved on into the religious order and spent the remainder of his life writing eloquent poetry. The sketchy information about his life stated he wrote in the Anglian dialect, but distinctly mentioned that he used Latin sources and, apparently, was well versed in the Latin language.

There are times when people know divine providence has stepped into their lives. Cassandra was having that feeling as goose bumps flooded her skin and the hair on the back of her neck stood up. Had Cynewulf chosen to write Magnus's words in Anglian, she and AJ would have had no clue as to what the scrolls revealed. For some reason, this ancient poet had written the telling of Kingdom Hill in Latin—the one ancient language AJ could read. It confirmed her innermost feelings that she and AJ had an entwined destiny waiting before their lifetimes even began. She closed her eyes as the tears dripped down her cheeks, and she did something she stopped doing when her mother died; she thanked God.

Just as she stepped into the water to go back under the hill, AJ swam out.

"Bathroom break," he said with a little grin.

She had dried and changed by the time he reentered the room. He was telling her how much he enjoyed the cooler climate as he unzipped the wetsuit and started removing it when it dawned on her; he was about to undress right in front of her—and there was no way his damp underwear was going to stay up when the suit came down. For a split second, she hesitated; then she turned around to face the table.

"Ah crap. I'm sorry, Cass," came his apology.

She kept her back to him, "For what?"

"We've been changing clothes so many times around each other, I almost got a little too comfortable."

"AJ, can I tell you something?" she still had her back to him, and things became noticeably quiet after her question.

"Yeah, if you want to."

"It's not from the past. I just want to tell you that you're—you're beautiful. I've never said that to a man, maybe because I've never met one like you, but when you were in the shower the other day, I—I watched you for a couple of seconds. I just saw your backside, but... Well, anyway, I'm not big on compliments, but I wanted to tell you what I thought about you and to apologize for doing it without you knowing."

"Can I tell you something?"

She nodded.

"When you turned your back to me yesterday and changed, I couldn't take my eyes off of you."

"At least you keep yourself under control, but, me, I—"

"Did you lose control in the sleeping bag last night? Come on, Cass, you deserve more credit than you give yourself."

"Last night was one of the best nights of my life," she spoke it so softly it was barely audible, "I've never met a man with your willpower."

His arms wrapped around her from behind as he kissed her temple, "If you want to know the truth, I never knew I had that much willpower either, but I'll have however much it takes for you to feel safe when you're with me." He squeezed her a little tighter, "How about the next scroll?"

They made themselves comfortable as AJ opened it on his semi-reclined lap. She was tucked against him, infinitely more relaxed than she'd ever been, but at the same time apprehensive about what they would learn from this scroll.

I asked my father if Emiline could be moved into or near the palace, so she might undergo tutelage from one of the palace women (as to whatever women might teach to young girls). Someday, I wanted to ask for her hand in marriage, but I wanted her to be confident in her ability to be my bride and queen. Since she had no mother and was but a mere fourteen years of age, it seemed logical that some form of schooling would be in order. I had no concept as to what kind of schooling women endured, but she did not strike me as feeble minded in any conceivable way.

It was agreed and she was placed in the care of Bernatha, an elderly woman who had taken care of me from birth until I was about ten years of age. I knew her to be prudent and wise, caring and compassionate for the souls of others. I was happy with the arrangement, and happier still I would now get glimpses of Emiline on nearly a daily basis. Occasionally, I would have the pleasant surprise of actually speaking with her.

Within a month of her arrival at the palace, word spread of invaders whom had landed on the western shore and were marching overland to reach Northumbria. I was ripe for battle. Given command of my father's army, I strategized our attack and prepared my soldiers to march. Earland was to be my second-in-command, but within a day ere embarking on the adventure of our young lives, he became desperately ill and unable to keep any sustenance within himself.

I did not wish to leave him behind, but in his condition, he would be of no use to me or even to himself for that matter. Leaving him with my prayers for a return to health, I took the ranks and led them out to battle. I had assisted my father in putting down several small skirmishes in the past, but this was much different. My father had not stomach neither for war nor me; I wondered if he harbored hopes for my demise, but I would not, could not, be defeated. As I left the borders of Northumbria behind me, I saw a countryside both rich and beautiful. Peasants, yearning for the protection of a warrior king, were scattered across the land. I garnered support and information as I advanced. The confidence of my men increased as they witnessed my diplomacy with the inhabitants and the bite of my sword against the enemy.

We were returning victorious after four months away from our homeland. My military commanders, though older than I, began to urge me to force my father into abdicating his throne, but I saw a new country which held more promise than Northumbria. I said nothing, but my plan to create a new kingdom began to form. What I did not realize at the time was an event, yet unbeknownst to me, would propel me to launch my plan almost immediately.

The face I yearned to see forthwith upon my return was Emiline's, but matters of State demanded I first meet with my father. After our meeting, he told me Bernatha succumbed to an illness similar to that which Earland had been beset with; Earland recovered, but Bernatha died a fortnight following my departure. Emiline, he said, refused any other tutor. Concern for her filled me so deeply that I bid my father my leave and went directly to her side.

I knocked at Bernatha's residence but received no reply. "Emiline, are you in there?" I heard a faint whimpering beyond the door but still no answer. "Emiline, it is Magnus. Please allow me to enter."

The latch slowly lifted, and the door cracked open. I could only see a small portion of her face, but it appeared pale and drawn; her hair tumbled all about her shoulders. Tears glistened on her cheek, and it felt as though my heart broke into two pieces at that moment. "Please, dearest Emiline, let me in," I crooned. "What is wrong? Tell me, please." I knew these tears could not be due to her loss of Bernatha; it had been too long. Something else was upsetting her horribly.

"No, my Lord. It would not be good for you to—to see me this way."

"What way? Tell me what is the matter with you? Are you ill?"

The sound of her crying increased, "I do not wish to see you ever again. I will be leaving for my father's house on the morrow."

Shock and confusion filled me. I could not imagine a life without her presence. "Emiline, I will not leave. I intend to take you as my bride. I—"

"Go away, Magnus!" she tearfully exclaimed, "I am fit to be no man's bride! Leave me to my shame. I would rather God take my life than for you to know what has happened."

The door was still ajar, and I had to see her to uncover what madness imprisoned her mind. I pushed it open as she quickly turned her back to me and cowered down toward the floor. I gripped her shoulders as tenderly as possible and turned her toward myself. "Sweet heaven above, what has happened to you?" One side of her face was bruised and swollen, her lip thick and cracked. That was when I noticed her dress: torn at the bodice, a torn undergarment exposed, and a dark red stain upon her skirting. She crumpled against me sobbing and crying, begging and pleading for me to thrust my dagger into her heart to end her shame. My beautiful Emiline had been brutalized by a man.

AJ still had a small portion of scroll to finish reading, but he stopped when he realized the reaction Cassandra was having.

"I need some air," she said, sounding as if she was fighting nausea. She stood and went immediately to the water's edge, but he stopped her.

"Cass, don't. You'll ruin your dry clothes. If you have to go outside, let's change and go out together."

She nodded in apparent agreement as he attempted to rub her back. "Don't—please," she said, as she moved away from him and picked up a bottled water, taking a few sips.

"We can finish this tomorrow."

"No. I don't want to start tomorrow like this. I'm okay, I just needed a break. Go ahead and finish it."

He went back to their reading spot and picked up the scroll, but she didn't return to her place beside him, "Do you want to sit?"

She shook her head no. She paced back and forth in a small area, her arms tight across her chest, her expression pained.

Nothing could prepare me for the news when I ordered her to tell me who had done such a thing. My blood boiled within me, and I readied myself to kill whomever she would name.

"I cannot! Please, do not make me," she pled, "He told me he will deny it. He said you would never believe me. He said he will tell you all manner of ill about me to turn you against me. Please don't make me, Magnus, please, just let me go and forget you ever knew me."

"I could never doubt you. You hold my heart, Emiline, and I love you. If you love me as well, tell me who committed this atrocity."

She looked at me through tear-stained eyes and uttered the word that cut me to the marrow, "Earland."

AJ looked up at her, "I knew that was coming."

"Me, too," she softly agreed, "Is that the end of the scroll?"

"Yeah. Are you okay now?"

She didn't answer him as she opened her phone, "That one took awhile. It's check-in time again." She glanced around the room and then back to AJ, "I think I have enough wire in all my gear to put a satellite out one of the lower vents and a hookup for signal under here." She hoped he'd take the hint that she *did not* want to discuss what he just read.

"That would save a lot of swimming, but what about keeping everything charged?"

"I have that covered. I'm a bit of a science geek, so I tinkered with my batteries. Phone technology is pretty good anyway because it lasts about three days from a full charge. I jazzed up my laptop, so I can get about ten hours. And, since I only use it for about thirty minutes a night, I'm good for four or five days."

"Cass, about the scroll—"

"How about dinner tonight? I'd like to take a drive and get some real food."

"Cass—"

"Can we *not* discuss this right now?"

"I need to say something, but it's not what you think."

"You don't know what I think!" she suddenly snapped. She instantly regretted her bitchy remark, "I'm sorry. Go ahead."

"I was actually thinking we should start the next scroll tonight."

He was right; that wasn't the comment she expected, "Why?"

"We both have a good idea what's going to happen. We can finish it tonight, so tomorrow won't be, I hope, quite so rough on you."

She tried to swallow down the lump that formed in her throat, "You probably don't realize this, but I haven't cried in a lot of years. I meet you, and I'm a wreck; I'm blubbering all over the place."

"Tears are good for you, Cass," he said, as he reached out and wiped her cheeks. "They're going to help wash away that hard wall you've built."

She rolled her eyes and pulled away, "And—and when you're gone, AJ, what then? You'll have taught me to lower my defenses and I'll be vulnerable. *I don't ever want to get hurt again*."

"I think it's time I tell you what Bobby and I talked about."

She didn't like the sound of what was coming, "I don't want to know."

"Maybe you don't, but what hurts worse than knowing I won't be here much longer is thinking that you might end up back with some idiot like Dirk. You deserve so much better than what you're settling for, Cass."

She was becoming angry. She didn't want Dirk—she never wanted Dirk—he'd just been someone she didn't scare away. The man she wanted was standing right in front of her, and she couldn't fathom the moment his eyes would close and never reopen, "You can't pass me off to him like some trinket in a will."

"All I want is for you to promise me you'll give him a chance."

"My God! You're serious?! Did you actually tell him to try to put the move on me when you're gone?!" She jerked away from his touch and backed up a few steps, "Maybe I was wrong about you; maybe you aren't different, just twisted."

"It's not twisted to want you to have someone good in your life! He and I have been friends since I was twelve years old. I have never met someone as honest and good, kind-hearted and truthful as Bobby. He'd never hurt you, and he'd never let anyone else hurt you, either. He'd kick Dirk's ass all over the place if he tried to get near you."

She gave a scoffing laugh, "Dirk? You must be kidding."

"He may be shy around women, but I haven't seen a man yet who can push him around. I want you protected, and loved, when I'm gone."

She could hear him swallow hard as the sound of tiny bubbles rose in his throat. As tough as it had been to listen to his viewpoint, it evidently had been even harder for him to express it.

"But I don't love Bobby—" she started to quietly tell him.

"Give him a—"

"I love *you*." She actually said it out loud. The feeling that had been building inside her finally had a name, and its name was love. She didn't doubt it any longer. She had fallen in love for the first time in her life.

He closed the space between them and very gently cupped her face in his hands, "Tell me you trust me, Cass, please."

"I do," she whispered.

His mouth touched hers, softly at first, almost like a butterfly's wing brushed against her skin. He came back again just as tender as the first time. She'd never felt lips so warm and compassionate. She wondered what his kiss was going to be like, but she never imagined it could be so perfect.

"Cass, I love you. I really do love you."

The kiss came firmer this time; his lips sought her response. She parted them slightly to let her tongue brush his mouth. His lips parted as he met her curiosity. The kiss went deeper—exploring the emotions inside each other. She pulled away for a moment as she tried, unsuccessfully, to catch her breath. If this was suffocation, she was ready to welcome it to the point of passing out as his mouth covered hers once more.

When their kiss finally ended, she was shocked to realize she was on the floor, wrapped in his arms, fully embraced against him. But old demons don't die easily, and she found herself pushing against his chest, asking him to let her go, yet clinging to his lower body with her legs. She hadn't expected him to stop; no one had ever stopped at this point.

"Let me go, Cass. We aren't ready for this yet."

She was confused; he was asking her to let go? The game wasn't played this way.

"We have to stop," he reiterated.

Her eyes closed as she tightened her legs and raised her pelvis to grind slowly against his. "You don't have to stop," she whispered, eyes still shut.

"Look at me. Cassandra, open your eyes."

Her eyelids fluttered open.

"Did you mean it when you said you love me?"

She nodded.

"And when I asked you to trust me, did you mean it when you said yes?"

She nodded again. Her frenzied emotions were starting to cool; the grip of her legs easing.

"Then trust me right now; you're not ready for this yet."

"But I want it."

"Listen to what you said. You want 'it.' You want sex, not me. If this happens between us, you're going to have to want me, nothing else. This has to be about making love, not just having sex."

"But, AJ—"

"It's not going to happen any other way."

"I've never made love," she whimpered, her body starting to tremble in fear, "it's always been about the sex."

"Not this time, beautiful. It's going to have to be about you and me, and what we feel for each other." He placed a final soft kiss on her mouth, "Let go."

She turned him loose, and he helped her to her feet. She glanced at her cell phone. "I—I missed check-in time."

"And I bet you'll find each one of them left what you need in your voice mail."

"I really would like to have dinner with you somewhere tonight, but I agree about getting through one more scroll, too."

"Then let's do it. We should get back here with enough time for me to help you run the wire for the satellite, download your data, and then we'll spend the rest of the evening reading."

She beamed a huge smile as she stared at him.

"What?" he asked, wrinkling his forehead in curiosity.

"I had no idea falling in love could feel this incredible."

He drew her against himself for one more kiss. "God willing," he breathed, "it's going to get even better."

CHAPTER SIX

It was close to nine by the time they settled in to read the next scroll. Their evening had been perfect, but now she was feeling apprehensive again. She could tell AJ sensed it, and knowing he cared so much about her and about her feelings completely blew her mind. All evening long, as they ate dinner, ran the wires, checked the progress of the teams, all of it, one thing stayed on her mind: she was going to find the finest aneurysm specialist in the world because she couldn't let him go without a fight.

He pulled the sleeping bag up around her shoulders as he began.

I was in utter disbelief when she told me who had attacked her. I asked, as gently as possible so she would not think I doubted her, whether she was certain. Did she truly know who Earland was? As far as I was aware, she only met him on the dance floor the night of my party.

"Yes, it was he. He visited me often once you brought me here. Bernatha, God rest her sweet soul, did not like him. She said he looked at me with indecorous intent. The poor dear took pity on him, though, when he became ill. I believe it was her undoing. She tried to care for him but bore his illness when it was finished. Once she passed away, he visited more frequently, and I began to be uncomfortable; he liked to be here with me alone."

I said nothing as I listened; my heart hardened like a stone toward my once good friend. How could he do this while I battled for our kingdom, risking my life to keep Northumbria safe?

"When the messenger arrived yesterday saying that you had been

victorious and were nearly home, he came immediately to me and asked..."

"What did he ask?"

"He asked me to go back with him to his father's house and become his wife."

"But he knew that I—"

"I am sorry, dear Magnus. I understand if you do not believe me."

"I cannot doubt you any more than I can doubt the heart that is beating in my breast which loves you without question."

"When I told him I only wished for his friendship, and you were my true love; he flew into a horrible rage."

Once again, she began to weep, and I did not know whether she could continue, but she gathered her bravery and resumed.

"He said he would have me first, for you would not desire a soiled woman. I told him you would be furious enough to kill," she said then slowly gazed up at me. "He was unafraid. He said you would believe anything he told you. He said you were simple and easily led by his stories. He said he would tell you all manner of unscrupulous ills about me, and I would be doomed by your hand."

"He told you that I—I would kill you?"

"Yes, sweet Magnus, he said you would end my worthless existence by his urging. And then he—he..."

She crumpled like a crushed flower against my breast, as I tried to sooth her. I told her she needn't tell me more; I was already angry enough to kill him. I needed no further provocation, but she continued.

"When I tried to fight him off, he struck my face, sending me sprawling to the floor. Before I could rise, he was upon me, ripping at my gown and exposing what should have only been for your eyes. I tried to stop him. I scratched at his shoulders, but he held me down and then hurt me, Magnus. I did not know a man's body could be so forceful. My insides were in so much pain. My blood soaked through my garments. I knew I could no longer hope to marry you; I am no longer chaste. I felt I had no other choice than to agree to marry him after what he had done, but he—he laughed at me," she wailed out, "and said I was no longer worthy to be his wife, either."

I was so filled with fury; I felt as if my body might explode, "You are worthy in my eyes! I do not care what has happened here. You will be my bride; I will have no other. But I must go for a little while. I must confront him and make him atone for this sin against you."

I had to comfort her for a while longer. She wanted me to stay and hold her in my arms. She wanted to stay pressed against me and asked repeatedly whether I would be gentle with her when our time finally came to be together. I had to leave. I could not allow my passion for her to become unbridled, as did Earland. I felt her innocence calling out to me to show her tenderness and intimacy.

"I must go, sweet Emiline."

"You will not tell anyone what happened here, will you? I would be ashamed beyond living should anyone know."

"No one will know."

I left and stalked to my father's hall to announce that Earland was a traitor to Northumbria.

"After I kill him, I am leaving with as many soldiers as wish to accompany me to build a new kingdom."

I still recall the look upon my father's face. He was seated in conversation with Ceolwulf, his young cousin.

"Are you mad?" My father asked.

"I am not."

"Earland and his father are from noble lines. What proof do you have of this act of treason?" Ceolwulf asked.

"I have my proof; no one else need know."

"Everyone else need know! You must prove his guilt," Ceolwulf continued.

"My son, if you do this thing without known reason, I will have to renounce your heritage to the throne."

"I care not for your throne, Father. And you have never cared for me to be your heir. You can adopt Ceolwulf, and let him be your successor. I shall be king of a land far greater than Northumbria."

The last thing I heard as I stormed from the hall was Ceolwulf telling my father that I was indeed mad. I went to the captains of my soldiers and told them, if they wished to follow me into glory, to be prepared to ride out for a new land when the sun rose the next morning. They were to bring their families and possessions. "I feel no anger toward you if you do not wish to join me," I stated. "A greater kingdom is my dream, and it can be yours, as well, if God so moves you."

When I reached Earland's home, I was surprised to find that the coward who took delight in destroying the innocence of a young girl would have the audacity to be awaiting my arrival. My sword was already drawn as I dismounted.

"I am unarmed," he said, as I approached, "You must listen to me, my friend; all is not as it appears."

I took my first swing at him with my sword, but in my rage, my aim was imperfect. "You forced yourself upon the woman who was to be my bride!" I grabbed another sword from my mount and threw it at him. "Arm yourself," I growled.

He caught the sword but then laid it on the ground, "She is evil, Magnus."

I swung again, this time barely missing him, as he dodged my fury.

"Listen to me, please. We have known each other since boyhood. She was the reason I could not go into battle with you."

I paused for a moment. I would let the traitor confess before dying. "I believed you ill, but I think now perhaps you made yourself ill to stay behind with her."

"No. She poisoned me. She invited me to Bernatha's and offered me drink, saying she wanted to talk to me about protecting you on our journey."

"Liar!" I shouted, and charged him again.

"She hated Bernatha and I believe she killed her with the same poison—only a greater amount."

"She loved that saintly old woman, you..." This time he was not quick enough to miss the edge of my blade as I caught his shoulder. He cried out in pain, and for a moment, I regretted my mission.

His father heard the skirmish and ran out, but Earland bade him to stay back.

"I did not realize what she was doing until it was too late."

"Too late for whom? Too late for her, after you beat and raped her?"

The look on his face told me he was genuinely surprised by my words.

"I did not do such a thing!" he said with a clear and innocent voice, "She seduced me!"

I stuck my sword into the earth and charged for him, slamming him hard against a near tree. I drew my dagger and pressed it to his breast as he winced under my hold. Earland was stronger than I, and a better swordsman, but he refused to defend himself. "You took away the virginity she would have offered to me as my queen!"

He straightened himself and looked into my eyes with clear intent, "She was no virgin when I took her."

I do not recall shoving the blade through his heart, but I do recall his father's cry as Earland fell dead upon the ground.

With the last word spoken, AJ went totally silent.

Cass sat so motionless during the reading that her body felt riveted in place, but she had to move. She had to shake off the imagery that filled her mind while the story had unfolded. She slowly stood and opened her cell. "It's after midnight."

"Are you doing okay?"

She nodded but then glanced around as the lantern light dimmed, "We'll need a fresh battery tomorrow. I know it's a stupid thing to complain about, but I have to go pee and I don't want to get in the water."

He got up and went to their stash of supplies and returned with a Ziploc bag. "I've been thinking about that. You know, these things are good for more than keeping stuff dry."

She smiled and then pressed her hands to her face. "It's amazing that you can still make me smile even after what we just read. Thank you," she said, reaching out for the baggy.

They spent the night in their combined sleeping bag again, and, just as before, all he did was hold her. She woke early, mainly because at some point AJ rolled flat on his back and began to lightly snore. She welcomed the sound because it reassured her that the most important being in her world was still breathing. She slipped quietly to the far end of the room and hooked her computer up to the newly rigged satellite line and muted the sound. She started at six in the morning, and stayed on it until she felt his touch on her shoulder, a few minutes before nine.

"What are you doing?"

"We're flying out to St. Paul, Minnesota tonight."

"What?!"

"I have an appointment set for you for tomorrow afternoon at The National Brain Aneurysm Center."

"But—but, Cass, I've already been to—"

"Yeah, I know where you've been, but this place specializes in cerebral aneurysms. They have a doctor on staff who handles hundreds of these every year from all over the world."

"But what about the scrolls?"

She stood up and wrapped her arms around him, kissing him to shut him up. It worked because he started returning the kisses. "AJ, I can't lose you, at least not without a fight. This place will be waiting for us when we get back. It hasn't gone anywhere for thirteen-hundred years. *Please*. Do you want to stay with me? Do you love me enough to try?"

"Cass, before I met you, I gave up. I figured I'd live out what I had left as if nothing was wrong with me. My parents wanted me to move back home and give up working for the magazine, but that sounded like sitting around waiting for the bomb to go off in my head. And then I met you, and it felt like my whole world changed in an instant. I never wanted to die, but now I have a beautiful reason to live."

"So you'll go?"

"I may need some more kissing to seal the deal, but, yeah, I'll go."

She'd never been the jump-up-and-down-and-squeal type of woman, but, then again, she'd never been this happy.

"What time and which airport?"

"We're flying out of Glasgow at seven p.m. It's a ten hour flight, but there is a five hour time difference so we'll arrive in Boston around midnight. We have an hour layover, and then we board for a short flight to St. Paul. We'll catch some Zs at a hotel, and then your appointment is at two in the afternoon. Why are you grinning like that?"

"Because I purposely wanted to see just how detailed you'd get, Miss Over-Organizational."

"Oh, that is just the tip of the organizational iceberg. I reserved a hotel room near the airport tonight so we can clean up, I've paid for the tickets, pre-paid the parking for the Land Cruiser, planned where we'll have breakfast and lunch and—"

"And all before I agreed to go."

"But, AJ, why wouldn't you?"

"I'm kidding, Cass. Do we have time for a scroll in your pre-planned schedule?"

"Yes, we do. Are you feeling okay?" she noticed he was starting to grimace.

"I have a headache, but it isn't really bad," he added quickly, so she wouldn't worry. "It's probably just a little bit of eyestrain because I haven't been using my glasses."

"I didn't know you used glasses. Let's skip the scroll today," she quickly added. She hadn't thought that reading might actually be bad for him, but considering how much concentration he had to put into it, and how long each one took, perhaps it wasn't a good idea.

"I'll take a pill and put on my glasses. I'll be fine."

"No, please," she said, bordering on whiny, "we'll just be lazy today and rest."

His face became very serious as he tipped her chin up so she had to look into his eyes. "I've made it this long by *not* living my life like I'm walking on eggshells. Doing what I would normally do is what keeps me going. I don't want you to get crazy on me like my parents and suddenly think I shouldn't do anything other than 'take it easy.'"

The tears filled the bottom of her sea colored eyes as she gave a small nod, "You get the scroll. I'll get you a pill."

His kiss came as slowly and sensually as the very first time, but it was different. She could feel his need and desire like a warm blanket wrapping around her physically and emotionally. When he took his lips off of hers, she had to ask, "Or would you rather show me how to make love this morning?"

"Oh, Cass, you have no idea how badly I want to make love to you, but you have to come clean. You have to trust me enough to tell me what you're hiding. I know there's a whole lot about yourself that you just aren't saying."

"Please, AJ, I can't. I don't know how much time we have together, and I don't want something to happen and we never get the chance."

"If something happened right this second, and I hit the floor, this would all still be worth it. To make love is a beautiful experience, but to be in love is so, so much more. If I could choose right now which I'd rather have before I die, it would be to use my last breath to tell you that I love you."

She couldn't say anything in response; she just cried as he held her and gently swayed back and forth. She finally raised her head and wiped her eyes, "Did you bring your glasses?"

"Yeah, they're in one of the outer zipper pockets on my pack."

She turned him loose and went to get what he needed while he removed the next scroll from the wall.

With a pill down and his glasses on, they settled into their reading place and stepped back in time.

It did not surprise me when I returned to the palace to learn three quarters of the guard stood ready to join me in creating a new kingdom. I had Emiline quickly gather her things and I placed her in a cart with a driver. The entire kingdom was in upheaval. Word spread quickly that I had killed Earland, had been disowned by my father, and I was no longer to be his rightful heir. Yet, many wished to follow under my leadership rather than to remain under my father's rule. I do not know the number, but many of his subjects became mine and followed me to the east.

We were welcomed by those who had longed for a king to give stability to the eastern region. We traveled on until we reached this beautiful place. I knew when I saw Emiline's smile we had found our new home. There was good land to the north from whence to quarry stone for building, fertile ground in all directions, several springs, and abundant game. I devised an ambitious plan for the kingdom. I would not simply build a palace. I envisioned a fortified palace. A protected, large, sprawling structure with high walls to keep out invaders and a place where even the peasants could retreat if the kingdom came under siege. My subjects embraced the work with surprising vigor and fortitude. I not only commanded, but also laid my hands to the task. My first order of business was to assure Emiline had a safe place in which to live. Once completed, I gave her some of the peasant women to have as housekeeps, chamber maids, and such.

Emiline asked me often when we would wed, but I felt in my heart she was asking for my sake and my needs, but I assured her when the time was right, I would take her as my queen. In truth, I wanted her to have time to overcome what happened. I could hardly believe she wanted to be exposed to the needs of a man after all she had been through.

After two years of heavy labors, the inner and outer walls were completed. Our inner walls contain four towers at a height of thirty cubits each from which the land could be surveyed far and wide for signs of danger. One of the towers had become my quarters and I began to long to have Emiline join me. I had the workmen shift to completing the palace church, and as soon as it was finished, I had two official orders of business. First was my formal crowning as King. The land, a hundred or so years earlier, had been name for King Rheged, but I was not to be tied by that name. We christened the land as Valderegnum, to mean Great Kingdom. Once I was crowned King of Valderegnum, I fell upon my knees to show the greatest respect to ask Emiline to be my Queen.

The celebration of my crowning and subsequent marriage lasted a fortnight. My kingdom was well pleased with their king and queen. During the festivities and celebrations, I touched her not. Her staff came with her to the tower and prepared what had been my quarters into our wedding chamber. I had waited years for my beautiful Emiline, and she was eager to be consummated as my wife. I was surprised to learn she was not timid in accepting me. She was now a young maiden of seventeen years, and she told me she had waited for me long enough; there was no need for shyness. She challenged my strength and ability with her need to be a woman; a woman for my pleasure and my love. We did not reappear before our subjects for three glorious days.

AJ had a slight smile as he finished reading, "Well, this one was much shorter and definitely ended on a—a happier note."

"How's the headache?"

"Better. The glasses and the pill helped."

"Let's leave early for Glasgow, so we can enjoy our hotel room for a little while before we fly out."

"Cass, I didn't say anything this morning, but it's kinda bugging me that you've evidently already paid for all of this."

"Why? You didn't ask me to make this appointment; it was my idea."

"I realize that, and I appreciate it more than you know, but I'm starting to feel like a moocher."

"You're not, so don't even go there. I make pretty good money doing what I do, so I can afford it."

"Well, yeah, I guess nine million for six weeks' work isn't too shabby."

"It won't be anywhere near that figure. Half goes for all the expenses, crew salaries and bonuses. Then Uncle Sam will get roughly half," she began to explain when he stopped her.

"Whoa. I wasn't trying to figure out how much you'll personally make. I was just saying—"

"You know something? You are the only person I've ever felt like discussing my finances with. Now hush up and let me finish."

He rolled his eyes and crossed his arms, "Go ahead."

"Okay, the corporation gets half of that. Then what's left is divided into thirds. I'll get roughly four-hundred and fifteen-thousand, but then I get to personally pay Uncle Sam about half of that, so when all is said and done I'll clear about two-hundred-grand."

"Why thirds? It's you and your dad. Who's the other party?"

She'd been so busy spouting off facts and figures, she didn't consider she might be opening a personal door of a different kind. "Family," she stated without her previous energy.

"And that," he said, sounding like he had a degree of certainty, "is something you *don't* want to discuss."

"I have three half sisters and—and two half brothers."

"Younger than you?" he evidently was thinking about the three step-moms she told him about already.

"No," she answered quietly, and then looked away, "they're all older than I am."

He touched her chin and turned her to face him, "I'm sorry, Cass. I'll stop digging."

"My dad was married twice before he met my mom, and Mom had been married once; that's where they all came from. I'm the last."

"You're the baby?"

She nodded.

"Do they all work for... I'm doing it again."

"No, it's okay. I can handle this much. None of them work for my dad. He's always insisted they be included in the profits. They divide a third of any profits five ways, which I think is totally wrong, and it pisses me off. I honestly believe he's just buying time with his grandkids. You know, if he cuts off the gravy train, they won't bring the grandkids around anymore. I was the only one who wanted to be part of his world. I was the one who put it back on track when he was nearly broke," she sighed. "And now I work my ass off, and they ask Daddy, 'When is our check going to be deposited into the bank account?'"

"Yeah, I think that would piss me off, too."

"What really hurts now is two of them want an equal share in the corporation—not just the profits. They've been telling him they want to help 'run' the business, when they don't know their asses from a hole in the ground! If my dad lets them talk him into it, I'll—I'll... I don't know; I guess I'll quit."

"Does your dad know how you feel about all of this?"

"Yeah, but Dad's not always logical. The booze has fried a few of his circuits."

He softly touched her cheek and then ran his fingers into her hair, "How about that hotel? A steamy shower sounds good right about now."

She finally smiled.

The only thing they did when they left was remove the underwater line, the external satellite, and threw some sod over the three ventilation openings, just in case someone should stumble across this secluded spot and snoop around.

The ride to Glasgow didn't take long, but during the short span of time, the weather turned ugly. It was windy and rainy when they pulled up to the Holiday Inn. They had about five hours before they needed to check-in at the airport, and for those hours, they would relax.

AJ plopped down on the comfortable bed and motioned toward the bathroom, "Ladies first. Wake me up when you get out."

She took her time, enjoying the warmth of the shower—and the soap. They may have been in water several times a day, but it wasn't the same, and it left her smelling like a pond, so soap and shampoo were luxuries she missed. She wrapped herself in a towel and padded quietly out to wake him, but he was lying there on his back, stripped down to his boxer briefs, with his tattooed arm behind his head and a smile on his face.

She looked at him quizzically and then bent down to kiss him, "The bathroom is all yours."

His smile grew.

"You're getting stubbly," she laughed, "*everywhere*. I've never told this to a guy before, but baby, you need to shave your legs."

His deep laugh rolled, "Cass, I hate to tell you this, but I paid you back."

"For what?" she said with a furrow to her brow.

"Moffat."

She cocked her head sideways.

"The business with the shower."

Suddenly, what he was talking about hit her, "You—you peeked?!"

"Just for a few seconds; it sure is making it hard to see you in that towel right now."

She stared at him with a serious face.

"Are you mad at me?"

She smiled, "No, but I thought the exact same thing when you came out in a towel."

He raised his hands and gripped the tucked corner of her towel but then stopped. He let the first growl escape she'd heard from him.

She offered no resistance.

"Not yet," he whispered, but it sounded like he was saying it to himself.

"AJ, I want to do something."

"Yeah, me, too but not until—"

"Not that, although it is a definite thought right now; I want to shave you."

His eyebrows went up and stayed, "Oh, Cass, I don't think we can manage that without going too far."

"I won't get in the tub with you. I'll just sit next to it. Please."

"You're serious?"

"Yes."

"I'm going to have to wear my boxers into the tub?"

"No, make it a bubble bath or put a hand towel over your lap."

"Did you shave your legs already?"

"I didn't take a razor in there with me."

"Go get back in the tub and tell me when you're ready. I'll do you first."

She filled the tub with hot water and bubbles and then sank to the bottom. She'd never done anything like this before, and she was actually nervous. She was hesitating to tell him she was ready when he gently knocked at the partially open door and asked if he could come in.

When he entered, he had a towel around his waist, a razor in one hand, and a small can of shaving cream in the other. "I hope this is okay," he said, referring to the shaving cream. "I don't have anything fruity smelling, so you may come out of here smelling like a guy."

She laughed, which was all it took to take away her case of nerves. She raised one long leg with toes pointed and bubbles running down her thigh, "I don't think I'm going to be paying attention to the fragrance."

His eyes widened, "Me neither."

What a sensual and special experience to allow him to do this simple thing for her. The wonderful part was—since he was skilled at shaving his own legs—he knew where to be careful with the razor; no nicks or cuts on her shins, ankles, or knees.

"Your turn. Hand me my towel."

Instead, he simply held her towel open and motioned her out. She stood up slowly and stepped into his waiting arms. He tucked her into the towel, removed his own, and stepped into the bath. She caught her breath; he was nude, and he was flawless.

Shaving him took considerably longer. She started with his legs, but when she moved to his chest she realized he wasn't taking his eyes off of her. He wasn't smiling or speaking, just watching as she carefully worked. When she moved to his arms, he held her free hand as she shaved him. She had him roll over in the tub as she finished and then kissed the top of his head and told him she was done. He turned over and grinned, "You forgot something."

She swallowed so hard it was audible as she glanced to the part covered in bubbles, "I—I didn't think you wanted me to shave *that* area."

"Cass," he said, causing her to stop staring at the bubbles, "my face."

"Oh," she felt the blush rush into her cheeks, "I forgot about that part."

She applied the shaving cream and began, but quickly realized faces weren't as easy as other parts of the body, "I don't think I'm doing a good job."

"Hand me the mirror," he said, gesturing to one sitting on the sink.

She tried to hand him the razor.

"No, you hold it. I'll guide your hand."

And that was precisely what he did as he showed her the proper way to shave a man's face.

She stood up and grabbed his towel, holding it open just as he had done to her.

"Give me a second to rinse off." He turned on the shower and stood up as she watched.

She had viewed the male physique frequently during her lifetime, but his body was different to her. There was no ugliness, no vulgarity, nothing dirty, or shameful about him; he was like artwork. It was more than just what she saw with her eyes, it was the man she was getting to know with her heart. And she suddenly knew he was right about sex and being in love because what she felt in her heart was the greater hunger of the two.

He stepped into the towel she was still holding, "Thank you for suggesting this. I didn't think we could handle it, but I loved every minute."

"Me, too."

They spent their last hours tucked under the blankets in the comfort of a soft bed until the front desk rang the room with their wakeup call.

Check-in at Glasgow International wasn't hard, mostly because all they had were two carry-on bags. She reserved first class seating, but even with first class amenities, the trip was long. She watched him grab a notepad and pen and begin to write.

"What are you writing?"

"I was working on my story about your survey job."

"The story about the hill is going to be better."

"But what if we decide not to expose what's there?"

"I can't really see why we shouldn't. Do you realize William the Conqueror is the first recorded castle builder in history—in ten-sixty-six? Magnus had him beat by three hundred years."

"Magnus didn't call it a castle."

"I know, but only because there was no such thing at the time. He gave it the only name that made sense to him, a fortified palace, but it *was* a castle. He had it all from the walls and towers to the moat. I think word leaked from some of his subjects down through history about what had once existed, and William the Conqueror decided to build this fabled 'fortified palace.' It only makes sense he would have called it something else so he could claim original credit for it."

"I love your story angle there, babe, but it's their grave. I mean if the castle was empty and buried, I'd say dig it up, but—"

"Their bodies could be re-buried near the castle. I bet, since the castle basically hasn't been exposed to the wind, rain, and sun, it's probably in remarkable condition. And Magnus could take his rightful place in history."

"But that's what we haven't learned yet. I really think he *didn't* want it recorded in history. He may have achieved greatness, but the price for it was so costly, he decided obscurity was better."

"AJ—"

"Look, let's not make those decisions now. We need to read all the scrolls before we even start considering what to do."

"Okay, you're right. And besides, what we're doing right now is more important anyway."

For once he looked really worried.

"AJ, what's wrong?"

"I—I didn't want to tell you, but I'm scared to death about this."

"Why?"

"Every time I have it checked the news just gets worse. I don't want to know how big it is now, or how thin the vein has become, or any of the stats because according to the last doctor, I shouldn't be alive right now."

She squeezed his hand tightly, "But you are alive, and this is going to be good news for once."

"I didn't know you were an optimist."

"Usually, I'm not. I'm a realist."

"Me, too, that's why I'm scared."

"A realist is neither positive nor negative but finds the best answer. That is what we're going to do. He's the best in the world, and we're getting a straight answer."

CHAPTER SEVEN

The closer it came to his appointment, the more nervous he appeared. Cassandra was truly worried because he'd become pale, but she put on her best brave front and reminded him that she loved him and would be by his side the whole time. The center was located inside of St. Joseph's hospital, and she had to admit even she felt anxious as the clinical atmosphere surrounded them.

After Doctor Ericsson read her pleading email, AJ's appointment was scheduled as an emergency with the stipulation they might have to wait for a little while as they worked him in among his other patients, but it was not the case. No sooner had they signed-in and given his insurance information to the nurse, he was ushered back to meet the doctor.

Doctor Ericsson made both of them feel at ease as he listened to AJ explain all he knew about his own condition. He wrote the entire time AJ talked, asking brief questions here and there, and finally handed AJ a medical release form.

"I want all the records from USC and Doctor Kennabrook. I also want to get you admitted."

"Admitted?" AJ's voice was a few octaves higher than usual, "But I thought this was just a preliminary meeting?"

"Just overnight—nothing to be worried about. You're scheduled for an MRI in about an hour and then we'll have you stay here tonight, so I can perform an angiogram in the morning. I want as many detailed pictures of this aneurysm as we can get. My colleagues and I will review all the images, and then we can discuss this more knowledgably sometime mid-morning tomorrow. Plus, that'll give your records time to be faxed here."

"Can I stay with him?" Cass quickly asked. There was no way she wanted to leave him alone when she knew how vulnerable he felt in this place.

"Of course," Doctor Ericsson replied in a soft tone, "I don't know how comfortable our recliners are in the patient rooms, but you are welcome to stay all night if you like."

The next hour was a whirlwind of activity as they worked on admission, blood work, an I.V. line; all the things that make going to the hospital a regrettable experience. He was shot full of dye and sent in for the MRI. Cass wasn't allowed in the imaging room, so she pace the floor and waited for him to be wheeled out. Afterward, he was assigned a room and settled in for the evening.

"They could have just let me come back in the morning," he complained. "Now I'm wishing I'd eaten a bigger lunch before we got here," he said, referring to the fact they weren't going to let him have any food before his scheduled test. Then he looked at Cass and squeezed her hand, "You don't have to skip dinner because I do. I know they have a cafeteria in this place."

"I'm not hungry, and I'm not leaving this room. I just wish I could curl up with you in that bed."

"Personally, I think there's room," he said as he motioned to the side without the I.V. line running across it.

She walked around and lowered the rail, scooting in next to his warm body, "I had no idea they were going to admit you." She sounded very apologetic.

He sighed as he pulled her in a little tighter, "It's okay. Hey, at least if I blow a brain fuse now, I'm just a floor away from surgery."

"Don't you dare 'blow a fuse,' now or ever. They are going to repair it, and you may have the horrid job of watching me grow old and wrinkly."

He put his fingers under her chin and tipped her face up to his, "I can't think of anything better than seeing what you look like at sixty."

She rolled her eyes.

"I bet you'll still be gorgeous." He kissed her slowly and then laughed as his heart monitor beeped because his rate suddenly jumped. "I don't know why they insisted on putting that thing on me; my heart is fine."

A buzzing sound came from his clothing pile. "Would you hand me my cell?"

"Sure." She noticed the text message was from Bobby as she handed it to him. She didn't say anything as she watched him enter a response and hit send.

"I told him before we left what we're doing," he clarified.

"What did he say?"

"He said it was about time someone got my stubborn ass in for another opinion—and he said to tell you thank you."

"Can I see your phone?"

He didn't say anything as he handed it to her. She stayed beside him as she told Bobby she had the phone for the moment. They texted back and forth for several minutes; she explained what they'd done so far, made a comment about the lovely green, paisley-print hospital gown he wore and how it showed the cheeks of his butt when he had to get up for the bathroom. They bantered back and forth for a while longer, and she finally told him she was relinquishing the phone to its owner. "He may be shy in person, but I can tell that boy likes to text."

"That's the real Bobby. Once he gets to know you, he's a blast. He can always make me smile. By the way, you have that ability, too."

"What?" she asked with a disbelieving glance.

"You make me smile."

"I'm surprised I didn't make you want to run away screaming after I treated you so badly that first day."

"No way! You were all growl and snap, but I knew immediately I liked the woman behind the 'bitch' façade."

"I was horrible."

"You were intriguing, and you still are. We don't have a scroll to read, and I bet we have a couple of hours before they call lights out in this place. Do you feel like talking," he paused, "about yourself?"

She looked mortified.

"You'd rather trade places with me, wouldn't you?"

She nodded.

"Isn't there something you can tell me about yourself? I can see your pain, Cass, but there has to be some good stuff."

"There were a few good years," she admitted, though sometimes it was hard to remember they were there at all. "We lived on a farm in Missouri until I was almost five. Daddy hardly drank at all back then. He ran his survey business for the locals and worked the farm in between. When I was five, we moved to Texas to help out my mom's mom; she was losing her ranch to a foreclosure. Daddy stepped in with his life savings and paid it off. In exchange, she gave us the ranch; we were going to take care of her and live there like one big happy family."

"I take it that wasn't what happened."

"Nope. My mom's family had a fit, and they said Daddy swindled it out from under Grandma. I didn't understand what a lot of the fighting was about. Dad's youngest two kids lived with us, and Mom's two daughters lived there, too, but it didn't take long for her girls to side with their grandmother. Lillian was twenty; she married and got out of there. Penny was seventeen when she and Grandma moved out with some other relatives. Then it was just me, Tommy, and Lane for a while.

"Things calmed down for a couple years, but the feud on Mom's side of the family raged on. Soon, she and Daddy both started drinking heavily. When I was seven, Mom had a bad car accident on her way home from work; she split open her skull, mangled one of her legs, and broke her collar bone. She couldn't work, and surveying took a dive. Dad's savings was gone. I remember riding with him to the local grocery store, and we'd go out back to the dumpsters; he'd put me inside to get things." She exhaled softly, "You'd be amazed how much good food they throw away: loaves of bread, tubs of yogurt, damaged items. Sometimes, I think we ate better out of the garbage than we did before we went broke."

"Cass," he gently stopped her, "I said the good stuff. You don't have to get into what's painful if you're not ready."

"That *was* the good stuff," she said. She was completely serious. "But since I've gone this far, I guess I can at least tell you what happened to my mom."

He nodded, but she could see concern etched on his face.

"Anyway, Mom improved, but she didn't go back to work. When they became so broke they couldn't afford alcohol, my dad started making it out of anything and everything. He had hidden some cantaloupe wine in a bedroom closet, but Mom found it. We came home from school and just thought she was passed-out, drunk. It wasn't until bedtime that Daddy saw the bottle by the bed and knew she'd gotten into the wine. When he tried to wake her up and bitch her out about it, he realized she was dead. He'd screwed up the recipe and botulism took over. He's never really forgiven himself; I guess that's why he stays wasted."

"No wonder you didn't want to talk about it before."

She leaned forward in the bed slightly and turned to stare him directly in the eyes. She didn't need to say a word. She saw the comprehension in his eyes, as he realized that those memories weren't the monsters she battled on a daily basis; and then his expression changed.

She'd seen this look on his face before; he was bracing to ask her a hard question.

"Cass, what did your family call you when you were little?"

"It's not what you think," she said with a small, bitter laugh, "Pumpkin was my nickname. Daddy still calls me pumpkin, or pumpkin pie depending on how much he's had to drink."

He seemed puzzled, but he reached for her and pulled her back into his embrace. "You left someone out. You said you had three sisters and *two* brothers."

"I'm done, AJ, no more."

"Things got a lot worse after you lost your mom, didn't they?"

"I'm done. Don't make me get out of this bed."

He kissed her temple, "I'm shuttin' up because I don't want you going anywhere."

"Tell me how you met Bobby."

"I can do that. My family is Polish. I know, big surprise, right?"

She finally smiled as she stole a quick kiss, "I may have a thing for Polish guys from now on."

"Hey, just one Polish guy, please."

"True. I have a feeling you're unique."

"Anyway, my family lives in Virginia, but we have a ton of relatives scattered around the UK. My mom runs a travel agency, so every summer she'd book us to spend a month there. Bobby lived next door to my aunt in Northampton. We became friends right away. I spent my time being dragged all over the place by him, showing me everything fun a couple of young boys could get into.

"Our families became friends, and they started spending time in the states. I'd show him how American kids had fun. College rolled around, and he spent a year with me at George Mason University as an exchange student. He lived at my house, and every weekend we'd drive a couple of hours south to Cape Hatteras to learn how to surf."

"Bobby surfs?" she tried not to sound too shocked.

AJ chuckled, "Not very well. He thought it would be a great way to meet girls, but every time he thought a girl was watching him, he'd fall off the board. Bobby's got the surfer's build, so a lot of girls watched him—and he spent a lot of time in the water. As soon as we'd paddle to shore, he'd lose his nerve and be ready to go home. It was comical—

pathetic, but comical."

Cass was giggling as she tried to picture it.

"Anyway, I spent the next year as an exchange student in the UK. I went to Bobby's college, the University of York, and lived in his house. We were like brothers. But then we both had to get serious about school. We didn't get to see each other for a while. I met Kristen."

"Kristen?"

"The swimsuit model."

"Oh. She was pretty, huh?"

"Cass, I could put the two of you side by side in bikinis, and she'd be pretty; you're a knock-out."

"Major brownie points," she snickered.

He kissed her but didn't smile, "No, I wasn't after brownie points; it's the truth. I can only imagine how many guys were crazy about you when you were in high school and college."

She became still and somber, "Go on with *your* story."

"He was supposed to be the best man at my wedding, but instead, he ended up being the one who wouldn't leave my side when the news hit me," his voice cracked, and his eyes filled with tears. "He dropped everything and came to the states. He was the one who told me he wasn't going to let me crawl into a hole and die."

"But I thought you were the one who decided to keep living a normal life?"

"No. I was depressed and wanted to give up." The first tears spilled over his bottom lashes.

She didn't interrupt him; she just wiped his cheeks and offered a soft smile.

"Bobby picked me up and reminded me I wasn't dead yet; life was still out there; only God controls the end. We spent about a month together acting like we did when we were back in school and crazy. By the time he left, I was me again, and I haven't looked back since. I'll never forget what he did for me—or what you've done for me."

"Me? AJ, I haven't—"

"Yes, you have. I've never felt this way about *anyone*. Cass, I have to ask you something."

"It's getting late. Maybe you should get some rest."

"Cass, I have to know."

"We've said enough."

"How do you feel about God?"

The question was not what she expected—at all. "I—I'm not sure," she said, stumbling over the words. "When I was little, until about seven, Mom would dress us up and send us to the Baptist church. Looking back, I think she and Daddy wanted the house quiet for a couple hours. I liked it, but I wouldn't go with the other kids to children's church; I sat with the adults and listened. We stopped going after her wreck. I felt like He'd forgotten about me or at least didn't care." She felt the need to put her shield in place as she stiffened beside him. The anger and bitterness took hold like some kind of old and unwelcomed relative who moves in. Yet she wanted to finish telling him what would surely sum up her life without going into detail, "And then at nine years old, I stepped straight into hell and haven't seen the light of a good day until I met this awesome Polish-American guy in the UK. I think you are God's way of tapping me on the shoulder and reminding me He's still around. How about you?"

"When I found out about the aneurysm, I figured it was God's way of punishing me for pulling away from the Church, and I was so angry. In a way, I felt I probably deserved this."

"NO!" she snapped. "You do not—"

"Cass, it's okay; let me finish. After Bobby pulled me out of the dumps, I began a lot of soul searching. I never felt close to God before; it was all just mechanics, but suddenly I found myself depending on Him for every breath. A year after my diagnosis, I got saved and—and I know it may sound trite, but I've been at peace ever since—until just before I met you."

His remark stung a little. Had she somehow destroyed his peace with God?

"When I was flying in to start my vacation, I just knew everything was close to being over. I started praying."

Just barely above a whisper, and not turning to look at him, she asked, "What were you praying for?"

"I asked God for one more really beautiful experience before I leave this place. I didn't expect it to be love because I never imagined someone like you."

She wiped her tears from her cheeks before he could, "I think it's Kingdom Hill. You write it up and take credit for the discovery, and you'll leave your mark in history."

He sat up and faced her as best he could with all the wires and attachments. "You're wrong; *it is you*, and the only place I want to leave a mark is right here," he said, putting his fingers to her heart. He pressed the button for the head of the bed to recline; he laid his body on hers and kissed her with a passion that told her he wasn't going to be able to keep his needs in check much longer.

This was not the place where she envisioned their first experience together, but if he was finally ready, then...

At that moment, the door to his room burst open and two nurses rushed in and then abruptly stopped. In a split second, AJ rolled onto his back to cover his exposed 'ass'ets. All four of their faces were scarlet.

"Mister Lisowski," one of the nurses finally spoke up, "you just sent your monitors off the chart. I don't think this is the place for—"

"Sorry," Cass said, climbing out of the bed and pulling the railing up, "We were just—ah, saying goodnight." She sat in the lounger and did her best to look innocent.

"I'll bring you a sleep-aid."

"No," AJ quickly stopped her, "I don't need help falling asleep."

"Goodnight," the other nurse growled, and flipped off the light as they left.

She could hear AJ trying to silence his deep laugh which came out when he found something genuinely funny.

"What?"

"I'm sure glad they came in when they did."

"Why?"

"They thought my numbers were wild a minute ago? They'd probably been rolling in here with a crash cart if they'd given us any longer, and, wow, *that* would have been embarrassing!"

Cass tried to close her eyes and nod off, but every time she thought about what he said, she'd start laughing, and then he'd start laughing. Eventually, they did fall asleep.

CHAPTER EIGHT

His angiogram was finished by eight-thirty, and they discharged him. He and Cass went out to breakfast then back to Doctor Ericsson's office for the results. She knew he had to be nervous about what they would tell him because she was closer than she'd ever been in her life to freaking out, but she kept it under careful control, so he wouldn't know.

There were two other doctors in the conference room with Doctor Ericsson; they all looked very somber. Cass squeezed his hand, feeling the need to turn and run before they could say anything she didn't want to hear. His grip tightened.

"Okay, AJ, we have a lot to discuss," Doctor Ericsson began. "First off, I don't see any additional expansion of the aneurysm."

She felt his grip on her hand ease slightly.

"I don't actually think it can. Your brain is acting as a compression bandage on it. We're all amazed you aren't showing any physiological or psychological effects from something so large. As far as thinning is concerned, it hasn't changed, either. We've conferred and agree it is *not* inoperable."

At that moment AJ's grip went limp. He leaned forward in his chair, made a fist, and rested it against his lips. His hand was trembling.

"Yesterday, you told me Doctor Kennabrook said it was basically hopeless; it's not. Although very rare, we've successfully treated this type before."

"How—I mean..." he choked up, and had to pause.

"It's okay. Take your time," Doctor Ericsson said, as he rested his hand on AJ's shoulder.

"...how many patients and what kind of survival rates?" he finished the question.

"I don't like people to get hung up on numbers, but I understand why you'd want to know. We've had forty-three similar cases since we opened our doors. We lost two on the operating table and five in recovery. Thirteen survived several days."

Cass could feel her composure shattering; falling completely apart was seconds away, but then he finished.

"Twenty-three are still with us today with little or no permanent side effects. They're living normal, healthy lives."

"That's better than fifty percent," AJ said, sounding clearly astonished. "My other doctor said I'd be lucky to have three percent."

"When?" Cass finally found her voice.

"You mean schedule him for surgery?"

She nodded.

"We obviously don't want to wait too long, but we all agree we have a little more time than AJ thought, or, actually, didn't think he had at all. We'd like you back here in eight weeks. Judging from your previous records and the images we've taken, and remember these things are very unpredictable, we're guessing it might hold up for another six months or so. But we don't want a rupture; it's far too large, and the damage would be devastating."

"And if I don't have the surgery?"

She couldn't believe that question came out of his mouth! He finally had a decent chance at life. What astonished her was none of the doctors seemed surprised he'd ask such a thing. She just sat there with her mouth open and nothing coming out.

"It will eventually rupture. Even if you get to the hospital quickly, by the time they get you on the table, because of the size and location, your chances of surviving drop to about fifteen percent; surviving without complications would be in the zero to miracle range. You *need* the surgery, AJ. We'll give you a few days to think it over."

"Think it over!" Cass snapped. The bitch inside her instantly woke up. "Schedule it right now! We don't—"

"Cass—"

"What the hell is wrong with you?!" she said as she faced AJ; then turned on the doctors. "What's wrong with all of you?! He needs it or his chances are basically zero!"

"Cass, stop," AJ said as he gripped her arm, "you've got to give me a minute here to—"

"A minute to what? Think it over? We're—"

"Ms. Henley," Doctor Ericsson's voice was firm and sharp. "You have to understand what he is processing right now. I've just—"

"Bullshit!"

"Shut up and listen to me," the doctor growled.

She didn't expect that out of him, but it was enough to close her mouth.

"I've just told him that in eight weeks, his life will either begin again, or in eight weeks, it's all going to be over with, and he will die; that's definite, not vague. Surgery removes much of the guess work about his future. You have to let *him* decide. And trust me; it's not as easy or cut-and-dry as you think."

It was still cut-and-dry in her mind, yet she suddenly knew the doctor was right; only one person could make the decision.

"I'm sorry," she choked up, tears immediately rushing down her cheeks, "whatever you decide, AJ, I'll support you." She hated those words, but she knew she had to stick by them.

He looked at all three doctors, "Eight weeks. I'll be here."

Cass went weak; one of the doctors finally took notice she needed a tissue—badly. He handed her a boxful.

For the next ten or fifteen minutes, the three explained exactly how they planned to perform the surgery and how they would repair the vein.

"It's complicated, so we'll block eighteen hours for the operation. We're hoping it will only take ten or twelve. We do have one other issue, and although I'm not usually the one to bring this up to a patient, I volunteered rather than you having to go through all of this when you get downstairs. Your insurance," he said, taking a deep breath, "is nearly exhausted. Six years of treatments and doctors, and the policy limit only leaves about fifty thousand. We won't turn you away, but the hospital may require an investment upfront."

"How much will the surgery cost?" Cass asked before AJ could speak.

"Depending on the number of days in ICU, observation, and possible complications, perhaps a few months of therapy; you could be looking at a quarter to a half-million dollars."

AJ appeared stunned.

"It's covered," Cass said firmly, "I'm paying."

"No, you're not!" AJ started to argue.

"Who else do you know with my kind of bank account? And who else loves you so much that if you say no right now you'll break her heart? Please don't say anything else, AJ. Just nod your head and agree to let me do this, *please.*" She could tell he was reluctant but after a brief pause, he nodded.

They stood as Doctor Ericsson shook his hand, "You've made the right choice. Anything special you two have planned in the meantime?"

"Yeah," AJ answered, "we have a couple of jobs in the UK to finish."

She knew the doctor was alluding to either a nice vacation or perhaps a wedding, but he smiled and told them goodbye.

"So," she said, as they walked out into the balmy seventy-two degree air, "Are you calling him or am I?"

"Who?" he still looked like he was a little bit overwhelmed by everything he'd just learned.

"Bobby. I know he's been waiting all morning to get the report."

He opened his phone and brought up Bobby's number, "Call him from your phone. I need to call my mom and dad. They have no clue what's been going on."

She was on the phone with Bobby, explaining every detail, when AJ's conversation caused her to go silent.

Poor Bobby just kept saying, "Cass? Cassandra, are you still there?"

AJ didn't tell his mom about the pending surgery. The first thing she heard him say was, "I've found someone really special, and I'm bringing her by, so you and Dad can meet her."

"I'll call you back," she said, and closed the phone before Bobby could reply.

"Yeah," AJ continued, "you'll absolutely love her. I found a new doctor, too, and, well, I'll just say things have definitely improved. I can't wait to see you. We should be there in a few hours, depending on which flight we can get. Okay, Mom. Yeah, I love you, too."

He looked over and smiled, "We have an extra stop to make."

Although AJ was excited to have her meet his parents, they were understandably, most interested in his news about the aneurysm. When they learned it was Cass who talked him into going to the center, they turned their attention back to her. She smiled and chatted, but the whole while she was dying to get out of there. She knew it wouldn't take long before they would jump from learning about her to asking about her family. But AJ was quite gallant, and as soon as the conversation took a turn, he cut it off and told them they were running late for a flight back to the UK.

"But you just got here," his mother said, clearly disappointed they were leaving so abruptly, "I was going to make pierogies with potato pancakes."

He leaned over and kissed her forehead, "Next time, Mom, I promise we'll stay longer, and you can cook all you want."

"Cass," his dad said, reaching for her hand, "it sounds like my son was very lucky to meet you."

He had a warm, firm grip—just like AJ's.

She smiled, "Oh, I think I'm the lucky one. You've raised an extraordinary man, but thank you, anyway."

They didn't say much on the way back to Dulles International, but they were both smiling.

CHAPTER NINE

It was four in the morning when their plane touched down in Glasgow. They promised Bobby they would meet him for breakfast down in Carlisle. Cass had a ton of work to catch up on, and driving for a couple hours seemed like such a large amount of wasted time, so she handed AJ her computer.

"I'll drive and tell you how to enter the data."

"I could drive," he offered. He'd already explained to her that, once his aneurysm had become so large, he avoided driving whenever possible. It wasn't an issue of stress (he loved to drive), but more so should it rupture, he didn't want to be responsible for killing innocent people on the highway.

"Nah, that's okay. This shouldn't be too difficult, but I really want to see how they're doing." She missed three nights of data transfers, which was something she'd never done on a job. What she dreaded was calling Dirk to get the data download. He didn't have a clue she'd been missing them, but he did know she hadn't been taking check-in calls for the last several days. She figured he'd be awake and getting ready for the day's work, but it still surprised her how quickly he answered the phone.

"Where the hell have you been?" Was the first thing she heard.

"What I do is none of your business. I need you to turn on your computer and send me the data backup."

There was a small pause, "Why? Did your computer crash?" He didn't sound angry at this point, just curious.

She thought about lying; it would be so much easier, but he

was her employee, and she wasn't afraid of him, "No. I went back to the States for a while, and I didn't have time to—"

"Where? *Did you go home?"*

"No. Look, I don't have to explain this to you; I just need the data. *Now turn on your computer!"* She was using her don't-piss-off-the-boss tone at this point.

"You'll have to give me a minute. I've already packed it in the truck."

"Fine. I'll call back."

"No that's okay. Stay on the phone; I've almost got it. So what did you go to the States for anyway?"

She knew he was using the excuse about the computer just to keep questioning her, "I told you before; it's none of your business. Do you have it yet?"

"Hold on. It's booting up. We need to get together."

"No."

"Let me finish, would ya? We need to talk about a couple problems that came up with the job. We had a few snags getting access to a couple big tracts of land. Seems the owner doesn't believe we have sufficient privileges as Americans to—"

"We have all our permits. Give me their names and—"

"Yeah, well, the owner is the government and they checked with the RICS and can't confirm our permission."

"That's fine. I can take care of it this morning. I have a meeting in a couple of hours with B... Mister Rose. Just tell me which tracts."

"Really?" he genuinely sounded impressed, "Well it's good to know you are apparently still on the job. I figured you were spending all your time getting laid."

"You are bordering on being fired, you know that, right?"

"I ain't stupid, Cass. I really want to believe you wouldn't do that to me."

"We aren't a couple."

"I'm done with not being a couple, and I'm tired of your 'no claims' policy. I wanted to do this differently, but if you are going to keep avoiding me, then I'll just tell you."

"Punch the damn button first and then I'll listen." She glanced at the computer on AJ's lap, making sure her signal was good as they cruised down the highway, "I know your computer is booted by now."

"Fine. I hit it. Is it coming through?"

She glanced over and saw the transfer bar begin to fill with green squares, "Yes, it is. Now what is so friggin' important it can't wait a couple weeks?"

"I love you! And it's killing me for you to be running around with AJ!"

She wasn't prepared for that—at all. She saw AJ's head jerk up from the computer to stare at her when he heard what had been shouted through the phone. She didn't have a response.

"Cass, I've been in love with you for a long time now, and I finally went out and bought you a ring. I wanted to give it to you our first night here, but I lost my nerve. I'll be a son-of-a-bitch if you didn't take off with AJ, and I haven't seen you since! We're more alike than you and he will ever be, and you know that. You've always been a fuck-'em and leave-'em kind of girl, but for three years you've always come back to me; don't leave me now."

"Dirk, I don't love you. You've been..." she struggled for a word that wouldn't hurt him quite as badly as what she really wanted to say. "You've been a good friend, but—"

"No, no buts—we aren't doing this over the phone. I know I can be pretty rough on you, but you have to give me at least one more chance. Three years deserves a final chance, doesn't it? This has got to be face-to-face before you blow me off like every other guy you've known."

"We'll talk when the job is over."

"I can't wait that long—tonight, Cass. If I have to, I'll just track you down through your phone and find you."

All the company phones had GPS tracking installed, including hers, and Dirk had the code to get into the account. She was certain the only reason he hadn't done it before now was because her phone was set to beep if the tracker was turned on. The last thing she wanted was to have him show up at the hill. It wasn't so much that he would discover what was under the hill, but she was pretty certain a fight would break out. There was no way she wanted AJ in a fist fight.

"Okay," she conceded, "but I'm tied up today and tomorrow. I'll meet up with you on Friday evening. Give me the info on the tracts so I can handle that this morning."

When she hung up, AJ immediately told her she was not meeting him alone.

"Yes, I am. I don't know what kind of mood he's gonna be in, but I'm not going to have you end up in a fight."

"I saw the way he kissed you that first night just before you slugged him; he didn't ask, and I get the feeling he takes whatever he wants from you."

She immediately choked up, "I—I'm not going to sleep with him. I couldn't—never again—I—"

"Baby, I'm not worried about you wanting him. I'm worried about him forcing you. *I have to be there*."

"I'll meet him someplace public, but there is no way in hell you're going with me. Please, AJ, if something happened to you, I'd never forgive myself."

"And how do you think I feel? What if something happens to you? I couldn't take it."

"You asked me to trust you, but now you have to trust me. *You're not coming, and I will be okay*."

Silence makes for a long ride, and since this was a long ride anyway, it felt like an eternity before they reached the restaurant.

When they walked inside, she knew Bobby expected to see smiling faces, but there weren't any.

"Is everything all right?" he asked without hesitation.

Cassandra immediately launched into the problem her company was having obtaining access to three extremely large parcels of land. "I have the name of the man who denied us access. Would you mind calling him and straightening out this mess for me? Someone at the Royal Institute said we didn't have permits."

"Of course I will. I'll take care of this as soon as—"

"Bobby," AJ finally spoke up, "what are you doing Friday night?"

"Oh, no you don't," she started to say.

"Why not, Cass? If you're only worried about me getting hurt, you shouldn't have any problem taking Bobby."

"Taking me where?" he asked.

"Cass needs a chaperone for a date Friday night."

"It's not a date. I—I just have to tell him I don't feel the same way about him as he does about me."

"Who?" Bobby asked, thoroughly confused at this point.

"Dirk," AJ and Cass answered in unison.

"If you don't take Bobby, then you're taking me."

"I don't think that is a good idea," Bobby quickly stated.

She sighed. She truly did understand his apprehension about

her meeting with Dirk; she'd only refused to take him along out of fear for his safety. And if she had to tell him the truth at that very moment, she was scared to death to face Dirk alone.

"Okay, I'll take Bobby," she agreed, "but only if he's okay with it."

"Of course," he answered, "I agree with AJ; you shouldn't meet him alone."

AJ was finally smiling, which made Cass immensely happy. A mere nine days ago, she would have never believed the way someone else felt would affect her own emotions. Even stranger, she liked it. She often thought love would feel like a prison, but it was more like the first taste of freedom she'd ever known. She watched both men while they talked about the visit to the center. AJ was right; he and Bobby were more like brothers then friends. She smiled, squeezed AJ's upper arm, and cuddled closer to him in the booth. She stayed quiet through breakfast, so much so, even Bobby made a comment as they prepared to leave.

"Cass, I thought I was supposed to be the shy one. You haven't said two words since you agreed to take me with you."

"I just enjoyed listening to you two."

He held the door open for them as they stepped outside, "So what have you two been doing since…I mean, don't tell me what you've been doing. I just…I mean, if you're not surveying…" His face turned scarlet, "Never mind. Forget I asked."

AJ was looking at Cass, but she hesitated. She could tell Bobby was someone he trusted completely, but she had a twinge of uncertainty. "Not what you're thinking. AJ is a true gentleman."

Her admission didn't alleviate the color on his face, "Oh—no—please, that wasn't what I was—"

She reached out and put her hand on Bobby's, "We've made a monumental discovery, but we aren't sure what we're going to do about it just yet."

"Actually, Cass discovered it, I was just lucky enough to be with her when she did; we're talking about a thirteen-hundred-year-old kind of discovery."

That changed the look on his face, "The government gets rather sticky when you're dealing in antiquities, especially of that magnitude. No one else knows, do they?"

Cass shook her head, "Just me and AJ so far, but I'm guessing," she said, turning to study AJ's face as he nodded quickly, "he'd like you to know about it, too. *But*," she added watching his excited expression dissolve, "I need to know if your position with the Royal Institute could be jeopardized if we tell you, and you don't report it."

"Good thinking, Cass," AJ suddenly blurted, "You're right, and I don't want to get him in trouble."

"Everything in life has consequences. Besides, if we are caught, you two can say you *were* reporting it to me. But I do understand if you'd rather I didn't—"

"Friday," Cass stopped him, "if you can, come early, we'll meet you at the motel in Moffat and drive you to the site. Bring your swim trunks and a towel."

His head tilted slightly, "Seriously?"

"No, she just wants to check out your body," AJ laughed as he watched Bobby's expression. "Yes, you idiot, she's serious."

"Was his job your only real concern?" AJ asked as they pulled from the parking lot.

"I wish I knew him as well as you do, but, for a split second, no. All I could think about was the decision to make it public or keep it private might come out of our hands if we told him. You really do trust him, don't you?"

"A hundred percent; I trust him with my life, and, more importantly, I trust him with yours."

"I didn't want to meet Dirk alone."

"I *never* thought that. And although I'd like to believe I'm superman, I know a punch to the head might kill me. I wouldn't want to risk you witnessing that. But I'd take a hundred punches before I'd let that asshole hurt you."

"I have to know something."

"What?"

"When we were in your hospital bed, just before the nurses came into the room, it didn't feel like you were planning to stop."

"I didn't want to stop, but I wouldn't have tried to make love to you there; I just want to be with you so badly."

"I feel the same way. It isn't about the sex anymore; really, it isn't."

"Answer me one question: if I get you under the hill and tell you we can make love, is there anything you haven't told me that could come between us?"

She was silent.

"That's what I thought. Before we went to Minnesota, I figured I'd run out of time before you were ready. I'm hoping we have some time now—real time. Let's not rush it. I don't want anything in the way when I make you mine."

His statement surprised her. Normally, she would have been quick to dispute belonging to any man, but she wanted him to possess her. "That sounds permanent."

"You once told me you don't get into head games; 'hate them with a passion,' I believe was your exact wording. This is no game for me, Cass. I really do love you, and for however long God gives me, I want to spend it *all* with you. If you can't commit to me, tell me now because I don't want to get hurt any more than you do."

"Other than the business, I've never committed to anything. I don't think I'm worth that kind of promise, but once you really know me—if you still want me—I'm yours, every part, every emotion, and every heartbeat."

"There isn't anything you can tell me to make me not want you. Unless you're actually a guy, which would be a problem, but after seeing you in the shower, I highly doubt that."

She laughed, "Thanks for lightening the moment."

There was no more time for conversation because once they reached the hill, there was work to be done. She tied the rope back in place and transported some fresh supplies under the hill while AJ uncovered vents and installed the satellite. When he joined her inside, they did a little housekeeping and then pulled out the next scroll. Settling into their reading spot, he began.

I wondered how Emiline would take to becoming queen. I was inspired how she embraced it. Her mind was keen and sharp as she made and executed plans. She did not falter or waver; she commanded. As queen, her first order was the formation of the queen's guard. She said it needn't be large, but should we ever come under attack, she would have a devoted few assigned to preserve her at all costs. I would never argue the point; although, I told her I, myself, would be her shield and would lay down my life before allowing anyone to harm her.

"And shall you stay by my side, my husband, as if we were bound together with fetters? Nay. You have a kingdom to rule and work to be overseen. I should think myself lucky to see you at all."

"Fetters and chains bind my heart to you, sweet Emiline, but

you shall have your guard with my blessing."

I assembled my soldiers and made my recommendations, but the selection belonged to her. I cannot purport to know how a woman arrives at a decision, but I am certain one does not employ the same logic as the male mind. She had never seen these men in battle; she did not know their strengths or weaknesses, but her decision was impressive, nonetheless. She selected six men of imposing strength: one of keen intelligence, and the remaining five of less mental acuity but a greater degree of raw power and tractability. She had done well.

I pulled them from the ranks and dubbed them the Queen's guard. "You are under the queen's command. I expect you to accompany her in my absence and be ready, night or day, to defend her. You will follow her orders as you would mine." I have many regrettable decisions where Emiline was concerned, but this had been a grave error in my judgment. Had I given more caution to her request, I would have made the selection myself and assigned to her only those with the greatest amount of sincere loyalty to their King and country. As it was, she honed their allegiances to herself alone.

The construction of the Kingdom continued, and it seemed the work might never cease. I often wondered whether I had been too ambitious in my grand scheme. But as I watched the magnificence unfold, I knew I would achieve my desire of a kingdom greater than that of my father's. I learned of my father's death a mere year after my departure. As I had suspected, he gave his throne to Ceolwulf before passing. Ceolwulf lasted eighteen months before I received word that a remnant of those who felt I should have been their king had overthrown him. A messenger was dispatched to bear the news that Northumbria bade my return. I declined with utmost diplomacy and respect. Shortly thereafter, Ceolwulf was restored to power. Our kingdoms would coexist in peace.

Emiline grew to become a woman with even more alluring beauty than she possessed as a youth. She would attend to my needs and desires, but I felt her passion wane. I clearly recall the night she laid before me upon my bed, as I beheld her, and I felt her pull away from my touch. I questioned her. She surprised me in two ways. She said she was distressed that throughout all of our copulation, she had not conceived an heir for me, her Lord and King, and she was disheartened to the point of giving up. Her second revelation was although she yearned to bear my children, she feared it with great trepidation.

"I witnessed my chambermaid as she attempted to give birth. It was a violent and hideous affair which neither she nor the babe survived. There have been others since, and I believe in my spirit, dear Magnus, I would not survive the process. But I am yours to do with as you wish, my Lord, even unto my death."

I reflected upon the loss of my own mother and became keenly aware of how my father must have regretted the act of fulfilling his need at the expense of her life. "No, my beautiful wife, you are not a mere possession of which I can dispose to meet my physical desires. I would go so far as to agree to a spiritual union before I would continue to risk your life."

The look on her face, as she realized my intent was true, puzzled me. I believe she knew, at that very moment, how deeply ingrained within my heart was my love for her. It also gave her the opportunity to suggest what I now believe she hoped to achieve from the beginning, and, oh, how wickedly her plan would unfold.

"You should have an heir; you must have an heir for Valderegnum."

"No, I—"

"Would you want your splendid creation to fall into the hands of anyone less?"

"Of course not, but I will not risk your life."

"You shan't. I have given this problem great thought before this day, and I would like to present you with a gift, a gift to solve the issue for both of us."

I was mystified as I watched her rise and leave for the adjoining chamber, but I was shocked upon her return. She led in a young maiden. The girl was no more than perhaps eighteen years, but with an ample bosom and rounded hips. She was clad in but a sheer cloth which left nothing to the imagination. Her eyes were cast down to the floor, and it was evident she was trembling with great fear.

"Emiline, what have you done? It is not fit for me to look upon another woman this way."

"She is yours, my husband. If I am to be your spiritual wife, a concubine shall bear your heirs. Narcilla will fulfill the role I cannot. She is virgin, and she comes from a family of fertile women. Take her, my husband, in my stead. Fill her with your seed, and she shall bear children for both of us."

I wanted no part in Emiline's solution, but she persuaded me with her honey-sweet, yet contorted, logic. I agreed Narcilla would be my concubine. Emiline removed the girl's light covering and brought her to my bed. The look on Emiline's face was of a wicked bliss as she ordered her to lay and prepare herself to be 'made worthy.' I came to the sudden realization Emiline had no intention of leaving the room.

"I cannot. Emiline, you are my wife. I cannot betray that in your presence."

She gave a sinful smile and rose to press herself against my chest as she whispered, "I see no betrayal; she is an extension of my love for you. She will bear our child upon my knees. Take her and I will only see myself upon that bed. Take her," she urged again. "And think of the virginity you were denied from our union."

She kissed and touched me, arousing the passions inside me until she achieved the response from my body she sought. She led me to bed as she fanned the need inside me and then abandoned me to fulfill my desires with a strange woman. I knew not what horrors this would set in motion as she cunningly bid me to do her will.

AJ reached the end of the scroll, but he was shaking his head, "These things aren't getting any easier."

"Cynewulf pretty much warned us before we started when he described her, but I'm actually scared to go to the next one."

"We only have a few more; we might even have them finished by Friday. That could make things a whole lot easier when Bobby sees this place, don't you think?"

She sighed, "That depends. What if he thinks our choice is wrong."

"If he honestly thinks we're wrong, he'd have to convince me why. But, Cass, I really believe, even if he doesn't agree, he'd respect our decision. Do you want to go for the next one or save it for tonight or tomorrow?"

"I don't want to wait, but I need to play catch-up." She spent the next two hours working with her data, talking with crew chiefs, and finally confirming with Bobby the tracts of land would now be open to her workers. She re-ran her projection program and was pleased to see the figure dropped from thirty-eight days to thirty. The crews had been working fast and furiously. She'd never placed trust in her workers, just as she refused to trust a man; now AJ was enlightening her to the opportunities to find what was trustworthy. Bobby would be the next hurdle. She could only hope he was right about him, too.

She saved Teddy as her last phone call of the evening. She had his data, but she missed Charlie. He told her everything was going well and Charlie was doing fine.

"That's great. I'm hoping by Saturday I'll be ready to get him."

"Boss, ain't you coming back to the crew?"

"No, I'm gonna let you guys finish this one. I always thought I needed to push the teams, but you all are doing great without me."

"We still need you, boss," he reassured her, "but I'm glad to know you're happy wit' the job."

It was nine by the time they opened the next scroll. They were both yawing and tired. Cass was certain they wouldn't get ten words read before they called it quits and went to sleep, but once again, Magnus's story swept them back in time and held them spellbound.

Emiline insisted I should bed Narcilla every evening until we knew, by her natural cycle, if she had conceived or not. I agreed, but only if Emiline would not be present in my chamber.

"It is unnatural," I insisted.

"You were magnificent last night," she cooed. "I received almost as much pleasure in the vision as I do in joining with you."

"No, Emiline. I cannot. I agreed to an heir but—"

"You need more than one. I have another young woman who will also serve you, my husband."

"No! Have you gone mad? What manner of evil possesses you? It has been difficult enough to agree to one concubine, yet alone another."

She suddenly shrank back from me as large tears ran down her cheeks, "Forgive me, please. You must think poorly of me; I am very selfish. I long so desperately for children of my own that I... I'm sorry, my love, I am so ashamed that, in my desperation, I have made this about your heir when in truth, I pray daily to be surrounded by children—children I shall never bear."

Once again, she melted my heart. "I am the one in need of forgiveness, precious one," I said as I wiped away her tears. "I did not realize how deep your longing was for a child. Be patient but for a little while longer. Let us see if she conceives, before—"

"But, Magnus," she pled, "infants are fragile creatures, many not living beyond their first year. If we had several to love, our hearts could surely go on should the unthinkable happen."

"If she conceives, I will take another concubine for the surety of your heart's desire, but I must insist you give me those moments in privacy. This must be our truce."

She rested her head against my breast and clung to me, "You are so good to me. I only wish it were I who could bear these children for you, a palace filled with them, if God would grant it."

She did as I requested and left me alone with the young woman each evening. It was difficult, at best, to coerce myself into the act of procreation with Narcilla. She was not unattractive; she was actually a lovely creature who, once over her fear of me, tried to encourage pleasure between us, but she was not the woman whom I loved. I found the act, without love, to be unfulfilling. It was purely carnal yet strangely empty.

Several weeks passed, and her natural cycle abated. I was surprised. I knew in that moment Emiline must truly be barren. We had years of relations and she had not conceived. I suddenly felt her pain and loss. I thought she would be overjoyed to learn about the pending birth of our first child; instead, the very night after I told her, she ushered in another young female, Justine. Just as before with Narcilla, Justine was tremendously frightened at what her new duty in the kingdom had become, but she willingly submitted to my purpose. Weeks passed, and she conceived as well.

Emiline tried to encourage me to take more concubines using the Hebrew history in the Pentateuch as her defense. I explained that even though I was a King, I did not wish for more wives nor concubines as Hebrew kings had done. I admit, in truth, as the months passed, the sight of those two women bearing my seed enthralled me. Narcilla bade me to come near one day as I happened by, so I could feel the movement of the child she carried. I was stunned as I experienced what felt like a tiny hand pressed outward toward mine.

Nine months after Emiline first told me of her plan, Narcilla gave birth to my son. I named him Magnus the second and proclaimed a day of celebration. But the joy was short lived as within days of his birth, Narcilla passed away. I brought in a wet-nurse, but I was disheartened. A life was given, and a life was taken. Yet in such tragedy, my son flourished. Emiline refused to spend time with him, and I feared it was from sadness and guilt over the loss of Narcilla. When I questioned her, she told me she had sentenced Narcilla, although not truly wittingly, to death.

Weeks after my son's birth, Justine and the child who would have been my daughter, died during labor. Emiline's reaction left me aghast.

"This is why I told you, my husband, you need more concubines. I will find you more suitable women."

She was relentless in her position concerning heirs. If I balked, she cried until I bent to her will. By the next year, I had an additional six concubines, but three had already passed away due to complications with their pregnancies. I had twin daughters and two more children on the way and a queen who argued continually to bring me more concubines.

My son became the focus of my life, and I felt genuine happiness as I watched him grow. Yet, Emiline was dispassionate toward the children, including Magnus.

Word began to spread that my subjects were becoming fearful of their queen. I did not understand it at the time, but soon my eyes would be opened. The end, by my hand, would come swiftly for Valderegnum.

"What do you think she was up to?" AJ asked as he began rolling up the scroll.

"Honestly, I haven't a clue, but it doesn't sound like she wanted children."

"I know it's late, but I think we should try to wake up early tomorrow and finish the last of these."

Cass checked the time; it was one in the morning. She shook out their sleeping bags and broke a couple glow sticks as he put things away. She slipped into the silky comfort and asked him to turn off the lantern.

When he crawled in beside her and snuggled against her, she had to ask him something, "Have you ever thought about kids?"

"Hmm? You mean as in kids of my own?"

"Yeah."

She heard the slow breath he drew in as he began, "I never thought about having kids until my life was given an expiration date. At that point, all I really felt was a sense of loss, and at the same time, I was glad I didn't have any because I'd feel like I was abandoning them."

"Death doesn't count as abandonment, unless you off yourself."

"Maybe not, but I'm just being honest. How about you?"

"Never—until a few days ago."

"You mean yesterday when the doctor gave me better odds?"

"No, before then. When I thought there wasn't any hope, I wanted to keep a piece of you with me."

"You'd want to raise a baby on your own?"

"No, not *a baby*, but your baby I would. It didn't look like there was an option, other than being a single parent, before—now there is, so I wanted to know how you felt about it."

He softly smoothed her hair away from her temple as he rose up on his elbow and kissed it, "Raising a baby with you would be incredible, but Cass, I'm looking at a fifty-fifty chance here. It's a toss of the coin whether I'll make it or not."

"You will make it," she said with a stubborn tone.

"How do you figure that?"

"Because you have to, and I won't let go."

"Listen to me, Cass, listen closely because that sound in your voice scares me. If something goes wrong and I'm not me anymore, if I'm brain dead or a permanent vegetable, don't try to stop them from taking me off life support. I don't want to live that way."

"But what if it's temporary, or if you're still aware of what's going on, and they just don't know it?" she couldn't mask her frustration as she considered the possibilities.

He stretched himself across her chest and made sure he held her eye contact, "No. You have to understand; I made a living will a long time ago because I don't want to exist that way. My parents didn't like it, but they finally understood; the choice is mine to make right now. I don't want it to be in someone else's hands when I can't speak for myself. Don't step in and try to change it."

She didn't mean to burst into sobs, but that was not what she wanted to hear.

"Shhh—shhh. Don't do this. In that conference room, you said *whatever* I decided, you'd support it. This is part of the deal; support me on this, not just because I'm asking you to, but because you understand it's my choice, and I don't want it on anyone else's shoulders. Please, Cass."

She wrapped her arms around him and held on tightly, "Okay,

but if you die on me, I'm gonna be really pissed at you," she choked.

He started laughing.

"I'm serious!" she wailed.

He laughed harder, "I'm sorry, baby. I know you are." He tried to compose himself, but he kept laughing and finally rolled back onto the sleeping bag.

She propped herself up on her elbow and gave her best tearful glare, "What?!"

"I can just see me now arguing with Saint Peter that I've got to go back, or there's gonna be hell to pay."

She cracked a smile, "Don't make me laugh when I'm crying."

His laugh simmered to a sweet, soft rumble as he lifted his head and kissed her. "You're perfect, Cass, simply perfect."

She snuggled down and put her back to him as she pulled his arm over her side, "No, far from it, but I guess God put us together for a reason."

He squeezed her, "You're perfect for me, and I'm glad you said that because you're right. Goodnight and I love you."

CHAPTER TEN

Even though it was AJ's suggestion they get up early and try to finish the scrolls, she was surprised when she rolled over to find herself alone. The next scroll was out of the wall and lying on the table, and the wetsuit was gone. She checked the time; it was after nine. She heard the rippling sound of water and knew he was back.

"Where'd you go?"

"Nature called and there was no way we have enough ventilation in here for that conversation."

She smiled, "So why didn't you wake me when you got up?"

"You had a rough night, Cass. I don't know what you were dreaming about or whatever, but after all that rolling around, I figured you'd be tired this morning."

"Actually, I was awake most of the night. I need to call my dad."

His eyebrows rose, "I take it that's not something you normally do when you're on a job?"

"I know you'll never believe this, but I'm pretty independent," she teased.

"You're right—I'd never believe that. So what's the special occasion? And, no, I don't believe it's me."

"In a way, you are. I'm going to tell him the UK is mine, and I'm not sharing this time."

"You mean the profits from the job? But why?

"We don't do nine-million-dollar contracts on a regular basis;

something big like this comes along once or twice a year. Most jobs run from ten to a hundred thousand; those are the real bread and butter to our business because we can do them quickly with minimal expense."

"Cass, I really don't want you paying for my surgery."

"Well, that's just too bad because I am."

"It's going to drain you, isn't it?"

"I have an impressive bank account, but I'm like a lot of other people who make good money; I spend good money. I've spent weeks kissing ass to TNR and Rand McNally, putting together my bid, my permits, all the arrangements, and the crew. It's time I take what I deserve. The undeserving leeches don't need to benefit from what I've done. If Dad doesn't like it, then this can be my severance pay. He can bring in the other two idiots and watch his company go down the drain."

"And what are you going to do if he agrees, and you're out of a job?"

She smiled, "After I pay for your surgery and give you time to recoup, I'm thinking about a very long vacation. I dive; you surf, so Hawaii sounds pretty good or Tahiti or Bora Bora."

"What about my job?"

"It does take you to some pretty cool locations, right?"

"Definitely."

"I think we could work what you do into part of a vacation."

"Keep going."

Her smile grew, "I own some property in Texas, but if I give up the business, I won't want to live there anymore. I'll cash it out and go wherever you lead."

"Just like that? You're gonna let me call the shots?"

"Well, maybe not *all* the shots. I do have a major purchase planned, but I think you'll agree to it."

"And just what would that be?"

"A piece of land in the UK with an awesome hill; how does that sound?"

"It's—it's for sale?" he asked, clearly shocked.

"I looked it up last night after I got the data download. As close as I can tell, it was purchased by a sheep rancher, and he ran out of money; it's part of a foreclosure. I'm thinking we could build here and maybe buy something in the States, dividing our time between the two—you'd get to see Bobby a whole lot more this way."

"You know, when I first met you, your organizational abilities were a little annoying," he said, as he unzipped his suit, "but I'm really starting to like the way you think."

She grabbed the end of his sleeve and held it as he pulled his arm out. She was staring intently as she reached to offer her assistance with the other sleeve, "I haven't told you this, but you have fantastic arms."

"You mean the tattoo?"

"No, your arms in general. You know how some guys will say they're 'leg-men' or 'breast-men' depending on what part of the female anatomy they like best; well, I'm an arm-girl. A great pair of arms can turn my head pretty quickly. I absolutely love your arms. Their proportions are perfect," she said, as she gripped his left arm with both hands and began to massage his bicep. "Nice thick muscles, well defined, but not grossly overworked. The tattoo just adds a little 'wow' factor, but I think you have that naturally."

"You know, for someone who says she doesn't give out many compliments, I—"

She smiled, "Maybe I just never found someone who deserved so many."

"Do you want to start a scroll, or are you calling him?"

"It's about three in the morning in Texas right now," she laughed.

"Yeah, time zones, I forget about them."

"He starts his day early, but it still gives us about two hours, so—"

"I'm already on it," AJ stated, as he picked up the scroll and his glasses from the table, "reading time."

I still recall the night she stopped me and said she had another 'gift' waiting for me in my chamber.

"Remove her," I stated. "I am done with your plan. I have enough children, and my son shall inherit this Kingdom."

"But, my husband, he is not quite two years old. Children draw sickness more easily than others; what if something should happen?"

"No. My son is strong and healthy. He will grow to be King of this land; he is enough. And there are two more children yet to be birthed; surely I may have another son. You have done enough to ensure my lineage. Remove her." I did not often take a stern tone

with Emiline, lest I wished to send her into either a rage or one of her displays of sorrow.

"Then she shall be the last, my love. One more, and there shall be no more even should all your heirs perish. Please."

"Would you swear this to me? Will you swear not to coax and plead and beg for any others?"

"My word as my bond; she is the end." The words she uttered this night would prove prophetic.

I sighed and walked away from Emiline, entering my chamber expecting to see a maiden waiting, but my bed was empty. I glanced around the room in the dim light but saw no one. As I walked forward, I suddenly caught a glimpse of long, pale blonde hair blowing from my tower watch. As I approached, I was shocked to see this young girl perched in the opening ready to spring to what would surely be her death.

"Come away from there," I stated, but careful not to startle her.

"No, my King. I know the plans she has for me, and I would surely rather take death now than by her hand."

Her words stunned me. First, was her refusal to obey her king and secondly, death by whose hand? Emiline's? "No one will harm you. Please come away from the window."

"Harm me? What will you do with me, my King? Enslave me into the queen's menagerie?" She rose slightly from her crouched position and leaned into the air.

"Do not! I promise you, I shall not touch you. Come down from there and speak to me. Unravel the riddle you have spun. I will not harm you," I repeated.

She glanced around the room as if she were a frightened bird who had accidently flown into my chamber. She was a true beauty—so very different from Emiline. Her eyes were large and limpid, the color of rich emeralds. Her hair was the color of sundried straw that glistens in the field at noonday, and her mouth appeared soft, full, and pink. I suddenly desired my last 'gift.' "What is your name, my dear?" I asked, continuing to keep my tone gentle as I slowly advanced toward her. It was my thought to snatch her from death's opening should I draw close enough.

"Stay away," she warned. Her body leaning so far forward she could no longer stop herself from slipping off the ledge.

I lunged, and by a miracle of God, grasped her wrist, nearly pulling both of us to our deaths. I lifted her back inside. Her eyes were enormous as she tried to catch her breath; she had been prepared to die and was certain she succeeded, so standing there beside me was an utter shock for her.

"Please," she begged, "Please, let me go."

"Why do you fear me and my queen?"

"I do not fear you, my Lord. You are a good and Godly King. No one speaks ill of you in Valderegnum."

"And of my queen?"

"Please, my Lord," she whispered so softly I could barely hear, "the walls have eyes and ears. Would you take me from here to a place of assured privacy?"

I wanted privacy with her, but not for the reason she was asking. "Tell me your name," I whispered back.

"Sarai, my King."

"You are beautiful, Sarai."

I could see the fright fill her as she began to tremble, large tears filling her eyes. "Please take me from here," she begged.

I grabbed my cloak and draped it over her shoulders, "Come with me."

I led her immediately from my chamber at a fast pace from the tower to the lower hall, around the great banquet room, and down to the room where I often met with the captains of my guard. This place, I knew, was safe and quiet, "You are safe here, Sarai. Now, tell me this riddle you have spun."

"I spin no riddle, my Lord. Your queen takes young virgin women to bear your children, but she does not suffer them to live; some die before they can bear your seed and others shortly after, but she has no plans to leave any alive—neither women nor children."

I could not stop myself from being angry with her, but at that moment, I heard the sound of soldier's footsteps in the corridor. "Shhh," I whispered as I pulled her with me behind the great curtain. I feared no one, but if there was any truth in her words, I would take no chance of discovery. The door to the room opened. From the small space where the fabrics met, I could see Richard of Llyons, Emiline's chief guard, enter, look about, and then leave.

Had Sarai been right? Had I been under watch in my chamber? My anger over her accusation cooled. "Tell me how you know these things."

"You have had eight concubines, my Lord; five of them have already met their end. The villages are filled with women who birth children almost daily; there is no greater place for loss of life for females than within the walls of your palace."

"Many women die from child birth. You are speaking treason against my queen," I stated, anger once again flickering to life inside me.

"Not in these numbers, my Lord. And it is rumored some young girls from the village who recently disappeared were seen being followed by the queen's guard shortly before they vanished. I'm sorry, my Lord; if you must end my life for my words I understand but I speak truths, not treason."

"If you speak the truth, Sarai, your life is in danger."

"Yes, my King. I fear my only safety now is to remain in your presence. Should you leave me, I shall surely die."

"Then you shall stay with me, but it must appear I have become smitten with you. She cannot suspect any other reason for our time together."

I watched color fill her cheeks as tears dripped down her face, "I do not wish to be a possession in the king's collection of concubines. A life without love is a life without reason to live."

"Beautiful words from a beautiful woman. I wish I had considered such words before she brought the first young woman to my chamber."

She kept her eyes lowered in humility, "I wondered if you were as truly good as all believe you to be. Now, I believe, my Lord."

"Magnus," I spoke softly, "I wish you to call me Magnus." There had been no one, other than Emiline, whom I asked to call me by my birth name. Sarai was quickly becoming someone I longed to hear utter my name.

"No, my Lord, I cannot."

"Please, Sarai; speak my name."

When she raised her eyes to meet mine, I recognized something that had been missing every time I looked into Emiline's, and I did not notice it until now; goodness. Goodness was here in this beautiful face.

"Very well, Magnus."

I lowered my lips to hers and placed a slow and tender kiss upon her mouth as she trembled against me, "Do not fear me, Sarai. You are in my safety now, and I shan't let you go." The 'last gift,' as

Emiline called her was stealing away my heart and my love.

"Wow," was AJ's response as he finished the scroll, "that I didn't expect, yet I'm not surprised."

Cass just kept shaking her head, "I knew it was going to be twisted, but I never thought she was the reason those women died, or, at least, as far as we know right now."

"That one took a while, but we could go ahead and start the next one if you—"

"Not yet," she said, rising stiffly from the floor and stretching, "Dad is up by now and I really want to get this over with."

"Are you sure about this?"

"Yeah. I do love my dad, but I'm tired of feeling like the family pack mule."

She changed her clothes and dropped her phone into a bag and swam out. The computer worked very well off the satellite line, but she hadn't adapted it for her phone yet, so being outside was essential, and she certainly didn't want this conversation to drop right in the middle.

Within two rings, his familiar voice answered, "Pumpkin?"

She knew why he sounded surprised; she rarely called when she was working, "Hey, Daddy."

"Is everything okay? I was shocked when I saw who was phoning me."

"No, actually everything isn't okay. I need to talk with you about a couple of things. First, something has come up, and I need the profits from this job—just for me. I'm not splitting this one, and I hope you'll understand."

"But, pumpkin, I—"

"No, just hear me out. I'm tired of supplying a bunch of adults with money to play with. They all have jobs; they all have their own lives. We work hard, Daddy, and they sit on their fat asses waiting for the money to roll in. And I'm not going to stay a part of this business if Steven and Lane are stepping in. I'd rather—"

"Cassandra Diane."

That silenced her; her father rarely used her full name, "Yes, sir?"

"What are you talking about? Didn't Dirk tell you?"

That made her pause, "*Tell me what*?"

"Honey, just before he left to pick you up to go to the airport, I told him to have you call me. I told him I finally made my decision. You're the only one who ever cared about me or this business. It took me a while to see it, but I'm signing it all over to you. When you didn't call, I figured you just thought it was about time I got some sense in my head, and you'd talk with me when you got back to the States."

"That son-of-a-bitch!" she spouted, suddenly realizing why he wanted to know if she went home. He didn't love her. He was going to try to sweep her off her feet before she knew she'd just been given the opportunity of a lifetime. "I'm gonna kill him," she snapped.

"Dirk? Why?"

"Daddy, that asshole said he'd fallen in love with me! He bought me a ring and... Oh, that stinking weasel! He was gonna try to convince me to... Ah!"

"Slow down, honey. You didn't marry him, did you?"

"Hell no! Matter of fact," suddenly her temper cooled, "Daddy, I met someone over here; he's an American, and I'm so in love with him. There is a lot I need to talk to you about, but I don't want to do it all over the phone. I'm gonna call you as soon as this job is done and I'm headed home because I want you to meet him, and damn it," she said, her temper flaring once again, "I want you sober when I bring him home!"

"We do have a lot to talk about, but I want you to know the business is yours. When you get home, we're signing the papers. And I'm sorry I told that idiot before I told you, pumpkin, but I thought—I mean, you two have been together a while now, and—"

"Don't go there, Daddy. Your apology is accepted. But that asshole is in *big* trouble with me."

Their conversation ended, but Cass couldn't go back under the hill just yet. She was too busy shaking with anger to let AJ see her this way. She considered calling Dirk, so she could rip him up one side and down the other, but she thought better of it. She'd meet him and act as though she were clueless about what he was trying to do. She wondered if she'd be able to control her temper long enough to let him babble on about how much he 'loved' her. She thought about confronting him on Friday with what her father told her, but that might not be the wisest thing to do while they were still over here. She didn't want any screw-ups or delays on this job. She needed the money, and no one, besides herself, could push a crew as hard as Dirk. She smiled, deciding she'd tell him they would work on their relationship *after* the job was completed. Her smile widened as she thought about telling him if they could just get this job finished, perhaps he and she could stay a little longer in the UK afterward and have some private time together—although she had no intention of ever having time alone with him. Instead, when it was all over, she *would* fire him.

She was still fuming with anger when she swam back under the hill. She'd tried to cool down, but the longer she stood there thinking about it, the madder she became.

AJ must have recognized the pissed off expression the moment she raised her face out of the water. "It went that well, huh?"

She sucked in a big breath, "No problem. The UK is mine, and you want to know why it's mine?!" Her volume was unintentionally rising. She could see he was ready to flinch at whatever she barked out, "because the whole damn company is gonna be mine!"

"Cass, you didn't tell your dad you were taking the business from him, did you?"

"No, he's giving it to me!"

"Then why are you so mad? Isn't this a good thing?"

She exhaled, "I'm sorry, that's not what I'm pissed about. When I called him, he told me he had decided to give it to me *before* I left the States, but he didn't tell me. No, no, he told *Dirk* to tell me!"

She gave it a second for the information to sink in, but it didn't take him long to see why she was so furious.

"You said all along that he didn't love you. I don't friggin' believe it! He was trying to con you?!"

"Yeah. He must have busted his ass hurrying to buy me a ring before we flew out here. And the only thing he was genuinely angry about when I had him on the phone was that you might be about to blow his chance at owning half of my business."

"Fire him," came his unhesitant response.

"I'm going to, but only after he works his ass off to finish this job." She spent the next half hour explaining to AJ why she was handling it this way. Dirk had plans to use her in the worst way, but she was turning the tables.

"As long as you don't get near him other than to meet with him Friday night; then fire him when the job is done, I'll be happy."

"There isn't a man on this planet I want to be near, except

you."

"And Bobby," he added, but then explained himself, "for Friday night. And it wouldn't be bad to bring him along when you fire Dirk, either."

"He'll be fired right in front of the whole crew. He won't have a chance to—"

"Do me a favor, please. Let Bobby be there to make me feel better if nothing else."

"You really do believe he can take Dirk, don't you?"

"I know it. We've been in a couple scraps together, and all I can say is I was really glad he was on my side."

She finally started smiling, "Okay, but you two are it as far as I'm concerned when it comes to male trust."

By mid-morning, they were comfortably side-by-side as AJ unrolled another scroll, and they stepped back into the world of Kingdom Hill.

I returned to my chamber with Sarai but extinguished the torch light in the room and told her to remain silent. The only illumination was a shaft of moonlight coming from my tower window, but it did not fall where I slept. There were two things I had never done in my bed before that night; one was to sleep with my dagger at my side, and the other was to sleep beside a beautiful, virgin female and not touch her. Sleeping with the dagger was the easier of the two.

When morning came, I awoke facing a creature even more perfect than I had seen the evening before. I reached out to gently stroke her face, but she awakened with a frightened shudder. "Shhh—keep quiet. I want to know how you acquired your knowledge about the queen. I would like to get away from the palace, so we may speak openly but must know if you have ever ridden?"

"I can, my Lord, though not as a lady should. I have ridden astride my family's plow horse."

I tried not to frown. I could not take her riding in such a scandalous manner. "You will ride aside."

We barely made it into the corridor when Emiline came out from her adjoining chamber and asked me what I was doing. I could hear the sound of irritation and frustration in her voice as she kept her eyes steadily on Sarai the entire time.

"I am enjoying the gift you gave me," I answered lightly. "She

rides, so I'm—"

"She rides?" Emiline said with clear disbelief.

Sarai kept her eyes cast downward, and said, "Yes, my Lady."

"I spoke not to you," Emiline snapped. "I evidently gave the wrong woman to my husband if she does not know her place around royalty." Emiline reached out and gripped Sarai by the wrist to lead her away.

I watched panic wash across Sarai's face.

"No, my wife," I stated, pulling Sarai from her hold, "you have bestowed her unto me, and I have made her mine. It is not fit for you to retract her now."

I had never witnessed such wicked anger in an expression before that moment as I did in Emiline's face. "Then I shall lock her in a tower and wait to see if she conceived from your encounter last night; if not, she will go home."

"Emiline," I replied with a certain amount of shock resonating through my voice, "it is not the conception, but the consummating which makes her my possession. You shall do no such thing; she belongs to me to do with as I wish, and I wish to take her riding."

I was grateful the queen carried no weapons because surely she would have stabbed me at that moment. As it was, she turned with a crisp snap of her skirt and left us standing there.

It is apparently not as easy to learn the proper way to sit aside as I had thought. The stablemen assisted, and we moved her as far as the stable yard for all to view. I knew Emiline would be observing from some vantage point to witness whether this woman could indeed ride as I stated. But Sarai could not keep her balance and wobbled precariously as she tried to stay upon the mount. "If you would allow me to ride astride as you, my King, this would not be so—"

The pace of the horse quickened, and all I saw of Sarai was a pair of dainty shoes fly up in the air through a swish of skirting as she tumbled backward off the horse. I thought I had surely killed her by breaking her neck, but to my relieved surprise, she was unharmed but thoroughly unhappy as she rose from the ground. I dismounted quickly and grabbed the reins of her mount and offered her my hand, "You shall try again." Then I lowered my voice as I drew her close to me, "We must get to a place where we may speak without an audience."

She gave me a look I was not accustomed to seeing from a

woman, not even Emiline; it was something I had seen on the faces of my soldiers when faced with a problem whereby resolution is mandatory, and it told me she was about to take matters into her own hands. Her foot went into the stirrup, but instead of accepting my help to be seated sideways, she swung up as a man and seated herself. You could almost hear the collective gasp rise from the stable yard. I was stunned; I did not even realize she had taken the reins from my hand.

"And now we shall ride," she stated, kicking the horse's flanks and bolting toward the yet unopened pasture gate.

It only took me a moment to mount as I shouted for the stablemen to open the gate, but she was already upon it. I held my breath as I watched the horse gather itself and vault into the air. Surely, she would fall again, but this time I doubted her neck would survive the impact. In that instant, I wondered if killing herself had been her intention all along. The horse and rider landed gracefully on the other side as she pulled back the reins and stopped, turning to look at me. The stableman was about to open the gate when I told him to leave it. I would not be outdone by a female in the riding arena. I urged my mount to a gallop and jumped the gate, as well.

She smiled as I came beside her, "Lead the way, my King. I will keep up."

"I detect a challenge from you, dear Sarai."

Her smile widened, "Then catch me." In that instant, she pulled away from me at a rapid pace.

"Plow horse, my arse!" I growled, and the race began.

I had not had such an enjoyable morning ride since I raced through the woods as a boy with Earland in fast pursuit. It had been many years since I had given thought to his name; my heart ached when the memory rushed me. Had I not been so young and impetuous, I would have given more heed to his final words. Was it possible things were not as my love-blinded heart believed at the time? In my tangle of thoughts, I did not notice she stopped near a small stream and dismounted until she called out to me.

We allowed the horses their freedom as I took her hand and led her to a shaded place beneath a small tree. "And now you shall tell me everything you know and how you came to learn such things."

Her face grew somber, "May I trust my King to keep my words from anyone else's ears? I would die before bringing harm to others."

"I swear my silence, but you must stop calling me your King. I asked you to call me Magnus."

"It is difficult, my... I feel as though it is not my place to be so familiar with you."

"As far as everyone believes, you were intimately familiar with me by this morn."

"I find it shameful," she stated, lowering her eyes.

"You said a life without love is a life not worth living; did you love someone before you were brought to me?"

"Oh, no, my Lord—I mean, Magnus. My parents arranged my union, but I did not..."

"Did not what?" I asked gently.

"I do not love him. For that matter, I do not believe I could ever love him. I was strangely relieved when the queen appeared at our door and said I was to be taken to the palace to be your concubine; I would not have to marry Thamus. Instead, I planned my demise, and I knew my family would find compassion to forgive my sin."

"Tell me, in trusted secrecy, all you know to be true about my Queen." I was unprepared for what she was about to divulge.

"My great aunt has been employed by the Queen's service for several years, and she has bespoken to my mother of many suspicious things about the queen. Once, when alone, she found a large stock of strange herbs, plants, and potions. Some of which she recognized, but many she did not. But one, in particular, was kept in good quantity."

"What was it?"

"Wild carrot seed."

I had no idea the significance of what she told me, "Explain: what is its use?"

"A—a woman consumes it after—after relations with a man to prevent conception."

"But she would not feed that to..." Suddenly I realized what she was revealing. Perhaps Emiline's inability to conceive was not of nature, but of design. But why? Did she not tell me she longed for children of her own? "I see," I slowly stated, "You are saying perhaps my queen is not barren as I believe her to be."

"You have asked for my knowledge, so I must beg forgiveness should it trouble you."

I tipped her face up to mine, "You need beg me for nothing. If this is what you have learned, and believe it true, be unafraid to reveal it to me." I could feel her yielding under my touch. Her vulnerability was exquisite and powerful.

"I am afraid," she said, as she became ever more so defenseless under my hold, "Afraid of what I have heard concerning your concubines."

"Tell me, Sarai, please."

Her eyes met mine and held me without breath as she stared.

"I have heard each of them became dedicated in their service to you through their acquired love for you. I was told you behold a power over women, and I am beginning to understand your power."

I kissed her without the reserve I employed the previous night. She accepted me, and I elated. "I would have you, beautiful Sarai, but you deserve not to be a concubine, but a wife. As king, I can have more than one, but only one queen. Would you accept me for your husband?"

"I believe the queen would kill us both should you take me before the church!"

Her words were true; Emiline would not stand for another to be called my wife. But my long-time and good friend who pens my words, Cynewulf, was bishop of my palace church, and I knew he would agree to a private vow between Sarai and myself. "Then answer me here and now, and I shall pledge thee my love and loyalty. We need not the church, but our bond before God. Do you take me as your husband this moment?"

"My heart beats as the wings of a sparrow, and I cannot describe the fear that fills me, but it is not greater than the joy I express to you as I accept."

I had never made love in the expanse of the wilds, open before heaven, but it was, without doubt, the most beautiful experience of my life as I bared Sarai down to her lovely flesh. She was slight of figure, of a slim waist, small hips, and a smooth flat abdomen. Her breasts were neither small nor large, but erect and completely responsive to my touch. She assisted in the removal of my clothing, touching my chest and powerful arms in awe of this new experience.

"There is beauty in you, my King," she breathlessly stated. She looked into my eyes and realized her error. "You are glorious to me, Magnus. Make me thy wife in love and truth."

"In truth and love," I whispered as I laid my body upon hers. My concubines had all been virgins, and although not rudely forceful, I had taken away their gifts without honest tenderness. This gift,

however, was to be taken with all the tenderness I possessed. This was the experience I once longed for with Emiline but never achieved. Love was present in this moment as it had never been in any other. Sarai was not my possession out of duty; she gave me all she had to offer with complete surrender and willingness. In love I was accepted, and never had there been such a union of two hearts.

Cass covered her face with her hands, breathing a huge sigh as AJ finished what had been one of the longest scrolls so far.

"You're not crying are you?" he asked gently.

"No," was her flat response.

"What is it?"

"You *don't* want to know."

"Cass," he said, carefully pulling her hands away from her face, "tell me."

"I'm horny; okay? The last part was... Anyway, I could really use a lesson from you right now, but no," she said suddenly defensive, "I'm not telling you a damn thing!" He smiled and leaned toward her, but she gave him an ultimatum first. "If you kiss me, you're gonna lay me right here and right now. I need it, and yes I'm saying sex. I want to make love, but sex would do the job just fine at the moment."

He stopped short of her lips. She advanced, but he pulled away. Her frustration level was peaking.

"Are you always like this with other women? Do you have to know every detail before you sleep with them?"

"You aren't 'other women.' And to answer your question: no. You are unique, and I've never experienced anything like this."

"Unique as in strange?" she was trying to keep her temper out of her voice, but it was starting to seep in.

"I've always believed in following my instincts. I have some very loud instincts where you're concerned, but if you want to know the truth, I'm so damn horny right now I could almost give in. But love changes everything; we both need to wait. Unless you want to tell me why you like it rough?"

Her eyes locked on to his. It was the first time he'd said anything like that, but she knew he figured it out a while ago. "That's just it, *I* don't like it rough. Rough is all I understand; rough is what my body responds to," she said, the corners of her lips turning downward as they began to quiver, "You're the only guy who ever treated me like I deserve anything else. I just wish you weren't wrong."

"I'm not wrong, Cass. And when you're ready, I'm going to prove it. Let me kiss you, but don't go berserk on me," he leaned in once again.

"If you mean what you're saying, then don't kiss me right now, not with both of us feeling this way." Then she said something she never believed she'd tell him, "I want to wait."

His smile was enormous, "You *are* a good person."

"Hardly, but you're working on me," she conceded.

He leaned in for the kiss but placed it on her forehead.

"You're getting a headache, aren't you?"

A funny look crossed his face, "How did you know?"

"I'm starting to get good at reading your expressions. Do you want something for it?"

"Yeah, if we're going to read anymore, I'm—"

"Would a massage help? Nothing sensual," she added quickly, "just your back and shoulders and maybe your feet and calves?"

"That sounds great. We've been sitting so long my back is killing me."

"I'll get you a pill. You sprawl out on the sleeping bag."

For the next thirty minutes, she rubbed, pushed, kneaded, and worked his muscles. He was moaning in the beginning, but somewhere between finishing his shoulders and slipping down to massage the soles of his feet, he dozed off. She changed her clothes and swam out.

It was two in the afternoon and the day was spectacular. The sky was cloudless, and the sun beat down as best it could in the temperate climate. She grabbed a towel from the Cruiser and trekked to the top of the hill. She could see the highway far in the distance; occasionally vehicles traveled by, but the area was otherwise desolate and peaceful. She spread out the towel and stripped down to her bra and underwear. While he rested, she would, too—she'd just get a tan while doing it.

She drifted in and out of consciousness; her mind continually returned to the story of the great kingdom below her. She wondered what Magnus looked like. In all his descriptive language, he never described himself in detail. The only thing he mentioned (and it was what set her off in the first place) was that he had powerful arms. She rolled onto her stomach and fell into a light sleep. She dreamed of walking through the palace, lords and ladies abound, but she couldn't make out their faces. She approached a throne and knew she was about to meet the great King of Valderegnum. AJ was seated on the throne, but when he looked up and saw her, what he said woke her as quickly as if she'd been in a nightmare. He looked at her, smiled, and then called her by name: Emiline.

She jerked upright from the towel; her heart thundered inside her chest and tears immediately swelled over her lashes. Emiline didn't deserve Magnus. She was beautiful on the outside, but inside, something was terribly wrong. Emiline would eventually destroy the good things in her life and ruin the man who once loved her so deeply. Would Cass find herself someday doing the same thing to AJ? She believed with all her heart he would make it through the surgery, but would she end up ruining his life in the end? She dried her tears on the towel and looked up toward the sky, "Change me; I don't want to be an Emiline."

When she reentered the hill, he was awake and munching on trail mix.

"Where'd you go?"

"I just caught a little sun," she answered with an easy smile.

"A little too much sun," he said as he rose to leave a thumbprint on her shoulder, "you're burnt."

She glanced at her red skin, "Not too bad. I'll be tan by tomorrow.

"Can I kiss you now?"

"Yeah, I'm good. How about you?"

"Man, I am so relaxed after that massage and nap; I don't think I could get a h... Never mind. I'm good, too."

She giggled.

"Eat this first, though," he said, holding a scoop of trail mix to her lips.

She allowed him to dump it in, but then had to ask (somewhat awkwardly as she chewed), "Why?"

He grinned, "I don't want to be the only one kissing with peanut breath."

She had two choices as the laughter rose without warning: shower him in chewed peanuts, raisins, and chocolate, or choke. She choked, turning her back to him as he apologized and thumped her gently between her shoulder blades.

"I'm so sorry. Are you okay?"

It took her a minute to reply, "I'm fine—need some water, though."

He handed her his open bottle, and she took a couple of sips.

She gulped in a good breath of air and smiled, "All right, kiss me, you idiot, but no more wise cracks."

He was starting to laugh, so there was no way a kiss was going to work. He pulled her against his chest and nuzzled his face into the side of her neck. "It must be really nice outside," he said as his laughter ebbed, "Your skin is so warm, even after coming out of the spring, I can almost feel the sunshine on it."

"Let's put the next scroll in a bag—okay, a couple bags for safety—and go outside. We can catch a late lunch or early dinner and read while we watch the sun go down. Besides, this is going to be the last night on earth we're the only two people in the world who know what's hidden here."

He was finally composed enough for their kiss. And it was a very good kiss. "That sounds perfect to me."

It was a few hours before sunset; they were seated on top of the hill in lounge chairs they picked up from town. The lighting was infinitely better than under the hill, making her realize this would take the strain off his eyes. She reached over and worked her fingers into his hair as she super-lightly massaged his scalp. He smiled and began.

I believe I could have left it all behind after that moment. I needed no kingdom, no power, no glory, and no place for history to record my name. All I needed I held in my arms. Had it not been for my children, I would have taken Sarai away and never returned to Valderegnum. But we would return, and had I known what the future was to hold, I would have surely abandoned it for her sake.

"Are you sure you cannot ride as a lady should?" I asked, as I held her mount steady.

"Have you ever tried to ride that way?"

"Of course not."

"Try it. No one is here to bear witness," she urged.

I sighed as I considered her suggestion. I was prepared to tell her no, but I recognized she was not attempting to manipulate me; she simply wanted me to understand why she was disobeying. "Very well," I said, pushing myself up in the saddle and seating myself aside. "This is not so terribly bad," I started to say when she gave the horse an easy slap to put it in motion. Although I did not fall, I instantly had a better understanding of why she did not wish to sit in such a manner. I dismounted quickly and apologized. "You may ride astride. I know not what everyone in the kingdom shall think, but at least I understand."

She mounted but seated herself very lightly, "Could we please make it a slow pace for the return?"

I know my expression told her I was perplexed.

She winced to a small degree as she placed her hand on her lower abdomen, "You were gentle and good to me, Magnus, but there is still pain.

"Yes, of course, my love."

We walked the horses side by side on the journey back, which gave me more opportunity to question her, "Is your great aunt the only one who knows these things?"

"No, there have been others, but the queen is very selective with her subjects. But there is one member of her guard rumored to be unhappy. I know not which one, but I overheard my father saying one of the men is despondent; something to do with feelings of a stronger loyalty to his king rather than the queen.

"I do not profess to know the reasons the queen provides you with women only to kill them, but the rumor is well established among the peasants. There have been parents who hide their daughters when they know she is prowling about with her guardsmen. One family with three very beautiful daughters made all three cut their hair and changed their manner of dress, so they would not be immediately recognized as women."

"And what happened to you, sweet Sarai? How did she come to take you from your family?"

"She knew my family through my great aunt and has mentioned to my mother for several years how beautiful I was becoming. My mother said it made her uneasy. It was as if the queen was picking out a piece of meat for a meal instead of admiring a young woman. They arranged my marriage to Thamus so I might be saved. I was terrified when she arrived with her guard yesterday, only days away from my marriage. I wanted neither, but then I remembered my great aunt saying your chamber was in the high watchtower; I planned my demise."

"And how happy I am you did not succeed."

"As am I. Is it improper to tell you how much pleasure I felt as you made me woman?"

"Between us, Sarai, I hope there is nothing you cannot tell me."

"I did not know such feelings and sensations existed within me," her face filling with color. "Will it always be this way with you?"

"I hope I can make it even better for you as time passes."

We returned to the palace, and I sought after my dear friend and told him of my encounter with Sarai. He heard my confession and absolved me of my impatient vows, and agreed it would not have been safe to make such matters public before the queen. Cynewulf had suspicions about Emiline long ago, but at the time, I would hear nothing of it. I simply assumed he, as a man devoted to religious matters, would be inherently suspicious of our sins. He met with us that evening, in secrecy, to hear our vows and to tie the silken cord of unity to bind our hands in matrimony. Our joy was completed before God.

A fortnight I spent in the greatest pleasures of my life as I learned every intimacy of my new bride. When I was not consumed by thoughts of Sarai, I considered how I would discover which soldier desired descent from his rank in the queen's guard. I kept Sarai with me wherever I went, and I could tell it made Emiline most unhappy. After these weeks passed, she finally approached me just as I entered my chamber, requesting to speak with me in private. "Sarai is no more than an extension of your love for me." I said using the same words she had so long ago when she brought Narcilla to me. "We can speak in my chamber."

"No, my husband, I wish to speak with you alone. Send her out into the stairwell or down to the banquet room; I must have a moment of your time."

I gave my answer careful consideration, "Your chamber," I stated.

I watched the surprise fill her face. I had never ventured into her chamber, and she never wanted me to do so.

I watched her swallow hard.

"Give me a few minutes to prepare it, and I will bid you in."

She left the room as I turned and barred the outer door to mine. "No one can enter from the hall," I said, as I sat next to Sarai on the bed. "Take this and use it should anyone come in through the queen's chamber." I pressed my dagger into her hands. "Hide it under the pillow, and should you need to use it, do not withdraw it until they are so close they cannot possibly escape your thrust. Do you understand?"

Her eyes were wide and thoroughly filled with fright, yet she nodded.

Several more minutes passed before Emiline entered and bade me to her chamber.

It was a strange experience to be there alone with her. I once felt there would be no other who could touch my heart, but now I beheld my once most prized possession in a different light. I still loved her, but it was mingled with heavy suspicion and wonder. I looked around her room, knowing as I did, something was not quite right in this space. Furniture was in poor arrangement, and artwork hung oddly in some spaces. That was when I noticed Richard's gloves laid on a chair across the room. This was the first time I entered this space, but, evidently, not the first time a man had been in here. My suspicions grew as hot inside me as if I had grabbed an iron from the fire.

"I do not like all the time you are spending with your newest concubine," Emiline asserted. "You have never taken such interest in the other women."

I smiled, "I am enjoying this one. You did well by selecting her."

"I am feeling a bit neglected, Magnus. You hardly even look at me since you took her."

"She was given to me; I did not take her. And she was given by your hand," I added.

"I made an error, and I fear I am losing you to this strange woman."

I turned and walked slowly to the wall separating our rooms; the floor was worn sharply near a framed painting which hung too low.

She quickly inserted herself between me and the wall as she placed her hands on my chest, "I do not wish to be a spiritual wife any longer. I miss you terribly, and I want you to sleep with me this night."

That, I knew, would not work. I could not, would not, leave Sarai unprotected.

"And should you conceive in one night of passion?"

"We both know that to be highly unlikely, yet I would welcome carrying your child."

"Would you?"

"Magnus! How could you question me on such a thing?"

"You spend little to no time with my children, children whom you begged me to sire."

"I love Magnus, Arreanna, and Adelia. Just because I feel an awkwardness I never expected around children does not mean I do not love them," her eyes began to fill with tears.

My heart began to yield, and then I thought of all the times she molded me to see her view. "Sweet Emiline, forgive me," I feigned compassion. "I know you love me, but give me a few more weeks with Sarai to see whether or not she has conceived. When that is accomplished, and since there will be no others, we will spend time together."

She frowned, "I do not wish to wait weeks."

I wrapped her in my arms and pulled her to my breast, "Do you remember our first time in my chamber?"

She softened against me, "Mmm, yes, my love. You were such a perfect lover, so compassionate and determined."

"We waited years for that moment. Give me these weeks, and then we shall be together as it was when we were new at love."

"Do you promise me, Magnus? Look at me and tell me there is no other who claims your heart."

I was unsure how well I could convincingly lie. "Is anyone else my queen? Is there anyone else who can sway me with her sultry words and melt me with but a look? You are as beautiful as you are cunning."

"Cunning?" she asked innocently.

"Who else could have persuaded me to take nine concubines when I did not wish to have the first?"

She smiled, and I knew I was doing well to stroke her ego.

"All right," she conceded, and then gave a wicked look toward my chamber door. "Impregnate your cow and then put her away until she accomplishes her task. I await my husband's return."

I prepared to leave when she begged a kiss. I had forgotten her kiss during our time apart, and what I once found alluring, I now found to be staged and contrived.

I devised a plan in the following days and then called her guard to my military room. Richard of Llyons filed them in, but I could tell he was uneasy regarding the meeting. I was certain his loyalty was to my queen alone, and I believed him to be her lover. I observed them as they stood at attention before me: Berenger of Scotts, Sir Gregory, and Sir Ryland had been members of the queen's original guard, as had Richard, but Nyles of Dunfee and Sir Phillip were the newest members, replacing two who died from a mysterious fever. All of them appeared nervous.

"It has come to my attention two young maidens from the village disappeared some weeks ago." They all seemed to stiffen, but one, Nyles of Dunfee, refused to maintain eye contact with me. I watched Richard's sword hand slide almost undetected to his hilt, but I continued. "Since my queen insists to go out among the people on a regular basis to choose vegetables, fruits, and such, you have a vantage point which others may not. I command you to take extra precautions with my queen." The relaxation was miniscule, but I saw it nonetheless; they were relieved this was no accusation, but an assignment. "Also, I wish you to be the eyes and ears of the kingdom concerning this matter. If you can uncover anything regarding these disappearances, you are to report directly to me. I wish the queen to be neither concerned nor frightened by news with which she should not be troubled. Are we clear on this matter?"

Richard stepped forward bowing slightly, "Yes, my King. We shall see what we can discover without alerting the queen to our new task."

The other men gave their pledge, but once again, I watched Nyles. His face told me he was troubled. He looked at me briefly, and in that meeting of our eyes, I knew I had my potential deserter. Now the new challenge presented itself of isolating him from the others without raising suspicions.

The sun was touching the horizon as AJ finished the last words. "I was hoping we'd have these finished tonight, but I don't know if we can finish the final two now, especially if they keep getting longer."

"Are you tired?" Cass whispered in his ear as she kissed it.

"Yes and no. Physically I'm good, mainly because of the nap. Mentally, I'm bushed. All I can say is thank God Cynewulf had extremely neat penmanship, or this would have taken weeks to decipher."

"That and how they decided to store the scrolls. Do you realize if they had just made a shelf in the wall and put these on it, they would have been falling apart?"

"I've been thinking about that. Cass, if we decide to leave it secret, we'll have to seal everything just the way we found it. I'm pretty sure I can reheat the wax mixture and repack the holes in the wall, but I'm afraid to heat the coating on the shells that hold the actual scrolls; heat might cause damage. The only other way to preserve these would be to take them out and sandwich them air tight between panes of glass, but then they couldn't go back into the wall."

She didn't like that idea, "What if we put the scrolls inside the big zipper bags, suck all the air out, and then seal them in the holes? We could leave our names and the date we discovered them and our reasons for keeping them hidden."

The last sliver of the sun slipped behind the orange-gold horizon as she watched AJ's face.

He turned to her and smiled, "That's perfect. The scrolls won't draw any moisture through the plastic, and we get to leave our mark."

They were both still wide-awake by ten p.m. AJ decided he could handle one more scroll before they went to sleep. "If it's too long, I'll quit part way," he said, as he carved the wax from the hole and removed it.

The United Kingdom vanished as the Great Kingdom came back to life.

Separating Nyles would prove more challenging than anticipated. Richard never allowed the guards to gather in groups whose numbers were fewer than three, and he kept Nyles and Phillip with him the majority of the time. Strategically, his move was brilliant. No commander of any worth would allow newer and unseasoned recruits on the battlefield without thorough indoctrination. Loyalty was seldom natural; it had to be carefully honed, and that was what he was doing. Phillip seemed to embrace his new position with vigor; Lyles continued to show signs of hesitation. I would have to approach him soon before an accident or illness befell him.

In the meanwhile, I had to devise a way to keep Sarai safe in my household. I was glad beyond measure to learn she was indeed with child. If I placed her with the children and concubines, she should be safe. I would take extra precautions by assigning four of my closest guards to be added to the family wing of the palace.

None of the women ever died in the early stages of pregnancy, and if Emiline felt assured I was no longer devoted to Sarai, perhaps she would venture no ill plan for a time.

What I did not expect, but thrilled my soul, was Sarai's reaction to the children and even to the other women for that matter. She took to the children immediately. Young Magnus with his golden hair and sapphire eyes climbed quickly onto her lap and clung to her. My daughters, even at the tender age of fourteen months, were beyond beautiful. They were twins who appeared identical with the exception of Adelia's small red birthmark on her left shoulder. Their hair was medium brown and hung down in tiny ringlets. The women were going to shoo the children away from bothering me as I sat and watched, but I bade them to leave the children alone as they clung to the calves of my legs and smiled up at me. There was no resistance in my body toward anything these children should have want or need for. I picked each one up in turn and kissed them, but Magnus refused to leave Sarai's lap. I stayed for the day to enjoy the children, to watch her play games with them, and sing. My heart swelled so tightly I felt it would surely burst. This was what I had longed for, but never attained: a woman who would truly be a mother to my children and a true wife to her husband.

I thought Sarai might be uncomfortable with Evon, Melinda, and Cherrise, but the women were kind to one another. Sarai was filled with wonder as she talked with Melinda and Cherrise, both were nearing the end of their pregnancies. Melinda had three or four weeks remaining, but Cherrise was expecting any day to bring forth a child for me. And I saw something in these women's eyes I did not see before. When Sarai told me that my concubines became so through duty but continued in love, I did not believe it, but now it became very apparent to me she was right. These women genuinely cared for me not only as their king, but also as their provider and father of their children. Evon was the shyest of the three; she had lost her child a month before its birth when she came down with a terrible illness. Afterward, she stayed to serve as wet-nurse for my daughters, whom had lost their mother. We were a strange family but family nonetheless.

With Sarai secured as well as possible, I began the task of procuring the man who I believed could give me the most information about the true nature of my queen. I finally decided there were only two choices to speak with Nyles alone; either in the confessional of the church or in the garderobe. I set my hopes upon the confessional but somehow doubted Richard would permit them the privilege.

I asked Cynewulf to call a special service for my soldiers, offering it in small groups of twenty to twenty-five at a time. He would call them up one at a time to offer communion, allowing him to have a private moment with Nyles. If Cynewulf saw hope, he would tell Nyles which confessional to enter, where I would be waiting. The only thing that could foul my plans would be for Emiline to decide she wanted to go out among the villages on that day. Thankfully, she did not due to rain and cold weather. I made a special point to invite her guards to the early morning communion—and then prayed.

All went according to plan. He approached Cynewulf, but instead of the typical quiet blessing as he received sacrament, he was told if he valued his king and country more than the duties of the queen, to go to the confessional with the gold curtain; his king awaited him for a private moment. Immediately, Nyles rose and headed for the confessional, but Richard stopped him just beyond the curtain. I could plainly hear all their conversation.

"Where do you think you are going?" came Richard's strong yet quiet words.

"The Bishop told me to go in private to say ten Hail Mary's before partaking in the communion, sire."

"Are you sure you didn't tell him you need confession for your sins?" he growled.

I knew what was coming. Richard would want to see if the booth was empty. Very quietly, I went out through the hidden door that led to all the confessionals and eventually to the back of the church. But I did not go far as I continued to listen to the muted conversation.

"No, sire. I merely—"

I heard the curtain being pulled open as they undoubtedly stared into the empty booth.

"Make it quick," he said in anger, "I do not intend to spend more time than necessary on this mockery called religion."

I listened as Nyles prudently closed the golden curtain and entered the other side of the booth; he began repeating his Hail Mary's as I slipped back into the opposing side.

"Nyles of Dunfee, to whom do you pledge your loyalty?"

"To you, my King," he responded.

"I have reason to believe my queen is doing all manner of evil against God and kingdom; will you serve your king and tell all that you know?"

"Ay, my Lord, but I fear Richard of Llyons will know something is amiss if I stay here a moment more."

"We must meet privately; tell me when and where?"

I could hear heavy footfalls and I knew Richard was returning.

"In three nights, past the bailey by the southern gate as the moon is three quarters set."

I could wait no more as I exited the room undetected and headed down the darkened corridor to the back of the church. As evening came, I became restless without Sarai. Her absence was like a hole inside my heart that ached without ceasing. I could not consume my evening meal, and I could not concentrate for worry over her safety. When I reached the family wing, I was astonished to find Emiline seated on the floor playing with the children as the other women assisted. She looked up at me, somewhat surprised, and said she came down because Cherrise was close to giving birth, and she wanted to check on her, but became entranced with the children, instead. She was smiling and seemed, queerly enough, happy. She was even being pleasant to Sarai. I joined her for a few moments; then she rose and said she would return tomorrow to see if we had added another child to 'our' family. I was curious enough to pull her aside before she left and asked what was she really doing?

She didn't seem at all shocked by my question, "You said I didn't spend enough time with the children. Perhaps I find it awkward with them because I have so little practice. Will I join you in your chamber tonight, my love?"

"No," I stated quickly, wondering how was I going to explain myself. "I—"

"Soon, my love?"

"Yes, very soon, Emiline. Goodnight."

When I was sure she was well gone, I took Sarai's hand and asked her to please return to my chamber for the night.

Her smile beamed brightly, "Oh, yes, my husband," she whispered softly, "I was dreading a night without you by my side, but we have not eaten our evening meal yet, and I am famished."

"Nor have I. Dine with me in the banquet hall; no one is there *and all is quiet tonight."*

She kissed my cheek, and we left without another word.

When morning came, she was secure in my arms. I kissed her eyelids as she awakened.

"Time to go return to be with the other women," she stated drearily. "I love the children, and the other women are so kind, but I miss you terribly. Will you bring me back here tonight?"

"Emiline shall hate me when she knows, but I cannot be without you; yes, I will."

We were on our way to the family wing when one of the chamber women came running out and begged me to come no closer.

"They have all come down with a terrible fever, my Lord. Cherrise is near death and—"

Sarai gasped and took off at a run for the room before I could stop her. Several of the village women had already arrived and were trying to assist. I was shocked to see them, my concubines and children, all drawn and pale, yet consumed with fever. The children cried as they gagged with nausea, but nothing came up. I did not feel fear for myself, but I wanted Sarai to leave immediately.

"This is no sickness," she said in anger. "Look at them, Magnus. Look at their eyes; the blacks of their eyes have become enormous. This is the work of poison I tell you."

Immediately, I thought of Emiline's visit to them yesterday. Could Sarai be right? Could it be that Emiline was attempting to rid herself of all of them? I went to the children's beds and bent down as my son reached out to me.

"Stay back, my King," one of the elderly women stated, "it would not be good for you to become infected."

"Move away," I commanded.

She was reluctant, but she would not disobey.

I lifted Magnus into my arms and kissed his scorching head. He tried to call out to me, but nothing came from his dry lips. "Give me a rag soaked in water," I ordered. It was handed to me, and I put it to his parched mouth; he began to eagerly suck, and then to gag. The sapphire in his eyes was almost non-existent, as the black expanded to fill the colored space. I kissed him once more and laid him down then moved to my daughters. Their condition, though similar, was more severe; they were listless and unresponsive as I ordered the women to drip water into their mouths. I kissed them each, and with each kiss, my fury grew hotter.

Sarai let out a cry. I looked over as she sat holding Cherisse's hand; the last breath had been drawn as Cherisse's body went limp.

"Stay here!" I ordered, and headed at double-speed for the queen's chamber. Emiline would pay for this. I had not my proof yet of her involvement, but my suspicion for now was enough. I did not believe I could kill her, but I would make her confess then banish her from my kingdom.

I burst through her chamber door to see her still asleep on her bed. "What have you done?!" I bellowed as I turned her over and jerked her almost upright. I was not prepared for what would meet my eyes; Emiline was exactly as those I had just left. Her normally white skin was like chalk, her eyes completely black, and her lips dry. She tried to speak to me but fell limp in my hold. "Dear God, I am sorry, Emiline."

She choked as I gently placed her back on the bed. I grabbed the pitcher and trickled a small amount into her mouth. She gagged, but welcomed the liquid, motioning for me to give her more. I took a nearby cloth and soaked it, wiping her face and pressing it to her lips.

"Help me," came a tiny whimper.

I thought of all she had been to me, of all the years of preparation to make her my queen, my lover, and my wife; I had been prepared to accuse her when she lay ill in her bed unable to cry out for help. My heart broke as my tears fell. This was no poison; she had been with them yesterday and now was dying from the same sickness. But so had I, and so had Sarai; why were we not ill? I could think no more about this puzzle; Emiline needed me.

I tried to rise to get someone to come up and attend to her, but she gripped my sleeve in desperation and begged me to stay. Some time passed before her chambermaid arrived. I told her to take over for me so I could get more help.

The entire palace was in upheaval by the time I returned to the family wing. Sarai was holding Magnus, rocking back and forth whilst she sobbed. She had cried so much, the bodice of her dress was drenched in tears.

"This is no poison," I softly told her, "Emiline is also very ill in her chamber. She couldn't have done this, not to herself."

"Your daughters are gone, my King," she wept, as if she had not heard me. "Evon is gone as well. Melinda does not feel her child

moving inside her and is near death herself. Oh, Magnus, why? Why? Not the children. It is not right."

"Let me take him," I asked gently. "Give me my last moments with my son."

I could tell she did not want to let him go, but she knew the time was short as she placed him in my arms.

His eyes were open but his stare vacant as I kissed and held him close. My tears fell as I considered I had not been here as my daughters drew their last breaths. I would not make that error twice. I would stay with my son until he returned to me or heaven called him home.

Cass was shaking her head, tears running down her cheeks.

AJ rose up slowly. He was stiff from sitting and obviously very tired. He laid the scroll on the table and started to carve out the last hole.

"Don't even think about it," Cass said, as she took the tool from his hand. "It's three a.m. and there is no way—"

"Cassandra, I have to know if his little boy makes it."

"I want to know, too, but not tonight. You're gonna have one hell of a migraine if you don't stop and get some rest. Come on," she said, pulling him toward the sleeping bag, "we'll learn what happens when we get up."

He balked.

She pulled a little harder, "Please."

"You're right. And I am tired. I just want to finish it."

"You will—just not right now."

The lantern was turned off, and the room glowed with a dim green light. Neither one wanted to talk after all they had read. Kingdom Hill would soon come to a close and they both knew the ending wouldn't be easy to take.

CHAPTER ELEVEN

Despite the late night reading, they were awake early and tidying up for their visitor. Bobby would meet them at the hotel in Moffat at four in the afternoon, and since her meeting with Dirk wasn't until eight, this would give him plenty of time to see the hill and let them tell him some of the history. If the final scroll wasn't longer than what they read last night, they could finish with enough time to go out for lunch before meeting Bobby.

"I can't believe this is it," AJ stated, as he pulled the remaining scroll from its resting place.

She could tell something was different about it by the look on his face. "What is it?"

"It's heavier."

"Don't think we have to finish it before we meet Bobby," she said as she placed his glasses on his face and then slid them up the bridge of his nose. "I doubled-over the sleeping bag, so maybe we'll be more comfortable, set us out a couple bottled waters, and a snack; I think we're ready. Although I have to admit, I may not be prepared for the ending of the story."

"I agree, but we've come too far to not know what happened. Let's read."

It felt as if my world crumbled and fell apart beneath my feet. Within hours of rising up that morning, everyone, with the exception of Emiline and Sarai, was taken from me. I was still king of a vast empire, but it was hollow without my children and the good women who bore them for me. The only thread of hope keeping me from madness was Sarai. When I returned to Emiline's chamber, fully expecting to be present as she took her last breath, I was surprised to find Richard there administering a small dose of yellowish-brown liquid to her.

"What are you doing?" I demanded.

"I am trying to help, my Lord. My mother knew much about illnesses, fevers, and such. When I heard the queen and others had taken ill, I gathered a few things and headed here as quickly as I could. I am sorry I did not arrive sooner to help with the others, but perhaps I may at least minister to my queen."

"What are you giving her?" I noticed, whatever it had been, it was sufficiently bitter to make Emiline grimace, but moments later she appeared to relax.

"It is from the juice of the poppy seed. It will give her comfort, if nothing else."

"Opium? You are relieved of duty; there shall no longer be a queen's guard."

"But, my Lord, she is not dead. She is resting now."

"Why are you unafraid of this illness?" My suspicions were growing hot within me yet again. I considered that all the madness with the concubines happened well after the formation of her guard. Could it be he had worked, contrived, and conned his way into Emiline's heart? Could he be the source of my miseries? My anger bloomed to life like a flame when coals are stirred and given something to ignite; could he have seduced my wife? My hand moved to draw my sword.

"Magnus," Emiline's frail voice choked.

Richard observed the challenge about to take place, but he turned instead toward her, "You see, my King, I did not come to do harm. It is helping."

"Leave, now!" I demanded.

He seemed to hesitate then gave an almost undetectable bow and retreated.

Emiline's thin hand reached toward me.

"I can stay with her, my husband," Sarai stated, touching my back gently.

"No. If this is an illness, you are exposed enough. Wait for me in my chamber, and I will—"

"This is no normal illness; I still believe it poison. No illness can

come upon and take one so quickly."

"But if it is an illness, I would rather die than to watch it take you from me. Please, Sarai, my chamber." As king I was not accustomed to asking please, but rather to order and have my orders followed, but at this moment, I did not feel as a king, but as a broken and frustrated man, and, perhaps, more human than I had ever been in my life.

Sarai did as I asked without further rebuttal.

I pressed a cool rag to Emiline's brow, noticing as I did her eyes were beginning to show their beautiful blue color as the blackness shrank. I poured a small amount of water for her, which she eagerly accepted. She swallowed then struggled to speak.

"Quiet now, dear Emiline. I am here for you. There are many things I wish to know, but for now, I bid you rest." I stretched myself beside her on the bed, noticing her weak smile. I kissed her eyelids, whereupon she went completely limp in my grasp. For an instant, I thought it had been her last breath but then understood she simply went faint into sleep. I did not feel as though I had the energy to rise, but I had to satisfy my curiosity on at least one issue. I rose without disturbing her and went to the wall separating our rooms. I lifted the painting and immediately saw the defect. I bent down and peered into the opening. Though the wall was thick, and it was nothing more than a crack on the side in my chamber, I could clearly see into my room; the view was Sarai, lying upon my bed.

Emiline had been insistent to watch when she brought me Narcilla that first night, but after I refused her presence thereafter, she remedied the situation to suit herself. Once again, I was left asking myself why? Why did she wish to view such things? If she ever loved me, why would she want to see me taking pleasure from another female?

As she slept, I searched her room and found many curious things. I found a bag containing a few pounds of tiny brown seeds. I placed a pinch into my dagger sheath then continued my search. I also found two fresh poppy-seed pods in the bottom of a drawer near her bed and one small, round, black berry which appeared to have fallen and rolled under the edge of her bed. I checked her before leaving the room and knew the opium which Richard administered to her, had indeed relaxed and resolved many of her symptoms; she slept soundly.

I placed a chair in front of the small crack in my wall to prevent any further, unwanted observations from Emiline's room and then seated myself very slowly beside Sarai. But I was not gentle enough to prevent her from feeling my presence. She rolled over and looked at me, her eyes reddened, and the skin beneath them looked almost bruised from crying. I could not stop myself from feeling her forehead just to make certain she was not feverish, but her brow was cool to the touch.

"My heart breaks for you, my husband. Your sorrow must be more than you can bear."

"Were it not for you, I would not have the strength to go on."

She glanced toward the door leading to Emiline's chamber, "Do you believe she will survive this?"

"I do. Although she was desperately ill, I do not believe she was as severe as the others; the poppy resin he fed to her seems to be helping."

"How would her guard know what to administer? Opium does not cure fever. I have heard of those who use it for pains and corrections of the bowel, but not fever."

"I am as perplexed as you, and I have found two curious items in her room." I poured the seeds into my hand with the small berry, "Do you know what these are?"

"No, but there is a woman in my parents' village who treats the sick with herbs; perhaps she would know."

"I do not wish you to ride in your current state, but if I procure a cart, and you do not believe it will be too difficult on you, would you show me where she lives?"

"Have no fear for me, Magnus. I am strong; this child I carry is safe."

I could not stop the reaction I was having as my tears fell. She reclined on the bed as I pressed my face to her dress where I knew the miracle within her resided. I could barely speak for the blockage in my throat. "I will not lose either of you. I must send you someplace safe, a place far from Valderegnum."

"NO!" she quickly asserted, "I will be fine. I will stay by your side, sweet Magnus. No harm will come to me, and I shall birth our child here in this very room, while you hold my hand."

"It is not safe. Nowhere in my cursed kingdom is safe for you, my love."

"This kingdom is not cursed; do not speak such things. You have built the finest kingdom ever created. Your subjects are loyal to you

and would do anything you ask of them. Greatness is your destiny. But your happiness has been attacked from within this palace, and although I know she is ill and could have died from this as well, I still believe this attack came from your queen."

"I have many friends still in Northumbria; I will send you there, away from this madness."

"Please, I beg you; do not send me away. I am safe as long as I am with you. Let us meet with the woman from my village and see what she says. Please, Magnus, reconsider and allow me to stay. My heart could not stand to be away from you."

I kissed her lips and tucked her against my breast, "Cry no more, beautiful one. I will wait until I have gathered my evidence before I decide what shall be done to keep you safe."

My kingdom was in mourning over the loss of my family, and all was quiet; laborers stopped working in the fields, buying and selling in the villages ceased, everything came to stillness as they wept and prayed for me. There were few people about to see us leave on the horse-drawn cart. And, no matter what she told me, I was still concerned for Sarai as the cart jolted along the rutted paths toward her village, but she assured me she would be fine. When we came to the woman's hovel, she was astonished as to who was visiting.

"Please, dear lady, I need you to tell me what these herbs are which I have found." I scattered the seeds and berry into her hand.

"Wild carrot," was the first thing from her mouth.

Although Sarai told me what her great-aunt discovered, she herself did not know what a wild carrot seed looked like.

"And the other?"

She rolled the berry between her fingers, broke the skin and smelled it, touched her tongue to it and spat, "I do not know what it is called by others, but I call it the Devil's Cherry."

"What is its purpose? You have, no doubt, heard what happened at the palace this morning. Could someone have used this to take the lives of the women and children?"

"I heard it was a fever, my King."

"Yes, fever with extremely dry lips, sallow skin, gagging without spew, and—"

"Their eyes, my King, what did their eyes look like? Was the black of their eyes large?"

"Yes, almost to the point of no color at all."

With that, she tipped her head back and squeezed the juice of the berry into her eye. Sarai and I were both shocked as she dabbed away the juice with a rag.

"You will understand in a moment. Women who sell themselves commonly use the wild carrot seed, my King; it prevents conceiving a child. They merely eat a small amount, such as would fit in a dainty woman's palm after..." her tanned, withered cheeks blushed, "after relations. It works very, very well, but it does not make people ill. I do not believe it would harm even a child to eat it. That is, if they could stand the flavor and the coarse nature of the seed. Have you noticed what is happening?"

I had no idea what she was talking about at this point, but Sarai did.

"Her eye, my Lord. Look at the eye in which she placed the juice."

The black of her eye was expanding, creating an odd appearance to her because her other eye was normal.

"Does the same happen when the berry is eaten?" I asked.

"Yes, exactly, my King, but the other effects are what make eating it so very deadly. A tiny amount will calm a stomach spasm, or a breath of smoke from a leaf will help one who cannot breathe, but it is powerful; a little too much is deadly. Do you believe someone poisoned your household?"

"That knowledge is not for you, my good lady. And it is of utmost importance for you to keep my visit to you secret. Is that understood?"

"Aye, my King. These old lips have kept many things for less than kings. I am your servant and obey your command, good King." She paused, and her eyes became teary, "I also pray blessings upon your heart after all you have endured this day."

My embrace surprised her, but I wanted her to know how much I appreciated her heartfelt words, "Thank you. You have been of great help to me, my lady."

Just as we turned to leave, Sarai stopped me and spun around, "Could you tell us if there is anything that can cure one who has been fed the Devil's Cherry?"

She looked as though she was deep in thought for a moment, "Yes, but it depends on how much was consumed. A careful dose of opium will reverse the symptoms, but that, too, is a dangerous herb to toy with."

I had two possible people to blame for what happened to my family, one of which I was prepared to kill immediately, but the other? I could only pray she would not have done this willingly. Richard was the one who appeared to have the knowledge, as far as I could see. He must have known what was ingested and how to cure it. I could have him taken prisoner and tortured, but I would wait long enough to meet with Nyles of Dunfee. I had acted rashly in my younger life too many times. I would not make that mistake this time. I would gather all my facts and then exact perfect punishment.

Upon our return, the maiden who was caring for Emiline told me she had awakened a short time earlier and was calling for me. With Sarai secure in my chamber, I went forth, but my heart was heavy as I wondered about her involvement.

She was propped upon pillows, her face still quite pale, framed by thick, black hair pulled loose and cascading down to her waist.

"Magnus, I do not understand what has happened. I became ill last night, and could not call out for help. All I remember is you shaking me in anger, and then my chief guard telling me he was giving me something for my pain. What has happened, and why is everyone so somber?"

I was careful with my explanation, but when I told her the concubines and children were dead, she began to wail and sob. No tears would come as she screamed that her eyes were burning; then her voice gave out and she could not speak but in a harsh whisper.

"Water," she begged.

I held the cup to her lips while she sipped then dipped her fingers into the liquid and touched it to her eyes. "They burn like the sun, yet I cannot cry. What manner of illness is this?"

"It is no illness," I stated, once again being careful, "you have been poisoned, my Queen."

Her shock appeared genuine enough for me to believe her.

"Who would do such a thing?"

"I do not know, but I will discover who is responsible, and retribution shall be death."

"Is Sarai—is she... I thought I saw her in my delirium, but I must have been mistaken."

"Sarai is fine. She was unharmed." Now I had cause to worry as an aberrant cast spread across her face.

"She did not die with the others? She is well?"

"She did not stay with the concubines last night; she was with

me."

The wicked anger unique to Emiline seemed to wash over her, "Then you may have found your traitor."

I was aghast she should claim such a thing, but then she continued with sharp and cunning logic.

"She was with us all in the family wing. She served us tea as I played with the children, and she gave treats to the little ones."

"No, Sarai loved the—"

"Loved them? She barely knew them. Can you not see?" she said, taking another sip to quench her dry voice. "Who else would poison those close to you? She is apparently unhappy being a concubine, she would rather be queen!"

I did not like her accusation, but I was no longer comfortable with hiding the truth, "She is not my concubine."

"Yes, she is. You told me she is with your child."

"She is my wife."

She was so motionless I thought she fainted with her eyes open.

"I married her, Emiline. The law allows me to have more than one wife."

Her hand lashed out and slapped my cheek, but in her weakened state, I was impervious to her strike.

"How could you?! Magnus, I care not about the law," her voice cracked. "I am your queen. I am your wife—your only wife." She threw herself onto the pillows face down. "Go away," came her muffled sob. "I do not wish to see you. Go be with your murderous witch."

"Why do you have a bag of wild carrot seed? You never wanted to carry my child, did you?"

She rolled over and glared at me, "What insanity do you speak? What is wild carrot seed?"

I opened her wardrobe and threw the satchel at her. She looked at it as if she had never seen it before.

She opened the bag and poured seeds into her hand, "What are these? Is this how your witch poisoned your family?"

"It is not poison. You know what it is used for. Do not play ignorant with me, Emiline. It is taken to stop conception."

"You tell me, my husband, where did you learn of your 'wild carrot' seed? Could it be something Sarai told you about and then placed in my room to make me appear guilty?"

She was filling me with suspicions about my new wife, and all of them made sense.

"How did Richard know what to give you to counteract the Devil's Cherry?"

"You are speaking as a madman. What are you talking about now? What Devil's Cherry? My chief guard is a good man, unlike my husband," she snapped. "His mother was a healer. I should think he saw something in my illness that struck a memory for him. Do you regret his knowledge which saved my life? I am done with your insanity, my once husband, leave me. I would have rather died than to be saved to learn how you truly feel about me."

My mind was flooded with mayhem. I did not know what to think at this point. I did not wish to believe Sarai to be at fault for any of this. I loved her with more strength than even my love for Emiline had once been, but now my heart beheld the shadow of doubt. I was exhausted as I rejoined Sarai but told her nothing. She pressed herself to my side; her head resting on my shoulder as she dozed to sleep. Sleep was something I craved with a deep passion but I could not. Tomorrow, I would learn all that Nyles knew and then, and only then, would I make my final decision.

At some point, I did slumber, but it was a troubled and restless time in my soul. I dreamed of my children as I sat on the floor and they played around me; I heard the cooing laughter of my daughters and the sound of my son as he called out to me. The women were there, all of them, even sweet Narcilla, who had been the first to give me a child. And then, like a storm, my thoughts were assaulted with images of Earland's expression as he died, Emiline's face as I told her I had taken a new wife, and even Sarai as she told me immediately the illness was the work of poison.

The next day, after a special mass, the children and mothers were buried. My subjects were the most compassionate people upon the face of the earth as they offered me their heartfelt sympathies. There were days of mourning scheduled as all activities within my kingdom ceased. Emiline did not join me for mass. She was still weak, but I did not believe she would have accompanied me anyway in her fury. Instead, Sarai stayed silently by my side as I wondered about all things.

"We have to stop," Cass said as she placed her hand over the scroll to interrupt his reading. "This one is too long, and it's almost time to go meet Bobby."

He squinted as he removed his glasses, "I want to keep going, but you're right. There is no way we can finish it before we leave. Damn it, Cass, we're so close."

She pulled him to lean his head on her chest as she kissed his hair, "You need a break. When he takes me to meet Dirk, I want you to get some rest; no reading ahead without me."

He grinned, "How about you leave me your computer, so I can send my boss a sample? My vacation ends in a few days. I'm hoping he'll let me make your survey a feature story."

"And if he doesn't?"

"The next stop for me is Jeffrey's Bay in South Africa."

"And what's in Jeffrey's Bay?"

"Wild coastline, rainforest, rare animals, and—and the coolest surfin' on the Dark Continent!" He was clearly excited, about the surfing part, anyway.

She raised her eyebrows and laughed, "You talked him into that, didn't you?"

"There are a few benefits to the boss knowing his best writer could kick-the-bucket at any moment."

"Ah! I can't believe you would work *that* angle," she was trying to sound angry, but she wasn't doing a good job.

He pulled her close as he went from light-hearted to serious, "How about you, Cass? This job is going to last at least three more weeks. It won't matter if you're here under this hill downloading data or laying out on the beach in Africa with a satellite hookup. *Come with me*." He kissed her, slowly and deeply, his tongue teasing against hers. "I'm addicted, Cass; I need you, and I can teach you to surf," he added in a lighter tone. "Maybe I'll even talk you into a tattoo while we're down there."

She frowned, "I don't think they're quite as sexy on a girl. Come on. We have to go or we're going to be late." She didn't answer about Africa, but the whole time she was thinking there was no way she could function without him around. She wondered how she went from massively independent to feeling as though the man beside her was her literal connection to life. She stopped frowning, and giggled as she gave him a quick kiss.

He drew her to his chest one final time. "Don't let him kiss you while he's lying about how much he loves you," he said, resting his forehead against hers, "Those lips are mine now, and I don't like the idea of sharing."

She nodded, "I'll be fine. Bobby will keep me safe." It still felt like he was stalling and she began to wonder if he was having second thoughts about showing Bobby the hill, but she tugged one more time, and he finally moved.

Bobby brought his Land Cruiser from the RICS because AJ told him he would be driving through a field, so his car might not be the best idea. He followed them across the gorgeous green landscape as they parked and got out.

"Well, what do you think?" AJ asked, as he watched the perplexed expression on Bobby's face.

"You wanted to show me a spring—in a sheep field. Are we really going swimming?" he asked.

AJ was already stripping down and laying out his wetsuit as Bobby stared. "The cold water gives me a migraine, but Cass figured out a way to keep my body temperature from fluctuating."

"We are really going swimming?" he repeated.

Cass laughed as she began unbuttoning her shirt, "I never told you, but I love your English accent. Come on; strip, English boy. Let me see those white legs."

His eyes were huge as she pulled off her top.

"It's okay, Bobby," AJ stated, as he clapped down on his shoulder, "after a little while, it gets easier to watch her undress."

"I really should have bought a swimsuit, but this works. I'll have to change these wet underclothes for dry before we leave to meet Dirk. Catch," she yelled, throwing Bobby a mask.

He snatched the mask from the air and then finally started removing his clothes but kept watching as she slid her jeans to the ground. She glanced over and was surprised to see he wasn't as lily-white as most of the folks in the UK. And AJ had been right; Bobby had an awesome build, not as awesome as she found AJ's to be, but he was a stunning man.

"All right, enough staring," AJ said as he pushed Bobby over when he was attempting to get down to his shorts. Bobby stumbled, and then went for AJ's legs, and they began to wrestle.

Cass looked at them and sighed as she stepped into the water up to her knees. "Boys! Hey, boys!"

They finally paused their tussle long enough to look up.

"I may have to get out of these wet things in a few minutes. Are either of you going to be paying attention?"

They were tumbling over each other to get to the water when

she laughed and dove for the rope.

The expression on Bobby's face when he came up into the lantern-lit room was so good; Cass wished she had a camera.

AJ swam around him, "Are you just going to keep treading water, or are you actually going to get out?"

"It's a—a castle!"

"That was my reaction, too," AJ laughed.

They spent the next hour showing Bobby the scrolls and explaining a condensed version of what they learned about the kingdom.

"Do you understand this place changes history?" Bobby asked. "It's the first castle—three hundred years *before* the first recorded castle."

"Yes, we know that," Cass said, "but King Magnus suffered so much; he decided he didn't want to be remembered in history."

"But—but it is so perfect; the scrolls are impeccable, and the structure, from what I can see, probably has no damage."

"We considered that already," AJ added, "and we're almost finished reading the scrolls, but I'm leaning toward not exposing this place to the world."

"But National Geographic would pay you a fortune to break this story. Your name would be all over the news."

"That's what I told him, but he isn't interested in fame," she said as she leaned over and kissed AJ's head.

AJ looked up at her, "It's your find, Cass. It's your decision, not mine."

"And I've made my decision."

Both men looked up.

"If AJ doesn't want to write the story, it's going untold, and Valderegnum stays buried."

"Actually, Cass, I *have* decided to write the story."

"You have?" she couldn't believe it; he'd changed his mind and waited until now to tell her? "But you just said you were leaning toward not exposing this place."

"I won't. I've always wanted to try writing a novel. No one will have a clue it actually existed at one time. It's a win-win; the story gets told, and the castle stays buried."

She actually liked his solution. Plus, this idea showed he was starting to think about his future, his future *after* the surgery.

When Bobby and Cassandra pulled away from the hill, they left

AJ typing on the computer. The first part of the drive was quiet, but Cass finally got him talking when she asked him how he met AJ. She already knew the story, but it broke the silence between them and loosened him up. They parked in front of the hotel restaurant, and Cass reached over to put her hand on Bobby's.

"I think I'd like us to go in separately, if you don't mind. He's liable to freak if he thinks I've brought a bodyguard, and I actually want him to believe everything is copacetic so he'll keep working."

"Whatever is best for you, Cass, but if he gets out of line then expect to see me standing at your table, all right?"

"Thanks, Bobby, and I really do appreciate you doing this for me," she kissed his cheek and climbed out. She glanced back to look at him and realized the kiss caught him off guard; his face was beet red, but he was smiling.

She opened the door to the restaurant and saw Dirk seated in a booth in the far corner. She was trying to remember to keep her cool, but it was difficult when she knew what he had been up to. She was wondering now why she'd ever slept with him. He wasn't an ugly man aesthetically, but it didn't take a person long, being around him, to discover he was an ugly person on the inside; he was rude and crass, difficult to get along with, demanding, over-bearing... She had to stop, as she suddenly felt sick; she was describing herself. He was right; she and he were more alike than she and AJ. But she wanted all that to change: she begged God to let her be the kind of person AJ saw when he looked into her eyes. There were still some very dark things they needed to discuss, but for now, she would concentrate on getting through this meeting, and then she would worry about the other.

"Hey," she said as she approached the table.

Dirk rose quickly and leaned toward her for a kiss, but she turned her cheek to him before he could reach her lips. "What kind of fucking greeting is that?" he snapped.

"It's the kind that says don't start your shit with the boss, kind of greeting," she hadn't meant to begin this in anger, but he was asking for it. The humorous part now was since she knew what he was up to, she could see him purposely working to restrain his temper.

"I'm sorry, Cass. You've been away from me for too long—and—and I missed you, baby."

She wasn't giving his words any heed as she slid in on the side opposite from him, but she did observe Bobby enter the restaurant and seated himself a dozen tables away. Dirk, she knew, would not notice him because he rarely paid attention to things around him. She sighed as she considered it was an asset when it came to work; he was focused on what he was doing and that was it.

"So, you've got to tell me what you've been doing," he continued. "Cass?"

Her mind was adrift again: she was thinking about AJ and how she didn't take into consideration until this very moment that she did not like him being alone. What if something happened? What if his aneurysm burst when he was under the hill with no one to help him or get him to a hospital? What if—

"Cass?!" he reached out and grabbed her hand, "what the hell is wrong with you? You're never like this. You said you weren't sleeping with that asshole, so what's he doing to you? Feeding you drugs or something?"

She snatched her hand back, "Get friggin' real. No—I—I just have a lot on my mind right now."

"Like what?"

It was time for a little acting, "I've been thinking about how Daddy is considering letting Steven and Lane become partners, and I've decided I'll quit before it happens."

His eyebrows rose, "Don't worry about that. Matter-of-fact, don't even give it a thought while you're here. Let's just get this job done, and..." His hand reached into his shirt pocket as he withdrew a small, blue velvet box. "...then start thinking about us." He opened the box to reveal a diamond solitaire. "I considered getting down on one knee for you, but I know you're not that kind of girly-girl, so I guessed the direct approach was best. Cassandra Henley, I love you, and I want you to marry me."

She wanted to laugh so badly; she had to bite her tongue hard to hold it in. Which, in turn, actually hurt, and her eyes started watering.

"Oh—don't cry, baby," he said grabbing a napkin and handing it to her.

It just became funnier because it was freaking him out to see her that way; he'd never seen her cry.

She covered her face with the napkin and made a choking sound. He couldn't see her for the moment, and that was good; it sounded like she was about to start sobbing, when in truth, she was about to roll with laughter. She took a couple deep breaths, composed herself, and lowered the napkin. "I—I'm a little overwhelmed. Where did all of this come from? You were bar-hopping and happy-go-lucky before we left Texas."

"I just realized I'm never going to find anyone else like you, Cass. We're perfect together, a little rough, but perfect. And I'm planning on changing the rough part starting tonight."

That snapped her head upright to attention, "Wha—what do you mean?"

"I rented us a room in the hotel, so we can celebrate. I'm gonna do you so good tonight, Cass, whatever it is you're doing with AJ is gonna be long forgotten."

"Slow down, Dirk. *I didn't say yes,*" she planned to leave him tonight with the hope she might say yes when the job was finished, but her tone clearly indicated otherwise. She could see the angry red filling his face but could also see he was trying hard to restrain it.

"If you've been telling me the honest-to-God truth and you haven't been sleeping with AJ, or anyone else, then I know you want sex by now *even if you aren't ready to say I do.*"

She was thinking about swearing on her mother's grave that she hadn't been sleeping with AJ, but she had been, there just hadn't been any sex involved.

He saw her hesitate, "Son-of-a-bitch! You have bagged him, haven't you?!"

"NO," she answered a little too loudly, "Although it really shouldn't be something I need to explain to you; I swear on my mother's grave: I have not had sex with him." There, that was the truth.

"Then is he gay?"

Okay, she couldn't restrain the laughter this time. "No—no, he's not. He's just..." she paused, struggling for a word that wouldn't indicate just how badly she did want to sleep with him. "...different."

He reached across the table, this time gripping both her hands, "Come with me, Cass. You can go back to Mister Different tonight, but let me love on you a little bit first. And at least try this on to see if I got the size right." He pulled the golden ring from the box and pushed it hard onto her finger.

"Ah, you idiot; it's too tight," she said as she gripped it and tried to pull it off. "Now it's stuck!"

Dirk laughed, "Then I guess it was meant to be, huh?"

"Great! I have to go to the bathroom to get soap to get it off."

"Yeah, and then I'm gonna get *you* of in the hotel," he said with a wink.

She gave him one of her throat-slicing glares. "I'm not going to the hotel with you. I'll give you the answer to this," she said holding up the ring lodged on her finger, "when our job is finished."

"I'm not waiting that long. I'll get those long legs of yours apart and I'll have you screaming yes before you know it."

She huffed an annoyed sigh, snatched up her purse, and made her way toward the sign indicating where the restrooms were located. She was surprised that the door led to the outside corridor between the two buildings, but it was only an immediate right and she was in the bathroom. The stalls were empty and she was alone to grumble and complain about the ring. After applying plenty of soap, she tugged it off but it left a bright red mark. She slipped it on to her pinky, so she wouldn't drop it, dried her hands, and opened the door to walk out—right into an unpleasant surprise: he had followed her.

"Time to sweep you off your feet," he said, immediately scooping her off the ground.

"Put me down!" she demanded, kicking and flailing, but he just laughed. Her right arm was trapped around his back, and he was trying to contain her left as he started walking.

"I'm glad I got a room on the ground floor."

She finally twisted her left wrist out of his hold and punched his face. It stunned him just enough to make him lose his grip on one of her legs, and he almost dropped her.

"Let me go. I'm not playing, Dirk!"

He slapped her face with swift, stinging force and then he gripped her lower jaw too firmly. "Maybe you would rather stick with the rough stuff tonight, huh?" he panted, giving her face a shake as he tried to lift her again. "That's fine with me, baby; the harder you fight, the rougher I'll get."

At that moment, she heard an angry male voice.

"Put her down!"

Dirk turned and faced the intruder with a menacing look, "It's okay, buddy. She and I are just play... Hey, you're the guy from..." Suddenly she could see the connection being made in his mind.

Anger flooded his expression. "AJ's friend," he growled.

Cassandra struggled from his arms; she got her feet on the ground, but he kept a firm hold on her wrist.

Bobby advanced.

Dirk let her go and took a swing at Bobby's face.

He ducked the blow and punched Dirk in the ribs, sending him to his knees gasping for air.

"Are you okay?" Bobby asked, as he reached up to touch her cherry-red cheek.

She didn't have time to answer; Dirk sucked in a breath and lunged for Bobby's mid-section.

The fight was on.

Cassandra could only watch as the two men rolled on the ground, pummeling each other with punches. At one point, Dirk got Bobby below him and shoved his head back to smack the concrete. It stunned Bobby long enough for Dirk to get a good grip on his throat and bore down as he straddled him.

"So this must be the son-of-a-bitch you've been sleeping with!" he spat.

They were starting to draw a crowd, but it seemed no one wanted to step in.

Cassandra kicked toward Dirk's head, but he caught her foot, twisting it quickly and throwing her down. Bobby knocked Dirk's hand from his throat and came back with a punch like a hammer, busting Dirk's nose and sending blood everywhere. This fight was getting ready to end; Bobby was going to make sure of it as he scrambled to his feet. He jerked Dirk upright and then slammed him against the building. Two more hard punches and Dirk slid down the wall as if he were suddenly made of Jell-o.

Bobby helped Cass to her feet, "I am sorry; I should have come out here sooner when I saw him follow you."

She tried to put weight on her ankle, but it was painful from the twist Dirk had given it. She didn't have to say anything as Bobby bent and placed her arm around his neck to give her some support, "It's okay, and thank you for your help."

"Cass," Dirk called from his stupor as he struggled to get to his knees, "what the hell is wrong with you? I wanted to fucking marry you, you bitch!"

She turned to face him as she pulled the ring from her pinky and threw it at him. "You never wanted to marry me, you lying, sneaking, asshole! Do you think I'd be stupid enough to marry someone like you?!"

"Cass, please," he said, as he rose on wobbly legs, "I love you, baby. Don't—"

"Love me? No, you loved the idea of stealing half my business." She watched the surprise come over his expression, "Yeah, I know all about it. I talked to Dad. I was going to wait to do this, but not now. You're fired! Give me your keys and company phone."

"I ain't given you shi—"

Bobby moved toward him; Dirk threw his hands up in submission. He apparently didn't want any more of an ass-whooping than he'd already received. He threw the keys to his rental truck and his cell phone on the ground in front of her. Bobby leaned forward to pick them up—and Stupid charged. Bobby was ready for the dumb move, and he came up with an uppercut under Dirk's chin so hard that it lifted him off the ground and laid him out.

Their growing audience cheered and clapped.

Cass looked down as Dirk's eyes blinked open. "I'll have one of the guys from the crew get your stuff and pick you up. You'll get a ticket home. I suggest you take it. I'll mail you the balance of your pay. And Dirk," she stated as he tried unsuccessfully to lift his head, "don't ever show your face around me or my business again."

She put her arm back around Bobby's neck, and she tried to hobble away.

"Let me, please," Bobby stated, lifting her from the ground, "it's my fault anyway."

"No, it's not, don't even think that. This is embarrassing," she said with a small laugh, as the crowd parted, and he carried her toward their vehicle. "Would you mind taking me to his truck? I'll drive it back to the crew and let them know what happened and where to pick him up."

"I'll follow you and drive you back to the hill."

"You don't have to. One of the guys can—"

"Yes, I do. AJ will want an explanation; besides, what will you tell your crew? 'Just drop me off in this field, and I'll be fine.'"

"Yeah, you're right about that." She leaned her head against his shirt. Her cheek was throbbing, and she could feel her lip swelling.

"Can you drive with that ankle?"

"It's my left so I'll be okay."

"Maybe I should take you to have a doctor look at that," he said as they reached the rental truck where he gingerly placed her on the ground.

The concern on his face was so sincere; she felt a small tug on her heartstrings. He was a good person, just as AJ told her. "I didn't feel anything snap. It isn't broken, just sore." She opened her purse and pulled out a tissue, dabbing blood from his lip and cheek.

"I am going to look pretty bad by tomorrow, huh?" he asked with a little grin.

Cass laughed, "Yeah, but you know something? Dirk's gonna look worse."

They both laughed as she climbed into the truck.

She called one of the guys on Dirk's crew and found out where they were staying. Fortunately, it was a small inn, and she wouldn't have to go driving off into the woods in the middle of the night. She told them to give Dirk his duffle and his passport, and then she gave them enough cash to cover a ticket back to the States. Rubio volunteered to be the one to go back and get him.

"Take him straight to the airport and drop him off, got it?"

"Yes, ma'am."

She didn't expect it to take so long, but by the time they returned to the hill, it was after one a.m.

As soon as her head cleared the water, AJ was talking.

"It's about time. What did you two... Shit! What happened?"

Bobby immediately vaulted into how he felt responsible because he didn't get to Cass quickly enough, but she interrupted and explained that Bobby couldn't have known Dirk was headed for the ladies' bathroom. As they dried off, Cass gave AJ the entire story, including the round of applause Bobby received when he laid Dirk out at the end.

"I need to go," Bobby finally said, as he wearily stood up, "it's a long ride home."

"Too long," AJ stated, "you won't make it before sunrise. Cass and I can fit in one sleeping bag; you take the other. We'll have breakfast somewhere before you leave."

"No, I couldn't, really."

"Yes, you could," Cass chimed in. "It's like a four-hour drive back to your place, and, besides, how many times in a lifetime can you say you were able to sleep in a thirteen-hundred-year-old castle?"

"Very true," he laughed, "although I can't tell anyone, it is something I would like to add to my experiences in life."

After a little more conversation, they turned off the lantern and went to sleep. The only problem for Cass was, although they had been sleeping together and cuddling before, this was a much tighter arrangement. There was no giving each other a little space when things started feeling too good. AJ was pressed to her back, and it was extremely obvious that being glued to her ass was more than superman could take. He was rock hard and trying not to move, but it was almost impossible.

He breathed a very quiet apology into her ear and then kissed her neck. He also appeared to be having a problem as to where to put his hands: a little too high and there were two obstacles, a little too low and... She was about to break a sweat from wanting him to go low, which, in turn, made her squirm and that, in turn, made him moan. It would take them a while to get used to the effects of being so close, but they did eventually fall asleep.

CHAPTER TWELVE

When her eyes opened, she had already planned her day. They would go with Bobby into Moffat for breakfast then return and finish the last portion of the scroll. She considered inviting Bobby to stay and hear the end of the story, but it was a special experience for her and AJ; she couldn't share it. They would remove all their items from under the hill and repack everything into the wall as planned. Tonight, they would sleep in a motel and she would decide about Africa, but most importantly, she would tell him everything about herself. It frightened her to her core to expose what no one else on earth knew, but she couldn't go on any longer without a sexual connection. She only hoped, after he heard it all, he'd still want to make love with her.

As soon as they emerged from the spring into the blast of morning sunshine, her phone alerted that she had messages. The first message wasn't good. Rubio called from the motel where he was supposed to pick up Dirk. Dirk punched the hell out of him and took the rental truck and Rubio's company cell phone.

"What's wrong?" AJ and Bobby asked in unison when they saw the look on her face.

"That friggin' idiot beat-up Rubio and stole his truck and phone. Who knows what he's gonna do, but I just bet I'm going to end up with a bill to replace a sixty-five-thousand-dollar Land Cruiser. Damn it!" she snapped as she punched the button for her next message. This one dropped her to her knees, and she began to sob uncontrollably.

"Cass!" AJ said, as he tried to tilt her face up to look at him. "Honey, what happened?"

"Charlie!" she cried out, "Teddy said Dirk—Dirk called and said I wanted him. He—he showed up and—and took him! Teddy tried to get in touch with me, but..." She was choking and crying at the same time as she considered her faithful friend who didn't deserve to get hurt in any of this. "He'll kill him; I know he will."

Bobby looked wide-eyed and confused.

"Charlie's her dog," AJ answered without being asked, "That sorry bastard took her dog."

"I can turn on the tracker on Rubio's phone," she said, a little bit of sense returning to her distraught state. "He'll probably pitch it as soon as I do, but at least we'll have an idea where he is."

AJ helped her set up her computer as she accessed her cellular company and pressed the button to find Rubio's phone via GPS. Within moments, she had a blip on the map: Glasgow.

"The International airport," Bobby stated. "I doubt he has found a flight out already if he was running around doing all that. Let's see if we can find him; maybe we'll find your dog."

Bobby drove while AJ held Cass against his chest to let her cry. He broke every speed limit along the way, and they made it to Glasgow in forty-five minutes. "Where would he get a flight to, Cass? What city?" Bobby asked.

"We live in Tyler, Texas, but he'll have to go to New York and get a connecting flight."

"We'll go inside and check the flight schedules. It's a big place, but we'll just keep looking."

They were a rag-tag threesome: Bobby with his swollen and bruised face, Cass limping along, and all of them with wet, unkempt hair from the spring. The guys could actually get away with the spiky, wet look, but Cass knew she looked a little crazy as people turned her way.

"There is a flight boarding in fifteen minutes down terminal B," Bobby stated, grabbing a nearby airport wheelchair. "We're going to have to hurry, so you've got to ride, Cass. We'll never make it with your bad ankle."

She wasn't about to argue; as she sat in the chair, and they began flying toward the terminals. The good thing about being in a wheelchair is people tend to get out of your way—quickly.

As they neared the terminal, Cass tipped her head back to see

Bobby's face, "Don't let him get into a fight," she said.

"Absolutely not."

But, by the expression on AJ's face, she could tell he was ready to kick Dirk's ass; he was furious.

They spotted Dirk waiting in the boarding line. When Dirk saw them, he took off running with AJ and Bobby in hot pursuit. It was AJ who tackled him to the floor, but Bobby was on him before the first swing could even be considered. This was not a place where people avoided becoming involved in a fight. There were plenty of people who would join in—all of them in uniforms.

The police escorted them away from the terminal to one of their stations in the airport and began to sort out what happened. Cass explained everything to them, telling them about last night and early this morning.

Dirk rolled his eyes, "I didn't steal anything. The truck is sitting out there in airport parking with the phone inside."

"And where," one of the officers asked in a deep Scottish brogue, "is this lady's dog, mind you?"

"Don't know. I didn't take her damn dog."

Cass flipped open her phone and played the message for the police officer.

"Would you be thinkin' about rephrasing that statement?" the officer asked. "Where is this lady's dog? We can hold you on animal cruelty charges."

"I didn't do anything with her damn—"

AJ lunged, but Bobby and another officer kept him back.

"Give me your parking tag and the keys to the vehicle," the officer stated. He turned to one of the other officers and told him to check the truck for any signs of the dog or any signs that something happened to the dog.

"I didn't do anything to him," Dirk spat. "I stopped to get gas in Larkhall, and the little bastard jumped out. I couldn't catch him. The people at the gas station saw it happen."

The officer called the Shell station listed on Dirk's gas receipt, and the lady who answered said she did remember the pissed-off American. She said the little black-and-white dog jumped out, and when the man couldn't catch him, he tried to run it over. The dog took off through the parking lot toward the back of the building, and the man drove away. She said she went out behind the station to look for the dog, but it had vanished into the neighborhood.

Cass was relieved and upset at the same time. Dirk didn't get a chance to hurt Charlie, but now he was loose on the streets of a town in Scotland. She doubted she'd ever see him again.

The police had to release Dirk. Perhaps it had been his intention to hurt the dog, but as it was, the animal escaped, and they couldn't hold him for that. The only thing left to do was to drive to the service station in Larkhall to see if they could find Charlie. The Glasgow police called the police in Larkhall and faxed them the picture Cass carried of her four-legged companion along with her cell number—just in case anyone should report finding him.

They searched for Charlie all afternoon with no luck. By late day, AJ booked them a room at a bed and breakfast and told her to rest; he and Bobby would continue looking. Her ankle was swollen, and she knew all she was doing was slowing them down, so she agreed.

It was after dark when they showed up. The only thing they had in their hands was some fast food for dinner.

"We're going to find him," AJ stated as they propped against each other on the bed, her head resting against his chest.

"No, he's a good little dog. If he didn't get run over, someone is going to take him in and keep him." She was tired of crying, but she couldn't stop the tear that trickled down the end of her nose and dripped onto his shirt.

"I don't know, Cass, people can surprise you if you give them a chance." He turned on the television to the evening news.

She closed her eyes. She didn't want to watch it. She was exhausted, and all she wanted to do was curl up in a ball and sleep—until she heard something that popped open her eyes.

"...and in other news this evening, a National Geographic reporter has been combing the streets of Larkhall today in search of this little guy, who was stolen from his owner."

"Writer," AJ sighed, correcting the 'reporter' on the television.

She looked and saw her picture of Charlie. "Ah," she gasped, as she sat up and listened to the newswoman explaining how Charlie escaped from his dog-napper and fled into the relative safety of their town.

Bobby was grinning, "It's amazing how well a local television station will work with someone who has something to offer."

"AJ," she asked with surprise, "what did you offer them?"

"Well, I called my boss, who called one of his bosses, who called one of *his* bosses with our television producers, and their local station gets to air a National Geographic program—free of charge."

"I can't believe you did that. Thank you." She started crying again.

"Cass, you have to turn off the water works. I'm wetter than if I'd spent the day swimming under the hill," he teased, and then gave her a squeeze. "They're going to air it again in the morning, and they'll call to let us know if they find him."

She hadn't felt like eating earlier, but she couldn't stay upset and miserable after they had done so much. She sat up and asked Bobby to pass her a hamburger.

AJ kissed the side of her head and whispered he loved her. "When you're done, you could take a hot shower and—" He stopped because his cell phone was ringing. Charlie had been found, and he was fine.

CHAPTER THIRTEEN

Their weekend had been like some kind of crazy marathon, but it was over. Sunday morning, they purchased a small dome tent and pitched it under a tree, next to a familiar stream, in the shadow of a very large hill. Bobby was finally ready to go home, but it was obvious, no matter how crazy the weekend had been, he enjoyed being with them. He mused it was one of the wildest adventures he'd been on in a long time. He kissed Cass's cheek and gave AJ a hug and told them not to leave the UK without coming down to his house to say goodbye. They assured him they couldn't possibly forget to do that. He also told them he was arranging some time off from work, so when AJ had his surgery, he would be there for both of them.

Cass watched his vehicle as he drove away, "You were right about Bobby; he is a really good person. And he kicks ass," she laughed.

"Told ya," AJ said as he bumped against her shoulder. "Did you tell your dad what happened?"

"Oh, yes. I called him and told him to make sure everybody who works for us knows Dirk is *not* to be coming around the business."

"So are we reading inside or outside?"

"Let's clean everything up, remove all our stuff from under the hill, and read the last chunk outside. Charlie will appreciate that, won't you, boy?" The dog was stretched out on the grass in total comfort. "We can seal the holes tomorrow and, I guess, get ready for Africa."

"You mean it?" he asked, utterly surprised. "You're coming with me?"

"It's like you said, it doesn't matter where I am when I'm just gathering data. I don't know how well I'll do surfing though; my balance is a little off."

He pulled her in tightly, kissing her forehead, eyes, nose, and ending on her lips, "Cass, I can't wait anymore. I want you so badly."

"You won't have to. Before we leave, I'm going to tell you..." she swallowed hard, "*...everything.*"

"You're finally going to trust me with all of it?"

"I've trusted you for a while now, but I'm still scared."

"Let's get this done," he said, motioning to the hill with his eyes.

Later in the afternoon they were ready for their final venture into the realm of Kingdom Hill. Cass had no idea that her promise to tell AJ everything hadn't been necessary because the story of this once great place was about to rip it straight out of her heart.

That night, I lay awake waiting for the hour I would meet Nyles. Sarai knew of my meeting, but she was so depleted, mentally and physically, that she slept while I watched the time draw near. I did not like leaving her alone, but no one should know of my absence. I silently slipped away once the moon moved to three-quarters across the night sky. I was grateful that it was but a slight moon, hoping no one would be up to see me cross the bailey and head for the southern gate. The grass was wet with dew as I moved over it on bared feet. I took no chance in making noise; I removed my garments even down to all but my inner robe. As I approached the gate, I noticed a figure tucked tightly against the shadow where the wall jutted from the gate hinge; it was Nyles.

There was a small arms room at the base of the southern tower, and I ushered him in, so we could speak unexposed. What he would tell me would both anger and relieve me.

"I must know everything you have learned about my queen during your time as her guard."

His face was pale, and he was so frightened; he trembled all over. He drew and then handed me his dagger. "When I am done, my King, spare not my life. I should have never kept my silence so long. I should have come to you before her madness took hold of me."

I held his dagger and told him I would pass judgment whence he had expounded all he knew. "Is my queen a traitor to me?"

"She is wicked, my Lord. She seduced me the day I joined as her guard; she slept with me and told me I belonged to her alone. She said I would never be allowed to leave unless I wished for death. She has been a lover to all her guards," he said with a hard swallow, "even the two she killed."

"Why did she kill them?"

"She was testing a new poison and gave them too much, Sire. We are all hers to do with as she pleases."

"What did she know of my new bride, Sarai?"

I could tell the word 'bride' did not surprise him.

He continued, "She hated her vehemently. She ordered Phillip to follow you when you took her riding. He came back and eagerly reported to her all he witnessed and overheard. It was then I knew she had plans to kill her, but I did not know, my Lord, she would poison all the women and children in her effort to kill Sarai. But I should have because of her anger toward you for spending time with the others. She cursed you every moment you spent in the family wing. She hated them all."

"But why would she insist for me to have concubines and children if she hated them?" I knew, in that moment, he would rather take the dagger to his chest than to tell me, but I pressed him to go on.

"She—she enjoyed watching you as you—as you ended their virginity. Richard was the only one allowed into her chamber on those nights. He would pleasure her as she spied through a place in the wall that gave her vantage to see the—the act. But recently, it was not enough for her, my King. The two young maidens," he stated as tears filled his eyes, "she had them taken prisoner to a private place toward the east. She insisted we all partake as she watched. God will not forgive me for what I have done under her command. I do not deserve life after serving such wickedness."

My grip on his dagger tightened as I considered whether he was right; none of them deserved to live if they could be commanded to perform such evils. "Is this all you know? Is there anything else she may have told you or done that—"

"Yea, my Lord. She spoke often of how easily you would conform to her desires and her will. She spoke, with pride, of a time

before she was your wife and queen, a time when she goaded you into taking the life of an innocent man. She said she knew at that moment she would command you, and she would truly rule by using you as a pawn. She is a master of deception and manipulation, my King, and you had no way of knowing."

"Did she give his name?" I knew of whom she had spoken, but I had to hear it.

"She said he was your best friend, Earland. She told how she manipulated him, poisoned him, and then seduced him. She faked an attack on herself with the help of someone, but she would not say who." He lowered his eyes, "She said you did exactly her bidding and killed him. I know no more, my King. Take my life in exchange for what she has done through me."

He dropped to his knees before me, curling forward to give me the best place to drive the dagger through his back and into his heart. My hand rose, but then I paused. I am not sure how long I stood there but at some point, I came to my senses.

"Nyles of Dunfee, you have been no more than one who was her pawn, as was I. We are both guilty before God, but only He shall determine our fates. Rise and tell me if you will serve your King as I kill those who had neither the wisdom nor courage to come forward as you have done."

He looked up at me in disbelief, "I deserve not this chance, my Lord, but I will serve you now with all the breath and life that God has given me, until He removes it from me; I shall loyally serve you."

Before the dawn arose, he took me to the place where he stayed with Ryland and Phillip when they were not on duty. Although I told Richard there would be no more queen's guard, he did not disband his group. Richard, Gregory, and Berenger were hidden at the palace on the last watch hour, awaiting whatever Emiline would bid them to do.

The attack was swift as we disposed of the men and headed to my guards' quarters. I awakened two of my captains and told them of the treachery that was afoot. I did not want a large contingent which could disturb the entire household and alert those we sought as to our mission; this would be a battle of four against three, but in truth for me, the battle would be one-on-one as I considered Richard would die by my hand alone. Nyles knew where they were to be stationed, but they were not there. My heart suddenly panicked as I thought of Sarai lying unprotected in my chamber. When we entered my room, she was still asleep upon my bed. In silence, I left my captains in the room with her as I went around to Emiline's outer chamber door. "Your post is here," I whispered to Nyles. "I will confront my queen in private, and we will search for the other traitors once she has been locked away."

The dawn's first light was beginning to color the eastern sky as I entered Emiline's room. No cunning words or clever plots would change my heart this time. She would go to the gallows for the perfidious evils she brought upon and within my kingdom. But I would speak with her and tell her that I knew of all her deceit and lies before sending her to the dungeon.

She was still asleep. How incongruous that such perfect beauty could contain such perfect evil. I wondered, before she became one to mold others, who first molded her into the wretch before me now? I felt not pity toward her, only sorrow over what could have been had she been a different woman on the inside. For many years, I had loved her with the entire essence of my being, and I would have done anything to help heal the brokenness inside of her. But, alas, she clung to what had perverted her heart, instead of accepting and trusting in my deep love for her. When I gripped her shoulders firmly, her eyes opened without hesitation.

"Unhand me," she snarled.

"Nay. This morning, Emiline, you shall go to the dungeon for your wickedness."

She gave a small but disquieting laugh, "So you decided to believe her above me?"

"I know it all, Emiline. All your wicked ways from Earland to Richard were laid bare to me 'ere this dawn. You tricked me into taking the life of a good and kind soul, and you have played the harlot to control your guard while you plotted your sins from within your black heart."

She seemed only mildly surprised. "Dear, sweet, Magnus," she cooed, "of all my fools, you continue to be the easiest to manipulate."

My grip tightened so hard she winced but then smiled again, "You cannot hurt me. I have grown up knowing far greater pain than you can even hope to inflict."

"Tell me now, before I decide to take your life by my own hand, why did you bid me to kill my best friend?"

"Stupid man," she laughed, "I needed an excuse for not being a

virgin. And I needed to know which one of you would believe me without doubt. After I slept with him, I tried to convince him to destroy you. I explained to him how he could overthrow your father to take the throne, but he would hear nothing of it. I told him you forced yourself on me and that was why I was not a virgin when I took him to my bed. But he refused to believe anything I said." She laughed again, and then stared hard into my eyes, "He said he had faith in your goodness. I told him you would kill him, but the fool did not believe."

"And Bernatha? What had she done to you to deserve death?"

"That ignorant old woman watched me like a hawk. I could do nothing she did not observe. But I must admit she did do me a great service when I asked her to teach me about herbs. I already knew of the benefits of wild carrot seed; my father forced me to eat it regularly. But she taught me which plants to avoid and which plants were poison—now, that, I needed to know," she said with a look of wicked fire in her eyes.

"Your father? What man would give such a thing to his daughter?"

Her laugh was bitter and icy as she studied me, "Wickedness spawns wickedness, fool. I watched him end my mother's life; then he made me take her place within his bed to satisfy his vile needs. I was but a child, yet he taught me all his cunningness as together we plotted how to ensnare a future king. He even helped me falsify my battered, raped body for my best performance." The look in her eyes grew darker, "I paid him for his service when you left to kill Earland; I plunged a sword through his throat."

"Oh, God," Cass breathed, "no." Her eyes closed as she shook her head, "No, please not this." She stood on shaking legs and walked to the edge of the stream.

AJ set down the scroll and came up behind her, gently touching her shoulders, but she pulled away. "What's wrong, Cass? I know it's hard to—"

"A man," she said with a voice thick with emotion, "should never do that to a child. Don't they realize what it does to a little girl? We aren't animals."

"Don't tell me this is it, Cass. You've been hiding the same thing haven't you? Talk to me, Cass, please."

She turned and stared at him, but she wasn't the same woman

who looked at him before the final story unfolded. He wanted her to talk to him? Suddenly, she seemed to realize he was a man. What a novel idea to discuss something like this with the enemy.

"Your dad," he started to say.

"No, Daddy is a good man. Mom's family accused him of killing her because when she died, our money problems were solved; he had a quarter-million-dollar life insurance policy on her. I don't believe he would have hurt her on purpose; it was an accident—an accident that put him back in business. But it would have killed him to know what was happening to me."

Her heart was softening. AJ wasn't just a man. He was the one man she truly trusted with everything. He held her heart in his hands, and she was getting ready to place her scars there as well. But she couldn't look at him and say these things; she had to look away. She hated these memories with such bitterness; she could taste their flavor in her words, "You asked about my other brother, but I didn't want to tell you. Steven is sixteen years older than I am; he's my dad's only child from his first marriage."

"He's the one? He's the reason, isn't he?"

"He's not all of it, but he was the beginning. Everyone said I was such a beautiful girl, and he thought so, too." She wiped away a tear that escaped—freed from the place in her memory she swore she'd never cry over again. "He moved to Texas when I was nine. Said he wanted to be close to the family. Said he wanted to help Dad. He was twenty-five and had a wife and three kids, but when he held me, or hugged me, or touched me, for some reason, I knew something about him was different."

"Did he—did he hurt you, Cass?"

She could tell he was trying to word it carefully, but hurt could mean so many things. "He liked to touch me, but it was always wrong, and he talked to me and told me how grownup I was. By the time I was ten, he'd have me babysit his kids, and then when he'd tell his wife he was taking me home, he'd take me somewhere we could be alone, instead."

"I can understand why you don't want me to touch you right now, but would you please turn around and look at me."

She didn't want to see his face. It would be easier not to cry if she didn't see his face, but she knew he wanted to help. She turned around. "He'd buy me wine and cigarettes and tell me how grownup I was. Then he'd take nude pictures and videos of me. And when he touched me, he called me Cassie, over and over, repeating my name it seemed a hundred times for every time we were together. When I started to understand how wrong what he did to me was, I hated the sound of my own name, and I wouldn't let anyone call me that—except him," she said with a mournful expression. "I couldn't make him stop saying it."

"Cass, I don't know how to ask this question, but was he the one who... Was he your first?"

"No." Her eyes closed for a second and then reopened, "You see, you probably thought he was the bad part of my life, but it just got worse. I realized men liked me. For just a touch, I could get whatever I wanted. But it never went further than touching. When I was thirteen, I started working with Daddy. He said none of his other kids wanted to be in the business, so he'd teach me. The guys on the crews liked me, but no one touched because they were afraid of him. And then, one day, one of the men stopped being afraid. He told me he was crazy about me—said he was falling in love with me—he wanted to teach me things I didn't know. He had separated from his wife and two little girls. He told me he was going to divorce her and marry me. I believed him. He made me feel clean and beautiful, really beautiful; *I trusted him*," she winced at the words.

"He had his girls for the weekend and asked my dad if I could watch them because he had something to do. He picked me up from my house with my dad's approval. But I didn't know the something he had to do would turn out to be me." She tried to choke back her tears, but she'd never told anyone what happened before; the pain wouldn't stay down. "He raped me that day, but what was even worse was he did it right in front of his kids. They were little; one was two-and-a-half, and the other was almost one-and-a-half, so I guess he figured they wouldn't understand what was happening to me.

"He beat me and hurt me, but he was careful not to hit my face so my dad wouldn't know. He worked my body until I couldn't take it anymore. Then he took me home and told me if I ever said anything to my dad, he would tell him I was the one who begged for it. I was the bad person who made him do it. And you want to know something, AJ? I believed him. I felt it had to be my fault. That was why my half-brother and all those other men wanted to touch me, because it was something I did; it was my fault."

"Will you let me dry your tears?"

It amazed her that he wanted to reach out to do something so simple, yet he asked first. She held on to his hand as she closed her eyes and allowed him to dry her cheeks with a gentle stroke of his thumbs. She reopened her eyes and looked at him. The only thing she could see was he cared for her.

"I'm glad you finally told me, Cass."

"You said you didn't want anything between us. It's not over—not if you want it all."

"Oh, baby," he whispered, his voice cracking and swollen with emotion, "how could anyone have done anything worse to you?" By this point, he was crying, too.

"After that, there wasn't anything anyone else could have done; I did the rest to myself. I wanted to destroy what little bit there was left of me, so I started drinking and doing drugs. When that wasn't enough, I tried twice to commit suicide. By the time I was fifteen, Daddy had burned through most of his money, and the business was in trouble once more. It was my first year in high school, and I was his only kid left; everyone else left us. He couldn't keep a wife when he was stinking rich, and he surely couldn't when he was broke again.

"We had a chance for one big contract, but Dad was too drunk to make it to the bid meeting. I decided to stop trying to kill myself because if I succeeded, it would kill him, too. Anyway, I skipped school that day and dressed up like a woman, not a girl. I took two of our best surveyors, all the paperwork, and went to the meeting myself. It was a half-million-dollar contract, and I was in the arena with the big boys. My bid tied another company that had more experience, so they had us go out and compete on two small parcels of land. I threw down the fastest, most accurate survey of my life. I won, and the man with the money chose me." She could tell AJ didn't fully understand. "He told me I won the bid, but he chose me because he knew I could 'sweeten' the deal for him.

"It didn't make sense then, and it still doesn't today. I competed mentally against bigger companies and beat them, but just because I looked the way I did, I couldn't be the winner unless I gave a little extra. It was basically the same thing as prostitution, but I got my dad the job. I hated men, and I hated sex, but I could use both of them to clinch a deal. You said you could just imagine how many guys were crazy about me in high school and college. No, you can't because they weren't guys; they were all men. I ran the business while I went to high school and then through college. We went from a couple-thousand in the bank to a company now worth millions. We finally earned a reputation for being the best geomatics company out there, but it took years of working on my back before they started respecting my work in the field. I haven't had to seal a deal that way in seven or eight years now.

"And even though I hated what they did to me, I hated myself more; I'd get violent when a man would take me." A pitifully deep choking sob followed by a shallow inhalation stopped her for a moment. She couldn't keep looking; she had to turn away. "They all liked it when I did and—and then I learned to like it, too." She crumpled down as she sat by the water's edge. "Now when I want something, I pick him out and take it and walk away. I get off on the ugliness, pain, and the violence. I hate myself, and my body loves it. I've had a couple guys try to be easy, but it doesn't work for me. I can't get pleasure unless it's mentally dirty and physically abusive. How," she said as she looked up at him, "can I possibly be the right person for you? I'll never be *right* for anyone."

"Don't you dare believe that, Cass," he said, as he dropped beside her. "It can be beautiful for you. You have to stop listening to the memories and the lies."

"I dreamed the other day you called me Emiline and I—"

"No," he said. This time he didn't ask but reached out and gripped her shoulders. "You're not like her. She ruined this kingdom because there wasn't any love inside her. I see love and compassion inside you, and you would never do to me what she did to Magnus."

The fact he understood her fear blew her away, "I do love you, and I don't ever want to hurt you. What I started to tell you was that when I woke up from that dream, I asked God to change me. I'll never get rid of my past—that part can't be made right—but I want to learn how to experience love, real love, if you still want me."

"I told you there was nothing you could tell me that would end me wanting you. I meant it, Cass. I want to be the one who teaches you how to really make love, and I understand it might not be easy to close the door on your memories, but like you said the first time we spent time here, I can be pretty stubborn, myself. We'll close it together. I won't give up on you."

He wrapped her in his warm, muscled arms and held her, rocking gently back and forth, whispering sweet, yet indiscernible words of love, patience, and hope. And as he held her, she realized the most beautiful thing: there was no barrier between them anymore. When he was ready, she would yield, and he wouldn't pull away.

She softly gripped his tattooed arm and kissed his bicep, "We need to finish the story before we have to do it by lantern light."

"Are you sure you're ready?"

She nodded, "We've come this far. We need to finish it."

They returned to the ancient past and steeled themselves for the end.

I never knew evil could have such depths! But as I considered her sins, she smiled at me.

"You are too easy for me, Magnus, and I shall miss you terribly when you are gone. You did not really believe I was asleep, did you? Have you not wondered why you could not find the other half of my guard?"

It felt as if my heart stopped beating. I heard the unsheathing of a blade behind me. Without looking, I drew my dagger swiftly and spun about, pressing it hard to Emiline's throat. I knew before I saw him it would be Richard standing behind me.

"Lower your sword or I'll end her miserable life," I threatened.

He was immobile as though he were made of stone.

Emiline laughed even though my blade was pressed tightly against her skin, "Can you not count, Magnus? Two guards are missing. Do you not wonder where I might have hidden them?"

But for a second in time, I wondered if they were hidden by the tapestries draped behind me, but then I realized of where she spoke—my chamber!

"If you do not remove your blade from my throat, she will die, Magnus."

"You first, my Lady," I said, and pressed harder.

"What will you gain?" she whispered. "Let me go and at least I will allow you to be with her once more before you meet your end. If not, Richard will give the signal, and she will be dead before you can remove your sword from its sheath. They have her right now, Magnus, and I am sure she is frightened."

I could not defeat her. She planned this moment well. I lowered my blade.

"Just to show you I am not completely heartless, my once sweet

lover," she motioned Richard to open the adjoining chamber door.

"Let me kill him," he growled.

I knew it was the wrong thing for him to do. Emiline followed no one's commands.

"Open the door! I will let him be by her side when she dies. I wish him to see it before his own end."

Reluctantly, Richard threw open the inner doors.

Sarai was seated at the foot of my bed wide-eyed and still. The bodies of my two captains lay upon the floor. They had been slaughtered in utter silence as they were attacked from the shadows and their throats slit almost to the point of decapitation. Gregory and Berenger stood on either side of her, armed with crossbows. Their bloodied daggers, sheathed.

"She has remained silent, just as you said she would, my Queen," Gregory spoke.

"Is that not so thoughtful, Magnus? She was told if she made a sound, you would be executed before she could see you again. How droll and predictable that the two of you would use your last defenses to behold each other. She could have screamed to warn you, and you could have sliced open my throat then charged Richard. No wonder you find yourself in such terrible messes—bad decisions."

She and Richard moved to face us as I joined Sarai's side. She held my hand tightly, and I could tell she was brave and ready for whatever would be our fate. Gregory moved with his back to the queen's chamber as Berenger stepped forward to place his bow in Richard's hands. That was when I saw Nyles. They were unaware of his presence, as he had crept into the queen's chamber. For once, I was glad a soldier disobeyed me and left his post. He had two swords; one he gripped by the hilt in his right, and the other he held by the blade in his left. I could read his intention before he struck. He would attack Gregory from behind as he threw a sword to me.

The moment the bow was about to be exchanged, Nyles struck, running Gregory through with his sword, sending the crossbow to the floor. The other sword flew through the air into my waiting hand. As I gripped the hilt and began to lunge forward, I used my free hand to push Sarai flat down to the bed to make her less a target.

Richard had two targets, but Berenger stood between us, so he turned to fire at Nyles. It was not a deadly shot, but it did pierce his sword arm, and Nyles fell to the floor. Berenger had not a chance as I sliced through his backbone in one swift and mighty swing. I finally faced the one I wanted so desperately to kill. Richard's bow spent, he dropped it and drew his sword, and the thunderous sound of clashing irons filled the palace.

"Magnus! Watch out!" Sarai's screamed. I turned to see Emiline with Gregory's crossbow in her hands, pointed my direction. There was a swish through the air. I thought the arrow had been launched, but it was Nyles. He had thrown his dagger, lodging it deep into Emiline's back.

"Emiline!" Richard cried out, as her body stiffened in mortal pain.

It was enough to take his attention from our battle; I sliced the sword from his hand and then drew my dagger, plunging it into his chest. I lowered him to the floor as I watched the life leave his eyes. The battle ended, but Emiline remained upright gasping for air, her eyes wide with shock. She raised the bow for a final time in my direction.

"No!" Sarai wailed.

That was all it took.

Emiline was too far for me to reach her as the last wicked thought entered her mind. I lunged, but it was too late. The arrow was spent as it made its mark. It went straight to my heart. She knew exactly where my heart was beating: right into the breast of Sarai.

Emiline collapsed.

I ran to Sarai's side as she gasped for air, the arrow sticking completely through her. "No, no, Sarai, you cannot leave me. I cannot live without you," I cried.

"I will never be gone," she whispered, as the color washed from her beautiful face. "I shall always be right here," she said, as she placed her hand against my heart. Her eyes closed, her breath stilled, and her hand fell limp. Heaven gained the most perfect angel.

I turned to Emiline as she writhed on the floor, the knife working deeper with every struggled movement. She was in pain, yet wore a blissful smile. The bloody puddle below her was small, and I knew the dagger itself was keeping her from bleeding to death. She suddenly shuddered; fright filled her face as she reached out for my hand.

"To the depths, witch," I growled, as I pulled the blade from her back and watched the red run wild beneath her.

Her eyes grew wider. She gasped and seemed to freeze; her final expression was one of disbelief.

Valderegnum should have been a place of great accomplishment and great joy, but it had been a Kingdom of tragedy. I called all my subjects to gather at one time the following morn. I gave the greatest speech of my reign as I laid my heart bare before them and asked for everyone to put their hands to the task of burying this place of sorrow. I would divide my royal treasury among each family in exchange for their work and for their respected silence concerning this once great place.

It had taken nine years to complete the construction and one full year to bury it. They dug a great lake to the south. Slowly, they filled the palace from the bottom up to the highest towers, careful to leave no space empty. When all was done, my chamber in the final tower was filled. Sarai's body had been carefully wrapped and preserved; she was laid upon my bed and the chamber almost filled; an opening was made in the tower roof. All was complete.

Slowly, the subjects moved away to different lands; only three remained. I have left my story here for whoever finds this as a warning Sarai once gave me, "A life without love is a life without reason to live." Emiline lived a life without love. All she desired she craved with her physical being, and in doing so, she destroyed the lives of many. I ask for no memory of my name or for my kingdom. All I have want for is buried in this place. Keep it sacred. Grant me my only dignity of resting in peace beside the woman who loved me in this place once called Valderegnum, but now I pray, forever, Kingdom Hill.

Orthellous Magnus, 782 A.D.

There was a space after his signature. Cynewulf finished the scroll.

My dearest King and friend passed into glory within eight months of the final recording of his words. There were two of us left to bury him; myself and Nyles of Dunfee who had become a faithful servant and true friend of the king in the years that followed his confession. We dug down through the last remaining exposed piece of the palace, and placed him, as was his wish, beside his sweet

Sarai. Upon his burial, we remained to cover completely the last tower, the entrance to the springhouse, and to seal these words in stone. We are departing for whatever God has left for us. May peace and wisdom, but more importantly, love guide your decisions and your life. God be with you.

Cynewulf, Bishop of Valderegnum

"I can't believe it's over," Cass said, her voice full of wonder. She rose from her chair, feeling the need to move; AJ stayed seated. "I felt like I really knew him—like he was here while you were reading."

"It was incredible and heartbreaking, yet, at the same time, I'm glad we know what happened."

"AJ, were you serious about turning this into a novel?"

"I've already started it."

"I thought you were working on the survey story?"

"I wrote my sample piece and emailed it to my boss. He likes it, but he doesn't want it for a feature story; he wants it for filler."

"What's the difference?"

"If he had let me make it a feature, I would have been given an extra camera guy and a few more weeks to work on it. When it's filler, I take my own shots, and the story will be smaller. He said I could take another day or two, but he wants me in Jeffrey's Bay no later than Thursday. Cass..." he hesitated, "...I hope you won't be mad at me, but when I was using your computer, I noticed you like to write, too."

"You read some of my stuff?" she wasn't angry, but she was surprised.

"You're good. Did you minor in journalism in college?"

"No. Math and science were my forte. I've never shared what I write. What did you think about it?"

"Dark, very dark, but beautiful at the same time. You've seen a side of life most people wouldn't have made it through, and I saw that in your writing. I want to know if you'd consider writing the novel with me?"

The story about Kingdom Hill contained a lot of darkness, and he needed her for that. She wasn't offended by his offer; she knew it had been intended as a compliment. "I don't know how good I'll be, but I'd love to help." She looked up at the cotton-candy colored sky, as the sun began its descent. "It seems weird knowing we have a night where we don't have anything to read. Do you want to build a fire?"

"Yeah," he stated slowly.

She could tell he was deep in thought, but he didn't say more. She turned and started to walk away when she felt his hand grip hers.

"Where're you going?" he asked softly.

"I'll go gather some sticks."

He kissed the back of her hand then rose from his chair, "Not that kind of a fire. I don't want to rush you, Cass. I'm ready, but I understand if it's too soon for you. Tell me no, and I'll wait. Tell me yes," he barely breathed the words as he placed a gentle kiss on her lips, "and this is our night."

She returned the kiss, sultry and slow, savoring it as if this was the first time their lips had met. "I don't want to wait anymore," she whispered. She pulled from his hold then unzipped the tent flap. "We need to get in here, anyway," she said, smiling, "I felt a midge."

The tiny biting midges hadn't been a problem under the hill, but the summer swarms would begin in a few weeks, making camping out impossible. Her crews would be finished with the job before the bugs became too bad.

He followed without speaking.

It was strange to know they were getting ready to take the step she wanted so desperately their first night in a motel, but he had been right: she wasn't ready then. She wasn't even sure she was ready now, but if there was one thing she had confidence in concerning AJ, it was that if she couldn't handle it, he would stop. This wasn't going to be like anything she'd ever experienced.

They spent time simply being together, basking in the warmth and glow of their closeness. The tent was called a Stargazer because the upper part of the dome was made of an almost invisible fine screen which allowed them to watch the night sky as it unfolded—and it was an incredible sight. The stars made their appearance, slowly at first, but as the darkness deepened above them, millions of twinkling pin-pricks shimmered in the heavens. The moon hung low in the evening sky, bathing Kingdom Hill in soft, ambient light.

"If I do anything wrong, Cass, don't be afraid to tell me," he whispered as he rolled from beside her, up onto his elbow. He smoothed her hair as his mouth descended, sending her mind far away from anything other than the sensual, deeply need-filled kisses they shared.

She had been careful before not to touch him when they were this close, but she wanted to explore all of him tonight. She reached under his tee-shirt to feel his warm, muscled stomach; her hands slipped around his sides then moved upward along the sculpted erector muscles in his back, and finished by curling her palms over his shoulders. Her left palm felt the ridged pattern of the tattoo on his skin. Damn, he felt wonderful.

He pulled away from her touch and began unbuttoning her blouse. She noticed his hands were trembling, but she had a feeling it wasn't fear; this was anticipation—the kind of tremor that takes over when you're about to receive something you've wanted so desperately. He lifted her gently to a seated position as he finished removing her top. She did the same by gripping the bottom edge of his shirt and pulling it over his head. His handsome face disappeared as he buried into her hair, his mouth moving hot and determined for her neck, kissing, suckling, and licking her skin. She felt his hands dancing up her spine. Instantly, her lacy bra popped loose—he'd unhooked it.

He kissed his way back to her lips, his breathing deepened as soft moans started rolling up from his throat. He teased her mouth for a response then backed away and gripped her shoulder straps. The bra fell; her breasts were exposed. It was natural for her to reach up and massage her heated mounds, her nipples tightening immediately under the touch of her hands.

His eyes lit up, but his face remained serious, "Cass, you are so beautiful, I'm almost afraid I'm gonna screw this up."

She didn't answer him, but simply took his hand and lifted it to cup her breast. His free hand went behind her, and she felt the sensation of being tipped backward as he laid her down in the thick silk of the sleeping bag. She closed her eyes and raised her ribcage toward him, feeling the decadence of allowing him to explore. A shockwave tingled through her as his lips covered her nipple and drew it slowly into his mouth. She suddenly needed air; her lips parted and she inhaled quickly.

"Are you okay?" he asked, stopping after her reaction.

"Yes," she swallowed and nodded at the same time, "don't stop, AJ. It feels good—so good."

This time, he gripped both breasts and began to tongue and roll her pebbled nipples against the edge of his teeth. Instantly, she wanted more—she wanted it all. She wanted him hard and fast. She wanted his groin slamming into hers. She began to twist and writhe under him. She positioned her hand over his as she gripped with too much strength, trying to force him to squeeze down on her.

"No, Cass" he whispered, sensing the change in her. "Nothing about tonight is going to be hard or rough; you're—"

Her other hand went immediately to his jeans. His eyes widened as she clutched against the erection hidden under the fabric, "Whoa, Cassandra."

"But something *is* going to be hard," she stated sharply. Her breathing picked up speed. "Take off my pants," she demanded.

He attempted to stop her from thrashing under him, but pinning her only made her wilder in his grasp.

"No, Cass."

"Yes!" she demanded.

"Stop it!" He backed off and pulled away.

She gave a wicked laugh and tried to bite him.

"Cassandra, don't."

She took a swing, but he caught her hand—just in time.

Everything came to an immediate stop.

Her angry gesture held inches from the side of his head.

"I know you don't want to hit me, Cass. I won't hit you. I love you, Cass—listen to me, baby—listen, please. I'm not going to be what every other man has been for you. We have to do this my way or I sleep in the truck."

Her eyes were locked onto her fist. What if he hadn't stopped the blow? She felt the shame and the disappointment over her ugliness well up and fill the bottom of her lashes. "I—I'm sorry," she choked. "I—I didn't mean to..."

"I know. Cass, maybe this is too soon for you. Maybe I should just hold you tonight. If you're not ready..."

"Please," she whimpered, "I'm ready here." She placed his hand against her heart, "But you have to help me change it here," she said, pulling his other hand to the side of her head as she kissed his open palm. "I love you, AJ," she said, her tears dripping down her cheeks. "Don't leave me, please. Teach me what to do."

"Ah Cass, baby, I'm not leaving you. I told you I'm stubborn—stubborn in love with you—but we can't hurt each other—that's not love. You have to trust me. We can try again, but if you go off on me, then you need more time."

She didn't want more time, she wanted AJ. How could she cage the side of her that had no control? There was only one thing that was going to help her at this point, and it was something she'd never done in her life: she had to surrender—and it had to be without question or resistance to whatever he showed her tonight. The monsters from her past had to die *this* night or she'd never be free, or have a new future with the man who owned her heart.

"I trust you. Tonight—I can't go on without you."

He smiled gently and kissed her. He said he would hold her for a little while then they would try again. She was pressed against his chest as he placed kisses on her face and stroked her hair for what must have been fifteen or twenty minutes until she finally relaxed and began to simply enjoy being near him.

"Ready to try again?" he whispered.

She nodded, afraid to speak.

He moved carefully back to her full breasts as he kissed, suckled, and caressed them. She'd never felt them ache so desperately for the touch of a man. She needed to learn how to accept his gentleness, but she also needed to learn how to give it. She kissed his throat, tasting the sweet flavor of his maddeningly male scent then she moved down his chest to kiss and tease his nipples with her lips. He moaned, and she knew he liked what she was doing. Pleasing him this way, with tenderness and sensuality, felt incredible—and it was giving her the strength to fight off her demons, instead of AJ.

He tipped her face up and lowered his. He kissed her with a little more passion and depth then broke away to study her. "Don't slip away from me, Cass. We're going a little further, but don't lose it, baby," he said, as his fingers reached down to undo the button to her pants.

Just the thought of him removing her pants caused a heated rush to pool between her legs. Her abdominals tightened, and she unconsciously held her breath as she listened to the zipper go down.

His lips moved to the center of her chest, then slipped lower to the hollow of her stomach.

She'd never felt this kind of fire inside. It was as if every nerve ending suddenly had been hit with a jolt of electricity, and she was alive—everywhere. She raised her hips as he pulled her pants and underwear off, his mouth traveling downward, kissing and pressing his warm, full lips against the center of her heat.

He reached under her thighs, bringing them to rest on his thick shoulders, his biceps lifting her hips, his hands stroking her abs. When his scorching tongue dipped inside her, she gasped for air and plunged her fingers into his hair. She could tell it thrilled him to go down on her, but she wasn't ready. Losing control was seconds away. "I can't—" she cried out, "can't handle this yet, AJ."

He raised his face to look at her, but he wasn't disappointed; instead, he wiped his mouth and smiled. "Do you realize what you just did, Cass? You stopped me before you slipped." He kissed the inside of her thigh, closing his eyes briefly; he allowed his cheek to rest against the place he had just kissed. "Baby, I can't wait to get you off. You're intense, Cass—and I can't even imagine how good it's going to be with you." He returned to face level, and kissed her, "Maybe that was too much for you tonight—but son-of-a-bitch, I'm gonna love it when you let me tongue you into ecstasy."

"As much as I want to let you do that tonight, some things may take me a little more time before I'm ready. I don't want to lose it with you."

"I love you so much, Cass—this is exactly what I want. Trust me, feel safe with me; say what you feel instead of hitting and hurting."

Her heart rate was still in overdrive, yet she was glad she'd done the right thing; and, more than anything else, she was glad he was pleased with her.

"Take off my jeans, Cass" he whispered, as he rolled over onto his back.

Now she was the one with trembling hands, but she was scared. She'd seen him naked, but she'd never touched his bare body like this. His jeans came down. She reached for the waistband to his boxer briefs then hesitated, "This is okay, right? You want me to take them off?"

"Yes, I do," he said, raising his hips slightly to make it easier.

She removed them and, for the first time, raised her hand to stroke the bare flesh of his manhood.

His eyes closed as his head slowly tipped back, "Damn, that feels good." Suddenly, he curled forward and gripped her arms. "No, Cass."

She didn't understand. She wasn't losing control. All she did was kiss what she was caressing. "But I'm okay."

"No, baby, it's not you this time; it's me. I've wanted you for so long, and I'm afraid you're going to push me over the top before we even get started."

"Oh," she said, suddenly, understanding. She brought herself back to being face to face with him, allowing her body to glide against his, skin to skin, as she did. They were finally completely bare, and she was finding that surrendering to him was like opening a door inside her soul, baring what had at one time, felt as though it would never see the light of a beautiful moment.

His breathing was faster and his face a little pale. Suddenly, something dawned on her she hadn't considered. "AJ, it is okay for you to have sex, isn't it? This isn't bad for your aneurysm, right?" She craved this experience more than anything she'd ever wanted, but she realized her focus had been selfish—now it changed, leaving only one person in her universe—and, surprise of surprises, it wasn't her.

"Cass," he said with a small smile, "Seriously? Baby, I'm pretty sure this is safe." His smile broadened.

Her curiosity was piqued, "Why?"

"Because I don't think there is an ounce of blood left in my head." His deep laugh was starting to come out. She must have looked perplexed, so he continued. "It's all somewhere else right now."

She caught the drift and looked down, "Yeah, I can believe that." She found herself laughing with him. How beautiful; laughter and joy could mingle with passion and physical need. She'd *never* experienced this, and she loved it. The demons faded, dying in the light of true love.

"Ah Cass," he sighed, "even if it wasn't, I wouldn't trade this moment for anything. Have you ever heard the song, Your Guardian Angel?"

"I don't think so," she whispered, cuddling against him. "Who sings it?"

"Red Jumpsuit Apparatus."

"No, definitely not. I think I would have remembered that name. Why?"

"Because it's running through my head right now."

"Sing a little of it for me."

He chuckled slightly, "I can't sing. But there is a line in the chorus that goes something like 'I will never let you fall,' something,

something, something, 'I'll be there for you through it all, even if saving you sends me to Heaven.'"

She frowned, "If sex isn't safe for you then we're stopping because I don't want you going anywhere without me."

"Cass, my doctor told me I could enjoy as much as I wanted." Her doubtful expression prompted him to continue, "I'm serious." He gripped her arms gently and brought her down as he rolled above her. "And I *am* enjoying this; I don't think anything has ever felt as incredible as being with you."

"I need you to tell me something, AJ," she whispered, as his body moved to rest against hers.

"Anything," he replied.

"What's your real name?"

He seemed thoroughly surprised.

"Your first name," she clarified. "You put AJ on everything at the hospital, but it must stand for something else."

He softly moved her hair away from her face with his fingers. "It's Adam."

For some reason, his response wasn't a surprise. It was as if her heart had already guessed it. Immediately her eyes filled with tears.

"What's wrong, Cass?"

"Nothing," she said with a little choke, "It's just—I mean your name: First man. That's what you are for me: the first *real* man who has been in my life. The first man I've fallen in love with. And—and now this... I'm sorry, I didn't mean to cry, but you're just so perfect to me."

"And you have no idea how very perfect you are to me." She turned her face away, but he made her turn it back, "You are. *Please* start believing that." He paused for a second and started again, "Cass, not to trash the romantic moment, but I never asked." He paused.

"What?"

"You are on birth control, right?"

Her bag was an arm's length away as she dipped her hand into an outer pocket and produced a condom. She gave a tiny grin, "I guess you could say I am. It's just that mine comes in a little foil package. I've always believed it was safer." She watched a look come over his face that could only be described as panicked, "What's wrong?"

"You don't take anything else?"

"No, I... Why?"

"I can't use a condom, not most condoms anyway. You were with me when I put my allergies on the paperwork at the hospital, but I never thought to—"

"Latex," she said, instantly realizing why he had that look on his face. "You're allergic to latex."

"Yeah, I'm sorry, I should have thought ahead."

"We don't need it," she said quietly, slipping the package back into her bag.

"Yeah we do—if we don't want something else to happen here tonight."

"AJ," she said, getting his attention, "Please don't stop what we're doing. I'm okay with this. If something happens—"

"I'll pull out."

"No, I don't want you to do that. I'm begging you; don't stop what's happening between us. Everything about our relationship has been a miracle; let's not stop now."

"Cass, are you really sure?" he asked, allowing his groin to press firmly between her legs.

She inhaled and arched her back, "I've never been surer of anything in my life. Make love to me, AJ. Show me how."

His erection fit perfectly against her aching mound. It was a different sensation for her to feel bare skin intimately touching bare skin. The heat alone was about to push her sensations over the top.

He was being maddeningly slow as he rubbed and stroked himself through her passion. She fought the urge to force the moment; realizing she had to submit to however he wanted to control her body. She had to put her body and her trust completely in his hands.

Suddenly, she could feel the length of him widening and deepening her slick, aching canal—a final thrust and he was deeply and fully seated inside her—he was taking over and she was letting go. How extraordinary to be claimed in love.

She closed her eyes as she began to raise her knees.

"No, Cass, don't do it. Open your eyes."

She couldn't breathe at the moment as her pulse skyrocketed. Her heels dug into the sleeping bag as her hips rose up like a wave underneath him, lifting him.

"Open your eyes and look at me; do it now, baby."

She gasped and opened her eyes at the same moment. It was

as if she had been underwater and was just getting her first breath of air.

"There aren't going to be any ghosts from your past or any memories between us. You have to keep your eyes open. You have to know who it is who loves you this way. Please, stay with me. I love you—don't slip away."

She'd never felt a connection like this before as he began to move inside her, never taking his eyes from hers. He had a powerful and perfect rhythm, his stroke pushing her to her first orgasm. She'd never had one that wasn't associated with something wrong or bad. This was a completely new level, a whole new experience. She breathlessly called out his name as the sensation shot through her like a white hot, shooting star splitting the night sky, vocalizing her pleasure at becoming his possession.

He kissed her long and deep, his breathing coming faster, his rhythm moving in perfect sync with their bodies unified craving for this incomparable need, this perfect collision as he and she fully became one.

She was rising to the peak once again, but she sensed that this time he was going to join her in the elation. She felt him hesitate, realizing he was thinking about pulling back. "No, don't do it, AJ," she begged. "I can't take it if you leave me now, stay with me," she pled.

Hesitation vanished and he tightened down on her, his pulsing thrust going even deeper than before, and she knew he was committed to staying inside her. She reached the end of her ability to control her sensation, as he gave in to his own. They cried out at the same moment, as together, they were swept over the edge of the most satisfying answer to desire that either one had ever known.

CHAPTER FOURTEEN

Dawn came with startling brightness. Their previous mornings had been in darkness under the hill, but today, with their clear-topped tent, every brilliant ray showered them in illumination. She faced him, wrapped in his arms and more content than any other time in her life. She brought his hand to her lips as she began to kiss, caress, and suckle each finger. She watched his sleepy expression as his eyes fluttered open.

"Hey, beautiful," he whispered.

"Good morning. Did you sleep okay?"

"Uh-huh," he moaned.

"No headache?"

"Actually, I did get one last night, but I just went to sleep, and I'm fine now."

"Did sex give you a headache before?"

He grinned, "Last night was pretty intense for me, Cass."

She smiled and grabbed his tattooed arm as she rolled over and pressed her back to his chest, pulling his arm over her shoulder, "I thought it was pretty intense, too, but that's only the beginning. I was planning a little intensity for you this morning."

He moaned again, "That sounds interesting, but I've got to ask you something. Are you double jointed—maybe in your back or your hips?"

She thought the question was a little odd. "I don't think so, but I know I'm really flexible. Why?"

"I've never been with someone who can move like you do. I

swear to you, Cass, last night was a surfer's dream."

She turned back over. She had a feeling she needed to be eye to eye for this explanation. "A surfboard is hard, flat, and inflexible; I'm not getting the connection."

"No, baby," he whispered, a laugh on the brink of coming out, "not the board; you were the wave. When you rolled your body up to meet mine, or whatever it was you did, it was like catching the perfect wave. I had the urge to stand up." That was it; he couldn't hold back his laughter any longer, "God it was amazing."

"Well I'm glad you didn't stand, unless you'd taken me with you. I would have rather died than to have broken the connection to you last night." She gave a little grunt and moved to sit Indian-style beside him, "Do you mean to tell me, with all the women you've slept with, none of them—"

"Cass, you make it sound like a large number."

She swept her hair away from her face, "With your looks? Please, AJ, I figure you've been laid more times than asphalt on the highway."

He sat up. "If I accepted every opportunity presented to me, yeah, then you could say that, but I've always been... He seemed to be struggling to find the right word.

"Picky?" she offered.

"No, it's not that."

"Only took the best-looking ones?" she offered again.

He gave an annoyed sigh, "Definitely not. I've met some amazing women most guys wouldn't have looked at twice, but I guess what I'm trying to say is I've always looked for the one who... Cass, I can't describe it, so I'll just tell you it's you. When I met you, the feeling that went through me was inimitable."

"Stop right there, Mister I'm-a-big-shot-writer. I'm above average on brain cells, but you're not allowed to use words I don't know the meaning of, especially when you're describing something that has to do with me."

"It means matchless; something too good to be imitated or copied. I've been looking for you ever since my first hormone raged out of control, causing me to finally notice girls. I've met a lot who were willing, but I immediately knew they wouldn't be right for me. When Bobby brought me to your camp, and I stepped out of the vehicle, I thought, *I don't believe it; there she is.* And the feeling that hit me was—was inimitable."

"That was your honest first thought when you met me?"

His smile broadened, "Honestly? My very first thought was *Good job, Bobby!* What did you think when you first saw me?"

"I was a little shallower; at least, I think I was. I went immediately for your looks, those biceps under your shirt and then decided I liked your handshake. And, naturally for me, I got mad at you."

"Yeah, you didn't seem happy at all about allowing me to follow you around."

"No I wasn't, but I've been thanking God ever since I stopped being pissed off." She pushed him to recline on the sleeping bag then slid down his body as she began kissing from his stomach and moved lower.

"What are you doing, baby?" he breathed.

She could tell his body was eager and ready for her touch. She kissed from one side of his hipbone to the other, "I'm getting ready to give you a new meaning for inimitable."

She could hear him take in a lungful of air as his head tipped back, and he started moaning out her name. She would have thought the pleasure this morning would be all his, but she found herself enjoying his experience just as much. Love changed every sexual act into true passion and sensuality—the higher she pushed his emotions, the greater her personal satisfaction and desire to please him.

She draped the tent fly over the sheer top to give him a little darkness to relax in. He was snoring, so she knew he was comfortable. Their only jobs today were to put the scrolls in Ziploc bags, leave a note, and reseal the holes. She packed everything into the truck, and then swam under the hill for the final time. She had just wrapped the last scroll in plastic when AJ emerged from the water.

"You should have woken me up and let me help."

"You do get to help. You write the note and seal the holes."

"That isn't much, but I did clean out the tent and put it in the truck."

She smiled, "So where do you want to stay tonight?"

"Northampton. I got a text from Bobby and told him we were finished here. He said we might as well stay with him. We can fly out of Heathrow in London to Cape Town Wednesday morning." He walked around behind her and wrapped her in his arms, kissing the side of her neck. He swayed slowly back and forth, his hips rubbing firmly against her body. "You have the most fabulous ass. You're firm everywhere," he said as his hands explored, "do you workout when you're not surveying?"

"Surveying is pretty physical, but I run and hike when I'm not working. I used to like the time alone." She turned and slid her arms around his sides and up his back, "But I don't want to be alone anymore."

"Me neither, matter of fact, I can't even imagine being alone now."

"Yeah, I think we've been super-glued at the heart. Are you ready to start writing?" she handed him the pen and paper.

With the note written, he warmed the ancient wax and packed the holes. It was done. The only thing left was to pull up the rope; leaving no trace anyone disturbed this place.

"Cass, I want a picture of you for the survey story," he said as they emerged from the spring.

She cut him the first nasty glance she'd given him in days, "I'd prefer not."

"Just a shot of you using the Total Station. I don't have to have a full face shot, although I'd like one, but I doubt you'll go for that."

"You're right."

"How about a silhouette? Come on, Cass. I want *you* to be in my story. If Henley Geomatics is going to get national press, then the one who makes the company tick should be in the story. Please."

"You're cute when you're begging."

He offered a big smile.

"But no."

The smile fell from his face.

"I'm kidding," she laughed. "We'll catch one of the crews when we head south and you can have your picture."

They met up with Norton's crew about an hour away from Northampton, and she allowed AJ to take a couple of shots before they continued on their journey to Bobby's flat. She talked with the crew for a little while then unloaded everything from their Land Cruiser, with the exception of their clothing bags, into Norton's vehicle so she could return it to the rental agency at the airport. It didn't take too long before they were back on the road.

"What's wrong?" she asked, as she drove, glancing at AJ's face as he worked with his camera.

"I can't use any of these."

She didn't expect the look she was seeing, "Why? Is there something wrong with the camera? Did you have your finger in front of the lens?" She was teasing at this point, trying to get a smile out of him, but he was still so serious.

"I mean, look at this," he said, turning the display toward her.

She stole a glance. It was the close up shot he took as she looked through the Total Station. She didn't see anything wrong with it.

He took the camera back and flipped to the next picture.

It was a silhouette shot of her leaning forward looking through the same piece of equipment. Once again, there wasn't anything wrong with the shot.

He went through several more pictures, and each time, she couldn't see anything wrong with them.

"They look fine to me," she finally said.

"Yeah, they are fine, and they're gorgeous and sexy and... I can't put you out there like this."

At first, she was angry; she hadn't asked to be in the story. Then she realized his concern about her was genuine. He didn't want to cause problems for her from men who would hire her company solely to meet her—for all the wrong reasons; he wouldn't put her in that position. The solution seemed simple, "Then don't put a picture of me in the story."

He looked unhappy with that option, "I'll Photoshop the silhouette and just use from your shoulders up."

She reached over and gripped his hand, "Thank you."

They weren't far from Billing Street, where Bobby lived, when AJ asked her to pull into a small drug store. She didn't question him at first, but when they stepped inside and headed down the feminine aisle, she had to ask what he was looking for.

"Polyvinyl," he stated, as he stopped in front of their family planning supplies, "or lambskin."

She didn't mean to get upset about it, but emotion instantly washed over her. "But I don't—"

"This will do," he said with a box of Trojan lambskin condoms in hand. When he looked up at her, he saw she was on the verge of tears. "Cass?"

"I don't want to use anything," she swallowed when she said it.

She knew what she wanted; it had been a giant step for her, and one she thought he understood last night.

"Cass, you don't mean that."

Her tears spilled over the rim, "Yes, I do, but I thought you knew. I'm sorry; I thought you wanted this, too."

Standing there in the store with people milling around, he put the box back on the shelf and wrapped her tightly in his arms, his mouth coming to rest by her ear, "I thought you just didn't want to wait last night. I didn't realize you were hoping for something else."

She pulled away and picked the box back up, "It's okay. I understand if you don't want—"

"Cassandra," he breathed, "I can't believe you would want to carry my baby but—but, oh God, yes, if you're sure. I can't even begin to explain how much I want this. I didn't realize... I mean, this," he said pulling the box out of her hand, "wasn't meant to hurt or insult you. I just didn't get the big picture last night. And now that I do, it blows me away. Let's get out of here."

"There is one thing I do want from this section," she said, as she picked up a home pregnancy test, "I'll just save it for a while."

Now it was his turn to tear up as they headed to checkout.

Bobby's two bedroom flat was new and modern. He wasn't due home for another hour, but he'd hidden a key for them, so they could let themselves in and relax. The relaxation came in the form of a hot shower—a shower for two. The water rained down, and the steam rose as they satisfied their new passion for each other. She thought it would be difficult to let go of the past, but she found her surrender the night before had given her more liberty than she could have ever imagined. She was completely dependent on him, and at the same time, independent from the stigma she had attached to the physical act. Where sex ceased to exist for her, his love and compassion replaced it.

"I want you to relax for a little while," he said as they dried off, "I had an extra nap this morning. Now, it's your turn."

"But I thought we were going out to dinner with Bobby?"

"We will, but you are going to get a massage and get some sleep. We'll make it a late dinner."

"No, I'm—"

He put his hands on his bare hips, "Are you turning down my massage? I don't offer this to just any woman."

She laughed, "I'll accept as long as you promise never to offer it to any other woman ever again."

"I don't know, baby; bartending, surveying, and writing don't pay nearly as much as I earn massaging."

"You'd better be teasing."

He just laughed as he picked her up and headed for the bedroom.

When her eyelids opened, it was close to dark outside and Charlie was curled up at her feet. She could hear the guys talking as she stumbled around in a half-sleep stupor and pulled on her clothes. She brushed her hair and pulled it back into a ponytail, wishing the whole while she'd brought some makeup along on her trip to the UK. She didn't wear it often, but AJ was bringing out the feminine side in her. She did carry a little bit of shaded lip balm in her purse, which would have to do.

"Good morning, sleepy-head," AJ said as she walked out.

"Morning?" she said glancing quickly out Bobby's balcony to make sure the glow was in the western sky.

"I'm kidding, but for someone who said she didn't need a nap, four-and-a-half hours is almost a night's sleep."

"You should have woke me up," she moaned as she plopped down beside him on the couch, "now I've got a cotton-head."

Bobby gave her an odd look.

"You know," she explained, "cotton-head, spider webs in the brain, muddled—"

"Muddled," he echoed, catching her meaning. "Now there's a term I understand. Good to see you again, Cass," he said, leaning over and giving her a hug.

"So did you guys already eat?" she asked.

"Nope," AJ spoke up, "We were waiting on sleeping beauty, and I'm starving."

"Give me a few minutes to walk Charlie, and—"

"I already did that. I kind of wondered if he woke you up when I put him back in the bedroom fifteen or twenty minutes ago."

Bobby wanted them to try a small pub not far from his flat that he swore had the best fish and chips in all of the UK. The night was fun as they talked and enjoyed the meal, but it seemed to her that AJ was edgy. When he ordered a glass of ale, she knew he was nervous about something. Two additional glasses of ale down and she was getting a little worried about him. They finished their meal and were just about to leave when he turned to her and asked if she wanted to get something to take back to Bobby's place for later.

She puffed out her cheeks and gave a single pat to her stomach. "Are you kidding? I'm stuffed. What'd you want, dessert?"

"No," he said, turning to face her and then dropping down on one knee right in the middle of the restaurant, "I'd like to take a wife with me." He pulled a small black box from his pocket and opened it to reveal a beautiful diamond ring. "Cassandra Henley, would you do me the honor of marrying me?"

She just stood there unable to react, as it seemed that every pair of eyes in the restaurant turned their direction; the place went silent.

"Say something, baby," he urged.

"But—but why, AJ?" she stammered. "You don't have to do this because—"

He rose and pulled her close as he rested his mouth against her ear, "Cass, that's not why I'm asking, but I'm not going to wait, and if you do end up pregnant, I won't have you think you forced me into this. I want this; I want you." He kissed her cheek and pulled away, "Will you *please* marry me?"

The knot in her throat blocked her ability to speak. All she could do was nod her approval. The place broke out in cheers as he placed the ring on her finger and swept her into his arms for one dramatic kiss for the crowd. Teary-eyed Bobby was hugging them both, congratulating them.

They were walking out as she kept staring at the ring on her finger. "But when did you have time to buy this?" she finally asked.

AJ grinned, "Why do you think I wanted you to take a nap?"

"Yeah, well what if I hadn't slept so long?"

"Bobby was there and ready to give you a load of baloney about where I went. But," he continued, as he reached over and gripped Bobby's shoulder, "he didn't have to because you were out so hard I think a train could have gone through his apartment, and you'd have never budged."

They spent the last of their evening sitting on Bobby's couch as the three of them talked about the future. AJ said he hoped to find someone to marry them before they took off for Africa, but Bobby told him that wouldn't work.

"Americans can get married over here, and it's perfectly legal when you get back to the States, but as Americans, there is a lot of paperwork involved, and you'll have to wait at least a week or more to file it all."

"You sound pretty knowledgeable about marriages," Cass teased. "There must be someone in your life who made you look into that before. Stop blushing," she said, as she poked his ribs. "Blushing is unnecessary around friends; you just say whatever you're thinking."

He blushed harder. "I'm sorry, that's just me. No, Cass, I've never found the girl who was the right one for me. Thought I did," he said leaning forward to look around her at AJ, "but my best friend fell for her instead."

She didn't catch on at first and was ready to ask who was she?

AJ spoke up as he gripped her shoulders and pulled her against his chest, "Yeah, and I'm not giving her up."

"Oh," she said, suddenly realizing he had been speaking about her, "but you're such a good looking guy. Surely, these English girls must be gaga over you. You have that 'Prince William' look. Don't you date?"

AJ laughed.

"What?" she asked.

"He couldn't even talk to you. He sent me to scope you out. Cass, that has to say something."

Bobby reached across and frogged AJ's thigh. "I have so mustered up the nerve to talk to girls and," he said with an indignant huff. "I do date. I just haven't found the one who gave me that feeling of instant attraction until..." he raised his fist to give another playful thump on AJ's leg.

AJ caught the fist before it could bang down, "Yeah, yeah, I know, but I'm still not giving her up."

"All right," Cass stated, trying to part the two who were fighting practically right over top of her, "if this is turning into a wrestling match, let me out of the middle."

They paused as she struggled from between them, and then she watched the match resume, as if someone had dinged an arena bell when she rose to her feet.

"Don't hurt him too badly, Bobby," she laughed, as she started to walk away.

That must have fueled AJ's desire to win as they tumbled from the couch and he pinned Bobby to the living room floor. "I said he could fight," AJ yelled after her, "but I never said he could beat *me*!"

"I'm going to bed," she announced, without turning around.

She could hear the scramble as the bodies untwined.

"Goodnight, Bobby," AJ called back to his friend, as he followed her into the bedroom. "Cass, you can't be tired," he said, as he shut the door.

"I'm not," she said as she began undressing, "how about you?"

He gave a slow smile, "Not at all." He unhooked her bra then slowly pulled the straps from her shoulders.

"Are you sure you want to marry me? It's not just because I don't want to use any protection, right? You seemed nervous about asking me."

"I needed a little liquid courage. I wasn't sure if you were okay with it or not—drinking, that is—I really hoped you be okay with my proposal," he added with a grin.

She nodded, "I gave up drinking, but I completely understand. I just don't like it when someone doesn't know when to cut it off."

"You don't have to worry about that with me; I promise. And if I could marry you tonight, I'd do it. But it looks like we should wait until we get back to the States."

"How long are we going to be in South Africa?" she asked.

He was kissing her throat, his lips moving lower with each touch to her skin. "My boss has two cameramen assigned to me," came his muffled explanation. He was down to the small expanse where the rib cage separates, kissing, nibbling, and teasing her skin. "I have them for about a week, and then he'll give me another week to fine tune the story." He had moved to her belly button now, his warm hands firmly holding her hips. "I could do my fine tuning in the States, which would make him happy, so I don't bust my expense account—" he'd just reached the bikini line as he paused and looked up, "—again."

She was taking her index finger and poking his shoulder.

"Ouch! Cass, what are you doing?"

"I'm looking for the mute button because in a few seconds I'm not going to hear a word you say anyway."

He laughed as he rose up to kiss her and then lifted her body off the floor and laid her down on the bed. "This is going to be a very long night," he crooned, and he started all over again from her neck and worked lower.

And it was exactly that. There were pleasures and tender secrets to be learned as they explored the depths of their need for each other. Hours of feelings and sensations that, at times, overwhelmed both of them. For her, it was all new; for him, it went to a level he'd never attained with anyone else. By five a.m., they were comfortable, satisfied, and drowsy in each other's arms as they heard the sound of Bobby's alarm clock going off in the other room.

"Goodnight, baby," she whispered, at the point when her eyes refused to reopen.

He pulled her snuggly against himself as he tucked the comforter under her chin, "Goodnight, Cass."

When they woke, she began checking all the arrangements National Geographic made for him in Jeffrey's Bay. Pets were not allowed at the place they booked, but she did find a great condo only twenty meters from the beach that did. He said he had a little flexibility with his expenses, but she covered the additional charge. His airline ticket with British Airways had been purchased, and although there were still seats remaining on his flight, they weren't near him. She upgraded his ticket from business to first-class, so they could sit together, and made all the arrangements for Charlie. She would take care of the return of the Land Cruiser when they arrived at the airport, but other than that, everything was complete. Well, almost complete—she was in the middle of washing all their dirty clothes that had accumulated over their time spent at Kingdom Hill.

"We fly out at eight a.m. tomorrow morning," she stated, as he helped her fold clothes. "If we have everything ready tonight, we can just get up when Bobby does at five and leave out. Are you okay? You've been really quiet."

"I was just thinking," he stated softly, "the next time I see Bobby, I'll be getting prepped for surgery."

"Yeah, that's right. And the next time after that will be when you're waking up in the recovery room. AJ," she said, her voice getting shaky, "I really didn't understand how hard the decision was that day at the hospital. It didn't hit me until later; the doctor was right about surgery taking the guesswork out of the future. Honestly, I don't know how you've kept it together all these years, especially with your other doctor telling you there wasn't anything that could be done, but this is your chance—your only chance..." she couldn't continue for a moment. "I hope I didn't push you into this. I mean, maybe—"

"No, Cass. Don't think that. You gave me the first ray of hope.

I'm just scared. I've been trying hard not to even think about the surgery."

"I've got an idea that might help get it off your mind."

"Oh, yeah, that works," he smiled. "I wasn't thinking about anything other than you last night."

She laughed, "No. I'm not talking about sex." She reached into her bag and pulled out her laptop and handed it to him, "Start your novel."

He leaned over and kissed her forehead, "That's a great idea, but I do have my own laptop. I just left it here with some of my other stuff when Bobby asked me to check-out, and I quote, the most fabulous woman he'd ever met."

"He really called me that?"

"Well, in his defense, I think you were much politer when you were in his office trying to get what you wanted."

She couldn't stop the big laugh that bubbled out. What he said was the absolute truth. When she was after something for the business, she could be convincingly and deceptively sweet. "I bet when he dropped you off at my camp and saw my claws come out, he wondered what the heck he'd gotten you into."

"Hold up a minute," he said, as he pulled out his phone and began punching buttons. After a few seconds, he turned it so she could see what he had been after. It was a text message from Bobby dated ten days ago. The screen read, 'ANFSCD! IMS'

"I don't text quite that much. I know the IMS stands for I'm sorry. What's the first part?"

He looked at her and started laughing as she tried to get him to reveal the meaning.

"I'll just Google it," she finally stated, taking back her computer.

"It means," he relented, "And now for something completely different!"

She smiled, but then an interesting thought crossed her mind, "So what was your response?"

She could tell by the look on his face, he never expected her to ask; the battle over his phone ensued. She honestly didn't think he was giving it his best as she pried it from his fingers. And when he wrapped his arms around her from behind and kissed her neck, she knew he'd been teasing.

The reply message simply read: 'That's OK—I like her.'

"Don't cry," he whispered, kissing her ear "It's like I told you; I knew you were the one for me from the moment I met you."

"Twenty years," she stated, as she wiped her cheeks, "I've been a desert, and now all you have to do is look at me and I tear up." She tipped her head back to look at his face. "Thanks, for this," she said handing back his phone. "It wasn't that I doubted you, but yet, at the same time, I still have trouble believing you stayed."

CHAPTER FIFTEEN

Early the next morning, they said their tearful goodbyes to the guy who was now a good friend to both of them then left for Heathrow Airport in London. It took eleven hours to get to the southernmost tip of Africa, but it was a comfortable flight that seemed to pass quickly while AJ worked on his novel and Cass caught some rest after another long night of passion and discovery. She was worried about him though because she knew he needed sleep. The problem was that ever since she suggested he start the novel to get his mind off the pending surgery, he'd become a little possessed with it. And although he'd asked for her help initially, he was now refusing to allow her to see what he was doing.

They only had a forty-five minute layover in Cape Town before they boarded a much smaller aircraft for Port Elizabeth, just east of Jeffrey's Bay. The short flight was turbulent, making her wonder how Charlie was doing in the cargo hold. He'd never been airsick when he traveled, but they'd never been on a flight quite this rough. But he was a little trooper; happy as usual to see her when they handed over his crate. With their baggage and Charlie collected, they moved to the rental desk.

"Give me your confirmation number," she said, holding out her hand to AJ.

He unfolded the piece of paper that had been in his pocket, but then hesitated.

She reached over and removed it from his grip.

"But, Cassandra—"

"Here you go," she said handing it to the lady at the rental desk, "What kind of vehicle did they reserve for us?"

"But—" he tried to interrupt again.

"A Fiat Panda," the lady answered.

She turned and scowled at AJ, "You've got to be kidding." She turned to the clerk, "That won't do. I see you have Jeeps. Do you have anything besides the Wrangler? How about an Unlimited?"

"No, ma'am. I'm afraid the Wrangler is the largest four-by-four we have."

"Cass—"

"How about a Wrangler with a hardtop and a roof rack? I hear vehicles get broken into pretty often down here."

"Yes, ma'am. I have one hardtop left, but it's a manual transmission."

Cass smiled, "That's perfectly fine; I can drive stick. Cancel the Panda."

"Cassandra," AJ crooned with an unusual extra smooth quality to his voice, but it was weird enough to get her attention.

"What?"

"That's not my reservation."

The lady looked down at the printed confirmation, "This was ordered by Tim Mathers with National Geographic for Garrett Weston, correct?"

He finally smiled, "I was trying to tell you, that's my photographer's car. The boss sent me the confirmation because my flight was arriving before his. I don't drive, remember? The boss figured Garrett would be my driver."

"Should I cancel the Jeep?" the clerk asked.

"No, definitely not," she said reaching across the counter and picking the confirmation up, "Mister Weston can have the Panda; I'm still taking the Jeep. You didn't tell your boss you were bringing your own driver?" she questioned with a little grin, as she dug out her credit card and identification.

"No. I haven't discussed my *new driver* with him, yet. The last time I spoke with him, I told him I needed bargaining material for a television station in Larkhall, Scotland; he didn't ask why."

Cass grabbed the keys and paperwork from the clerk and headed for the nearest bench, "So, we have to wait for your photographer?"

"Yup. His flight is coming in from Johannasburg in the next few minutes. The other guy, Machi, lives here. I've done several stories with him. He's going to meet us tomorrow out on Paradise beach."

Cass looked down at Charlie. He was whining and shivering. "He never goes in his box, and I know he's dying to go potty. I'll take him outside and find a grassy median."

"Cass, it's dark outside, and I don't completely trust their airport security. Hold up, I have an idea." He went to the rental desk and spoke with the clerk then returned, "Okay, let's go outside and find our Jeep. Charlie can go potty, and we can unload our bags."

"What'd you tell her?"

"The first place Garrett will go is to the rental desk to find out if I've been here. I left her my cell number and told her to have him call me."

It didn't take long after they found their vehicle, and let Charlie have his needed break, before his phone was ringing, "Yeah, I'm out in the rental lot right now. Okay, see you in a few minutes." He flipped his phone shut and smiled, "I can't wait to get to our place because I am exhausted."

She reached up and wrapped her arms around his neck, kissing his temple, "It'll be about an hour drive. You need to recline your seat and relax; no writing on the way." She had a scolding tone on the last part.

"My battery is dead anyway, but you were right about the story taking my mind off... Well, off *other* things. I want you to start writing, too."

"You mean start writing *with* you, right?"

"Not yet. I want you to write everything you remember, in first-person story form, from Magnus's point of view."

"But isn't that what you're doing?"

"Hey, AJ!" a male voice shouted.

Cassandra let go, so he could turn and face the man approaching.

"Garrett, how are you, buddy?" he said, giving the stocky man a quick hug.

He appeared to be in his mid twenties with light brown hair and a rather unkempt blonde goatee. He had a wide chest, thick arms, and a narrow waist which gave him a body builder appearance. He wasn't much taller than Cass, and he seemed thoroughly surprised she was with AJ.

He spoke up before AJ could make the introduction, "So what

are you doing? Mugging this poor girl?"

AJ laughed, "Garrett Weston, I'd like you to meet my fiancée, Cassandra Henley. Cass this is Garrett."

The surprise on his face was immediate, but he still reached out and shook her hand, "Fiancée? When did this happen? You were single a few weeks ago."

"Ah, you know how it is when some chick comes along and just sweeps you off your feet," he teased.

"Yeah, I do, and the next time I'll be more careful," came his odd reply.

They talked for a few more minutes, then drove from the lot and headed out for North 2 toward Jeffrey's Bay. Cass took the lead, mainly because she had her own version of GPS, and there was no way someone with her qualifications was going to get lost in Africa. She explained that she and AJ changed their accommodations to something a little more posh, but that they could drive together until they got into town. Garrett seemed content to follow, although he did mention not going too fast so his little Panda could keep up.

AJ followed orders, reclined his seat slightly, closed his eyes, and nodded off almost immediately. In all honesty, she knew the only reason he agreed to rest was because it was nighttime and all the great scenery was obscured by darkness. They had just reached Jeffrey's Bay when she turned off for their place on the beach, giving a wave out the window as Garrett continued into town. She checked out several places before deciding on where they would stay. This one was only three units, but they were luxurious and located right on the ocean. The section of beach in front of the unit was listed as one of the spots for experienced surfers, but when she talked to the woman handling the rentals, it was explained that one could travel any direction on the long stretch of coastline and end up with everything from areas suitable for beginners, all the way up to the pros and kamikazes. AJ told her he was dying to try Paradise beach, which was listed as to only be attempted by the pros and kamikazes—basically by the suicidal. She reminded him the dying part could be real if he got carried away.

She pulled up to the gated and covered parking area and pushed the button. Within a few seconds, a man with a heavy British accent answered.

"Hi," she shouted into the speaker box, "I'm Cass Henley. We have reservations for this week."

"Oh, yes, Ms. Henley. I'll buzz you in. Just pull straight ahead into the first spot in our car park. I'll be down in a moment."

A dull buzz sounded, and the iron gate slowly creaked open.

As soon as she turned off the engine, she leaned over and kissed AJ's cheek, "Hey, we're here, sleepy-head."

His eyes barely blinked open, and then shut immediately. "Just a few more minutes, Mom," he mumbled, trying to turn his back to her.

She laughed as she reached over and grabbed his crotch. That woke him up. What was even funnier was she could tell he really had no clue where he was or who was tinkering with his private toy.

"Sorry," she said, continuing to laugh, "but, I'm not your mother."

"Ah, crap, Cass! You scared the..." He looked around in his stupor, "We're here?"

"Yep," she said, opening the door to the Jeep to hear the sound of crashing waves twenty meters away. She inhaled deeply, "Wow, smell that salty air."

He stretched and yawned, "I'm still bushed."

"In about fifteen or twenty minutes, you are going to bed but we have to get upstairs first."

"Ms. Henley?" came a voice from the rear of the Jeep.

She turned to see an older, overweight man, with a balding, red scalp, and a big double chin. He was pushing a luggage carrier, and smiling.

"Hello, I'm Wally. You spoke with my wife, Meredith, on the telly yesterday."

"Hi, Wally. I'm Cass and this is my..." she paused for a millisecond. She'd never called anyone her fiancé before, but since he was, she continued, "...my fiancé, AJ Lisowski."

"Oh, yes, you are the big shot reporter with the magazine."

AJ gave a faint smile, "I'm a writer."

Cass could tell Wally was oblivious to the difference, and she could almost pick the words 'What's the difference?' off his slightly puckered lips—which he wisely kept closed.

"Well, all righty then, let's open the boot and load up your bags on the trolley here and—"

When Cass opened the back of the Jeep, Charlie barked, causing Wally to jump.

"Oh, yes. I recall my wife did say you have a little doggy. Cute little fellow," he continued. "She did tell you we can't have barkers, didn't she?"

"Yes, and he rarely ever makes a peep, he's just tired of traveling."

They loaded their bags and Charlie's crate then headed for the elevator. Cass was surprised such a small place would even have an elevator, but it was pretty posh, and posh rarely likes to walk up and down steps.

"There is a dog run on the west end of the building you can access from inside the car park. It is safe to venture in there after dark—well, safe as long as you watch where you step," Wally chuckled as the doors opened on the second floor. "But we don't recommend you leave him out there alone. Such a nice little fellow could bring a pretty penny. And make sure you keep your vehicle locked. We don't have problems due to our secure car park, but around town you will want to be remembering that tidbit. Crime is what happens in a moment of opportunity, and the guv'nor says if we have no opportunities then we'll have no crime."

"Good philosophy," AJ agreed.

Wally opened the door to their spacious unit and placed the key in AJ's hand. "Enjoy your stay. We have a small office on the bottom, east end of the building. Mornings until ten we have fresh fruit, juice, tea, coffee, and fresh made pastries and muffins. You can sit out on our beach patio and..." He droned on.

It dawned on her that Wally loved to talk, insensitive to how late it was, or how exhausted they both looked. "Thank you so much, Wally," Cass said, smoothly slipping a tip into his palm as she gave him a nudge out the door.

AJ smiled when the door closed, "I thought for a minute he was going to come in and have a seat."

"Huh," she said, rolling her eyes, "I haven't been a bitch for days now, but I think that would have set me off. I'm going to feed Charlie then take him out to the dog run. Why don't you relax in the shower and get ready for bed?"

"I'll do the dog; you do the shower," he said trying to pull Charlie's leash from her hand.

"You know I didn't realize how very protective you are. Have you always been like this?"

"Nah, just ever since you wanted to drive off on a four-wheeler and I asked to tag along. I don't know why, but I couldn't take the thought of you being by yourself then, and I still can't. Weird, huh?"

She wasn't letting go of the leash.

He tugged a little harder, "I won't rest if you're outside, so you might as well let me do this."

"All right," she caved, "but let me give him a small container of moist food while we put away our bags, that way he'll have something he needs to do when he gets down there."

"Deal."

She took his bowl to the kitchen. Charlie usually ate dry dog food, but she kept small cans handy for treats and nights like tonight. He ate with hardly pausing to taste it, and then lapped down several ounces of bottled water. He would be okay for ten or fifteen minutes before he needed to go out, so she headed for the bedroom and found AJ hooking up his computer.

"Oh, no you don't."

"Cass, I'm just putting it on charge; no writing tonight, I promise."

"Wow, check out the balcony," she stated as she opened the big sliding doors and felt the bite of cool night air flood the room. She gazed out on the moonlit beach, watching the swells blowing ashore.

He came up behind her and wrapped her in his arms, "Even in the dark, it's beautiful."

"Too bad it's too cold to skinny dip."

She was teasing, but he took her seriously. "No way. You'd be a late night snack for a big shark. These waters are teaming with whites."

"Is that what your feature story is going to be about?"

"My boss would kill me if it was. No, I'm doing the feature for our travel magazine. Billabong and another group of sponsors contacted the magazine to see if we could generate more press for the upcoming pro surfing tournament. My article will be on the cover story coming out two weeks before the tournament."

"Oh, I see. So, mentioning these waters are like the ocean-predator version of McDonalds wouldn't send a rush of tourists down here, huh?"

"Actually, it's kind of like NASCAR. People have a morbid inner nature, whether admitted or not. They go to the races and secretly hope to see a bad wreck. I told my boss, I could pitch it with the shark angle and the place would be filled."

"Of those secretly hoping to watch some pour soul be eaten?"

"Yeah, but honestly their record isn't bad. Florida has triple the number of attacks, but when you throw the words great white shark out there, people freak."

Cass laughed as she considered why, "Yeah, because a black tip taking a taste of you sounds survivable; but a great white taking a sample sounds catastrophic."

"True."

"Have you had any run-ins with sharks?" she asked. She shrank her shoulders under his warm biceps as she pulled his arms to cover her.

"Several, to be honest. I did a story in Bali a year ago, and I figured I'd do a little surfing while I was there. They basically don't have man-eaters, mostly just reef sharks which are insanely curious. I wiped out on my board and was just about to get back on when I felt a hard hit to my right side. It was a damn tiger shark, which is rare for there; he peeled up my side. It looked like I had a bad case of road rash."

"You didn't have a suit on?"

"Nah, the water is warm there; I like warm water," he said, kissing her temple.

Charlie came out and weaved between their legs, and stared at the scenery; his blunt little nose taking in all the scents on the air.

AJ looked down, "You gotta go outside?"

Charlie looked up at the mention of going outside and emitted a very small bark.

"Shhh," AJ said as he pulled the leash from his pocket, "you'll get us tossed out of here, buddy—then who would Wally talk to?"

While AJ walked the dog, she unpacked their clothes and placed them in the dresser, and then stripped down to her undergarments and headed for the bathroom. The entire condo was beautiful, but the bathroom was a dream for two. There was a gas fireplace, and an oversized, round hydrotherapy tub in one section, but what made the bathing area even more impressive was a massive shower head about two feet in diameter located in the ceiling above the tub. In the corner of the room was a glass enclosed rain shower with steam heads, and a waterfall ledge. She found the controls for the fireplace and the dimmer for the bathroom lights, and then dashed back to the bedroom for the shaving bag; she would have a little surprise waiting for AJ when he returned.

He took longer than she expected but it worked perfectly with the filling of the tub. She had just slipped into the water when she heard him walking into the bedroom. Quickly, she turned on the overhead fixture and stood under the raining water as she waited for him to come around the corner.

"Sorry that took so long," he was saying before coming through the bathroom doorway, "but, believe it or not, Wally caught me outside at the dog run. I guess he knew we'd..." he stopped mid-sentence when he saw her.

She had a shaver in one hand and her shaving cream in the other, and water rushing over her body. "Sorry," she began, "but I don't have anything that smells manly, so you may come out of here smelling like a chick."

He laughed as he started stripping, "I don't think I'm going to be thinking about the fragrance."

What a perfect and relaxing way to end what had been a very long day. She positioned herself facing away from him, between his legs, as the jets pounded his tired muscles, and she lathered and shaved his legs. For his arms, she simply reclined against him and brought them around her shoulders then she turned toward him and finished his chest. "Okay, I'm turning the shower on, and I'll wash your hair and you can rinse and go crawl in bed."

"But, baby, what about you? I thought I'd do your legs."

"You're so tired you can barely—"

"Please. It won't take long, and I want to."

She relented, partly because she could tell he'd be disappointed if she said no, and partly because she enjoyed it so much the last time he did this for her, "All right, but then you hit the hay."

They changed positions as she leaned into the jets and let him work on her legs. It was so comfortable; her eyes began to grow heavy as she tipped her head back on the deck surrounding the tub.

"Okay," she said as he finished, "turn on the shower and I'll wash your hair."

He hit the release for the tub drain and stood up.

"No, don't drain it just yet; I have to finish something before I get out."

"What?" he asked as one eyebrow rose.

"I was gonna—I have to trim my—my bikini area," she stammered, yet wondered why it was so hard to tell that to him.

"Let me do it," he said, clearly excited with the idea.

"Look, you're good with that razor, but—"

"Trust me," he said, giving her a very sultry look, "I can handle it."

"I—I don't know."

He lifted her onto the rim of the tub and told her to recline on the deck.

"You have no idea how bad a razor nick can hurt down there."

"I won't nick you. Trust me, Cass," he said again, "lay down."

Reluctantly, she did as he asked, closing her eyes as he began to carefully work. It didn't take too long before he was telling her he had finished as he helped her to stand up in the tub, and turned on the shower head. They washed each other's hair as the tub drained, then grabbed their towels and climbed out. They were standing in front of the bathroom mirror as he kissed her neck and offered to hang up her towel. As soon as she turned loose of it, she saw what he'd done.

"You—you—"

"What?" he asked innocently, his hands slid around to her abdomen.

"You trimmed it in the shape of a heart."

"I thought it was really cute."

She twisted in his grip to face him, smiling slightly, "I take it you've done this before."

He gave an impish look, "Swimsuit models have to keep things well trimmed. You're not mad are you?"

She seemed to be considering his question when she went back to smiling and told him no. "Come on. It's late, and you've got an early morning."

They curled up under the thick comforter, safe, warm, and happy.

Charlie woke her in the morning. He was used to being up early, but sunrise in South Africa in June wasn't until a quarter to eight. The weather wasn't much different temperature wise from when they left the UK. It had been late spring there, but here, south of the equator, it was the end of fall, so as the temperature warmed in the UK, Southern Africa cooled off. They were entering their winter short days where the sun rose late and set early, but

Charlie's internal clock told him they should have been up a while ago.

Cass felt his stubby nose and round head nudge up underneath her hand, trying to force her to pet him. As soon as her eyes fluttered open, he happily advanced to her face. She held him back; doggie breath first thing in the morning wasn't the best aroma. She sat up, glancing at the bedside clock. It was a couple minutes to seven.

She figured she let AJ sleep a little longer. Even though they behaved themselves last night and actually went to sleep instead of making love, she knew he had some extra rest to get caught up on. She grabbed the clothes she set out and tiptoed to the bathroom. They were meeting Garrett and Machi out on Paradise Beach by eight thirty, giving her enough time to make a pot of coffee then slip downstairs and pick up something for breakfast from the office.

But, unfortunately, Charlie had other ideas. She had just made her way back into the bedroom when she saw him bull-dozing his head under AJ's arm. Before she could grab him to make him stop, AJ's eyes blinked open.

Thanks to Charlie, they made it early to Paradise. Although AJ was writing the story, he still brought his camera along to take a few shots of his own. The only problem was every time she turned to look at him, the camera was pointed her direction. She finally threatened him sufficiently and he went back to shooting scenery. It wasn't hard to spot Garrett when he pulled into the beach parking lot in his bright orange Panda. He had another man in the passenger's seat which Cass assumed would be Machi. But when he climbed out of the car with a very expensive video camera, Cass had to ask under her breath, before the two reached them, why didn't Machi have a regular camera?

"He's a videographer; Garrett is the photographer."

She was clearly uncomfortable, "Is this going to be on television?"

"Relax, Cass. He usually shoots the scenes for the infomercials that run on the Travel show to highlight what's coming up in the next magazine. He rolls film constantly and then he takes stills from what he shoots for the story."

Having someone 'rolling film constantly' would be difficult to stomach for someone who didn't even like having her picture taken. He was filming them as he approached, but then lowered the camera when they were feet away.

"Machi! How are you, my friend?"

The tall, thin, black man's face spread into a wide grin as he hugged AJ, "I am well, lion tamer. Who is this beautiful woman?" he asked with a thick accent.

"Machi Okorie, this is my fiancée, Cassandra Henley. Cass, this is Machi, and you already met Garrett last night."

"I am pleased to meet you," Machi stated with an outstretched hand, "You are a very lucky woman to have such a good man."

Cass accepted his handshake, which was firm and warm even though his hand felt a bit leathered. "Yes, I realize that. It's very nice to meet you. AJ tells me you've done several stories together," she said, as she released Machi's hand and shook Garrett's.

"Oh, yes. Did he tell you that he saved my life on the last one?"

Cass could feel her eyebrows rising as she turned to AJ.

"Hey, I couldn't let that lion eat the best video man in the company. We were—"

"Let me tell it," Machi interrupted. "He may write a good story, but I *tell* a good story. We were doing a piece on the lions of Kruger Park, in Mpumalanga about seven months ago. We were driving along when we came across this big male and two cubs sleeping in the shade. AJ tells me, 'he must be *babysitting'* because there is no lioness around, you know," he said and then glanced around as if he was actually looking for one to appear on the beach.

"It was kind of funny to us, so we get out and sneak up to get some good shots. We are downwind, crouched in the brush, getting some very excellent pictures, when we both hear heavy breathing. We turn and there is the lioness. She had been sneaking up on us, as we were sneaking up on them! But she was licking her lips; I think I even saw her mouth watering," he said with a nervous laugh.

"AJ whispers to me that our only chance is to stand up and make lots of noise, hoping to scare her off. Me? I wanted to run for the truck, but he says, 'No, no, Machi, don't you dare run or she will eat you!' I do not want to be eaten, but my legs really want to run. We jump up and yell and make big noise like AJ said, and she turns away and starts to leave. I think, in my mind, it is okay now to run for the truck, so I run, and—"

"And," AJ spoke up, "she went after him."

"I know the lioness she is fast, but I was so scared I thought I would be faster. She was *very* fast. Before I knew what hit me, I am on the ground, on my back, screaming like a little sissy girl with the lioness's teeth in my shoulder. She is planning to invite me to her family dinner where I will be the guest of honor." At that moment he peeled back his shirt to reveal a horribly scarred shoulder.

Cass flinched without thought as she stared at the jagged pink marks against his chocolate brown skin.

"But no, my good friend," he said, as he gripped the back of AJ's neck, "he is not going to let me die so easy. He grabs my camera and starts bashing that lioness like a crazy man. He is yelling and shouting. I am looking and I see the big male lion heading our way, and now I am thinking that we are *both* going to be lion food. But she lets go and runs about ten meters away. Here comes the big papa," Machi's pitch was rising with the excitement of the story. "AJ, he still has my camera and he throws it like one of those American baseball players, and BANG!" he shouted, clapping his hands together. "He bounces it right off of big papa's nose. Before I can even think, AJ has me in the truck and we are driving away."

"I'm guessing you don't run from lions anymore," Garrett added with a grin.

"Me? No, no—I tell my boss I need a new camera. I say I want one with a better lens and better zoom because Machi is not playing with the lions again!"

They all laughed at his statement.

Cass bumped her shoulder into AJ's, "So, you're a hero, huh?"

"Nah, I just couldn't stand to lose the best videographer in the business; I knew I'd need him again someday," he teased.

AJ explained what he wanted to do with the article, and the kind of shots he was hoping to get while Cass took in the beautiful scenery. They decided to do a flyover for the first leg of their work, and then to head to one of the local surf rental shops so AJ could grab a board and they could get some actual surfing shots.

They hired a pilot from the Paradise airfield and took off in a helicopter for an early morning flight. It was spectacular as they watched a pod of dolphin frolicking in the surf, and a pair of Southern Right Whales with a calf. The pilot wasn't afraid to fly as low as they wanted, and at one point Cass thought he was going to dip the skids into the ocean, but he stayed just above the water. On their final pass along the coastline, they got to see their first great white swimming slowly about two-hundred meters off the beach on the western end of Paradise as surfers geared up to hit the water.

The pilot turned around as he considered a way to warn the surfers, but the white made an abrupt left and headed toward the deeper water to the south and disappeared from view. It was a little after eleven when they made it back to the airfield.

AJ hadn't been kidding about Machi shooting continual streams of video; it was as if he and the camera were one piece of equipment. It was a little nerve racking at first, and she had to bite her tongue a few times to keep her 'other' personality from coming to the surface, but eventually she became comfortable with it.

AJ told Cass he would teach her how to surf, but she refused. She knew how badly he wanted to get out on the waves and she wasn't going to put a damper on his fun while he tried to teach her the basics. "I'll hire the pro at the surf shop. He can teach me while you have some fun on the water. And who knows, maybe by tomorrow I'll be ready for you to take me out on a few waves." He'd already explained to her that learning to surf was a long process which he was still honing after years of practice, so it was doubtful she'd make any progress in a day.

"Are you sure?"

"I'll be fine. Go see if you can catch that elusive perfect barrel," she urged. He told her he'd dropped onto several barrels in the past, but had never been able to ride out of one before the tube collapsed.

The look on his face showed he was genuinely torn between staying with her and surfing.

"Go," she gave him a push, "besides, I want to watch you surf." She was lying through her teeth; she was going to be a nervous wreck the whole time he was out on the water. If she wasn't thinking about great whites, then she would be thinking about him getting hit in the head. "Go on. Show me how it's done."

He gave in; with a huge smile, he took his shortboard and headed for the surf.

The surf pro seemed more than happy to be her instructor for the afternoon, but said he wouldn't be able to start until he finished his shift in an hour. It was fine with her. She'd sit on the beach with Machi while Garrett used a water-proof camera and paddled out onto the waves with AJ. They were in an area designated for experienced surfers, but there were quite a few out on the water who looked like novices. Fortunately, they stayed out of the way of those who demonstrated obviously better skills.

She watched him paddling out in his wetsuit, even at a distance she could see why he had such fabulous arms; he really had to work to get out to where the bigger waves were breaking. Eventually it became more difficult to see him until Machi offered to let her look through his camera lens.

"This camera has excellent optics—see for yourself; watch him."

She knew he was being kind because her tension was apparent, but she gladly accepted his offer. Now she could see him clearly, even his expression as he started catching waves—and his expression was one of bliss. He had a determined smile each time he paddled for a wave, and then the smile would turn into some kind of serenity she'd never seen before as he rose up on the board and rode out the wave, snaking the backend of his board up and down the cresting water, pulling a few showy stunts just for the sheer joy of it. She didn't know all the surfing terminology, but Machi was explaining as they watched him, pointing out what was a cut-back, a tailslide and, at one point, a backside-tailslide.

"He's really good at this," she said in amazement, not that she doubted he would be, but it was so much more obvious in an ocean full of surfers that only a handful could do what he was doing.

The offshore breeze hovered around eight to ten knots when they arrived, but it was steadily picking up speed. Pretty soon, Cass noticed the incoming waves were getting taller and many of those without skills were exiting the water to sit on the beach and simply watch. There were a half dozen guys and one girl left to watch as the waves continued to grow. At one point, a really perfect wave, at least from a visual perspective, began to crest as AJ and another guy caught the wave at the same time. When AJ saw the other surfer, he turned off the wave and temporarily disappeared behind it.

"Now see," Machi stated, "another surfer might have beaten the hell out of that guy for dropping-in on his wave, but not AJ."

"Dropping-in? I thought that's what you did when you caught a wave?"

"No, no, that's just called to drop on a wave. Dropping-in is when another surfer steals someone's wave. AJ had the rights to the wave because of his position near the crest. He is very good at holding his temper, although I have seen him lose it before."

Cass was thinking about the look on AJ's face the day he tackled Dirk at the airport, even then he seemed well in-control.

"What made him lose it?"

"We were doing a story about one of the tribes in Madagascar when a young boy, maybe eight to ten years old, was brought into the camp. He and his father were from a rival tribe and had crossed over into their territory when they were hunting. His father ran away and left him behind. Several men from the village were very rough with him, and AJ, through our interpreter, asked them to stop. Two of the men stopped, but the third man had a mean spirit; you could see it in his eyes that he did not like AJ interfering. He began to jerk the little boy around by his hair. AJ grabbed his arm, and I thought to myself we are going to die. But the other tribe people just watched us with curiosity. He asked him again to stop.

"This boy was no threat to anyone, and AJ said he and I would return him to his village. The man looked at us, and then he turned back and punched the little boy with his fist. AJ went crazy! He beat the man to a bloody heap. I have never seen him so angry. Later, we found out the reason why the others in the tribe just watched and did not attack. Although AJ did not know it at the time, he was challenging their top warrior. Once he beat him, they considered AJ the top warrior."

"What happened to the little boy?"

"We took him back to his village. His father was very ashamed, and yet very grateful at the same time."

"Sounds like you and AJ have really had some wild adventures together."

"He is like my brother, my white brother," he laughed.

"I'm starting to learn that about him; he doesn't make friends, he makes family."

"You are a very special woman, and I can see in your eyes how much you truly love him. I have prayed for a long time for him to find a good woman. Most of them like him for what they see, but when they…" His voice faltered and he went back to watching them surf.

"What, Machi?" she asked as she rested her hand on his warm arm.

"I know what you have done for him," he said, tears filling his eyes. "The hope you have given him. He called and talked to me about you the other day. He said he was picking out a ring for you at the time. He said you were very special; I can see that now. I thank you so much for helping him get another chance at life." He put the camera down as he embraced her, both of them ready to sob.

When he released her, he suddenly smiled and began to shout, "Look! Look! He has caught a big wave!"

She held her breath when she saw him. It was a *huge* wave, and as he began to slide down the face of it, the wave curled completely over him creating a barrel. Her heart was beating a million-miles-an-hour as she wondered where he was. She couldn't see him, and all she could think about was him getting tumbled under all that power and force. Machi put the camera back in her hands and told her to look. She could just make out the tip of his board shooting along the water at the ever-lengthening end of the barrel. Suddenly he emerged, just ahead of the mouth of the tube as the crowd on the beach cheered him on. The barrel collapsed, but he rode out the last of the wave and then kicked up the backend of his surfboard and gave a victory jump into the water.

"Oh my God, he did it!" she said, back to crying again as she gave Machi another hug. "He said he's been trying to ride through a barrel for the longest time."

"We must celebrate this with him tonight! I know a wonderful restaurant both of you will love, if you wish, of course."

"Definitely. You know if AJ is your white brother than that means you're going to be my brother-in-law, and we can't have a celebration without family."

He gave a big laugh and nodded his head as he went back to filming.

She was aware of something she'd never felt in her life: family in this context was a good word. It had never been good for her before. Being part of AJ's world was changing her in ways she never imagined. She told him she wanted to carry his baby, and she meant it with every fiber of her body, but now it filled her with hope, hope for a family, a real family, not the dysfunctional, hell-riddled mess she had been raised in. There was a chance now that she would finally discover what a real bond between people could mean. Real love, real connection, and real concern between human beings washed over her like the big wave that covered AJ. She liked it.

Eventually, the surf pro found her sitting on the beach. She'd completely forgotten about signing up for the lessons in her AJ-watching oblivion. He was an Australian, appearing to be in his mid-forties. He wasn't a bad looking guy, but certainly one who you could tell held a very high opinion of himself. She'd seen that swagger many times from men who thought they were impressing her with their manly charms.

He started with the fundamentals, explaining to her about the surfboard parts: the deck, the rails, and the fins. He talked about using wax so her feet could grip the board. The whole time, she was wondering when she would get to put it in the water.

"Now you're going to learn the proper way to paddle the board, and... Where are you going?"

"I'm going to go up to the bathrooms and put on my wetsuit."

"No, love, you're not gonna be in the wat'a just yet. You learn to paddle on the beach, first. You won't be in the wat'a t'day."

She leveled her eyes at him and growled, "Wanna make a bet?"

She spent the next hour learning how to mount the surfboard, how to lay on it and paddle, how to make it through oncoming waves with either a duck dive or a turtle roll, and how to turn the board onto a wave. She learned all of this while on the beach—which she thought was dumb—the water seemed the more logical place, yet he swore this was how everyone learned. He was ready to teach her how to pop up and take the proper stance on her board when she turned to look at Machi, surprised to find AJ and Garrett sitting with him. Evidently, they had been out of the water for a little while and were observing her take lessons.

She was ready to quit and join them, but AJ told her to keep going. She was still facing them when her instructor said it was time to figure out if she was a regular footer or a goofy footer—and he promptly shoved her forward toward the guys, nearly knocking her face first in the sand.

"You son-of-a-bitch!" she snapped, as she turned on him.

"You're a regular footer," he stated, putting his hands in front of himself just in case she took a swing. "Sorry, love, but that's the easiest way to tell which is your dominant foot."

AJ was laughing, "Don't kill him, honey. He's telling the truth."

He went on to explain that because she stepped forward with her left foot, her right foot was actually dominant and would be used to control the back of the surfboard. Then he helped her with the proper stance, bending at the knees, arms out, and hands horizontal. But when he gripped her hips and saddled up too close behind her as he talked about balance, AJ suddenly appeared at her side.

"That's enough. I'll teach her the rest," his tone left no room for doubt that he wanted the guy to get his hands off her.

He seemed to ignore AJ at first, but he cautiously stepped from behind her off to the side. "That's really up to you, love," he began, "you have me for anotha' hour. I think you're right, I could get you in the wat'a t'day."

"No, I'm done," she said, as she reached backward and grabbed AJ's hands, pulling him against her back, "my personal surf pro can teach me the rest."

He gave her a look which seemed to say he felt there was no way AJ was better at this than he was, but then he sighed, "All right. Good-luck, love." He turned to AJ, "I haven't told her about undertow, rip tides, and such; I hope you know what you're doing, mate."

"Believe me," AJ stated as his grip on Cass tightened, "I'm not going to let anything happen to her."

"I saw you in the barrel," she whispered, as she felt him place a slow, cool kiss on her neck.

"It was freaking awesome! It was the perfect green room. I wish you could have been in there with me."

"So, was it better than sex?" she asked, quiet enough that Machi and Garrett wouldn't hear her. She had been studying up on surfing before they got to Africa and one thing which struck her as interesting was many people wrote that surfing the perfect barrel or tube was the greatest high, even better than sex. "Everybody says it is," she continued. She could feel his pelvis pushing hard against her ass as his breath fell on her ear.

"All I can say is those poor saps never had sex with you. No, it wasn't; it was really good, but not quite that good. But you know what's funny," he went on as he kissed her ear, "I don't know if it was shooting the barrel or watching you up on this board, but I'm so horny right now I think I could do you on this beach in front of everyone."

"AJ," she whispered.

"What?"

"You'd better act like you're teaching me how to surf because if you step away from me right now you're going to have a big and very obvious problem," she said, referring to the fact she could feel exactly how aroused he was at the moment. And considering the tight fit of the wetsuit, it wasn't going to leave anything to anyone's imagination.

He laughed and then suddenly leaned hard with his right foot causing the board to tip slightly on the hump of sand under it, "Okay, baby, here we go." He rocked and swayed the board with his hands on her hips, telling her how to improve her stance. By the time he was done, they were both laughing.

"Okay, I've got the mechanics down," she stated. "I mean, with all the engineering and physics I know, I understand how it's supposed to work, but I just over-think the whole balance thing. Do you want me to get my suit on?"

AJ turned and looked back at Machi and Garrett, "Hey guys, what time is it?"

"Almost three," Machi answered as he looked at his phone.

"Well, I'm starving, so I'm sure everyone else is. How about we hit our rooms for a little while and then meet for dinner? We can get more shots tomorrow."

"Sounds good to me," Garrett stated as he rose from the sand. "The salt is making me itchy anyway. I guess you'll have to wait to get into the water, Cass."

She only smiled. She knew why AJ wanted to call it an early day.

"I am buying dinner," Machi spoke up. "Where are you staying?"

Cass gave him the address to their condo. He said he and Garrett would be there by six p.m., and then he was taking them to The Potters Place for a night of music and good food.

They carried their boards to the Jeep and secured them onto the roof rack, then he told her to give him a minute in the rental shop and he would be back. When he returned, he was carrying an enormous surfboard that must have been ten feet long.

"What in the world do we need that for?" she asked as she helped him lift it up onto the rack.

AJ pulled the strap over it and fastened it down, "This is a classic longboard. Tomorrow, you and I are going to do a little double surfing on it so I can teach you about balance."

"Well, I hope you bought a helmet because if you're going to balance me on that thing I have a feeling we'll be spending more time under it than on it."

"You might be surprised how easy it is to use this giant, even for a beginner."

She had her doubts, but she kept them to herself as she drove back to the condo.

Since it was daylight, AJ didn't give her too much guff about walking Charlie. She took him down to the dog run and let him enjoy himself for a little while. Wally was outside, but he was trimming hedges, so he didn't have time—thank goodness—to stop and talk. She took the stairs up to the second floor just to give Charlie a little more exercise. He had been cooped up most of the day, so a trip outside was something she knew he craved. Once back in the condo, she refilled his dry food and then tossed his tennis ball across the floor a few times before retreating to the bedroom. AJ had his wetsuit and beach clothes air drying on a hook out on the balcony. He was parading around in the buff as he laid out his clothes for dinner.

She came up behind him and allowed her palms to glide smoothly from the center of his backbone up to his shoulders and down to his hips. "Your skin is pretty cold for someone who had on a suit," she commented.

"Yeah, the water here is chilly, and the fact that I was out there for quite a while doesn't help. Anyway, a hot shower is going to feel really good." He turned and looked at her, "That is as soon as we get you out of those clothes."

He tried to offer his assistance, but she refused his help, and instead did a slow striptease all the way to the shower doors. She turned on the water and pulled him inside as the hot rain rushed down, and the steam heads began to smolder. He had such a serious expression that she wondered if he was feeling okay.

"I just want you so badly right now, baby," he said as he pressed her against the wall. "I wanted to wait until I could get you in the bed, but damn it, Cass, I've got a fire going that just won't go out." He buried his face into her neck and bit down on her skin. "I'm going to try really hard not to be rough."

She cupped his face in her hands. His eyes seemed as dark and turbulent as the need she felt coming from him. "I'm not china; I won't break. I'll tell you if you do anything wrong, but I want you, too. I trust you, no matter what," she said, wrapping her arms around his neck and tasting that burning need in his kiss.

He lifted her off the floor, and she wrapped her legs around him. He slowly slid her down as their bodies connected. It was intense and almost painful as his hips thrust upward and her weight came down. She cried out and then bit her lip when he paused.

"Don't stop," she choked, "I'm okay; you're just really deep right now. I like it; don't stop."

He wedged her between the wall and his body. She reached up and gripped the towel rings on either side as his stroke flooded her senses with pleasure. She was able to touch the floor at this point, but just barely as he continued to push her upward. Her mind was tangled in thoughts, but they were all about him. She could see him on the waves, she watched as he emerged from the barrel, the feeling as his body was press to hers on the surfboard, the look on his face the first night when she told him not to pull away, his expression in the store when he realized she didn't want protection, the long night meshed in each other's arms in Bobby's apartment, they were all there, all cumulating inside her as he pushed her body to the peak and then seemed to hold her on the edge without ending the sensation.

Then, like the water rushing over them, she screamed down the other side of pleasure as the feeling rocked every nerve ending in her body. She released the towel rings as his muscled arms wrapped around her ribcage. She felt so tiny in his hold at the moment—enveloped by him as if he was a giant, and she was nothing more than a wisp of air.

"Lay down," she pled, still gasping for breath from the sensory explosion that had rushed through her veins. There was a long, teak bench off-center inside the shower where the steam was thick and hot. He obeyed as he laid back and watched her straddle his hips. She grabbed the bench as she began to allow her body to wave against his. She didn't know how she did it, it just came natural for her as the motion rose from somewhere in her thighs, through her buttocks and pelvis, and into her spine.

He was getting loud as he told her how incredible it was to be part of her body. Telling her how fabulous she felt to him, and how he loved her so deeply. She sensed his intensity climbing as she built toward her second height of ecstasy. She wanted her orgasm to be timed with his, but the sensation was too strong to be suppressed. A powerful spasm of sublime pleasure stopped all motion; it was so intense that her muscles seemingly lock down on him, refusing to allow her to move. She felt his hands gripping her, then the sensation of movement as she found herself with her back on the bench and he was above her.

"Don't let me hurt you," he breathed in a panted rush, pushing her legs wide apart, his hands gripping her knees as he seemed to drop all his power inside her.

This time she cried out in genuine hurt, but she sunk her nails into the cheeks of his ass to keep him from backing off. It was the perfect blend of pleasure and pain, but yet without the violence and ugliness she'd always known. This was another new experience with him, and she wanted more. She would have never believed she could advance through the sensations as quickly as she found herself, once again, ready to dive off into the center of elation. It was a dive she wouldn't make alone. She felt him cresting as he told her he couldn't hold back any longer. On his final thrust, she tumbled over the edge and joined him somewhere in a perfect emotional sea for two.

They were both breathing hard as they stayed in the lover's embrace long after the sensations passed. He kissed her between breaths, and told her he was sorry if he hadn't been gentle enough.

"Adam," she said, immediately getting his attention by using his first name. "Don't say you're sorry for something so flawless. Am I going to be sore? Yeah, I think so. Did you hurt me? Not in any sense of the word that's bad. There was nothing ugly. It was like every experience I've had with you; it was new and perfect."

He put his head down on her chest, swallowing loudly, "I'd never forgive myself if I did something to bring up old memories for you. I don't know what got into me, but it was like I was on an adrenaline high. Ever since I watched the guy from the surf shop put his hands on you, I got so freaking amped, I wanted to do two things: tear him into pieces, and disappear inside of you."

She rose to a seated position on the bench, taking him with her. She tipped his chin up, but didn't say anything.

"Cass, have I told you how beautiful your eyes are? I thought when I met you that you had colored contacts in, but I eventually realized that really is the color of your eyes. They remind me of the inside of the barrel—just a stunning blue-green like the ocean. If you get pregnant, I hope the baby has your eyes."

"It's funny you used the word stunning because that was exactly what I thought about your eyes when I first met you. I've been hoping he'll have your eyes, and your nose, and cheeks, and face, and—"

He laughed and gave her a big smile, "And if it's a girl?"

She didn't have an answer at the moment as she considered it.

"Do you think it's too soon to use that tester?" he asked while she was temporarily speechless.

"Yeah, I'm pretty sure it is way too early. My period should start in another eight or nine days, if it doesn't, I'll take the test."

"And you're sure this is what you want?"

"About as sure as you said you were when you gave me this," she said, holding up her left hand.

"Then it has to be one hundred percent," he said, and kissed her. "Do you suppose we should actually take a shower while we're in here?"

She burst into laughter as she stood to her feet, "That might be a good idea."

They got dressed and ready for their evening out, but decided to cuddle together on the bed for a little while—the next thing they heard was AJ's cell phone ringing—they had both fallen asleep.

"Sure, come on up," he said into the receiver, "I'll open the door and be standing on the walkway."

Cass went out and seated herself on the over-stuffed couch, waiting for their visitors. Somehow she wasn't surprised when Machi came through the door with his camera rolling. "I know you aren't shooting anything for the magazine," she said with a hint of gruffness.

"Ah, but people like to see what kind of accommodations are available, so perhaps this will be in the magazine. May I look around?"

Charlie rounded the corner from the bedroom at the sound of a strange voice and began to bark at Machi and Garrett.

"Charlie; come," Cass said as she snapped her fingers. Charlie immediately quieted and ran to her side, shivering as he grumbled and growled at the intruders. "It's okay, they're good guys."

Garrett dropped down to sit on the floor, and he picked up Charlie's tennis ball. "Come on, boy. Want this?" he said as he shook the ball back and forth. Charlie stopped growling; he watched the ball intensely. Garrett rolled the ball across the floor and Charlie ran after it. He seemed a little torn as to what to do with it when he picked it up though.

"Come on," Garrett encouraged him, patting his thigh, "bring it back. Come on, Charlie."

Hearing his name called, he must have decided Garrett

couldn't be too bad as he slowly brought him the fuzzy green ball. After that, they made a tentative friendship, but he still seemed really suspicious of the tall man with the strange piece of equipment growing out of his head. AJ walked Machi through the condo and then, to Cass's relief, the camera came down. Even Charlie seemed relieved to see it was a man and not some strange creature. He approached cautiously and sniffed Machi's pants. Machi lowered his hand and allowed the dog to sniff it, then carefully scratched between Charlie's ears.

Cass gave Charlie a few more minutes to get acquainted and then told him it was time to get in his box. He was well trained and well mannered as he ran immediately to his crate and got inside. She latched the door and pushed a small treat through the bars.

"He is a smart little dog," Machi observed. "I have never seen one do that on command."

"Well, you know what they say guys; smart owner, smart dog," AJ quipped.

"Is that so?" Garrett questioned with a sly grin, "Does this mean Cass is going to eventually have you that well trained, too?"

They all laughed, even though Cass felt a little insulted by the remark, but AJ's laugh was more of a 'ha, ha, very funny,' sarcastic kind of laugh.

Dinner was a little unusual, but extremely delicious. The Potter's Place was a combination of a restaurant, coffee house, performing arts building, and shop. They finished their meal and then feasted on a sampling of incredible homemade cakes and pies served with piping hot coffee. The restaurant had a guitarist, Guy Buttery, playing who was, according to Machi, quite famous in South Africa. The music was good and the camaraderie excellent as Machi filmed and the guys talked about different things they had done while working for the magazine. Garrett had only worked with AJ twice before, but like everyone else, they made a close friendship in a short period of time. She was surprised however, to learn Garrett was the one who accompanied him down to New Zealand and witnessed the tattooing of AJ's arm.

"That was the wickedest thing I've ever seen," he confessed. "They went through this big ritual, and then they brought out that funky chisel and started hammering the design into his skin. What a bloody mess. They kept smacking the chisel, and one of the women kept mopping up the blood. I personally thought he was crazy. He never said a word but I could tell how much he was hurting. Then, when it was time to pack it up and head back to the States, he couldn't leave because of the infection. It looked like voodoo-medicine to me, but they eventually cured him."

"Yeah, and when I get past all this brain surgery business, I'm taking Cass down to visit my Maori family, and I'll let them do my other arm so she can see it for herself."

What he said surprised her so thoroughly she couldn't believe it; he was finally seeing himself as having a future. She felt, even though he hadn't said it out loud, he'd viewed the surgery as the end. She knew he didn't believe, until now, that he would wake up once they put him under. Now, he was seeing a glimmer of hope. Hope, she knew, was as essential to his recovery as the surgery itself. She wanted to cry, but at the same time she was so happy she couldn't tear up. But, she could offer him something.

"And right after they tattoo you, I'll get one, too."

His eyebrows went up, "I thought you said they weren't sexy on a girl?"

"Well, I want one now, on one condition."

"What?"

"You make the decision about what I get and where I get it."

"Whoa," Garrett said with a small laugh, "you're either crazy or you trust him completely."

She leaned against AJ as he leaned back, giving each other a brief kiss. "I trust him," she said quietly. She would have stated it louder, but the tears finally found her eyes, and if she'd given it anymore volume, they would have washed down her face.

"So when is the big day?" Machi asked, pointing to the ring on Cass's finger.

"In about five or six days," AJ said with a huge smile. "As soon as our feet hit American soil, I'm finding a courthouse and making it official."

"But most women want a big wedding," Garrett stated looking at Cass. "I'm sure you want both of your families and friends to—"

Cass couldn't help the unintentional stiffening that washed over her when Garrett mentioned the word family.

AJ caught it quickly and cut him off, "No, we both want it now, and we want it *private*." The way he stated it left no room for Garrett to doubt he should drop the subject.

Machi caught it too, and he decided to lighten the moment by lifting his glass. "Here is to the start of a beautiful life together."

The glasses were raised and clinked in agreement.

"So, where are we going in the morning, boss?" Machi asked.

AJ frowned, "Don't call me boss. We're going to the Point. I hear that's a great spot for longboarding. Cass and I are going to try a little double-team on the surfboard."

"The writer is always the boss on a shoot," Garrett stated matter-of-factly. "And you should be happy because as soon as you tie the knot, she's gonna be the boss," he laughed. "She'll have you trained better than that little dog of hers."

"I can't stand it anymore," Cass said, the sound of ire climbing into her voice as her inner bitch was aroused. "You don't have either a very high opinion of women or marriage, or both."

His face turned scarlet, "No, it's... I'm sorry, Cass. I guess you could say I got a bad taste in my mouth from my short marriage."

She noticed, from the corner of her eye, AJ seemed to be turning red as well. "What?" she finally asked.

"We had a mutual acquaintance," AJ stated, "that was how we met, then I helped him get a job with the magazine."

"Who?"

"AJ's first fiancée," Garrett said looking down at the table.

"Kristen?" she asked, suddenly understanding why all the embarrassment. "You married—"

"Yeah, but I didn't know AJ at the time," he quickly added. "The two of them had broken up and I was helping with a swimsuit shoot for another magazine. Seems that girl had her wedding already planned out and was just missing a groom."

"And in stepped—"

"Stupid," Garrett finished the sentence for him. "I met AJ at the wedding. He offered to help me get something permanent with National Geographic. Kristen turned out to be a huge mistake," he said, shaking his head. "I thought she was a little bossy before I married her, but I swear as soon as she slipped that golden band on my finger, she put another one through my nose. She wanted her way all the time, and if I didn't do exactly what she wanted, she made me suffer, badly. Six months later, I was filing for divorce."

"When he told me how she treated him after they got married, it was the first time I could honestly say I was glad I had my aneurysm. But," he added with a smile, "I had a feeling all along what she was going to be like. Cass is a different creature entirely.

There won't be any bait-and-switch after the altar; I'm going to be happy for the rest of my life."

"And I can see that," Garrett threw in. "I'm sorry about the negativity, Cass. I was pretty much an optimistic guy before she came along. I can tell you're very different, in a good way. Don't be afraid to remind me if I say something out of line again."

"That I don't have a problem with," she said with a small laugh. "Matter of fact, if anything, I think AJ has found the reverse with me. I was 'bitch extraordinaire' when we met, but somehow he saw the person I could be under the anger."

Machi burst out laughing as all eyes turned toward him. "Sorry, sorry, it is just I was thinking about when the Aussie from the surf shop pushed you. I think I saw the other side of you."

They all laughed in agreement.

CHAPTER SIXTEEN

The next morning found them suited up and trying out the longboard while Machi filmed from the beach, and Garrett paddled along side. It was a whole new animal being out on the water. Suddenly, Cass was very aware of why they started new surfers out on the sand. Knowledge and logistics were one thing, but putting them into practice was another. She managed to dump them in the water the first dozen times she tried to stand on the board, but AJ was a patient and encouraging teacher, and she told him exactly that as they sat together on the board and waited for the next wave to come along.

"I think, if you ever give up the magazine, you should try teaching. You'd be fabulous; you have the knack."

"Yeah, I think I could eventually see myself as the surf pro for a—"

"No, silly. I don't mean give up the magazine to teach surfing, I mean teaching for real—in a classroom. You're patient and innovative, kind and supportive; you'd be a great teacher."

He leaned across her shoulder and placed a kiss on her salty, wet cheek, "That's one I haven't tried, but it doesn't sound too bad; I'd have all summer to surf."

She laughed as another wave came their way and he told her they were going to try again. They turned the board toward shore and began to paddle hard as Cass felt the surge of the wave coming up under them and he simply told her, "Now!"

This time, she didn't tip the board when she popped up, but

she knew he was doing all the work to keep them balanced. Something clicked in her mind, and she felt she finally resolved her issue of leaning too hard to one side. It wasn't easy, but they caught their first wave and were actually upright and surfing down its face. What a thrill! Now she knew why he enjoyed it so much. This wasn't mechanical, or man-made; there was a pureness to this sport between man, Creator, and creation. It was an almost religious experience as the wave dissolved to foam—then she lost it, tipping them over once again.

She only allowed him to give her a few more lessons before begging him to go grab his board and have some fun on his own. The wind was picking up and the waves farther out were growing taller. He relented with a kiss and a smile as they paddled for shore.

She didn't get to watch him quite as much as yesterday because she grabbed her funboard and was busy trying to put all she learned into practice. She did manage to get herself upright on one nice wave, but her elation only lasted about two seconds before she was tossed back into the surf. She had enough. She figured she had swallowed at least half the ocean, and tumbled more times than a pair of dice in Vegas. Her body felt as if it weighed twice its normal weight as she drug herself from the water to collapse into a grateful heap on the sand. Machi was there with a video camera, a smile, and a bottled water to rinse the salt from her mouth.

The remainder of the week was more work than fun. AJ and the guys spent two days without her as she contacted her teams in the UK and caught up on their progress. Rubio was now in charge of the information downloads, and when he transferred it to her, she was pleasantly surprised to see the teams were making steady advances without her, or dumb-ass Dirk, pushing them along. She spoke to the leader of each team, and handled the few problems that had cropped up in her absence, one of which required a phone call to Bobby.

He was excited to hear how the work was going in Africa, and about AJ finally getting to shoot the perfect barrel, actually numerous barrels over the last several days. She also asked him to put an offer in for her on the property where Kingdom Hill was located. An American could buy land in the UK, but (like everything else) it was paperwork intensive and a bit clogged by bureaucracy. Bobby wouldn't have those kinds of issues, and she knew she could trust him to do this for her. She would provide the money, and he would provide the citizenship.

Someday, when everything settled down, she and AJ would go through the governmental hoops and assume ownership, but, for now, she wanted the property secured. And although she told AJ she wanted to buy it long before they left the shadow of Kingdom Hill, he had no idea she actually started the process. She wanted it to be a surprise, one she knew, without doubt, would thrill him.

The last thing she did after she finished her work for the business was to start the story of Kingdom Hill as he had asked. Her last day in Africa was spent sitting on the balcony of their room with a computer in her lap and a story pounding through her head. AJ didn't go to any other location today, he simply surfed right off the beach from their condo. She could look up and watch him then go back to reliving the beautiful telling of a tragic story. How ironic for her to be able to see both sides of the beauty and the brutality.

She wrote from Magnus's point of view, and was literally shocked by how clearly it all came back to her. Mingled in the memories of the story, were the moments she spent with AJ under the hill—every moment, from the ache in her chest that she didn't realize was the beginning of falling in love, to the moment he told her he was dying, their first night in each other's arms, to learning she could trust him not to be like every other man in her life, to the first kiss she shared with him—they were all there. She changed in that place, and she would never go back to being the person she had once been. He may have captured her heart, but what he really did for her was to set her free, and she would love him forever for that precious gift.

AJ still refused to allow her to see what he was writing. Every evening she would ask him if he was working on his piece for the magazine and, every evening, he would get this sheepish look on his face and say, "No, not yet." He told her he couldn't turn off the novel he started, but that he would (reluctantly) stop and write his piece for the magazine *before* his deadline. He did, however, read what she was writing, and said she was doing a phenomenal job.

They were flying from Cape Town back to London's Heathrow and from there to Miami. AJ decided he wanted to marry her in Florida. She suspected it was because he wanted to get in a little more surfing, but he swore he wasn't going to touch a surfboard on their honeymoon. He did a little internet investigation on his own, and decided they would spend a few days after the 'I do's,' at a spa and resort called Little Palm Island. It was pricey, but it was also secluded and private, accessible only by boat. Charlie would not be joining them. When they arrived in Miami, he would continue on a flight bound for Texas.

It would take thirty-five hours before their feet touched American soil. AJ took one long, six hour nap when they left London, but all the rest of the time was spent on his computer. Just before the plane touched down in sizzling Miami, he announced he was finished.

"With the novel?" she asked, clearly shocked.

"No, baby; I finished my story for the magazine. The boss gave me another week, but I want this week to be all about us, not me trying to meet a deadline. Machi emailed me some fabulous stills, and Garrett gave me his choice pics before we left. I wrote the story, made my photo selections, and transferred the whole file to my boss in D.C. He's already emailed me back and said it was perfect—and he thanked me for not busting my expense account."

"Do you do that a lot?"

"I kinda like to... Yeah, okay, I do, but I prefer to think they simply don't make my account large enough in the first place. I promise, I'm not a high maintenance guy."

"Do you honestly think I'm worried about that?" she laughed. "If you don't have a problem having a wife who makes more than you do, then I don't have a problem with whatever *maintenance* you require."

"I guess, since my first expense on you is going to be the surgery, I actually am high maintenance, huh?"

"Nope, because once you marry me, it's *our* money, not just mine," she added with a soft smile.

"I didn't think about it before, Cass, but do you want a pre-nup? I wouldn't blame you."

She kissed him to shut him up, "You have to be kidding. We discovered a piece of ancient history worth multimillions, you earned my complete trust before you'd even kiss me, and you're asking *now* if I want a pre-nup? All I want from you is a promise that someday, when we have our first really big fight, you'll still be there for me. Don't ever leave me, AJ—I couldn't take that."

"Until God takes me home, Cass, I'll always be here for you."

People were disembarking from the plane, but they had to take a minute for one deep, heartfelt kiss.

When their lips parted, AJ smiled, "Let's go apply for that marriage license."

There was a three day waiting period, and the days passed quickly as they explored Miami Beach and worked on their respective writing projects. But nights were a different matter entirely. With a great degree of difficulty, they restrained themselves from sex for three endless nights. It was AJ's idea. He said he wanted to build up the tension leading to their first night as a married couple.

Cass thought it was difficult to use restraint during the early part of their relationship when he was waiting for her to reveal her past, but this was excruciating. She knew now what it was to truly and honestly make love. He created a need inside her, a need which craved to be a part of him with a necessity beyond primal and into the realm of something as essential to her as oxygen.

She didn't want to tell him that she didn't like his idea, but when they crawled into bed each night and he wrapped her in those muscled arms, she would lay awake for hours. When she could tell he was safely asleep, she would roll over and simply study his face. Eventually, she would doze off and, usually, when she woke in the morning he would be staring at her, apparently doing the same thing she had done in the night.

She wasn't nervous when their waiting period ended; she wanted to be his wife more than anything she'd ever wanted in her entire life. Bright and early on Monday morning, they stood before the courthouse notary who walked them through the exchange of the rings, and a simple set of traditional vows, finishing with their acceptance of each other.

"Do you Adam Jacob take Cassandra Diane to be your wife – to live together after God's ordinance – in the holy estate of matrimony? Will you love her, comfort her, honor and keep her, in sickness and in health, for richer, for poorer, for better, for worse, in sadness and in joy, to cherish and continually bestow upon her your heart's deepest devotion, forsaking all others, keep yourself only unto her until death do you part?"

"I will," he responded in deep sincerity.

"Do you, Cassandra Diane, take Adam Jacob to be your husband – to live together after God's ordinance – in the holy estate of matrimony? Will you love him, comfort him, honor and keep him, in sickness and in health, for richer, for poorer, for better, for worse, in sadness and in joy, to cherish and continually bestow upon him your heart's deepest devotion, forsaking all others, keep yourself only unto him until death do you part?"

"I will," she said through quivering lips as she fought back the tears.

"Then by the power vested in me by the State of Florida, I now pronounce you husband and wife. Congratulations, Mister and Misses Lisowski."

They left immediately from the courthouse and went to the marina where a seaplane was waiting to take them to Little Palm Island in the Keys. In little less than an hour, they were pulling up to the dock at the beautiful island resort. Attendants waited to take their bags and show them to their grand bungalow.

She had let him make all the arrangements because he said he wanted to surprise her—and he did.

It was incredible.

He rented the largest suite on the island. It was decorated in tropical charm with thatch on the roof, plantation shutters, slate floors, wrought iron chandeliers, wooden ceiling fans, imported island furnishings, and a private hot tub on the verandah overlooking the blue-green waters of the Atlantic Ocean.

"Oh, AJ, this is perfect," she marveled, as she stood on the balcony and stared at their section of private beach. "I think maybe I should let you make all the travel arrangements."

"Nah, I'm not that good. But this I knew had to be special, *Mrs. Lisowski*," he said as he guided her back inside toward the bed.

"I know you're never going to believe this, but would you mind if we waited until tonight?" It wasn't that she wanted to wait, but she had a surprise of her own planned, and tonight seemed more appropriate.

His forehead raised as a quizzical grin crossed his face, "You don't want to make love?"

"Oh, trust me, I do, but we've been patient for three days and it just seems—"

"It's okay, Cass. Yes, I'll wait. I booked us a massage anyway, so let's get comfortable and then head down to the spa."

"You went all out on this, didn't you?"

"Oh, yeah, baby. I decided I could get just as good on the details as you. We have a couple hours booked in the spa, a light lunch, and a snorkeling trip on one of their reefs, and then it's back here for a private dinner on Harbor Point Beach. How'd I do?"

"Mister Lisowski, you've been holding out on me. I had no idea you were so organized. I figured you to be more of a shoot-from-the-hip kind of guy," she giggled.

He pushed his groin into hers and wrapped her in a warm embrace, swaying his hips slowly back and forth, "Ooh, Cassandra, I *do* like shooting from the hip. I threw plans out the window when I didn't figure there was much left to my life, but now..." He swallowed and his eyes reddened. "Let's just say, you've got me planning once again."

Just one kiss and she was ready to throw *her plans* out the window and take him to the bed right now, but he put the brakes on.

"You must have had a reason for saying you wanted to wait, so let's wait, Cass."

The remainder of their day was luxurious and comfortable. The spa treatment included a Thai herbal therapy, a soaking tub for two, and an intense massage with hot river rocks being placed on the skin. Both of them fell asleep during the massage as every tension over the last several days melted into nothingness. The reef excursion was fun. Cass preferred diving to snorkeling, but AJ wasn't certified, and she knew with his aneurysm, it would be dangerous to descend even one atmosphere. She wouldn't take the chance of letting him get hurt.

Their wonderful day came to a close as they sat outside in the after-sunset glow and enjoyed a sumptuous meal on the beach. The table was placed in a private location with candles and tiki torches lighting the way. The food was exquisitely prepared, and served with minimal interruption.

Cass debated when to surprise him with the gift she had, and decided to wait until later, but she ended up being the one with the surprise. When they returned to their bungalow—after he insisted that he carry her through the doorway—she discovered he ordered a turndown package. While they had been having dinner, the staff placed dozens of roses in their room, scattered rose petals, and placed candles everywhere, and, on a table by the bed, sat a bottle of chilled champagne with a small tray of chocolate truffles and strawberries beside it.

"Damn, I'm good," he said with satisfaction, as he read the

expression on her face.

She tried not to laugh, but she couldn't help it.

He started to pour her a glass of champagne when she stopped him, "I don't drink."

"I know, Cass, but I thought tonight maybe just one glass to toast with."

She didn't say anything as she left his side long enough to go to her suitcase and pull out a small package wrapped in cobalt blue paper and tied with a silver ribbon.

"What's this?" he asked, as she handed it to him.

"A wedding gift," she replied.

"Is this why you wanted to wait to make love until tonight?"

She nodded, big swells of tears filling her bottom lashes.

He turned the package over in his hands and paused, "Cass, I didn't know we were supposed to buy a gift for each other."

"I don't think the bride and groom generally do this sort of thing, but I really wanted to give this to you, so please don't feel like you should have something for me. And besides, this whole honeymoon excursion couldn't have been a more perfect gift from you." She paused, and then reached out and touched his hand, "Open it."

He led her to the bed as they seated themselves on the edge. He removed the ribbon and paper to reveal a long, blue velvet box. He grabbed the hinged lid and started to open it then stopped, "It has to be a watch. That's the only thing that would fit in this box."

"Open it," she pled, bumping her shoulder into his.

The lid creaked open, and he simply stared at the contents. For a split second, she could tell he was mystified—then it hit him.

"Oh my God—oh my God," he breathed, "Oh, Cass, are you serious? Is this for real?"

"It's supposed to be ninety-nine-point-nine percent accurate, so yeah, it's for real—we've made a baby."

They both began to cry.

AJ struggled to speak, "How—how long? When did you find out?"

She wiped her eyes and smiled, "I knew I was late the day we touched down in Miami. I took the test the first night in our hotel room, but I wanted to wait and surprise you with it. I would toast with you, but I don't think alcohol is a good idea right now."

There wasn't any need to say anything else. This night would be long and good, gentle and slow. The days of waiting, their marriage, and now the news about the baby brought them closer than they had ever been, and neither one had ever been happier.

CHAPTER SEVENTEEN

The days and nights on Little Palm Island were a complete respite from the world. Other than the time they each took to write, nothing else invaded their time together. They slept late, relaxed on the quiet beach, and discussed baby names. Cass was convinced it would be a boy, and, if it was, she wanted him to be named after AJ.

"Then if it's a girl, she has to be named after you," he stated matter-of-factly.

"No," her reply was simple, fast, and stated with one-hundred percent conviction. "My old life isn't coming anywhere near this baby, even if it's only in name. She'll be an AJ."

"You want to name our daughter Adam Jacob?" he stated with teasing surprise.

"No. I want to come up with a girl's name, but using your initials, like Ashley Jean, or—"

"Don't use Ashley."

"Why not?"

"Old girlfriend issues."

"Oh, yeah, that would be bad. Do you have any ideas?"

"I have an idea, but I want to check some meanings on the internet before I tell you."

Cass only smiled. Nothing more was mentioned about baby names until their last night on the island. They were packed and ready for a flight to Texas in the morning. She needed to straighten out some things at the company, and there was the matter of her dad wanting to sign the business over to her, as well. She would take care of that before the crews finished in the UK because profits were still setup to be split three-ways—and she had no intention of sharing that massive check.

Her father said he didn't want a settlement from the business; Cass had built it up on her own, and he knew it. She'd made him a wealthy man, and his bank account was, according to him, fat enough without taking from the business. He never said he'd quit when he signed the company over to her; he still wanted to work and help her, but he would do it as her employee instead of her partner. He said that way he could bow out whenever he wanted to retire, and wouldn't have to worry about all the paperwork.

She wanted to believe that having AJ meet her father wouldn't be too difficult, but she was sick with nerves, or perhaps this was the start of the nausea that came with being pregnant, but in either case, she didn't feel well.

It must have been apparent to AJ because he was being extra sensitive to her needs. Ever since he learned about the baby, he wanted to cuddle and hold her all the time. It was some kind of instinctive protection thing, but now there were two people in his world to protect, and she could tell he liked the feeling of being their protector, their shelter from the world, and the person whom she and the baby depended on.

"Can I get you anything before we turn out the light?"

"No, I'm fine," she paused, and then confessed, "actually, I hate to say it, but having you meet my dad is bothering me."

"Cass, it's going to be fine. Did you tell him you married me?"

She shook her head no. She knew AJ told his parents what he was doing before they left Africa, but she still hadn't told her dad. All he was aware of was that Cass said she was bringing home someone very special to meet him, and that was it.

"You don't have to be worried about him being drunk. I've bartended enough to know how to deal with someone who's had a little too much alcohol."

"It's not that—okay, maybe it is that—but it still bothers me."

He kissed her tenderly and stared into her eyes for several quiet moments, "Please, don't let it bother you. It's going to be fine. Cass, no matter what happens in Texas, it isn't going to stop me from being in love with you."

He was pretty intuitive because he pinned her fear down to

exactly what was causing her anxiety. She felt all along that if he stepped one foot into her world, he wouldn't love her anymore. In his world, people were basically good, they cared about him, and about each other. Her world was different. Her family was in it for whatever they could take from each other, no matter the cost.

Her dad was actually the only one in their family who realized that without Cass and the business which she kept running, they would have scattered, and none of them would even think to speak to the others. As it was, what held her misfit group called 'family' together was the fact that she earned the money they fed off of like a pile of leeches—and she was getting ready to bring her most treasured possession into the blood-sucking group of parasites.

"I picked out a name," he whispered.

She understood what he was doing; he was planning to take her mind off the trip to Texas. She smiled, "Okay, so if it's a girl, what is her name going to be? Just remember, she's got to be an AJ."

"I liked the French spelling of Amy. So her first name should be A-i-m-e-e, Aimee, which means beloved."

"I like Aimee," she smiled. "And her middle name?"

"It has to be what you are to me. I told you I asked God for one more beautiful experience, and that's what you've been to me, Cass. It took a little while to dig out the real you from under the rubble, but I knew there was a jewel there. Her middle name should be Jewel. Aimee Jewel means beloved precious one. That's what you are to me, and that is what our daughter will be, too."

There wasn't any sense in fighting the tears or trying to hold them back. "Aimee Jewel is perfect, just like Adam Jacob."

AJ had this really mischievous grin on his face as he wiped away her tears.

"What are you thinking?"

His grin widened, "I was just thinking: what if it's twins? We might get to use both names, huh?"

"I don't feel so good," she stated as a sudden flood of nausea washed over her. She could tell he thought she was teasing because of what he'd said, but she really did feel sick—she needed to get to the bathroom—now! Her only thought at the moment was about all the hot butter she consumed with the stone crab claws she had eaten for dinner. She rose up and rushed away from him, but he was right behind her.

It had been years since she'd thrown up, and she'd forgotten just how much she hated it. But AJ was there gently rubbing her back and offering her a cool washcloth. She hoped this was something from dinner that didn't agree with her, but he ate the same food and wasn't feeling sick. She sighed as she hovered above the toilet, hoping and praying the whole time this was *not* how pregnancy was going to go for her. He helped her back to the bed, tucked her under the covers and then left her alone. She missed having him snuggled against her, but she was so miserable at the moment she could appreciate the time alone.

When morning came, she was awakened by a gentle kiss, and found a breakfast tray sitting beside the bed. Thankfully, she was feeling better.

"Eat your toast," he said, lifting it so she could take a bite. "I did a little research on the computer last night, about how to prevent nausea when you're pregnant."

"I think I ate a bad crab claw," she stated, defending her volatile tummy.

"I think the crab was fine. You had too much greasy butter."

"Ewe, please! Don't mention butter right now."

"Like I was saying, I read up on this last night. You need to eat crackers or dry toast throughout the day, and eat several small meals instead of three normal meals. Lots of fruits, lean meats, veges, grains, low-fat dairy—"

"And sex, lots of sex," she interrupted him, pushing away the toast.

She could tell she surprised him, but then his deep rumble rolled up out of his chest as he started laughing.

"Actually, yeah, lots of sex. Pregnancy is supposed to sharpen your senses, all of them," he stated with a double rise of his eyebrows, "but only when you're feeling up to it."

She was up to it, into it, and onto it as she pulled his willing body into the tangled bedding.

They made it to the airport for their flight to Texas but with absolutely no time to spare.

The flight to Dallas passed too quickly for someone who was dreading the trip.

"Are we taking a rental car?" he asked, as they waited in the baggage area.

"Were taking my Caravan," she stated without any fanfare.

"A Caravan? Somehow, Cass, I would have never pictured that as being your vehicle."

"Really? Just what did you picture me in?"

"Well, you know what they say about first impressions; the first vehicle I saw you standing next to was a Hummer. I pictured at least some kind of big, over-powered, four-wheel-drive. I mean, after all, this is Texas. Doesn't everybody have a honkin' big four-by-four in the driveway?"

She only laughed, ignoring his question. Once they gathered their bags, she directed him to a small airport shuttle.

"Take us to the general aviation building," she said, as she flashed a card at the driver.

"What's that?" AJ asked, trying to take it from her hand.

"My pilot's license," she answered with a small grin, still trying to put it back in her purse.

"You're full of shit. Let me see that."

She handed it to him and watched his expression, "See, I really am a pilot. I have my Caravan stored down there."

When they reached the GA building, she spoke to several people, and then headed out on the tarmac toward a long white and red plane with the words 'Henley Geomatics' painted on the side.

"This is *not* a van," he said, sounding worried.

"I never said it was a van. I said it was a Caravan; a Cessna Grand Caravan to be exact." She couldn't tell if he was impressed or scared, or maybe both, so she kept talking. "Any big job within about five to eight-hundred-miles of home, I usually fly to myself. This plane can transport up to twelve crew members, or I can use it like a cargo plane and transport gear to a site. This isn't going to freak you out is it?"

"I—I think it's kind of cool actually, but I just never expected it."

They put their bags in the plane then he followed her around as she completed her pre-flight check list. When they boarded, she told him to come up front and sit in the co-pilot's seat. He lifted a Dallas Cowboys ball cap from the seat, arching one eyebrow at her for the unasked question.

"Oh—that's—that's Dirk's. You can throw it in the back for now. I'd toss it out the window, but the airport frowns on litter-bugs."

"So, he's the last person you flew in this plane with?"

She nodded.

"I never asked, but did you two live together?"

"Hell no," came her quick answer. "We flew here to catch the flight to New York. He really was only an employee. It's just that when we spent time together, we… Please, AJ, I really don't want to discuss it. Just believe me when I say we didn't live together, and we didn't have an ongoing relationship when we weren't on a job."

"Cass, it's okay. I'm not jealous, and I believe you completely if you say you weren't living together, but I had to ask."

"I understand. Put on the headset and I'll give you a little lesson on how to fly."

The flight to Tyler was short, but she could tell how much he enjoyed learning about the plane. She let him take control when they were about ten minutes away from landing. It gave her a minute to call her dad and tell him that she was back. She was clearly angry when she closed the phone.

He didn't ask, but she told him anyway, "He's drunk. We'll fly over the business then we're going to my house. You aren't meeting him today."

"I told you, I'm okay with it."

"Yeah, well I'm not!" she snapped, but then apologized. "It isn't even two in the afternoon! What really pisses me off is that I asked him to stay sober—just for one friggin' day—and he couldn't do it." But her upset expression changed to a gentle smile as they flew over the Henley Geomatics Corporation. It was a twenty acre commercial parcel, complete with a landing strip for the plane, and a four-thousand square foot main office, several additional buildings, trucks, trailers, four-wheelers, and even a few portable office units to take onsite when they had a big job. The place was alive and thriving as they flew low and received a few waves from guys on the ground.

"Damn, Cass, I'm impressed. You really do have a big operation, don't you?"

"It's the one thing in my old life that I'm actually proud of," she said, tearing up. "I can't even begin to tell you how hard I've worked for what you're seeing. And, I can't wait until Dad signs those papers because the only person I want to share this with is you. The rest of my lame family can kiss my ass."

He smiled and reached over, squeezing her shoulder. Her

home was about thirty miles away from the business, yet by plane the distance was only a matter of minutes. They touched down on a long, private, concrete strip leading to a hangar.

"Home, sweet home," she sighed as the prop slowly stopped spinning. "You know I never asked you where you live when you're not traveling around the globe for the magazine."

"I have an apartment in Virginia. I thought about buying a house, but it didn't make much sense since I travel so much, and—"

"And what?"

"I wasn't expecting to live much longer," he quietly answered.

They'd been so happy over the last several days that his questionable future had faded away for both of them. Now, she was sorry she made him bring it up. But she would remedy her error and see if she could get him smiling again, "Well, you have a home now. This is our place, unless you don't like it, then we'll sell it and buy something else."

She wasn't going to put the plane in the hangar just yet, but she did hit the controls for the door to go up so AJ could get her golf cart out because a twenty-five hundred-foot walk back to the house carrying suitcases wasn't her idea of fun.

"Wow, Cass, it's beautiful," he stated, as they pulled up to the treed and shady yard in front of her contemporary styled log cabin. "How many acres do you have?"

"We," she corrected him, "have forty acres that border the lake on the west shore. I have a dock down there with a couple jet skis in my boathouse." She hit the button for her garage door to go up. "And yes, you were right: everyone in Texas has a 'honkin' big four-by-four in their drive, or at least in the garage." The door went up to expose her carbon gray, H2 Hummer, and a sleek, red, Dodge Viper. "I told you I spend good money. I think I'm kind of like a guy in that respect; I like my toys."

AJ gave a sad sigh as he stared at the expensive vehicles.

"Is that bad?" she asked, worried that she had somehow disappointed him.

"People are going to say I married you for your money." He was totally serious.

She laughed, "We both know that isn't true. And if you've learned anything about me, you should know that I don't give a rat's ass what people think. I'm happier than I've ever been in my life and, as long as you are too, that is what's important to me."

He finally smiled; she knew he was happy.

"Where's Charlie?"

"He's back at the office. When I have to leave him behind, he becomes the company mascot. I'd let Dad take care of him for me but the last time I did that I found his water bowl full of beer and his food dish full of pretzels; I wasn't happy."

AJ started laughing, "I bet you weren't."

She unlocked the house and showed him around, then told him she was going to drive to the office and pick-up Charlie, and she'd be back.

"Let me go with you," he asked quickly.

"Tomorrow, not today. We'll get there early, before Dad gets soused. I won't be gone long." She could tell he did not like the idea of her going anywhere without him. *"Please don't give me that face."*

"So what do I do while you're gone?" he relented.

She rolled her eyes then smiled, "Your pregnant wife is hungry, and since you studied up on what I should eat... I have a gourmet kitchen and a stocked freezer. Can you cook?"

He wrapped her in his arms and kissed her, gripping her hips and pulling her tightly against his groin, "Oh, yeah, baby, I can cook."

"Food, honey? I know you can cook in the bedroom."

"Tell me how much time I have."

"I'll be back in about an hour-and-a-half, maybe two."

He frowned at the length of time, but then let a smile creep back onto his face, "Deal. I'll have something good fixed. Do you get the Food Network out here so I can get some ideas?"

She pulled the Viper key off a hook inside a cabinet near the garage door. "There's a TV in the kitchen. Knock yourself out, Iron Chef," she said squeezing his biceps and stealing a fast kiss, "I love you."

"You're driving that?" he said, referring to the key in her hand. "Be careful," he added before she could answer, "and, I love you, too."

She smiled all the way to the office. She had been able to afford the kind of lifestyle most people envied, but she had never been happy. She had been business all the way, hard-edged, difficult to get along with, and, in truth, miserable. But all that changed with a simple twist of fate when an English guy sent his best friend to check her out. Now she had the inner happiness to match the outward appearance.

Before getting out of the car, she sent Bobby a quick text message. They hadn't been in contact with him since they landed in Miami, and she suddenly wanted to let him know they were okay, and to thank him for basically putting her and AJ together. She considered telling him about the baby, but she had a feeling it was something AJ would want to do. His response was so rapid that she hadn't even opened the car door yet. She and AJ were starting to think alike because he said he'd just received a text from him, too—and then he was congratulating her about the baby. She didn't think even her drunk daddy could wipe the smile from her face as she picked up her purse and walked into the office.

She never wore that kind of expression, and for a moment the receptionist didn't seem to recognize her. She grabbed her mail then headed back toward her office, saying hello to staff as she went. Her secretary, Jill, wasn't surprised when she came around the corner. She'd called and told her she was on her way, and asked her to have Charlie ready. He was seated patiently by Jill's desk. His leash wrapped securely around the arm of her chair. He began to jump and twist when he saw her, barking in his strangely muted Boston terrier voice.

"Hey, buddy, did you miss me?" she asked as she untied the leash.

"So what brought you back from the UK so early? Are you—" Jill's eyes cut to Cass's left hand then froze in place.

"I haven't told Dad yet, so keep it down. Yes, I got married. Where is he at anyway?"

"He's—he's... You got married? To who? I know you fired Dirk."

"I'll bring him in tomorrow, and you can drool over him, but I need to know where my dad's at."

"He was in his office about twenty minutes ago then he said something about checking the ice machine. I haven't seen him since."

Cass sighed, she knew why he checked the company ice machine; it was where he stored his beer, or, occasionally, a bottle of scotch or rum. She took Charlie with her, heading out the backdoor of the building toward the equipment building. The drunker he became, the more time he spent out there; it shortened his distance between drinks. She crossed the lot and opened the door. He was seated on a stool next to the cooler with a beer in his hand, and the radio playing a sappy, ancient country song.

"Pumpkin pie! How's my baby girl? Where in the Sam-hell is this new guy you're all fired up about?"

She walked over to the radio and turned it off, "I asked you to be sober, Daddy."

"I'vent had more than foour or five beers," he replied—then burped.

"More like fourteen or fifteen," she snapped. "Do I ask you not to drink very often? No, I don't. I let you do your thing and I don't interfere, but you knew this was important to me, Dad." He wasn't saying anything as he studied the beer can in his hand, so she continued. "Have you had anything to eat today, besides pretzels?" she growled out, as she grabbed the small, empty bag off the top of the ice machine and threw it away. "Come with me and I'll run you up to Barney's; we'll grab a sandwich and take you home."

"Youuu're a good girl, pumpkin, just like your momma was when I met her. I miss your momma."

"I know, Daddy. Come on, let's go."

The Viper didn't have a lot of space, but Charlie was used to this routine; he curled up at her father's feet on the floorboard. She drove to the local deli and went inside, and ordered his favorite: roast beef with Swiss cheese, mustard and Bavarian kraut. She bought a bag of a dozen hard-boiled eggs for him to eat when he got up in the morning. She had tried to break his routine by giving him something healthy for breakfast, but it never worked. If he didn't have two or three boiled eggs in the morning, then he wouldn't eat, and the beer drinking would start early to fill the ache in his belly—and in his head.

Charlie was in his lap licking his face when she returned to the car. "Charlie, get down," she scolded.

"He's all right. He's just like you, pumpkin; he's trying to take care of the old man."

"I don't think sixty-five is all that old."

"Well, it sure as hell ain't young! So, tell me about this guy you like," he asked as she put the car in reverse.

"I don't *like* him, Dad."

"Wha'd ya do; break up already?"

"No. I said I don't like him; I'm in love, Daddy. For the first time in my life, I'm really in love."

"What does he do?"

"He's a writer for National Geographic."

"The magazine?"

"Yeah. Don't open that in the car," she fussed at him as he attempted to open the sandwich, "I'll have you home in a couple minutes then you can eat."

"So he's *the one*, huh?" he chuckled, clearly being sarcastic.

"He'd better be because I married him."

Her father seemed to sober slightly, "You did what?"

She showed him her left hand, "He's your new son-in-law."

"When the hell did this happen?"

"Five days ago down in Miami; three days after we flew in from Africa."

"Darlin,' you're confusing the hell out of my drunk brain. I thought you were in England, or Scotland, or somewhere over in the friggin' UK."

"We were. The magazine sent him to South Africa, and I went with him. We would have married overseas if it hadn't been a paperwork nightmare. Instead, we waited until we could get to the States."

"Why didn't you tell me?"

"Would you have been sober today if I had?"

He suddenly wore a guilty look on his face.

She knew he would have been drunk regardless. She pulled into his driveway and turned off the car, "Come on. Let's go inside so you can eat your sandwich."

She let Charlie out into her dad's fenced backyard while he munched on his dinner, and was, apparently, deep in thought. She opened the fridge to put the eggs inside but was disgusted by what she saw. Besides the fact that the majority of the space was taken up with beer, what little food there was inside was molded and gross. Suddenly, her stomach lurched and she felt sick. Making a mad dash for his bathroom didn't help at all. The bathroom was messy, and he evidently didn't flush the toilet after urinating in it either last night or early this morning. She didn't have much in her stomach except for the crackers AJ continually fed to her on the plane, but they came up.

Her eyes were watery and she was still gagging when she returned to the kitchen. She was going to grab a glass and get a drink of tap water, but the cabinet was empty. She braced herself, and opened the dishwasher. "Damn it, Dad! Did you fire Rosie, again?!" she growled as she slammed the door shut on the moldy dishes.

"That bitch said she was gonna throw out my beer!" he snapped back. "I don't need her to clean up after me. I'll find another friggin' Mexican to do her job; one that won't complain so damn much!"

"She is a good person, and she's the only one who will put up with you! Tomorrow morning you're going to call her, while you're sober, and beg her to come back, or I'm not coming over here again. I can't take the smell when I'm like this!"

"Like what?" he demanded, putting down the sandwich.

"I'm pregnant," she barked back. It wasn't exactly the way she planned to tell him, but the nasty house put her over the edge.

Now, he seemed completely sober. "That son-of-a-bitch knocked you up! That's why you married him?! I'm gonna kill him!" he bellowed.

Cass started to laugh, "No, Daddy. We—"

"Where the hell is my gun?!" he shouted, starting to rise from the chair.

She put her hand on his arm and then sat down beside him, "This wasn't an accident, Daddy—I wanted to get pregnant."

"But why, baby?" he asked, noticeably calmer. "You're too young."

"Dad, I'm twenty-eight. Half the girls I went to school with already have two or three kids. I told you, I'm so in love with AJ and—and I had other reasons why I wanted to get pregnant."

"AJ, huh? That's his name?"

"It's Adam Jacob Lisowski."

"He's a—he's Polish?"

She knew her dad had a pretty deep racist streak in him, but it usually only came out when he was drunk—which was all the time.

"What he is, is my husband, your son-in-law, and the most wonderful man I've ever met. He makes me happy, really, truly happy, and isn't that what you've always said you wanted for me anyway?"

Her dad finally smiled, but then immediately frowned, "Is he the reason you wanted all the money from the TNR project? I was going to give you the business anyway, but, pumpkin, if he's a leech—"

"Daddy our whole family is a bunch of leeches; AJ is nothing like that. But, in a way, yeah he is the reason, but it's not what you think. He doesn't care about the money."

"Then what other reason is there?"

She hadn't planned to tell him all of this, but he did seem considerably more sober then when she picked him up, "He's facing some serious medical issues in several weeks, and I'm covering the costs. He didn't ask me to; I told him I wanted to."

"What's wrong with him?"

She spent the next fifteen minutes explaining about the aneurysm and the risky surgery that was just a little more than a month away.

"Cassandra," her dad said in his most somber voice, "honey, why didn't you wait? You said it's only a fifty-fifty chance he'll make it; a marriage and a family, now? Cassandra Diane, you should have waited."

"You don't get it, do you, Daddy? This guy owns me, heart and soul. If he doesn't make it, and I didn't have this part of him to go on I couldn't—I couldn't make it. I'd rather die with him then to live in a world where no part of him exists." She couldn't prevent the tears from coursing down her cheeks as she laid her heart bare before her father. "I love him that much. But this baby isn't just to keep part of him around: it's also to give him a reason to pull through. I'm going to love this baby no matter what happens, but I'm really praying that he and I are going to get to raise this child together."

It had been a long time since her father put his arms around her and simply held her. Matter of fact, the last time she remembered this kind of heart-felt hug was when her mother died.

"You're the strongest woman I know, Cass. And the *only one* in my rotten, stinkin' life that I didn't let get screwed up. You're the one thing I did right, and that's why we have to get those papers signed with the attorney as soon as possible."

She swallowed hard. He had no clue just how screwed up she became while he spent her childhood in a drunken stupor, and she never wanted him to find out the ugly truth.

She kissed his stubbly cheek, "I have to get going; AJ's cooking me dinner."

"By the way, pumpkin, Steven called me the other day.

Somehow he found out I wasn't going to give him and Lane a share in the business. He was pretty pissed off, but he eventually said he understood, but he does want you to call him."

"I don't need to talk to him," she responded, bordering on a growl.

"He said it was important. He said to tell you he has some video for you, and said you'd know what he meant."

Her blood turned to ice in her veins; she suddenly felt weak, "What video?"

"I don't know maybe it's one from when you all were kids. Hell, that boy always had a camera or a camcorder in his hands."

"I—I don't have his number. I—"

"I have it. Hold on a minute," he said as he fumbled for his cell. He scrolled through his contacts then handed her the phone. As soon as he placed it in her hand, she could hear Steven's voice.

"Dad?"

He had accidently pressed the talk button, and the phone dialed.

Crap!

"Dad?" came Steven's voice again.

Her father urged her to put it to her ear—he had no clue why she didn't want to do it.

"Hold on a minute," she said into the receiver. "I'll be right back," she told her dad, and then stepped out the backdoor where Charlie was playing. "What the hell did you tell Dad—"

"Shut up, Cassie," came the reply that made her shudder. "What the fuck do you think you're trying to pull, little sister? If you think I'm just going to walk away from a multi-million dollar—"

"A multi-million dollar what? A business you had nothing to do with?!"

"He's my dad, too. He owes me."

"He doesn't owe you a damn thing. You never—"

"Cassie, you're either going to make me your partner, or you're going to wish like hell you did."

"You? Not you and Lane?"

"Fuck Lane."

"It wouldn't surprise me if you did." He gave a sick laugh, leaving her no doubt that at some point he had. "I'm not making you a partner."

"That's fine, Cassie. I kind of figured you'd be a bitch about this, so I put together a nice little video to give to Dad. It's going to surprise the hell out of him to see what you were really like when you were young and wild. You know he still thinks of you as being perfect."

Her hand went immediately to cover her mouth. She couldn't believe he would threaten to show something like that to their father. She tried to speak, but her words choked in her throat.

"Yeah, you were a dirty little slut back then. You'd do anything for a little attention, booze, or cigarettes."

"Do you honestly believe if he knew what you did to me that he'd turn around and give you a share in the company? I think he might shoot your stupid ass."

"First off, I didn't put *our video* in the clip. He won't have a clue about who filmed it. And I'll deny it, and just say someone gave it to me to show what kind of a person you really are. Of course, a friend of yours says you're still a dirty slut. He tells me you get into being slapped around now. I'd really like to try that with you, Cassie."

"D—Dirk?"

"Yeah, Dirk. He decided to give me a heads-up about the old man's intentions. I told him he just earned himself a re-hire and a raise as soon as I own part of the business."

"I—I won't work with you."

"Then you're going to give me the whole fucking company, and your buddy Dirk can run it for me, but either way, you play my game or Dad goes to his grave knowing his 'perfect' child was the worst one of us all."

She was sobbing so hard she couldn't speak if she tried.

"I'll give you a couple days, but after that Dad gets to watch a porn show—and you get to be the star."

She snapped the phone shut. She didn't know how long she stood there in the backyard trying to get it together. She wasn't even sure if she could drive home without wrecking the car. Thoughts of AJ patiently waiting for her to return filled her mind. How could she go home and tell him what happened? She wouldn't. She couldn't. She didn't want him to know because nothing good could come from him knowing what Steven was planning. He'd want to kill Dirk and Steven both, and she couldn't let him.

"I have to go," she said as she walked through the house and tossed her dad's phone onto the table. She had Charlie by the leash and was out the door before he could open his mouth. She looked into her vanity mirror and saw a pair of reddened eyes staring back at her. She couldn't go home this way. She stopped at the drug store and grabbed a box of tissue and a bottle of Visine. She cried and screamed until she was minutes away from home. She pulled off the road and flooded her eyes with drops, so it wouldn't be apparent how hard she'd bawled.

She made up her mind; she wouldn't fight him. He could have the business. She'd sell off all her assets to pay for AJ's surgery then she'd start another survey company far away from Texas. She'd most likely never see her dad again. Who would take care of him when she wasn't around? Who would make sure he ate once in a while? Would Steven even allow him to continue with the company, or would he simply fire him? She wouldn't put anything past that cold-hearted bastard. She wondered if he had shown his sick collection to Dirk. She never told Dirk anything about her life growing up, but perhaps he knew part of it now anyway.

"Hey, baby," came AJ's voice when she stepped inside the house.

Whatever he cooked smelled wonderful, but she was still so sick she didn't think she could eat. "I—I don't feel very good. Dad's house was a wreck. I'm sorry," she said as she began breaking down. *Stupid tears!* She couldn't hold them back. "I gotta go to the bathroom," she sobbed, clutching one hand over her stomach and the other over her mouth as she dashed for the stairs. She heard him following her up the steps, but she slammed the bathroom door in his face and locked it as he pled from the other side for her to open it.

She sat on the floor and bawled, "Go away, please. I'll be out in a little while."

All was silent.

She turned on the faucet in her big ball-and-claw tub then sat there watching the water rise. She took a long bath, as she calculated how much she would clear from selling the house and all her toys. It pissed her off that she had put the plane in the company name. It cost her over two million dollars, but there was no way she could get the money back out of it now. Her bank account was still decent, and if she could possibly hold off the transfer until after the TRN project, she'd pocket another two-hundred grand. She and AJ would be fine. She'd pay for his surgery and still have enough left to start another company. It would be tiny compared to the one she built over the last thirteen years, but she could do it again—as long as she had AJ, she could do anything.

When she finally emerged, wrapped only in an oversized bath towel, she found him sitting on the end of her bed looking worried. He held a handful of crackers and what looked like a cup of hot tea.

"Did you get sick?" he asked softly.

She nodded, "Dad's house was nasty."

"I thought you were just going to get Charlie?"

"I was but if I'd let someone from the business run him home, I knew he wouldn't get anything to eat tonight, or tomorrow morning."

"Open up," he said, holding a cracker for her.

He was just so damn good to her. She couldn't take it, and started to sob again.

He put the crackers and tea down on the nightstand and picked her up and laid her on the bed, curling his body against her back, and holding her securely. "Shhh," he whispered, kissing her neck and telling her how much he loved her. "I had no clue how hard this place was going to be on you."

He had just given her the perfect lead-in, and she had to take it, "AJ, I don't want to—to live here anymore." She managed it with one small stumble. "I have enough money without the business. Would you be disappointed if I just wanted to get out of here? I'll sell the house and all my junk; we'll move away."

He rolled her toward him; a serious expression filled his face, "All because of your dad?"

"It's a lot of things really. I just want to get the hell out of Texas for good." There was something in his eyes telling her he wasn't quite buying her story.

"Cass, I wouldn't care if you were flat broke and wanted to just live off what I make. Hell, I'd even find a second job just to get you a few 'toys.' But, baby, I have to tell you when we flew over the business today, I know what I saw in your face; you love what you do, and what you built."

"I'm not saying I'll give up surveying entirely. Maybe I'll start another company, one without so many bad memories."

"Whatever you want to do, but I don't want you to regret anything. Make sure, Cass, you're willing to leave everything you worked for behind. I want you to be happy."

She cried as he held her, swaying softly to and fro.

"Do you think you could hold something down? I made you some tea with ginger. It's supposed to calm your stomach."

"Sure, I'd love to try it. Dad fired his housekeeper—again. Everything was moldy, dirty, and gross." He handed her the tea as she took a tentative sip, "It's good. I don't have ginger tea. How'd you make it?"

"It's green tea; I added a little ginger from your spice rack. If you can keep it down, you can try dinner."

She was back to smiling on the outside, but inside it was killing her to lie to him about why she wanted to get out of Texas. "What'd you make?"

"Well, it wasn't easy because you don't have any fresh ingredients to work with, but I made Island Chicken with an orange, ginger glaze, over white rice. What I needed was fresh snow peas, water chestnuts, and shiitake mushrooms."

"I was kidding about the Iron Chef bit, but are you telling me that you really *can* cook?"

"Sometimes the bartender has to fill-in in the kitchen," he grinned.

She started laughing.

The meal he fixed was delicious, and he was right about the ginger calming her stomach. They finished the night listening to music in the great room. Since it was the wrong time of the year to have logs in her fireplace, she had a big, ten candle, iron candelabra with tropical scented candles burning in it instead.

She yawned, as she rested her head on his chest, "I'm tired. Are you ready to go to bed?"

He kissed her forehead, but then left his lips resting against her skin, "Cass, I want to ask you something, but I hope you won't get pissed off about it."

She pulled back slightly and looked up at him, "What?"

"Have you had many men here? I was thinking it might not be a good idea to sleep in your bedroom if—"

"I don't bring men here, ever," she frowned. "This place is my retreat from the world."

"Not even Dirk?"

"Especially not Dirk."

"You've honestly never shared your bed here with another

man?"

"No. You're the only one I've ever shared this place with, unless you count my dad and my half-sisters. Dad doesn't like coming out because I won't let him drink while he's here."

"I'm not saying I don't believe you, but it would really disappoint me if you weren't telling me the truth."

"AJ," she said, pulling away and sitting up, "why would I lie to you about this?"

"You said you had a *pair* of jet skis in the boathouse. If this place is just for you, why would you need two?"

"My half sisters, well two of them anyway, have kids. Lillian has two boys, nineteen and seventeen. Penny has twin girls, fifteen, and a thirteen-year-old boy. I don't see them too often, but the jet skis give them something to do when they come over."

"I'm sorry I doubted you. I started thinking about it today when I was here by myself, and it honestly bothered me. I know it shouldn't have; it was stupid and jealous."

"It's okay. With what you know about my past, I can—"

"Cass, I'm still sorry. I'd never bring up your past in a bad way, but I was wondering if it might be the real reason why you want to give all this up?"

A man *was* the reason she wanted to leave, but not one who slept with her in this house. She swallowed hard, "No, I just want a fresh start."

He kissed her temple and told her he was ready to make a beautiful memory for her in Texas.

CHAPTER EIGHTEEN

It wasn't daylight yet when Charlie jumped down from the bed and started barking. Cass groggily looked at the bedside clock, "Five thirty? Charlie, really? You couldn't hold it a little longer?"

AJ rolled over. "I'll take him out, baby," he said with his eyes still closed.

She was ready to tell him she'd do it, when she heard the front doorbell, "What the hell..."

AJ was on his feet and pulling up his jeans before she could finish her statement. "Do you normally get visitors this early?" he asked, grabbing his tee-shirt.

"I don't normally get visitors, period," she replied, slipping into her robe.

"No, you stay up here."

"I don't think so," she snapped. "Whoever it is, won't be expecting you to open my front door!"

"Exactly."

She wasn't about to stay put as she followed him down the stairs. The doorbell rang again before they reached it. She gripped his arm as he opened it.

"Dad!"

"You must be AJ," came her father's surly response.

"Dad, it's five-thirty in the morning! What the hell are you doing here?"

"Well, you did say you wanted me to meet him when I was sober, so I figured we'd better start early."

"Mister Henley," AJ said offering his hand, "it's good to finally meet you. I'm—"

"I know who you are," he didn't look terribly impressed, but he did accept the handshake—then he looked at AJ's outstretched arm, "You married a guy with a tattoo?!"

Cass growled her displeasure through the introductions, "Dad, this is *my husband*, Adam Lisowski, but he goes by AJ. AJ, this is my dad, Wade Henley."

"Would you like me to call you Wade or—"

"You'd better stick with Wade; I don't think I'm ready to hear you call me dad."

"I was going to say Mister Henley."

"Hell no! That's too damn formal. So, are you two going to invite me in or leave me standing on the front porch?"

AJ stepped out of the way, Cass just stood there until he tugged her arm.

"So, you knocked up my daughter, huh?" he grumbled as he stepped inside and headed toward the kitchen.

"Dad! I told you—"

"Pumpkin, I know what you said," he responded dismissively, as he continued to the breakfast bar. "I don't usually ask for coffee, Cass, but I could use a cup today."

AJ smiled and shrugged his shoulders as he looked at her then followed him to the kitchen, "I'll get you a cup, Wade."

"Well, at least the son-of-a-bitch has some manners," her dad mused.

"How do you take your coffee, Wade? Do you want espresso, latte, cappuccino, iced, frozen, or regular black?"

Cass watched her father's expression. He wasn't going to make this easy on AJ, or so he thought.

"It's supposed to get hot today, so frozen coffee sounds good."

While AJ had Cass's one-cup brew station making a fresh cup of coffee, he put ice in her blender then opened a can of evaporated milk which he'd refrigerated last night. He grabbed the bottle of vanilla extract and the powdered sugar. "We don't have any fresh cream right now; we haven't gone to the grocery store, so I hope this turns out okay. Did you want this to be mocha or just vanilla?"

"Mocha is fine," he replied and then winked at Cass.

Cass looked at her dad and rolled her eyes. If he thought he was going to fluster AJ over making this drink, he would be sorely disappointed.

With the coffee brewed, AJ poured it over the ice with the milk, sugar, cocoa, and vanilla then hit the button as the noise of the blender filled the house. In a separate bowl, he whipped cold milk, powdered sugar, and vanilla to make a topping. He drizzled chocolate syrup down the insides of a tall glass in a pattern, filled the glass with the frozen coffee and added the topping, finishing it with another light drizzle of chocolate.

"Cass, would you like one?" he asked, as he handed the visually appealing concoction to her father.

She gave a big grin, watching her father stare at the glass with a dumbfounded expression, "Make mine decaf, please."

"How is it, Wade?" AJ asked, after watching her father take a sip.

"Pretty damn good, actually. Where'd you learn to fix coffee?"

AJ glanced to Cass, and she gave him a small nod, "I bartend once in a while. I make quite a few different coffees when I do."

"A bartender?" his face was riddled in surprise. "Well, hell, pumpkin," he said as he put his hand on Cass's shoulder, "I think I'm actually going to like this guy after all. Got any whiskey? I like Irish coffee; it's the only thing the damn Irish did right."

Cass sighed.

"No, sir; her kitchen is alcohol free."

"Sir, my ass; call me dad."

The ice was broken; he began to warm quite nicely. He talked to them about AJ's job, the pending surgery, and the baby. He was being civilized, concerned, and caring, which surprised the heck out of Cassandra. She listened to the two of them as she sipped her glass of frozen decaf. She cooked breakfast, knowing if she put the plate in front of him, her dad would eat. She didn't get fancy, just scrambled eggs and buttered toast, but no one seemed to mind.

"When she told me she married you, I wasn't happy," Wade confessed. "Then she told me she was pregnant, and I wanted to kill you," he added, without a hint of jest.

AJ shot a fast glance to Cass.

"But," he continued, "I can see you two are happy together, really happy. Matter-of-fact, I don't think I've seen her this way since... Well, it's been too long. I may not be much of a father-in-law, but Cass makes up for that. She's a very special woman."

She had just put the last bite of scrambled eggs in her mouth, but she couldn't swallow after what he said. Her eyes became teary as she kept chewing.

AJ leaned over and kissed her temple, "She is exactly that, and I plan on keeping her happy for the rest of my life."

That didn't help the egg swallowing matter at all.

She picked up her napkin and turned away from them and spit out the last bite.

"You okay?" AJ asked, as he watched a tear finally trickled down her cheek.

Her dad appeared truly concerned because it had been years since he'd seen her cry.

"Yeah, I just can't eat if you two are going to get all mushy on me."

AJ wiped her cheek and pulled her against his chest, kissing her again, but this time on the forehead, "As long as you aren't getting sick, again."

"Ah, morning sickness," her father stated with a knowing nod.

"I'm usually okay in the morning, but by the end of the day—"

"Your momma was the same way. She'd sip a little ginger ale and nibble on crackers to get her through it."

Cass laughed, "AJ has me on a similar routine."

He thanked her for breakfast as he headed for the front door, saying he was going to the office. "Listen, honey, besides sizing up my son-in-law, I came out here to tell you that Nicholas has the paperwork drawn up and ready for us. If you and AJ want to come with me, he said he'd meet us there at eight."

Nicholas Ghelman was the attorney who handled legal matters for the business, but she was unsure how she would handle this, especially with AJ standing there. If she said okay, then he would wonder why she wanted to take the company only to give it right back when they moved. She had to take ownership at some point to turn it over to Steven, but if she told her dad to wait, then he'd wonder what was going on. Would Steven be satisfied if she only gave him her share in the business, and left her dad as a joint owner? That would protect her father's interest, but who knew if Steven wouldn't turn right around and show him the video anyway just for spite.

Her heart ached at the thought of her dad's reaction when he found out what she was doing with his gift of sole ownership. For a split second, she thought it would be a whole lot simpler if she'd just kill the rotten, stinking, sick, asshole who was, unfortunately, related to her. Murder would create as many problems as it would solve, but it would be so satisfying to see the look on Steven's face just before she pulled the trigger.

She gave a sad sigh. AJ gave her a gentle nod, expecting her to tell him that she changed her mind. "Can we discuss this later? I'm starting to feel queasy," she lied. She was planning to concoct a story in a little while as to why she needed to go into work, alone, and leave AJ home so she could handle the dirty deed in private. There would be no waiting for the TNR contract, but perhaps she could take a draw from the business bank account as a final stipulation.

"Sure, pumpkin," he said, as AJ opened the front door for him, "whenever you're ready, just call me. I'll—I'll try to stay away from the ice machine," he added sheepishly.

AJ appeared mystified, but she just smiled and thanked him.

"By the way," he said, turning as he started down the front steps, "what did Steven say to you yesterday on the phone that pissed you off so badly? Was it about the video?"

She felt faint as she watched a look of revelation wash over AJ's face—a look she'd never seen on him before. She knew the only thing that would satisfy his facial expression would be the truth, but how could she tell him?

Even her father appeared to realize something was amiss by their expressions. "Look, pumpkin, if he's said anything to you about the business that upset you, don't let it. He has his construction company, and he's never done a damn thing to help out our corporation other than to get free surveys out of us. I've been a fool long enough to believe that he, or any of the others, have any real interest in the business other than to drain money out of it. Everyone else understood why I'm giving it to you. Hell, if it wasn't for you, they all know it wouldn't even exist. Lane was mad, but she's always wanted everything given to her. I told her she is thirty-three, and it's high time she finds a real job. I gave her one, fifty-thousand-dollar draw out of my account to make her happy, but I told her that's it; the well has gone dry. And," he said pointing his finger at her, "don't you let her talk you into giving her any money."

"We don't talk," she sadly admitted. "I haven't spoken to her in two or three years."

"Yeah, I know," he acknowledged, shaking his head, "and I also know it has been every bit as long or longer since you've spoken to Steven. To tell you the truth, I didn't like it when he and Lane approached me about being partners, but... Well, I was hoping they were honestly interested in working with us. I finally realized they figured out I'm getting old and they might lose their gravy train. I'm sorry I even considered it. I know it insulted the hell out of you, and for that I apologize, pumpkin."

She embraced him and let the tears fall as she buried her face against his tee-shirt. Everything was going to fall apart. She'd have to tell AJ, and he wouldn't let her be blackmailed. Steven wouldn't care about the damage the video caused. He wouldn't care if it cut their father's heart right out of his chest. She loved, protected, and watched over her father for years; the business was her excuse, but she had done it all to make him proud of her. No matter what she did, someone she loved was going to get hurt, and it would be one, or both, of the men standing here trying to comfort her.

She felt his rough, gnarled hands patting her back trying to quiet her.

"Sorry, Daddy," she whispered through gasps for air. She still couldn't raise her face up to look at them.

"It's okay, pumpkin. Your momma was the same way when she was pregnant with you. The woman never cried, and then, all of a sudden, she turned into a frigging water sprinkler overnight. You'll be fine. You've found a good man, and you two are going to be happy for a long, long time. I won't pop a top until after noon, so if you feel up to it, call me before then and we'll get this thing settled. If not today, then we can do it tomorrow."

She felt AJ gently pull her away from her father. She put her head against his chest as he thanked him for coming by. As soon as her father was out of the driveway, she felt his fingers under her chin, but she didn't want to look up.

"Look at me, Cass."

She closed her eyes.

"Is Steven the reason you wanted to leave? What did he say to you?"

"*Please don't*," she cried, "I *can't* tell you."

"Cass, you know I'd do anything for you, and you know I love you but I will not accept anything other than the truth from you. If you lied to me, I'll tell you right now, I can't take it. I won't have secrets between us. That was why I waited so long to make love to you, and I'll be damned if I'm going to let you start hiding stuff from me now."

She looked up into those beautiful green eyes and saw more hurt than she could withstand. "I'm sorry I lied to you," she choked as she made her admission. "He is the reason, the only reason, why I want to leave. I have to give him the company."

"There is no way I'm going to let you give him what you've worked for your whole life! Why would you even..." What her father said must have finally sunk in. "Video—he mentioned a video." Absolute rage seemed to flood him, "Did that son-of-a-bitch threaten you?! Tell me right now! Did he threaten you?!"

She drew a shaky breath. She'd never seen him this angry. She nodded because she couldn't form the words right at the moment.

"Tell me *exactly* what he said to you, every word!"

Her knees felt weak as he helped her to the bench on the porch. She couldn't give him word-for-word; she could barely speak as emotion punctured her fragmented sentences, "He—he's gonna give Daddy a... If I don't let him have the business—he's—he's... Dad doesn't know! It'd kill him to know. He thinks I'm perfect—the only good thing in his life. I don't want my—my Dad to see me that wa—way, ever."

"He said he'd show Wade the pictures and video he took when you were a kid?"

She nodded.

"But then your dad will know what he did to you. He certainly can't expect to get the business after something like that."

She could feel the scarlet color filling her face as she looked down at her lap. "He didn't get in the pictures and videos with me—except once," she cringed. "He wouldn't take shots or video of me unless I smiled and acted like I was having a good time. He said if I'd loosen up and have fun with it, then he'd stop touching me—he'd run the camera instead. I didn't want him touching me." She finally looked up at him, "He said he'll tell Dad someone gave him the video to prove what kind of person I really am."

"Cass," came his soft words, void of anger and fury, "is there a video with him in it? Is there something you didn't tell me?"

"I told you enough," she said sadly. "You didn't say you needed every detail."

"I asked if you'd slept with him."

"No," she corrected, "you asked if he was my first."

"Oh God, Cass—did—did he sleep with you and—and film it?"

She lowered her face into her hands as she sobbed out the last secret of her life—the one she never wanted to reveal. "I told you I tried suicide twice after I was raped. I tried to suffocate myself the first time. I got drunk and put a plastic bag over my head. I figured I'd just go to sleep and never wake up. But, I must have flailed around too much when I passed out because I woke the next morning and the bag was tangled in my sheets. A year or so later, when the drugs and the alcohol didn't end my pain, I decided to use Dad's Colt 45, but it was gone. He'd given it to Steven. I went to get it from him, but he wouldn't let me have it. He knew I was desperate and, I think, he knew what I was planning, so he offered me something else instead."

"What?"

"He said he had sleeping pills that I could have, if..." she couldn't continue.

"If you slept with him?"

She nodded, "It didn't matter to me at that point; nothing mattered. I just wanted to die. His wife had left him a few weeks before; he said touching wasn't going to be enough. He set up a couple cameras—and—and when it was over he played it back and made me watch it."

"And he gave you pills?"

"Yeah, but they weren't sleeping pills. They turned out to be an aspirin based pain reliever; at least that's what they said in the emergency room. I went home and took them all. When Dad came in, I was having a seizure, and he rushed me to the hospital. They explained it was one of the side effects of too much aspirin at one time. When they asked me if I'd been trying to hurt myself, all I could think about was the look on Dad's face as he stared at me. I knew he felt responsible. He would have thought he was the reason. I couldn't let him believe that he was to blame. I told them I had a really bad headache and that I didn't know aspirin could hurt a person. They let him take me home. That was when I realized killing me, would kill him, too. I couldn't do that to Daddy, so I decided to find a way to help both of us. You know the rest. I'm sorry I didn't tell you everything."

"Don't be. You're right. I only asked if he was your first. You didn't offer everything, but I didn't press you for it, either. I understand why you left this out."

"But can you forgive me?" she asked through tear-stained eyes.

"There is nothing to forgive, unless you're asking for me to forgive you for lying yesterday."

"I figured you'd want to kill them, or at least beat the hell out of him and—"

"And who?"

She'd almost forgotten about the other party she didn't want AJ fighting. He was an intelligent man, so she didn't know why she didn't just come out and say it because he was already solving the mystery.

"Someone told Steven that your dad was signing the business over to you, didn't they? My guess is Dirk. Am I right?"

"Dirk knew I hated Steven, he just didn't know why."

"Does he know why now?!"

She could see the anger building once again in his countenance, "I don't know, but—but Steven did say Dirk told him I—I liked things rough."

"And I'm sure Steven liked that bit of information, didn't he?!"

She didn't answer.

"I want both their addresses—*now*," he demanded.

"Yeah, well I want you to be around when this baby is born, so you're not getting them!"

"I'll find both of them, with or without your help. They can't do this to you! I'm not going to let it happen! As far as Dirk is concerned, he's just after money. But Steven should be rotting in a jail cell somewhere with a big harry ape named Bendem Over for a cellmate."

"But—you can't... If the police get involved, Dad will know everything anyway. There'd be a trial. Everyone would know. I couldn't take it, AJ."

"Cass, you were nine-years-old when he started molesting you. Pictures and video amount to child pornography; he'll go to prison. He deserves that; actually somebody should kill him and put him out of everyone else's misery. And I know you probably don't want to hear this right now, but I'm sure you weren't the only young girl he did this to." He turned and headed into the house.

She followed him, wondering what he was doing. He went straight to her key cabinet, opened it up, and snatched the Viper key from the hook before she could stop him.

"No," she pled, trying to take it from his hand, "you can't drive, remember?"

"I choose not to drive. I'm perfectly capable."

This wasn't like the battle over the cell phone; she couldn't get it out of his hand. *"Please AJ, put the key back,"* she begged. "You don't know where to go anyway."

"Really? I bet your brother won't be too hard to find. His name is Steven Henley and he, according to your dad, owns a construction company; I'm guessing Henley might be in the name of his business, huh? Don't worry," he said, his voice growing sharper, "I'll Google him on my phone. I bet I can even get a map to his house! When I'm finished with him, he'll gladly give me information about Dirk."

"All right, fine—you win!" she shouted at him. "I'll—I'll call the cops and tell them what he did. It doesn't matter what people think about me anymore. *Just please don't go. I'll do anything—**anything** to keep you safe. Please don't leave me, AJ!"* She was going down to her knees but it was because they were giving out—this was more than she could handle.

"Baby," he said, dropping down beside her, "I'm not like him. I'm not going to make you do something when you have no other way out. I love you, Cass, and I don't want your name smeared all over the newspapers either. Let me take care of this. I won't get hurt."

"You don't know that," she whimpered. "I don't trust either one of them. If—if I tell you where they live then I'm going with you."

"No. Not in your condition."

"My condition! How about yours? I have to go, please understand."

He sighed, his anger relaxing slightly, "You'll stay in the car."

"I have to grab my purse. Would you please hand me the key?"

"You're just going to have to trust me, Cass. I won't leave you, but I don't like the idea of you coming."

She went upstairs, yet was relieve to see he was still waiting for her when she returned.

He was leaning against the Viper with his arms across his chest, his hands tight on his biceps when she entered the garage. His anger was building again, and his normal even-keel façade seemed to be peeling back. "I'm driving," he stated.

"Are you sure?"

"I need something to get my mind off of killing both of them, so yeah, I'm sure."

"I don't know if either one of them will be home, but I think we should go to Dirk's first." She knew Steven ran his construction remodeling business out of his house, but Dirk (she was hoping) had found a job and wouldn't be home—anything to give AJ's temper a chance to cool down.

He fired up the engine, and for a brief moment, he smiled.

"Feels good to be in the driver's seat for a change?" she asked quietly.

He dropped it into reverse and backed out. "I like your car," he stated and then burned the tires down the driveway.

When they pulled up to Dirk's place, her heart was pumping harder than the ten cylinders under her hood—his truck was in the drive. She put her hand on AJ's arm; his muscles had turned to rock and his jaw was clinched, "Let's try talking first. Don't just fly into him."

His head turned and he looked at her. He didn't need to say a word; he was ready to kick ass, "I'll talk first, if you stay in the car."

He hadn't even opened the driver's door when Dirk came walking out of the house headed their way with a CD in his hand. She couldn't sit still. She opened her car door and stood up.

But Dirk surprised both of them, "Cass, I didn't know. You've got to believe me. I'm not into the weird shit that he is."

AJ's hand went out to take the CD.

"Only if she's okay with you handling this," he stated, drawing back. "*I know* she isn't going to want you to see it."

She gave Dirk a small nod as AJ took it.

He immediately snapped the disk in half and threw the pieces into the car.

Dirk advanced toward her when AJ put his hand on his chest and stopped him.

She held her breath.

"Why did you go to her brother?" he demanded.

Dirk drew in a frustrated breath and began, "I was pissed at her, okay?! I know it was all my fault, and I deserved the ass-kicking your friend gave me. I guess I still deserve one for the business over Charlie."

"We found him," Cass said, finally speaking up.

He honestly looked relieved, "I'm sorry. I was just so freaking pissed off. But I swear to God, Cass, I had no idea when I came back to the States and told your brother what was going on, that—that..." His voice choked off. "I have some big debts to pay and I thought this would be a way to do it, but I'm not getting involved in that kind of..." his voice faded once again as he pointed to where AJ had thrown the broken disk. "People go to prison for even looking at that kind of shit. He brought it over to me last night. He said he thought I'd enjoy it. He told me I'd be managing the company for him pretty soon and then he left. When I put it in my computer..." Once again he couldn't continue.

Her eyes closed as her head tilted down and she fought back the tears.

"I didn't watch the whole thing," he added quickly, "I barely watched thirty seconds. I didn't even realize it was you at first, but it made me frigging sick. I called him and told him to find another manager; I didn't want the job."

All was quiet for a moment. She raised her head and took a deep breath.

"Can I speak to her alone for a minute?" Dirk asked.

"No," was AJ's unhesitant answer.

"AJ is my husband, Dirk. Anything you have to say to me, you can say in front of him."

The look on his face was as if she'd punched him in the stomach. His shoulders slumped, and he sat back on the bumper of his truck. "I really screwed up," he admitted, running his hands through his choppy blonde hair. "I'd been so focused on getting your money that I never stopped to think how good it was between us, when you'd let me," he added, "but it looks like I'm never going to get to make it up to you."

"Actually, you just did. You started out with all the wrong intentions, but I'm glad, when it came down to right and wrong, you turned him down. At least now, if I see you around town, I won't have to worry about AJ wanting to kill you."

"I have to ask you something," he said, looking really perplexed. "I thought—I mean, you kept saying you weren't sleeping with him," he said, pointing at AJ, "and the other guy was with you at the restaurant."

"Bobby is his best friend. I didn't want AJ getting into a fight."

"Oh," he replied, still puzzled as he slowly stood up. "I'm a little confused, but I'll tell you this," he said facing AJ, "you're one lucky bastard, and I don't mean about the money."

"I know that."

"I'm guessing you two are going to his house next, and, if this is a lynch mob, I'd like to be part of it."

Cass glanced at AJ's face, but she couldn't tell if he liked the idea or not. She looked back at Dirk, "Do you mean that? Do you really want to help?"

"I'm guessing that sick weasel has more copies of what he gave me; you don't deserve that, Cass. Yeah, I really want to help."

"If he sees me and AJ coming up to his house, he'll know something is up, and I really don't want him to know what's coming."

AJ still wasn't saying anything. He was studying Dirk.

"I know you don't have any reason to trust me," he told AJ, "but any man who can do that to a little girl deserves to have the hell beat out of him."

"Call him," AJ finally said, "and tell him that you've changed your mind, and you want to come over and talk to him. You drive up in your truck; we'll park somewhere out of sight. Keep him busy, and I'll surprise him. I'm sure he has a place where he stores his sick collection; you and I are going to make him show us where it's at."

"I can do that," Dirk said as he pulled out his phone and dialed Steven's number. It only took a second. "Hey, boss-man, you know the more I watch that CD the more I realize how much I like money—and how much I hate your bitch sister." He winked at Cass. "I changed my mind; I'm in. Yeah, she is one hell of a slut," he said, agreeing with something Steven said. "Has she caved yet?" he paused again. "Listen, I have some ideas. I think I can get her to give in faster. Would some current nude pictures of her help? Yeah I do, but I don't want to talk about it over the phone. No, I'll come to you. I'll be there in fifteen or twenty minutes. Hey, listen, by the way, is this all you have on her. It was pretty fucking good and I..." he paused again. "Yeah, yeah, that sounds good. Really? Yeah, I'd like to see that. I'll bring what I have. I'll see you in a few minutes. Bye." He closed his phone, shaking his head, "I'm sorry, Cass, but I had a feeling if I told him I had nude pictures of you as an adult, he'd be too curious to be suspicious."

"Cass," AJ began.

"No, man," Dirk spoke up, before she could respond, "I don't have nude pictures of her. It was only bait."

"Wha—what did he say to you?" she asked with a quaking voice.

He looked at both of them, and actually seemed to be getting emotional, "There is no way in hell I'm telling you what that sick bastard said. But after AJ and I get finished with him, that asshole won't touch anymore little girls."

AJ actually smiled.

The guys bumped fists, and they were on their way.

When they pulled down Steven's street, Dirk passed them and continued to the house. AJ parked the car a few houses away, "Stay here, please."

"I can't. I have to know you're okay. I won't get close enough to get hurt. I know neither one of you is going to let him get near me, but I'll go crazy if you make me stay behind."

He placed his hand on the back of her neck and kissed her, "Damn, you're stubborn, but I love you. Are you sure you're up to this?"

She nodded as she grabbed her door handle and gave it a pull.

She heard Dirk before she could see him. His truck was in the driveway and Steven's garage door was up. Then she heard the voice that made her skin crawl. AJ put his hand on her arm and whispered to her to stay put as he prepared to walk in on the two men. She did as he asked; her pulse skyrocketing through her veins. AJ slipped around the corner of the garage. Within seconds she heard Steven say, "Who the hell are you?"

She couldn't make her feet move fast enough when she heard the scuffle breakout. She stepped into the building and saw that AJ had Steven by the throat and had slammed him against the wall near the tool bench. Steven wasn't a small man. He was slightly shorter than AJ, but he had a much thicker build and outweighed him by at least fifty pounds. Dirk was a much closer match for Steven, but apparently AJ made his move first.

Steven's eyes were wide, until he saw her, "Well, well, little sister decided to play dirty," he sneered, and began to fight back. He swung with his free hand, but AJ blocked it then punched for his exposed ribs. As soon as he took the shot, Steven knocked AJ's hand from his throat, and the two hit the floor. They were too close together for the punches to have power, but AJ had the advantage when it came to wrestling. As soon as he maneuvered Steven into a manageable hold, Dirk jumped in and the two men pulled him to his feet.

"You just fucked up," Steven spat toward her. His lip was blooded and the side of his head scraped from the concrete, "Not only is Dad going to see you, but now I'll put it out on the internet and everyone will see, Cassie."

Dirk slapped Steven's face, hard, "Don't call her that, asshole."

Steven struggled violently, "Cassie likes it. Don't you, little girl? Cassie likes getting—"

Both men apparently had the same thought as, in unison, they slammed Steven face-first in to the concrete wall. The blow disoriented him. He staggered as they pulled him away. Blood was trickling down his forehead from his hairline, and from his nose which apparently broke on impact.

"If you want to keep talking," AJ growled, "we can arrange for you to keep kissing the wall until your face isn't recognizable anymore. We want every picture, every piece of film you have on her, do you understand?"

"Fuuck you!" he slurred.

AJ came unglued. He used Steven's body for a punching bag as he pummeled him with six or seven rapid strikes to the mid-section as Dirk held him. Dirk was struggling to keep Steven off the floor because Steven's knees buckled by the second swing. AJ gripped Steven's hair and tipped his face up, "I can do this all day, or at least until your worthless ass dies from internal injuries. Now, let's try this again, are you going to give us what you have on her?"

He nodded weakly.

"Good. Where do you keep it?"

He spat a mouthful of blood onto the floor and said it was in his bedroom.

They walked through the open door as Cass followed from a distance. It had been thirteen years since she'd been in this house, and although it had been modernized, updated, and added onto, she felt physically sick as the memories hit her. Where he was directing them wasn't where the master bedroom had once been. He had built a new master suite and bathroom onto the back of the house.

She turned away from where they took him, and went down the hall to what had been his bedroom years ago. He had walled in the windows making it completely black. She felt for a light switch and illuminated the space. A movie projector hung from the ceiling and an expensive, leather recliner was in the middle of the room. A fancy mini-bar was built into what had once been the closet, but otherwise it was devoid of furniture. There were speakers hung from the ceiling and a large projector screen hanging from the wall. She could just imagine what he spent his time doing in this room. The vomit came up in her mouth before she could move. She leaned over his chair and emptied her stomach. She was feeling weak in the knees, knowing she had to get out of this room before she was completely overwhelmed.

She walked into his bedroom, hearing voices coming from inside a walk-in closet. Dirk had Steven in a head lock, as he allowed him to have his arms free to open a large wall safe. It was, evidently, his second try as he worked the combination with trembling hands. He pulled the handle and the door swung open. She watched the expressions on Dirk and AJ's faces as they stared inside.

"Is this everything?" AJ asked with disgust clear in his voice. "I'll kill you if you lie to me." The threat wasn't void.

Steven tried to nod, but because of what Dirk saw, he had tightened his grip so hard that Steven was turning blue. His eyes rolled, and he passed out. Dirk couldn't hold up the limp weight as he let him drop to the floor then put his foot over the unconscious man's throat.

"Grab it all," Dirk said. "Cass, find a box."

"No," AJ replied, reaching inside carefully to make sure he didn't touch anything other than what he was after. He pulled out a container of DVDs marked 'Cassie' and then reached back inside for two more containers of loose photographs and small VHS tapes. "We'll leave the rest for the police."

Cass couldn't believe AJ would want to leave anything behind as she stepped over Steven's passed out body and looked into the space for herself. "Oh God," she cried, her hand covering her mouth. The safe was carefully arranged. There were clear shoe box containers organized by the first names of girls with dates beside the names. Photos and disks were inside the boxes. Steven had three children, two girls and a boy, all of whom were adults now. When his wife Regina divorced him she took the kids. Cass couldn't believe that she was seeing the names of his daughters on two of the boxes. Immediately she began to sob.

"Get out of here, baby. Let me handle—"

At that moment, she screamed. Steven had come to, and he reached up and grabbed her leg just above the knee.

AJ's hands weren't free, but he delivered a devastating kick to Steven's forearm as a resounding crack was heard.

"You broke my arm, you son-of-a—" Steven started to scream.

Dirk stomped down on Steven's throat so hard, she was worried he'd crush his windpipe, and then what had been a mission to retrieve her items would become a murder scene.

"Shut up, asshole," he spewed, "or you won't need to worry about your arm with a broken neck." He looked back up at A.J, "So, if we're leaving some of this, what's the plan?"

"Take this Cass," AJ said, carefully handing her the containers. "Go get in the car and wait for me—*go, Cass*."

She felt rooted to the spot. She was terrified at whatever he had planned for the man whimpering on the floor.

"Go now. I'll be there in a couple minutes." The look on her face must have told him every thought going through her head. "Trust me, please. I know what I'm doing."

She turned and started out of the closet when she heard Steven calling out to her.

"Cassie, don't leave me here with these guys. Cassie—Cassie..."

His voice faded as she put distance between them, exiting into the garage and running for the car.

It was near eleven in the morning, and the Texas sun beat down on the sports car, making it unbearable to sit inside. She placed the items on the floorboard. AJ had the key; she would just stand beside the open car door until he came out—and it seemed to take forever as she waited.

Suddenly a pop rang out, like the sound of a twenty-two caliber gun going off. It was followed by the most blood curdling screams and wails she'd ever heard. Her feet were in motion as she started to dash toward the house, but AJ came running around the corner headed toward her. Dirk was already in his truck and backing down the driveway. Several of the neighbors were coming out of their houses to see what was going on.

"Get in the car!" he yelled.

She obeyed, but she'd never been so terrified in her life.

"What did you do?!" she demanded as he cranked the car and spun it around in the street, with Dirk close behind.

"Not now, Cass. I'll tell you when we—"

"Did you kill him?" she choked out the question she feared asking.

"No, baby. He's not dead. I'll tell you in a little while. Sit tight and I'll have you home in a bit."

"Is Dirk—is he—"

"He's following us back to your place. I hope you're okay with that."

She nodded and then began to sob when she looked down. She'd kicked one of the boxes over when she jumped into the car; nude pictures of a little girl were scattered on the floor. AJ glanced and then looked back at the road as she rushed to put them in the box.

"It's okay, Cass, I don't think he has anything else. He had one more DVD in his computer that he gave me. But he swears he didn't save the files to his hard drive." AJ pulled the shiny disc from his shirt pocket. It was already broken in two.

"I—I heard something that sounded like a gun. It scared me so bad, I thought... I was worried about you."

He drew a long breath, "It was a nail gun from his workbench."

"Did—did you shoot him with it?"

"Maybe we should wait until we get to your house."

"Our house," she said softly.

"Our house," he agreed. "Are you feeling okay?"

"I'll be alright, but you look like you're in pain."

"I've got a headache coming on."

They wouldn't be at her house for another fifteen or twenty minutes and she could see he was struggling as he squinted at the road, "Pull over. Let me drive."

She wondered if he might argue, but he didn't as he drove the car into a service station and changed positions with her. Dirk was behind them, watching with a curious expression as they switched out. As soon as she sat in the driver's seat, she saw it. He had a bruise forming on the left side of his face. "AJ," she cried out. "Did—did you get hit?!"

"He got in one good punch," he said as he reclined the seat and closed his eyes.

She wanted to fall apart and start bawling but it wouldn't help.

When he attempted to crack his eyes open, her car was under the cover of the emergency room entrance to the hospital, and Dirk was getting a wheel chair for him.

"No, no, Cass," he said faintly as they helped him into the chair, but his attempt to resist was as feeble as his voice, "it's just a migraine."

Dirk sat in the waiting room, and Cass stayed with AJ until they took him away to be scanned. She went back out and sat beside him, trying her best not to cry.

"So what's wrong with him? Is this why you had his friend with you at the restaurant?"

She nodded, "He has an aneurysm in his brain. It's really thin. A—a hard hit to the head..." She let the tears fall and she couldn't continue.

She could tell it was freaking Dirk out to see her this way; it was a side to her he didn't know or understand. She explained more about AJ's condition to him as they sat and waited for the nurse to come out and get her. The longer the wait, the more nervous she became. She had to do something to get her mind off the terror filling every fiber of her body. "Tell me what happened after I walked out of Steven's house," she asked as she dropped her face into her palms, wiping her eyes.

"He didn't tell you?"

"He started to, but then... Just please, Dirk, tell me what happened with the nail gun."

"He said, after you left, that Steven needed to pay for what he'd done to you, and every other girl whose name was written on a box in his safe. I thought he wanted to kill him; I figured what the hell, my life has been in the toilet lately anyway, so I said I'd do it. He wouldn't need to take part. I owe you that much, Cass. You seem really happy being with him."

She gasped reflexively. She couldn't believe Dirk would have gone to that extreme for her. Before she could speak he continued.

"But he said he wasn't going to kill him; he said that would be too easy of an out for him."

"So what did he do?"

"We took him back out to the workbench," Dirk's face was starting to redden. "AJ grabbed a piece of cabinet trim board and wrote the words 'child molester' on it and then a line to tell the cops to look in his bedroom safe."

"You... He nailed it to him?"

Dirk's face became redder but a smile formed on his lips,

"Yeah, he nailed it to him, all right, but I don't know if I should tell you. I thought it was pretty damn creative."

"Please," she asked, resting her trembling, cold hand on his arm.

He covered her hand with his and gave her a tender smile, "I'm so sorry I was such a stupid asshole when it came to you, Cass." He took a long breath, but then lowered his voice to make sure no one would hear him. "He wanted to make sure Steven would have a painful reminder the next time he thought about little girls and sex, so he..."

She hadn't heard him. "What?" she whispered back.

At that moment, an ambulance pulled up to the emergency doors and the crew came rushing in with Steven on a gurney. He was moaning and crying, as they hurried him down the hall with a blood soaked drape over his bare lower half.

"He made him drop his pants, put the piece of wood over his dick, and then nailed right through to the workbench." Dirk smiled as Steven's gurney disappeared into a back room. He looked back at Cass, almost to break out in laughter. "He left him a claw hammer..." he added as if it had been a humanitarian step, but then he finished. "...slightly out of reach."

She finally smiled as she thought about Steven literally riveted in place as he struggled to get to the hammer before a neighbor or the police could see what was written on the wood. She was sure AJ would have made it close enough that he'd try reaching for it, yet far enough away so he'd never get it. The police came in right after Steven's entrance and headed down the hallway. It looked like her brother would finally get what he truly deserved. She felt bad for those whose images had been left at the house, but she was pretty certain the police would be sensitive about the privacy of his victims.

A few more minutes passed, and the nurse came out. She was smiling. "He didn't have a rupture. He must have had a little too much excitement today, and it gave him a migraine."

Cass breathed a huge sigh of relief.

"The doctor gave him something to manage the pain, but you should be able to take him home in a little while."

"Thank you so much," she said, choking up again.

The nurse walked away as Dirk turned to her, "What's different about you, Cass? I know this whole business with your brother freaked you out, but something is really different. You're not like this. The Cass I know is so strong, she would have nailed that son-of-a-bitch herself."

She gave a small laugh. He was right. If she'd never met AJ, and came home to this mess with Steven, she probably would have shot him. "I'm pregnant. I think it might have a little bit to do with my emotional handicap right now. Well, that and the fact that losing AJ scares me to death."

His eyebrows went up, "Holy shit! Really?"

"Yeah, and even though I'm bawling my eyes out lately, I've never been happier. Listen, Dirk, I'd like to offer you your job back. I mean, after today—"

"No, beautiful. I know me too well; I couldn't take being around you. I'd eventually screw up, and I don't want to hurt you anymore. I've got a couple of applications in with some other companies. I'll be fine."

"How bad is the debt?" she asked quietly.

"Don't worry about it."

"You might as well tell me, you know how stubborn I can be."

He chuckled, "Now you're starting to sound like the Cass I know." He looked down and scuffed one boot against the other, "I'm about ten grand behind on my mortgage. They started the foreclosure proceedings, but hell, the courts are so backed up with foreclosures right now it might take them a year or two before they kick me out."

"You know I seem to recall you had a severance package coming to you."

"We don't get... Oh. Nah, I'm a prick, and I deserve a little punishment."

"You seem to forget who the boss is Mister Blanchard," she said, getting back to her old self. "I said you have a severance package coming to you. Don't argue with me about it."

He smiled and gave her a hug. She wasn't ready to get *that* friendly as she pushed him back slightly. She watched the old spark light up his eyes, but then he sighed.

"Sorry."

"Good luck at whatever job you apply for, and just remember to put me on your reference list."

"Do you want me to wait with you for a little while?"

"No, I'll be fine. Go home, and thanks for your help today," she said as she glanced down the hallway.

Just before they released AJ, the clerk for the hospital sat with Cass collecting payment information. She knew AJ wasn't on her insurance, but that didn't matter. She would pay the bill, but she needed to get the clerk to walk away from the computer. She handed over her driver's license and insurance card, explaining that she and AJ married recently. She lied, saying that she hadn't received the new card with both their names on it, yet. When the young lady got up to make copies, Cass leaned over and changed the admission time on the computer screen from 11:20 to 9:20.

AJ was still in misery when they wheeled him out. He had a cloth covering his eyes to keep the sunlight from worsening his pain. The orderlies placed him in the passenger's seat, and she drove him home. He made it as far as the couch; he couldn't make it up the stairs. She drew the curtains, and tried to make him as comfortable as possible then slipped out of the room.

She didn't know if her dad would be sober at two in the afternoon, but she decided to give it a try. He answered his cell after two rings.

"Pumpkin?" he answered sounding close to sober.

"Hey Daddy, listen I know it's after twelve, but could you set the signing up for tomorrow morning? I wanted AJ to be with me, but I had to take him to the hospital today because—"

"The hospital? Is he okay?"

"He came down with a migraine, and it's pretty bad. That's why we didn't make it to the office," she lied.

"Sure, of course, I'll set it for tomorrow. Pumpkin, I want you to know I actually like him. I didn't think there'd ever be a man good enough for my little girl, but, if I could have picked out my own son-in-law, I couldn't have done any better."

"Thanks, Daddy. I—I love you."

"I love you, too. See you bright and early tomorrow morning. Is eight okay?"

"That will be great. We'll be there." As soon as she hung up, she decided to call Dirk.

He answered quickly.

"Dirk, I know several of Steven's neighbors saw our vehicles leaving his house, but I have an alibi. I just wanted to be sure you knew what to say in case the police show up."

"Actually, Cass, there is a sheriff's car that just pulled into my driveway, so talk fast."

"Say I called you just before nine a.m. to help me get AJ to the hospital. I changed the time on the hospital's admission record, so their computer will back up our story."

"Thanks, Cass. I got it." And the phone call ended.

An hour later, the sheriff's car was in her driveway. She walked outside before they could come to the door. "Sheriff Denton," she said as the elderly officer and a younger officer approached.

"Well, Cassandra Henley, look at you all grown up and pretty. I bet it's been eight or nine years since I seen you last. How's your daddy?"

"He's just fine. Drunk by noon most days, but you know that's my daddy," she said with a small laugh.

The younger man was giving her a thorough look over. It appeared he liked what he was seeing.

"So what brings you out here? No escaped prisoners or anything like that in the area is there?"

He gave a chuckle and said no, but then his face became serious. "Cass we had a little problem at your brother's house today."

"Half-brother," she corrected him. "You're talking about Steven, not Tommy, right?"

"Yeah, Steven. Seems a couple folks went into his house and beat the tar out of him."

"Really?"

"Yup, and some of the folks said there was a blonde woman there who looked like you."

"Couldn't have been me, I haven't seen him in ages."

"Well, it seems this blonde woman and a muscular, dark haired fellow drove out of there in a red Dodge viper. I ran your registrations and you own one. Doesn't that seem like a bit of a coincidence?"

"It sure does, and if I was in your shoes, I'd be suspicious too, but it wasn't me. I spent most of my day at the hospital."

"Is that so? What were you doing there?"

"My husband has a serious medical problem. I had a friend come over and help me take him in for a CAT scan."

"I don't recall anything in the local papers about you getting hitched."

"No, you know me, I don't like publicity. We married a week

ago down in Florida. I wanted to keep it quiet. You can check with the hospital, we really were there. We just got home a little bit ago."

"Let me talk to this new husband of yours."

"No. He's in a lot of pain, and I'm not going to let you disturb him."

"What's wrong with him?" the younger officer asked, sounding as if he expected to trip her up.

"He has a brain aneurysm," came her quick reply.

"Wouldn't he be dead?" the young man continued, "Bleeding in the brain is usually fatal."

"It is an aneurysm, not a rupture. A vein inside his lobes has a weak spot. You know like a tube inside a bike tire gets sometimes and bulges out."

The young man became silent.

"Cass, do you know anything about your brother having a problem, a sexual problem?"

She tried her best to appear surprised, "Steven has always been a little weird. He keeps to himself mostly. He's kind of the black sheep of the family. Why?"

"When he gets out of the hospital, we're arresting him for child pornography."

"That sounds really serious. Are you sure he's into that?"

"Yeah, we carted box-loads of evidence out of his house. We're pretty certain the two men and the woman who were at his house today may have removed some of the evidence. You know," he said, eyeing her carefully, "like they were trying to protect someone he molested."

Cass didn't say anything.

"Did your brother ever do anything to you? Maybe took some pictures or video?"

She couldn't answer, but all she had to do at this point was shake her head no and try her best not to tear up.

"All right, Cass," he said with a knowing nod, "I'm going to review those hospital records and see if your story checks out, but you do know no one would blame someone who'd been victimized, no matter what Steven says; the child is never to blame for a sick adult's misconduct."

She nodded her head in agreement.

"How did you know we were referring to your brother Steven,

instead of Tommy?" The other officer asked. Once again he was sounding like a dime-store Colombo.

"That's easy. I only have two, and Tommy lives in Georgia."

He was without a response, again, as the older man gave him an annoyed glance and then spoke up, "By the way, what's your husband's name so I can check the records."

"Lisowski," she stated and then spelt it for the young deputy who was writing it down, "AJ Lisowski."

The sheriff's eyebrows rose in surprise. He'd been the sheriff in their town for twenty-five years, and he was the one who investigated her mother's death. He knew her father only too well, "Did him being Polish set okay with your daddy?"

"To tell you the truth, Sheriff Denton, Daddy thinks he's wonderful."

"That's good, sweetheart. Maybe there is some hope for your poppa after all."

The tears finally filled her eyes, "Hope is all we have."

He patted her arm and then left.

By six p.m. the story about Steven was on the evening news. She watched it in the kitchen while she fixed a light supper, hoping the whole time she would be able to get AJ to eat something. This migraine was much worse than the one he suffered after swimming in the cold spring. She came out and sat on the floor beside the couch. She cooked a homemade chicken soup with rich broth, chicken breast meat, carrots, potatoes, onions, and celery, and made a small batch of tender biscuits. She'd been snacking as she cooked in the kitchen and, so far, her nightly nausea hadn't happened. She brought him a fresh, cold cloth for his cheek as she replaced the one he'd been holding against his head. The only light she had in the great room was candlelight in the fireplace.

"Hey, baby," she whispered, lifting the cover from his eyes, "do you think you could eat a little bit?"

He kept his eyes closed, "It smells good, but I don't know if I'm ready. Can you get me a Topamax?"

"The doctor said to wait until around eight," she reminded him.

"Yeah, but he doesn't have my headache."

She leaned over and kissed his closed eyelids, "I'll be right back."

She returned with the pill and held a drink for him as he

washed it down, "The bottle says it shouldn't be taken on an empty stomach. If I spoon a little broth into your mouth, can you keep it down?"

"As long as I don't have to chew, I'll try."

She put the first spoonful in his mouth and listened as he swallowed.

"It's good," he whispered.

She got another eight or nine spoonfuls down him before he said it was enough.

"Are you okay?" he asked, "Any nausea tonight?"

"No. I listened to Doctor Lisowski and snacked while I cooked."

"Did you want to talk about what happened?" his voice growing softer with each uttered word.

She could tell that even the simple act of speaking was a little too much for him, "No. You just rest. Dirk told me most of it. Are you going to be able to make it up to the bedroom?"

"Honestly, Cass, I can't move right now. Can you put the cloth back over my eyes?"

She covered his eyes and whispered how much she loved him. She put the dinner tray back in the kitchen then went upstairs and grabbed the pillows and blankets. She covered him up, put her pillow on the floor beside the couch, laid down, and went to sleep. He woke around midnight, still miserable, and took another pill. He begged her to get off the floor and go up to bed, but she refused.

Charlie slept beside her, and around six-thirty he began to nudge his head up under her arm and lick her face. AJ finally seemed to be resting comfortably as he snored, so she tried to be extra quiet as she slipped out the front door. When she came back inside, he was sitting up on the couch, looking haggard.

She told him about meeting her dad at eight, but even though she wanted him there, she said she understood if he didn't feel well enough to go.

"I want to come. I may not be the life of the party, but I want to be there by your side."

He took another pill, pulled himself somewhat together, and dug out his shades because the light was still too painful for him.

When they made it out to the garage, he went for the passenger's side of the Viper, but she quickly stopped him.

"We're taking the Hummer. The," she paused for a moment, "items from yesterday are still in there."

He nodded and went to the other vehicle. When they reached the office, she could tell he was starting to feel better. He lifted his shades and put them on top of his head, laced arm-in-arm with Cass, and they walked in. It was his first opportunity to see her business close-up, and she was hoping he'd be even more impressed than when they'd done the fly over. She didn't rush him as she made a few introductions, and they worked their way back to her office.

"And this is my secretary, Jill Musserman. Jill this is my husband, AJ Lisowski. He's a writer for National Geographic."

Jill smiled broadly, and shook his hand, "It's nice to meet you. Can I get you anything while we're waiting for Mister Henley: water, coffee, or a Coke?"

"Coke sounds pretty good and I think it'll help."

Jill looked a little puzzled.

"He's had a migraine since yesterday, and he's just starting to get over it."

"Oh," she said, suddenly understanding completely, "In that case, you're right. My sister gets migraines, and she usually takes her meds with a Coke then hits the bed. I'll be right back."

They went into Cass's expansive office, and she headed toward her desk. Her office was large enough to contain a conference table for eight, along with her freestanding large desk, book shelves, computer station, and a huge plotter for printing out surveys.

"Nice office," AJ remarked, sitting down gingerly in one of the thickly padded leather chairs.

Cass went around her oversized mahogany desk to put her purse in a drawer. "Yeah, but it's a little on the masculine side. The problem is that commercial surveys are big, so my furniture needed to be large enough to spread them out. I like it though, and I'm not much of a girly-girl anyway."

"Pumpkin," came her dad's voice from the doorway.

AJ started to get up when her dad told him to stay put, "Cass told me about the trip to the hospital yesterday. What the hell happened to the side of your face?"

"He fell before we could get him in the car," Cass replied before AJ could answer.

"We? Who was helping you?"

"Dirk, actually."

Her dad's eyebrows went up.

"He came over to apologize about everything, and ended up helping me get him to the ER."

"I don't know if I'd trust that boy's apology, pumpkin."

"Normally, I wouldn't, but he was sincere, and he was a big help with AJ."

"I suppose you heard about your idiot brother."

"Yeah, it's a little hard to believe," she stated, the words leaving a bitter taste in her mouth.

"I guess I should go see him and find out if he needs help getting an attorney."

Panic filled her as she thought about the two of them meeting, "Don't do that, Dad. I'll get Nick to find out if he needs any help."

"Sherriff Denton said they have a lot of evidence on him, hundreds of counts with seventeen or eighteen children, so to tell you the truth, I was thinking about staying out of it and just let the court system give the idiot a public defender."

She nodded, "I agree."

"I knew when I married Irene that nothing good was gonna come out of it. She was wicked and mean spirited, loved to fight, and slept around on me so much that I said the hell with it and filed for divorce. She pops up and tells me she's pregnant and, like a fool, I took her back. Steven was only two when I couldn't take it anymore. I never should have let her have custody. I'm sure that's why he ended so screwed up."

"Daddy," she said, reaching out for his hand, "you can't blame yourself for the way Steven turned out. He was able to make choices for himself just like the rest of us. He's the only one who can be blamed for what he did with his life."

"I suppose you're right, pumpkin. I'm just glad he never touched any of you girls—I would have shot him."

She gave a weak smile as she hugged him, "I know, Daddy, I know."

At that moment, the company attorney walked in the room, "Well, good morning boss lady," Nicholas said.

After she made the introductions, they seated themselves at the conference table and he explained what changes would occur because of the transfer. He had the accounting department draw up all the current financial documents on the business, so she could see the exact standing at the time of the transfer. It was impressive, even to her, and she already had a good idea what the balance sheet would look like. The corporation had fourteen-point-nine million in fixed assets and another five-point-two million in liquid assets. She was about to become the sole owner of a twenty million dollar corporation. Wade agreed to stay on for as long as she needed his help, which, with everything getting ready to happen with AJ's medical issues and the baby, could be quite some time. He would draw his normal salary, but was refusing the split of job profits. She'd be in control of it all. With the papers signed and handshakes all around, Nicholas left saying he'd have everything filed with the courts before the day ended.

"And now," her dad said after the attorney left the room, "go on vacation. I'll handle all of this. You only have a few weeks until the surgery, enjoy them and don't worry about this place."

"I'm still handling the UK," she said stubbornly. "It's wrapping up in another week or two."

"Pumpkin, I've got it. Anything that pops up, I can handle. I'll call you. Enjoy your husband and get the hell out of here."

She wore a big smile as she threw her arms around his neck. "Stay away from the ice-machine," she whispered in his ear, "and, by the way, did you do what I told you? Did you call Rosie and apologize."

He frowned, "Yes." But then he smiled, "You can come over now and not puke your guts out. She has my house spotless and smelling good. Go on, get out of here."

AJ hadn't said much through the whole affair, but he stood and wrapped Cass in his arms and told her he agreed with her dad. It was time to forget what she'd just become the sole owner of and spend some well deserved time alone with him.

The only thing they had to do, to complete their happiness, was to get rid of what was in her car.

That night they sat out on the patio and built a blaze in the outdoor fireplace. He told her he didn't want to see what she had to take out of the boxes, so he kissed her tenderly and told her he'd be waiting for her inside. She melted down the DVDs and pieces of DVDs first, watching the multicolored flames that the melting plastic created. Those weren't hard for her because she couldn't see what he'd put on them, but the master DVD he placed in a case by itself—she knew exactly what it contained. Angry and bitter tears washed down her face as she watched it dissolve into a molten puddle. The last to go were the photographs. She tried not to look at them, but it simply couldn't be helped as she watched the images of the slight, blonde-haired girl with the fake smile and large, frightened eyes turn black and then disintegrate into smoke and vanish. She even burned the plastic containers they had taken from his safe, marked simply with the word "Cassie" on the boxes. She'd never been so happy to see a name destroyed.

CHAPTER NINETEEN

She assumed that their lives would slow down for a little while, but between writing the story of Kingdom Hill, and trying to enjoy each other, there was so much to get ready before the surgery—which loomed ever closer. She decided they would live in St. Paul for a short time before, and quite a while after, the surgery. It would make things so much easier when he needed to be seen by Doctor Ericsson.

She found a perfect home in the historic district. It had been on the market for a while and the owners were finally ready to lease it out. It was a three story home built in the 1870's with a stunning view of the St. Paul skyline, and the best part was that it was only a mile from the hospital. The house had been completely redone and modernized with gorgeous hardwood floors, a gourmet kitchen, a sumptuous master suite and a big deck out back where they could sit and enjoy the view of the river. The backyard had a small fenced area so Charlie could enjoy the beautiful weather as well.

They would move to St. Paul two weeks before the operation. He was supposed to meet with his doctors ten days before the surgery to go through some additional testing and be briefed on what to expect. Since the fight with Steven, his headaches reoccurred on a regular basis. At first, she thought it stemmed from the hit he'd taken, but as the time to the surgery drew closer she realized it was his nerves; he was petrified. She called Doctor Ericsson and told him how the stress was affecting him; he prescribed Valium to help him deal with the pending surgery.

She didn't like making him take a sedative, but once he, reluctantly, started using the Valium, he relaxed and the headaches stopped. He was suddenly AJ once again. He was happy and comfortable, and intensely curious—constantly—about the baby's development. Cass worked hard to keep the nausea at bay. She felt sick all day long, but she rarely threw up. She stuck with the plan of multi-small meals, crackers, ginger tea, ginger ale, nausea bands; whatever came highly recommended, she tried it.

Her dad ran the business and, according to Jill, who reported the office happenings on a regular basis to Cass, he was staying sober longer than he'd ever done in the past. He would hold off having his first beer of the day until about three or four in the afternoon—which was phenomenal for him.

Cass was happy with how everything was progressing, until she flew them up to move into the house in St. Paul. The airport was two miles from the house, basically just across the river. They had a few days to get settled in, and then found themselves in the familiar surroundings of St. Joseph's hospital. They wanted him to do another overnight stay for testing in the morning, but he refused.

"I don't have to be hooked up and lying in a bed in this hospital. I'll be here tomorrow, bright and early. I'll follow the rules of no food or drink after midnight, but I'm not sleeping here and making my pregnant wife sleep in the recliner because I know she won't, no matter what I say, go back to our place for the night."

"We'd prefer if you'd—" Doctor Ericsson began.

"No. I'll see you in the morning," he said, grabbing Cass by the elbow and heading for the door.

He surprised her, but she felt the same way. Staying in the hospital only caused him unnecessary anxiety, and why do that if he could just come back in the morning for the test? He needed a Valium in the next day, but he wasn't allowed to have anything in his system, not even water, so he had a headache coming on by the time they were prepping him for the angiogram. His CAT scan was scheduled for thirty minutes after the first test, but he was so miserable, they checked him into a room and medicated him to get him relaxed. Within a few hours they scanned him. An hour later, when he could stand being in the light once again, they met with Doctor Ericsson.

"What the hell have you been doing?!" was the first thing out of the doctor's mouth.

"What do you mean?" Cass asked, since AJ was a little slow on the draw under all the drugs.

"His aneurysm has grown by one and a half millimeters since he was here last!"

"He hasn't—"

"Have you two been overly active—sexually?"

Cass cut her eyes to AJ; he appeared just as perplexed as she was.

"Isn't sex safe for him?" she finally asked.

"Doctor Kennabrook told me I could enjoy as much as I wanted," AJ interjected.

"That's because he didn't figure you were going to live anyway," the doctor stated, sounding exasperated. "Why cut yourself off if there is no hope for a cure?"

"Then it's bad for him?"

"I didn't warn you two about sex because I didn't expect you to change your normal pattern of activity."

"Doctor Ericsson, we hadn't had *any* sex together when we came to see you. We didn't sleep together until about a week later," she stated.

"Didn't it give you a headache?" he asked

The corners of AJ's mouth turned into a slow smile as if he were remembering their first time in the tent, "Well, yeah. But it wasn't severe and it only bothered me a little after that."

"You never said... You told me you were fine."

"Cass, I wasn't going to worry you. They weren't migraines, just a dull throb that lasted a couple hours."

"A couple hours!" she snapped, "Every time?!"

"Yeah, pretty much."

She gave a frustrated, "Aaah," and closed her eyes, letting her head fall back on the top of the chair. She thought about the fact that they had sex last night just before midnight. That was most likely the reason his tests this morning set off a headache—his brain had only stopped throbbing hours earlier.

"So have my chances changed as far as how long I'll last before a rupture?"

"The vein has outlasted everyone's predictions, and even though it's slightly larger than before, I'd still say you have another three to four months. But," he added with a scold, "we aren't going to wait to find out how accurate my forecast is because you'll be in surgery in a week and a half."

"No, I won't."

Cass's head snapped so hard to the right to look at him, she actually heard a popping sound, "What?!"

"I'm not having the surgery."

Cass went to pieces immediately, "AJ, why? You won't make it."

He turned to her, cupping her face in his hands, "I've been thinking it over; I want to see our baby. If I have the surgery and something goes wrong, I'll never..." his voice choked.

"That's too long," Doctor Ericsson stated before Cass could speak.

"I—I won't have this baby for another seven to eight months. You can't—"

"I was supposed to be dead by this time last year; I'll make it."

"No you won't," Doctor Ericsson said with certainty. "The longer you wait, the more dangerous the surgery. We already know it's growing again, and that means it's thinning and stressing out the rest of the vein. You aren't going to leave us anything to work with when we get in there if you wait."

"What do you mean?" she asked as she finally took her eyes away from AJ's intent gaze.

"The vein isn't just weak in that one spot; he's stressing and thinning the entire length. We are planning to use a piece of vein from his leg to replace what we remove, but the thinner the vein, the harder it's going to be to stitch the new to the old. You're dropping your fifty-fifty chance to more like eighty-twenty if you put it off."

"*Please, baby,*" she pled, "don't put it off. You have a chance to come out of this, and you'll be able to be with me when our baby is born. If you wait, you won't even make it to the birth."

"It's a chance I'm just going to have to take; I want to see my child."

"If you're going to try to pull this off, you're going on bed rest," the doctor frowned, "and no more sex," he added.

"I can't do either of those, but I'll take it easy and hang around the house. We'll only have sex once in a while."

Cass wanted to tell him there was no way she was agreeing to anymore sex, but she was too busy sobbing her eyes out.

"If you won't do this for yourself, at least do it for her and this baby. Don't wait."

"Sorry, doc, no can do. I'll see you in eight or nine months from now."

It was a good thing the house was only a mile away from the hospital because she didn't believe she could drive any further without an accident. She pled and begged harder than she'd ever done in her life for him to change his mind. They went upstairs to their bedroom and lay down as he tried to explain why he had to wait.

"If it makes you feel better, Cass, we'll stay in St. Paul, so we won't be far from the hospital. I'll take it easy. I'll just be a lazy bum and watch you get fat." He was teasing her, trying to get her to smile.

"If I had any clue you were going to do this, I wouldn't be pregnant right now."

He became somber instantly, as somber as if she'd looked at him and said that she didn't love him anymore, "Don't say that, Cass, please. Don't regret the life we've made."

"I don't, nor will I ever regret this child inside me. But, AJ, if I had any idea this baby was going to change your decision about the surgery, I would have just told you to get me pregnant after the operation."

"It wouldn't have been the same, Cass. This baby's chance for life was a one-shot deal, and to tell you the truth, I believe with all my heart you conceived the first time I made love to you. I'm not giving up; I want to be here to make more babies with you after this one, but I just know *I've got to see this baby*."

"I'm not sleeping with you anymore," she whimpered.

He tilted her chin up and kissed her slowly.

She melted into his hold. She'd already told him since she became pregnant she was aroused all the time.

"You can try to turn me down, but it's just too good between us, Cassandra. I don't care what the doctor says, headache or not, I feel better every time I disappear inside of you. Making love to you makes me happy. Don't take it away—please."

They held each other for a long time as Cass eventually cried herself to sleep in his arms. When she woke, he was deep asleep. She slipped from the bed, left the room, and made a couple phone calls.

The next afternoon their doorbell rang.

"Can you get that?" she asked him as she loaded the dishwasher.

He looked a little puzzled, but said sure. When he opened the door, both of his parents, his brother, and Bobby were standing on the front stoop. He slammed the door in their faces and turned to look at her as he snapped, "What'd you do that for!"

She walked around him and reopened the door, inviting their company inside. "Because," she said as she grabbed her purse, "somebody has to talk some sense into your thick head!"

"You're not leaving," he said in a menacing tone, grabbing for her.

She looked down at the hand that gripped her arm.

His hold softened. "Please, don't leave," he asked, devoid of anger.

"I'll be back. You need to listen to other people who love you as much as I do—without me around." She walked out into the afternoon sunshine and stayed away until Bobby sent her a text asking her to return.

No one looked happy.

"We've reached a compromise," Bobby stated as soon as she sat down. "He'll—"

"I will," AJ interrupted, "have the surgery..."

She openly sighed, but she should have waited for him to finish.

"...in sixteen weeks."

"Sixteen weeks? That's four months!"

His mother reached out and rested her hand on Cass's arm, "You're first sonogram, so he can see the baby."

"I'll have it now," she cried. "We'll go first thing in the morning."

"Cass, I've already looked up fetal development on the computer; I don't want to see a pile of cells, I want to see our baby. Twenty to twenty two weeks should give us a perfect picture, after that I'll—I'll go to surgery."

Four months was the longest amount of time the doctor estimated he'd last. She wasn't happy about it, but it was certainly better than him waiting until the birth.

She told everyone when she called them on Wednesday that she'd like for them to stay Thursday night or longer, if they could manage it. His parents and brother had a flight back to Virginia the next afternoon, but Bobby, due to the long nature of his trip, would spend the whole weekend. The house, at twenty-five-hundred square feet, was more than adequate to accommodate everyone. There were three bedrooms and a queen-size pullout in the finished basement.

She made dinner reservations for the garden patio at W.A. Frost's. Like everything in St. Paul, it wasn't far away. They spent the evening in the comfortable night air under the soft lights, enjoying a delicious meal, and good company.

She would never tell AJ, but she felt like an outsider, listening as they talked and laughed about things that happened years ago in his life. He had his family memories, his boyhood memories, and memories of things he and Bobby had done as teenagers and young men. She felt like such a foreigner in this circle; she had known him barely two months, yet in that tiny span of time he showed her more love than she'd known in a lifetime. She found herself feeling strangely jealous of how much they'd been privileged to share with him.

She ached for the ability to turn time around, to go back, back to the time when he learned about the aneurysm, to the time when his fiancée turned her back on him, to a time when Bobby pulled his spirit out of misery and put him back on his feet. She would have liked to have stepped into his life at that point and let him heal her broken trust in humanity. She would have brought him here and, surely that early, these doctors could have corrected his problem, and right now they would have years and years of memories to sit here and reminisce about, and several children to love and raise together.

She was still deep in thought when she felt his kiss on her cheek and his whispered breath in her ear telling her how much he loved her. She smiled. He said he had been praying for God to give him a beautiful experience, but she knew she was the one who received the answer to his prayer.

"You're beautiful," she whispered back.

He had a puzzled grin but then squeezed her tightly.

His family left the next day, saying they would return when he went to surgery. Cass had nothing to offer Bobby as far as some fun adventure while he was in St. Paul because she wouldn't let AJ do much more than take a walk down to the river and back. She did take them for one, sunset flight, Friday evening in her Caravan—

which he found to be extremely cool. But he didn't seem to mind that they didn't have any big escapade planned; he was honestly happy to just be hanging with AJ.

On Saturday, she grilled steaks on the back porch. The guys had a couple beers and argued about sports teams, and which national sport was better. But all the arguing was done in jest; they were just having fun with each other. She did have to burst their manly bubbles though when she forbade them to start a wrestling match.

She woke early Sunday morning to cook them breakfast, and was surprised to find Bobby in the kitchen digging through the cabinets.

"What are you looking for?" she asked softly, but still managed to make him jump.

"Sorry, bad habits of getting up at five a.m. every morning die hard. I was going to start the coffee."

She opened the freezer and pulled out the bag, "It stays a little fresher this way."

"Ah, I see," he said accepting it and giving her a sleepy smile. "How are you holding up through all of this, Cass? It must be hard on you with the added stress of the baby."

"No, I'm pretty good. I feel nauseous all the time, but the doctor tells me another six or seven weeks and that should all be behind me. I just wish AJ wasn't going to wait four months before the surgery."

"Me, too, but there was no talking him out of it, and, to tell you the truth, if I was in his shoes, I—I understand wanting to see the baby."

"So how are you going to manage taking all this time off work?" she asked. He already told her he would arrive the week before the surgery and would stay with the two of them as long as it took to see that AJ recovered. He would be the one to help her, once he came home, with all of his needs. She told him AJ might have little to no side-effects from the surgery, or he might have to re-learn how to walk, talk, feed himself—everything we take for granted in our daily lives. Pregnancy would prevent her from doing the heavy work, and she said, if it wasn't so severe that he needed to be placed in a rehab center for a while, she would need to hire a live-in assistant; Bobby told her there would be no need, he'd be there for both of them.

"I told my boss I might need to take an extended leave of absence. I just wouldn't know how long until after the operation."

"But what about money? Isn't this going to put you in a bind, financially?"

Bobby blushed slightly and looked down as he started scooping coffee into the filter, "I have some money saved, but I told my mum I'd need to store my things at her house until I get back. No need in paying for a flat if I'm not going to be there."

"Ah! I don't want you to lose your apartment. You seem to really like your place."

"It's just a flat, Cass. Nothing special that can't be replaced. AJ is more important, and my mum understands."

"So have you always worked behind a desk with the RICS?"

"Oh, no. I graduated with a geometrics engineering degree and started with a surveying company right out of college."

"Really? That's my degree, too. So how did you end up being a paper pusher?"

He smiled, "I like how you never seem to be afraid to say anything."

She laughed, "Most people don't care for that trait."

"I like it," he stated with a darker blush. "My major was in geometrics, but my minor was in business administration. I had a friend recommend me when an opening with the RICS came about. After that, they said they would pay for additional college, so I went back to school and turned that minor into a Master's degree. AJ tells me your company is quite impressive," he added.

She couldn't stop the smile that formed on her lips, "If things go well with the surgery, I'll take him home to Texas to recover and you can see my operation." She paused, hoping what she was about to say wouldn't be taken the wrong way, "I appreciate everything you're willing to do for us, so I would like to compensate you for helping."

"No, please, Cass. It wouldn't matter if I didn't have a place to store my stuff and let it all go back. He's just too good of a friend for me not to be here."

"You're a wonderful man, Bobby Rose. AJ tried to tell me that not long after I met him, but... Well, let's just say I didn't believe trustworthy men existed. Thanks for everything," she said, rising on her tippy toes to give him a hug.

He turned red, again.

"But we have to do something about all that blushing," she teased.

"It's just the company," he admitted. "If you were a guy, we wouldn't have this problem."

Cass started laughing, "That's for sure, but I'm glad I'm not."

"Me, too." But he suddenly looked up at her, wide-eyed and surprised at himself for saying what he did, "I mean, I'm sure AJ's glad you're not."

"She's not what?" came a voice from behind them.

Cass smiled as AJ bumbled into the kitchen. She gave him a quick kiss, "We were just discussing the fact that I'm not a guy."

AJ shot a goofy look at Bobby, "Dude, you just figured that out?"

They all laughed.

CHAPTER TWENTY

The weeks passed as Cass's body began to expand to reveal the miracle she carried inside her. AJ didn't fuss about his restricted activity; instead he spent all his time 'talking' to the baby. He insisted that everything he read said a large portion of learning happens in the womb. He was playing classical music with earphones placed on her stomach. He would read to her with his head in her lap, so the baby could listen as well. And, at eighteen weeks of pregnancy, he was thrilled to tears when he felt the baby kick for the first time. Cass felt it several times, but he had never been fast enough to feel the sensation for himself.

Bobby came back to St. Paul the very day Cass turned nineteen weeks pregnant. He was shocked at the difference in her figure. The hospital arrangements for AJ had been finalized, and so had her appointment with a 3D/4D imaging center specializing in extraordinary fetal pictures. A week later, Bobby drove them there, but then tried to tell them he would just wait in the car. They both insisted he join them to see the picture of the baby.

Cass already told these folks how important this image was to her husband, and what he was facing once he saw his baby. She couldn't have asked for better treatment, as the nurses teased and fussed over AJ and Bobby. They made sure all three were extremely comfortable as they prepared Cass for the test. When the first images appeared on screen the baby's face was hidden, but her bottom end was not. The technician smiled as she congratulated them on the fact that they had a daughter.

AJ pressed his face against the part of Cass's stomach not being scanned at the moment and began to speak softly, "Hello, Aimee Jewel. I love you, baby girl. I can't wait to meet you."

There wasn't a dry eye in the room as everyone watched the baby respond to his voice. She rolled over, and suddenly her angelic little face appeared on the screen. It was a perfect picture as a small smile formed on her mouth. Her tiny hand came against her lips, and she began to suckle her thumb.

"Ah, Cass, she's so beautiful," AJ said through a voice filled with wonder.

"She looks like you," she responded, as she squeezed his hand, "she has your nose and your smile."

The technician took lots of photos, and spent extra time to make sure the images were as clear as possible. When the machine was turned off and the screen went dark, AJ looked at Cass and stated he was finally ready for surgery.

They would have tonight, and then, by seven in the morning, he would report to the hospital. After dinner, Bobby was in the kitchen cleaning up because he insisted she and AJ enjoy their time together tonight without daily tasks interfering. AJ left the room briefly then returned with a four-inch binder filled with pages; he placed it in Cass's lap. She had a good idea what he was giving her.

"Kingdom Hill?" she guessed. She had finished her portion a few weeks earlier and had given it to him. Now, she would finally get to see how he incorporated both versions. She had been intensely curious as to why he refused to let her see his rendition of the story beforehand.

He nodded, his eyes getting teary.

She opened the binder to the first page, but stopped after no more than two sentences. "AJ," she gasped, "this is—this is..."

"Yeah, it is," he said as his tears went over the rim of his lower lashes, "Since I don't know how it's going to end, I'm letting you finish it. You'll need to write the prologue because I had no clue what was going through your head before I came on the scene. And, you'll need to add in your thoughts here and there to make it accurate."

She turned pages in amazement as she stared at what he'd done; he'd written *their* story, basically from her viewpoint, from the moment they met up until the baby's sonogram yesterday. She began to tremble, as big tears rolled down her cheeks.

He took it from her shaky hands then turned to the place where they first discovered the scrolls—there it was—the story she'd written about Kingdom Hill had been inserted in the places where he had read to her. He put the manuscript on the coffee table as she crumpled against his chest.

"I can't write the ending," she cried. "You have to make it. You have to finish it."

He kissed her temple, telling her he wanted to go to bed early tonight.

She nodded, but then stopped him from rising off the couch, "You're not the only one with a surprise tonight. Bobby, can I get that item from you?"

Bobby disappeared into the guest bedroom and returned with a thick envelope. He handed it to Cass then seated himself across from AJ.

She gave it to AJ, and watched as he opened the envelope and pulled out the documents.

"What is this? Bobby, you bought a place?"

"Yes—with your wife's money."

His eyebrows furrowed together as he tried to solve the riddle.

"It's only land," Cass stated quietly, "but it has the most beautiful hill."

"Oh, Cass, are you serious? Is this the deed to Kingdom Hill?" he looked up, a smile waiting to spread across his cheeks.

"The rest of the world doesn't know what it is, only the three of us. The parcel is one-hundred-twelve acres of the finest sheep pasture in Scotland. It would have been too complicated for us to take ownership right now, but Bobby didn't have that problem, and I would have hated for someone to have picked it up in a foreclosure sale."

He wrapped her in his arms, and reiterated the fact he wanted to turn in early. She didn't argue.

After the doctor's advice, they'd been so careful about lovemaking, refraining to the point that over the last four months they'd only enjoyed each other eight times. Cass knew the number exactly because she cherished every time he took her in his arms. She knew he wanted to make love tonight, and she never needed him more than in this moment. They told Bobby goodnight and went upstairs to the master suite.

"No matter what happens," he whispered in the dim light of their bedroom, "I'm going to love you forever, even if it isn't here on this earth. But if that happens, Cass, and God takes me home, I want you to promise me you aren't going to stay lonely."

She started to shush him, but he put his fingers over her lips and stopped her.

"You said the first time you understood what I was thinking about you and Bobby, you thought I was twisted. I know love doesn't just happen, there has to be a connection, but give him a chance to see if it's there."

"I won't need to because you're going to be fine."

"We don't know that. I want to be fine with every cell in my body, but I'm okay with going home, if I have to, because He answered my prayer. You've been the most beautiful and incredible experience of my whole life. I can't even begin to describe how happy I've been over these last six months."

"Don't you dare leave me, Adam Jacob Lisowski. Aimee Jewel needs her daddy, and I need my husband, lover, and best friend."

"With all my soul, I'm fighting to stay; I just know it's not in my hands."

She started to speak when he kissed her. It was slow, deep, and intense. "No more talking, Cass. I want to love you so badly right now it's like fire in my veins. I need you, all of you, right down to the breath in your lungs. No more words, and no more tears tonight," he whispered, as he laid her back on the comforter and stroked her cheeks. "Give me your beautiful smile and tell me you want me."

"With all my heart," she whispered, and then answered his passion with her own.

What an exquisite night. There were two bodies present in that space in time, but only one mind as they fulfilled their deepest, unspoken needs.

CHAPTER TWENTY-ONE

They arrived on time at the hospital, and the admission process began. There were things that had to be done today to prepare him, and tomorrow morning, by eight, he would be on the operating table. His parents and brother made it by ten a.m. Doctor Ericsson met with them in AJ's room by eleven.

He said AJ wanted to go over some very critical issues with them all together. Each of them knew his feelings about living a life as a vegetable, unable to take part in the world around him; he made it clear he would not want a feeding tube. He also reminded them he would not want to be kept on artificial life support if there was no chance for recovery, and he stated he'd already given Doctor Ericsson's team the permission to use him for organ donations should anything go wrong.

He wrote each of them a long note, only to be opened if he didn't make it, and the final envelope he gave to Cass, which was also to remain sealed, saying it contained his wishes for his funeral service.

Then it was Doctor Ericson's turn to discuss what would take place before, during, and after the surgery. "Once we've shaved him, he'll be given something to relax him to a point of a twilight state. Just before we begin, he'll be given a stronger drug which will put him completely to sleep. We'll attach him to some special monitors so we can watch the aneurysm during the entire time in the operating room.

"Doctor Yuler will begin with the surgery to harvest the vein from his leg then Doctor Phillips and I will come in a little later and open the skull, and locate and shut off the blood flow to the offending vein. We'll remove the damaged section and suture in the replacement then slowly restore the blood flow, making sure there are no tears or leaks.

"After we're satisfied the surgery has been a success, and all his statistics are stable, we'll close him up and put him in the recovery room for a brief period before moving him to ICU. He'll be awake in roughly three to four hours after the operation, and should be surprisingly cognizant. We don't like to dope our patients too heavily because the best indicator of how they are doing usually comes from their own mouths.

"Kind of like the new mommy or daddy counting ten fingers and ten toes," he said with a smile directed at Cass. "You wouldn't want them to bring out the baby with its hands and feet covered, or you'd wonder what's wrong. It's the same way with brain surgery. We want him awake and alert with minimal medication, so he can speak clearly and show us that he still has all his faculties."

"It sounds like you're pretty certain he's going to come out of this okay," his brother stated.

His parents seemed so overwhelmed; they just sat quietly and listened.

"I wish I could tell you he's going to be fine, but this is a high risk surgery. Any number of things could go wrong. We rarely lose someone on the table, post-op is a little more difficult, but the two or three days following the surgery makes all the difference. He'll have nurses testing him every hour for any signs of problems, we'll do another CAT scan the following morning, and then we wait and pray for no bleeds and no vasospasm."

"What's a vasospasm?" Bobby asked before anyone else could speak.

"It's something that can happen when an aneurysm ruptures, or after brain surgery. Basically, all the blood veins in the cranium spasm and contract, shutting off blood flow to the brain. Sometimes it's brief and causes limited neural damage, most of the time it's devastating, and the damage is irreversible. AJ is young and in excellent physical health, so we're hoping for the best scenario."

"Which is?" his father spoke up.

"He'll make it through surgery, his first few days will be without incident, and then we can start talking about letting him get out of this place and on with his life."

They had numerous tests to run, and he asked his family to go back to the house and relax, he would see them all again just before surgery in the morning.

"I'm not leaving you here alone," Cass stated firmly.

"I'm not going to be alone. I've asked Bobby to stay with me for a while. Go home, get everybody settled in, take a little rest, and I'll see you later this afternoon."

"No," she replied stubbornly, "I'll give your folks the key to the house."

"Cass, please. I want to talk with Bobby for a while—alone. *Please*," he reiterated. "Besides, mom is dying to see the pictures of the baby from yesterday, and they're at home."

She gave a defeated sigh, leaned over and kissed his forehead, eyelids, nose, and eventually his mouth, "I'll be back by three."

"Make it five," he replied.

"Why do you need that much time?"

Then he said the words so familiar to her, words she'd come to love.

"Just trust me, Cass."

"With my whole heart," was her reply as she turned and led his family from the room.

Five o'clock exactly, she was back. When she walked in, Bobby looked up at her with reddened eyes. He appeared physically drained as if he and AJ had wrestled the whole time she'd been gone—and Bobby lost. She gave him the car keys and told him to go home and eat the dinner she'd prepared, catch a little rest, and then bring his family back by eight for the last of visiting hours because there wouldn't be much time in the morning to see him before surgery.

"You know, I think there's enough room for me up there," she said referring to his bed.

He immediately smiled and moved to one side as she climbed up and snuggled against him.

"So what did you and Bobby talk about?"

He kissed her forehead, "A lot of things, but mostly about you."

"What kind of things about me?" she asked quietly, keeping her head on his chest.

"I would never do anything to hurt you, you know that right?"

She nodded.

"He needed to know what I know about you."

She raised her head quickly and looked at him, *"You didn't.* AJ, please don't tell me that you told him *everything*."

"You said you trust me. I asked you if things go wrong tomorrow to give him a chance. I had to ask him the same thing, but he had to know what you'd never tell."

"No wonder he looked at me that way," she said as the sting hit her eyes. "I don't know if I can face him now."

"Cass," he said, putting his fingertips to her lips to hush her, "it broke his heart to hear what you've been through. He doesn't think less of you, he thinks more. He said he didn't know how you survived it. And, if Steven wasn't rotting in jail right now, I think he'd have headed for Texas and killed him. Don't be embarrassed to have him know. He thinks you're beautiful, strong, and perfect, just like I do. And I had to know how he would feel if you gave him a chance to be the other half of your soul."

"You're the other half of my soul," she defended, "I can't give away both halves."

"My half stays if I leave."

She started to argue, but he shook his head no to stop her, "But now, I have to tell you something about him that I wasn't sure of until just a little while ago. I've suspected it for a long time, but I didn't know for certain."

"He's gay," she let tumble from her lips.

His deep rumble rolled out of his chest and he burst out laughing.

They'd been so serious lately that she missed his beautiful laugh.

"Would you stop thinking that's the answer every time a guy doesn't try to jump you."

"He told me the last time he was here things would be easier between me and him if I was a guy," she defended.

"That's just because he feels so awkward around you. Cass, he's dated, but he's old fashioned, and has never been serious with a girl, they just make him too nervous. I had to ask him if—if he's still a virgin."

"He's not, is he?"

"Yeah, he is."

"AJ, I can't handle this. You're planning this as if you aren't going to make it. You have to stop and believe that you will."

"Cass, I *am* planning on making it, but I can't go into surgery if I leave things undone, especially where you and the baby are concerned."

"If something goes wrong, I'm the person who is going to be responsible for this baby."

"Will you let him help? He already told me that even if you aren't interested in him that way, he wants to be involved in Aimee's life. He said, if you'll let him, he wants to be there at the birth. He's my best friend, and he genuinely cares. He said he'd be happy if you could, at some point, just consider him *your* best friend."

She was too choked up; she couldn't respond.

"Just nod if you'll let him help."

She nodded then buried her face against his chest and cried.

"I love you, Cass—forever."

"Forever," she echoed, never moving.

When his family came into the room, Cass was just waking up. She'd fallen asleep pressed to his side. They spent the last hour as all of them talked, laughed, and enjoyed each other's company. AJ was as happy-go-lucky as if he'd spent the day surfing. He was cutting up and making jokes, threatening to get out of the bed and wrestle Bobby just to prove he could do it without exposing the cheeks of his butt in his stylish hospital gown. Cass felt he was putting on a brave front, but she was so glad to see him being himself. It was light hearted and happy, and everyone seemed relieved to have the heaviness of worry leave the room. When the nurse told them visiting hours were over, Cass announced she was staying the night.

"No you're not," AJ stated firmly. "You need your rest; they are going to be poking and prodding at me all night."

"I don't care," she snapped, losing her previous smile.

"I'll see you first thing in the morning."

"Yes you will because I'll wake up beside you."

"Actually, Mrs. Lisowski," the head nurse spoke up, "he needs a good rest tonight. We're going to give him something to help him sleep. It would be better for him if you came back tomorrow morning."

The growl was rising in her chest, when she felt his hand on hers, "Please, Cass, go home. The baby needs the rest, and tomorrow is going to be a long day; a day that I'll be glad to have behind me when I wake up and see your beautiful face."

He made her happy by phrasing it that way. She kissed him and walked out with the family.

The next morning they were all there, watching as the nurse prepared to shave his head. She ran the electric clippers against his scalp and all that beautiful, dark hair rolled off and hit the floor. But when the nursed grabbed the shaving cream and a razor, AJ stopped her.

"I want my wife to do this part."

The nurse didn't argue as Cass took the razor from her hand. She moistened his scalp and then applied the cream. Cass drew the disposable razor slowly across his skin, careful not to nick him, and within minutes, AJ was smooth and bald.

"Now you look like you did when you were born," his dad teased.

"No," his mother responded, "he had a little bit of hair when he was a baby. Now you just look—distinguished," she finished with a small degree of difficulty.

"You look weird," Bobby laughed.

His brother burst out laughing and agreed.

Cass kissed his bald scalp and looked down at him, "I don't care just as long as you're around to grow it back."

The anesthesiologist came in and said he was going to administer something to put him in a state of light consciousness.

"What are you giving him?" Cass asked as the drugs were administered into his I.V. line.

"It's a mixture of morphine and scopolamine. It's like when you're really tired, but not quite drifted off to sleep yet. He'll be really comfortable."

"I hate drugs," AJ complained, tensing as he watched the syringe empty.

The man patted AJ on the shoulder, "You won't hate it in a few seconds. By the way, nice tattoo; all the nurses are talking about it."

A large smile crept onto AJ's face as every muscle seemed to relax and his eyes started to droop.

"See what I mean," the man said as he faced the family.

They stayed with him a few more minutes until the orderlies came in and transferred him onto the gurney that he would be wheeled into the O.R. on.

They said their good-byes, everyone taking a minute to put a kiss on his head, and then he was gone.

A nurse came and showed them to the waiting room and told them to make themselves comfortable, it would be a long procedure.

They hadn't been seated more than thirty minutes when they heard an urgent call go out for Doctor's Ericsson and Phillips to report immediately to the O.R. She watched as personnel dashed down the hallway toward the operating rooms.

"No!" Cass gasped as she rushed into the hall trying to ask someone what was going on. Bobby had his hand on her arm, but he didn't try to stop her. "Please," she said when she saw the nurse who had been in his room earlier, "what's going on? Is this about my husband?"

"I don't know for certain. I know there was an emergency in one of the operating rooms," she paused looking down at Cass's stomach. "I'll find out for you. Just please have a seat, and I'll be back as fast as I can get you some information."

Cass turned and realized they were all in the hallway with her.

His mother's eyes were huge, and she appeared to be on the verge of crying as she asked if all the commotion had something to do with her son?

Cass wrapped her arm around her shoulder, feeling the need to be strong and supportive, "Come on. Let's go back in and sit down. They'll let us know something in a little while. It's going to be okay."

Bobby, AJ's dad, and his brother stayed out in the hallway, pacing the floor as they waited for the news. Cass comforted his mother and distracted her with questions about the pregnancy, but the whole time she wondered what could possibly be taking the nurse so long. An hour later she looked up, and the same nurse was ushering the men back into the waiting area.

"Doctor Ericsson said to tell you they did have a problem after they started, but everything is going well right now. Mister Lisowski's vitals are stable and the surgery is continuing as they planned. It's going to be quite a while, but he'll let you know everything that happened as soon as they're finished."

"How much longer?" his mother asked with a tremble to her question.

"Oh, ma'am, it will be at least another eight or nine hours," she said, clearly sympathetic to his mother's anguish.

As far as Cass was concerned, it might have just as well been days instead of hours for the endlessness that dragged it out. Lunchtime passed as Bobby tried to encourage her to eat something, but her stomach was full of butterflies and she knew whatever she put in it wouldn't stay down. He brought her a cup of hot tea from the vending machine which she gratefully sipped as she stared at the immobile clock hands. When five in the afternoon came around, AJ's brother convinced his parents to go with him down to the cafeteria and have something to eat, but Cass was still rooted to her uncomfortable chair.

"Please, Cass," Bobby asked, "if you won't go downstairs, would you at least eat something if I bring it up here?"

"Yeah. Thanks, I really appreciate it. I just can't leave this room yet."

He gave a smile that could only be described as completely compassionate, "I know. They have sandwiches; turkey or roast beef?"

"Turkey, please."

"I'll be right back."

When he returned, he had two cellophane wrapped sandwiches and a container of hot chicken noodle soup. She was grateful for the food because by this point she was starving. He sat with her, and consumed the second sandwich. She ate half of the turkey sandwich and finished off the soup. She knew he had to still be hungry as she offered him the second half.

"No, Cass, you eat it."

"I'm full, honest; the bigger the baby gets the less I can hold."

He accepted the sandwich and started to eat when she suddenly grabbed his free hand.

"Ooh! Feel this," she said as she placed his hand against her stomach.

He looked petrified until he felt the baby kick, "Wow! That is..." he readjusted his hand so he could get better contact, "...so amazing."

She started to smile, then she made an audible swallow as she teared up, "AJ thought it was pretty amazing the first time he felt it, too."

"He's going to be okay, Cass. He's strong, stubborn—and he has you," he said with a light blush.

"Thanks. By the way, that's much better, Mister Rose. You

didn't turn scarlet this time."

He smiled, "I'm working on controlling it."

Twelve hours after the surgery began, an extremely exhausted Doctor Ericsson came into the waiting room.

"What happened?" Cass asked before he could speak.

"Before I tell you what happened, I want you to know he came through the surgery with flying colors. He's in recovery."

Everyone breathed a collective sigh of relief.

"What happened was an amazing piece of timing. The aneurysm ruptured while he was on the table."

"What?!" Cass said, as the sea of voices began asking questions at the same moment.

"Calm down. If he had put this off, even by one more day, it would be all over for him, but he was on the table with the monitors running. The technician couldn't believe it. She said she has never, in all her training, ever watched one rupture. We had him opened up within ten minutes of the bleed. The rest was hours and hours of work, but there shouldn't be any damage from what happened. He scared the crap out of us," he stated rather unprofessionally, but it was obvious he was too tired to care, "but, other than that, it went off like a textbook case."

"When can we see him?" Cass asked.

"He won't be awake until around midnight. I suggest you all get some rest and come back in the morning."

His parents were exhausted, and even though they wanted to stay, Cass gave Bobby the key to the house and asked him to run them home so they could get some sleep.

"Cass, you're worn out," his brother remarked, "why don't you go home with them? I'll stay here and wait for him to wake up."

"You don't know how much I appreciate that, but no matter how tired I am, I have to be here."

He smiled, "I understand. Bobby, I can run them home if you want to stay."

"That would be great," he said, handing over the key.

They moved him into ICU an hour after surgery. Cass and Bobby sat next to his bed in the tiny cubical. His head was swathed in bandages, and his face was terribly swollen and bruised. Tubes, wires, and monitors ran to every seemingly available space on his body. Cass cried as she rested her cheek against his fingers.

"It's going to be a while before he wakes, Cass. Lean back and try to get a little sleep."

She kissed AJ's fingers and then leaned back in the chair. Bobby offered his shoulder; she accepted and closed her eyes.

It was one in the morning when she felt someone gently stroking her cheek. She and Bobby had fallen asleep propped up against each other in the chairs. Her eyes opened to a beautiful site: AJ was staring at her. He had awakened and reached out to touch her face.

She sat up quickly, which in turn woke Bobby. She reached out, gripping AJ's hand, kissing it and weeping.

"Hey, baby," she whispered, "you made it. How are you feeling?"

"As soon as this Mack truck gets out of my head, I'll let you know but damn it's wonderful to see you."

"Hey, buddy," Bobby said, reaching out and squeezing his forearm.

"Sorry," AJ whispered.

"For what?" Bobby asked with a puzzled expression.

"For making it. I guess we'll just have to find you another beautiful woman; I couldn't give her up."

Bobby laughed, "That's fine, having a best friend with a hot wife is okay, too."

AJ tried a chuckle, but it apparently was painful.

"You have a really adorable ICU nurse," Cass told AJ, "maybe we can hook him up with her, huh?"

Bobby was turning red.

"That sounds pretty good, huh, Bobby? You knock up the nurse then our kids will be old enough to play together in a couple years."

Cass laughed, but she was trying to keep it quiet so she wouldn't disturb the nearby patients. AJ must have been at least a little bit loopy from the drugs because he never would have said anything like that to Bobby had he been completely coherent.

"What time is it?" AJ asked looking around.

"One in the morning," she replied. "You're in ICU."

"Where are my folks? They aren't still here at the hospital, are they?"

"No, baby, they're at the house, but I know they'll be here as soon as it's daylight. You scared us all."

"What'd I do?"

She went on to explain how his aneurysm finally ruptured, on its own, when he was laying on the operating table getting the vein removed from his leg.

"We heard them put out the emergency call for your doctors, and people were running toward the O.R. Yeah, it was scary."

"I'm really glad you had everyone talk me out of waiting nine months."

She was about to agree when his nurse pulled back the curtain and stared at him. "Well, Mister Lisowski, you decided to wake up. Now we get to bug you for a while." And she wasn't kidding. It was a parade of people for the next hour. They checked vitals, poked, prodded, and talked with him to the point where Cass could tell he was getting upset.

"I don't care," he finally snapped to a question one of the nurses asked him, "I just want something for this headache and a little piece and quiet!"

The nurse laughed, "Actually, you did really well. Most people who have been through what you have would have told us to leave a long time ago." She turned to Cass. "His responses and vitals are excellent. I'm going to get him something for the pain, and hopefully he'll be able to get some rest until the doctor comes in to see him around seven."

Cass held his hand until the medication took effect and he drifted off to sleep. She was stiff and uncomfortable from the chair, but she was too exhausted to get up and stretch her legs. Bobby turned her chair to give her more leg room then turned his chair, so she could put her feet up on his legs. Her ankles were slightly swollen from her cramped condition, but the new arrangement was infinitely more comfortable as she closed her eyes, gave a tired yawn, and went to sleep.

Doctor Ericsson made it in early, but it worked well with the timing of AJ waking. He said the headache was lessening to a bearable level. The doctor said a headache was to be expected. He would, most likely, still be plagued by headaches in the coming months. But, to encourage AJ, he told him they would grow weaker and weaker until they faded out completely.

"I don't normally move someone to a regular room quite this quickly, but you're doing well and I think it would be a little more comfortable for your wife. I'm still going to have the nurses keep you on a one hour schedule. I know it's going to be annoying for a while to be checked on so frequently, but it's necessary."

He raised AJ's bed up so he could check the small shunt that had been placed to remove any buildup of fluid on his brain. Cass watched as the doctor peeled back a section of bandage so he could inspect the incision and drain. It had been weeks since she felt nauseous, but it hit her instantly when she saw the bruised and stitched skin with the small protrusion. She excused herself to the bathroom without indicating how she was feeling. It took her a little while to get herself together, and when she opened the door, Bobby was standing there.

"Are you feeling okay? AJ and I both noticed you turned white."

"I'm okay; it's just hard to see what they had to do to him."

"True, Cass, but it's the result that matters."

She smiled and nodded.

AJ was in a comfortable private room by the time his family arrived. His parents, who had been steady through the entire procedure, broke down when they saw him. Their relief overwhelmed them the moment they opened his door and he was sitting up and greeted them. It took his mother a good ten minutes before she could stop crying long enough to speak to him without choking up. His dad had to keep wiping at his cheeks as he listened to everything the doctor told them regarding his progress. They talked Cass into leaving and going home for a hot shower while they stayed with him. Bobby drove her home, but when she emerged after her shower, she carried a satchel.

"What is that for?"

"This is the last time I'm coming back here until they release him."

"Cass, he will have a fit if you do that."

"I don't care. The next couple days are critical to his recovery, and I'm not leaving his side again."

Over the next three days, he continued to improve. He said his headache had reduced to a dull throb and, with its reduction, he became more like himself with each passing day. He laughed and smiled frequently while he and Cass planned what they would do over the next several months as they readied for the arrival of Aimee Jewel. Bobby had been prepared to be a heavy-lifting nursemaid if AJ suffered any neurological damage, but every test revealed he had full function of his appendages. Doctor Ericsson scolded him saying that doing well was *not* license to overdo things;

especially when AJ started asking when he would be able to go back to surfing.

"Six months of rest, and then, and only then, can you start *slowly* reintroducing moderate physical exertion. If you're lucky by that time, I'll give you the approval to lift the weight of your newborn daughter."

"Doc," he laughed, "I'm holding that baby, I don't care if you give me the approval or not."

The doctor smiled; he'd been teasing.

Five days after the surgery, he was told they would release him to go home. He would have an appointment back here in a week, after that the doctor would lengthen them by an extra week each time, so he would have another fourteen days after the first, then twenty-one days, twenty-eight days, etc. When he reached the forty-eight day space between appointments, he would go to six months and then one year. After that, he would be free from ever returning to St. Paul.

"Unless you just miss us," Doctor Ericsson joked.

His brother left two days after the surgery, but his parents remained to get the house ready for his return. Cass stayed at the hospital day and night, and she was ready to get out of that environment. AJ was dressed in jeans and a button-up the front shirt because he still couldn't pull a tee-shirt over his bandages. The paperwork took an exceptionally long time. AJ fell asleep propped up in his bed while Cass dozed. She was sitting on a stool next to the bed with her head resting on his lap. Bobby left to gas up the car and then bring it around to the proper door.

Cass woke to the feeling of AJ's fingers softly moving through her hair. She opened her eyes and smiled up at him.

"Something beautiful," he simply stated.

"What's that, honey?"

"I thought they were going to let me out today?"

"They are. The paperwork just took a while, but it's done. Bobby went to get the car," she yawned as she raised her head.

"Why is it so dark? I must have slept a long time. It must be nine or ten at night."

Cass couldn't figure out what he was talking about; sunlight streamed in through the window, "No, it's not even noon."

He turned his face slowly toward the window, his head wobbling slightly, his eyes not following in a unified movement, "Is it going to storm outside? It's so black."

Cass's heart began to race as she reached for his hand, "AJ, are you okay, baby?"

When he turned to look at her, the ensuing panic tripled. His eyes were dilating quick and uneven. She heard Bobby's voice as he came through the doorway, but she couldn't look away from AJ.

Suddenly, he gripped her hand, hard. "I love you," he gasped with a rapid breath and then screamed out in pain as his eyes closed extremely tightly.

"AJ!! AJ!!"

Bobby grabbed the call button and mashed it down and then made a mad dash out into the hallway, yelling for help.

The room filled with hospital staff. They were trying to move Cass out of the way as the emergency call went over the loud speaker for his doctors. She was crying and begging him to keep listening to her voice and to hold on. She felt strong muscled arms wrap around her from behind, pulling her back; AJ's hand went limp, slipping from her grasp as the personnel crowded over him. She flailed and screamed, fighting against the person holding her back. Eventually, she listened to the sound of the voice, realizing it was Bobby. He was pleading over and over for her to stop struggling.

Doctor Phillips ran in, ordering them to get him to surgery immediately. He didn't even pause to look at them as he helped push the gurney out of the room. A nurse spoke to her, trying to calm her, but Cass didn't hear a word she said. All she knew was they wheeled her heart out of the room when they took him away.

Bobby led her to the same waiting room they had been in days ago. He stepped out to get a good cell signal, so he could call AJ's parents and tell them they needed to get to the hospital right away.

She shivered uncontrollably, clutching her stomach, and rocking back and forth. She'd never felt so utterly alone in her entire life. She closed her eyes and began to pray. Moments later, she felt Bobby's warm arm over her shoulders, and the sound of prayers rising from his lips. They prayed until his parents arrived, and then they all prayed together.

This wouldn't be as long as the first surgery. Within an hour-and-a-half, Doctor Ericsson entered the waiting room. Cass's heart shattered when she looked at the tears on his face.

"I'm so sorry," he began.

"Please, no," his mother wailed.

"He's going to be okay," Cass stated, looking at the doctor's face, refusing to believe what he was trying to say. "He was ready to come home. You said he was doing so wonderful. He can't be. Please, tell me there is some hope," she begged.

"Cass, I'm sorry. I know how much you loved him; how much all of you loved him, but we—we can't pull him out of it."

She sobbed harder. This wasn't real. This wasn't happening. AJ should have been home by now. They had plans for their lives, for the baby, and the future. "What..." was all she got out before she was choked and racked by grief.

"What happened?" Bobby finished for her, his voice off-pitch and strained, tears openly flowing down his cheeks.

"As close as we can tell, he suffered a vasospasm so severe it literally ripped the graph between the old and the new veins on both ends. When the cerebral veins lost that much pressure, there was no way for him to come out of the spasm."

"He's dead?" his father finally cried out.

"He's on life support, but—"

"But what?" Cass managed.

The doctor reached out and rested his hand on her shoulder as he took in a ragged breath, "His brain stem was destroyed from the damage." He paused and wiped his cheeks, "He can't function without a respirator keeping him alive. Physically, he's still with us, but his mind is gone; he's brain dead."

Everything stopped. The world as she knew it, no longer existed. There was a massive, gaping hole inside her chest that grew larger every passing second after what he told them sank inside her. She was certain she couldn't live through this; life had no meaning at all.

And then she felt it.

The baby was kicking and pushing stronger than ever before, and she knew AJ was sending her a beautiful reminder as to why she had to keep breathing, she had to keep living, and she had to keep going. Part of him was still with her, and he hadn't left her alone.

Everyone huddled and held each other as the grief flowed like a river. The doctor, several of his nurses and orderlies, all joined the family as they expressed their sorrow over the loss of such a remarkable man.

"He wanted to be a donor," Cass snuffled, unable to breathe out her nose, "is it too late for that?"

"No," the doctor answered, "we're going to let you all go in and see him, and tell him goodbye. The transplant teams have been notified and are on standby. You're his wife, and we all knew his wishes on this subject, but you have to give the okay."

Cass nodded, a fresh flood of tears hitting her, "He'll want to help as many people as possible. That's just the kind of person he is."

Fifteen minutes later, the family was ushered in by his side. The steady pulse of the machinery around him reminded them all there was no fight left in him; he was already home, safe, and watching over them.

They each took a turn at his side saying farewell; Cassandra was last. She kissed the back of his hand and gently rubbed the tattoo on his arm. She leaned over and pressed her lips to his, whispering how much she would always love him, how she would raise his daughter to know what kind of an incredible person her father had been, and she thanked him for teaching her how to trust once again. Reluctantly, she pulled away and said she was ready to go home.

Doctor Ericsson personally showed up at the house the next morning to tell her that, before dawn, seven desperate people received gifts of life in the night. He requested to be a total donor, so more people would be helped, but those who were critical and in deepest need had been saved through AJ's generosity.

His parents, after Cass opened the envelope he'd given her with his funeral wishes, were all ready making the arrangements. His body would be flown back to his hometown in Virginia.

Although he found salvation in a small, Baptist church years earlier, his family was Catholic and he requested, for his mother's sake, his service be held in a Catholic church of her choosing. St. Aloysius Church was in Washington, D.C., but just a few miles from the Virginia line and his parents' home. There would be no interment. He asked to be cremated with half his ashes going to his parents and half to Cass.

CHAPTER TWENTY-TWO

She became strangely numb as the days to his funeral ticked by. She and Bobby were invited to stay with his family. Everything she did was methodical, mechanical, and empty as if her heart died when his stopped beating. Her father flew up to Virginia to be with her, he was sober and somber, but was the only one from her family. Her other half-siblings sent flowers, but stayed away. The day before the service, she got an incredible surprise. Machi flew in from Africa with a gift.

It was a gift from AJ.

"He was very worried about the surgery," Machi said, his ebony orbs filling with tears as he spoke. "When he called me and told me he was bringing you with him to Africa, he said he wanted me to spend most of my time shooting video of the two of you, so you would have memories to keep of your time together. He helped me with the final cut, and he added pictures of himself from hundreds of old stories he had worked on. It is a most beautiful piece of film, and he wanted you to have it if—if he did not make it."

Although she wanted everyone to watch it, she asked she be granted some private time to see it alone before she shared.

She sat in the bedroom with the shades drawn as the DVD began to play. The first few seconds were of Jeffrey's Bay and the breath-taking ocean. And then, just like a dream, he was there in front of her smiling.

"Cass, I'm going to tell you the truth: I hope you never see this video. But, if you're watching me right now, then I've left you, and I'm so sorry there wasn't more time for us to be together. You've been the ultimate high in my life and I can't imagine being separated from you. But I don't want you crying and hurting, I love you too much for that, so here are some shots of us together, plus some before you knew me—I put a few special pics at the end. I love you, Cass—no matter how far apart we are, I'll always be as close as your next heartbeat."

Music began to play when the video started. The song in the background was *Where Ever You Will Go* by The Calling. He had never mentioned it to her, but the words couldn't have been more beautiful than if he had written them himself. The first video was AJ surfing the barrel as she held the camera and talked to Machi in the background, then video of her and AJ balancing on her surfboard on the sand after he sent away the surf pro, a video of them enjoying themselves at The Potter's Place, and the piece Machi filmed inside of the condo when AJ had shown him around. AJ motioned Machi into the bathroom, quietly talking to the camera as he told him to get a good shot of the shower. "Cass will know why," he said with a wink.

The music changed, and the song *Your Guardian Angel* began to play. It was followed by several other short video clips and then a host of images of AJ from six years ago, up to the present. She was stunned as she looked at pictures of him, shirtless and handsome without his gorgeous tattoo. But the final images made her heart yearn deeper for the man who was missing from her life: it was all the shots he'd taken at Kingdom Hill—including one he swore he erased.

He did a voice-over for the final pic: "Cass, whatever you do, don't blame yourself. I didn't have a chance for life before I met you. You didn't send me to Heaven—*you were Heaven*—I love you."

It was the first picture he'd ever taken of her—the shot of her standing on the top of a hill in Scotland, looking to the south with an expression that showed she was deep in thought as she wondered what was about to change in her world.

She had to smile; this wasn't a moment for tears. He was with her, just as close as he said he would be, and now she understood he always would be. She asked Machi if he could make a loop of the video for the funeral, minus the portion where he spoke directly to her; that part she would keep for herself.

The church overflowed with those who came to pay their last respects to him. She met his boss from the magazine, several producers, and other writers, as well as a plethora of staffers. And although his actual immediate family was small, he had a great number of relatives, most of which came from the Philadelphia area, and several from the UK who wanted a chance to comfort his parents and to say farewell. Her dad was uncomfortable in the throng of strangers, but he wasn't running away to find a can of beer, which was one of the sweetest expressions of sorrow over her loss he could have offered.

AJ requested a closed casket, with several favorite pictures displayed on top. There were a few childhood pictures, pictures of him and Bobby when they were twelve, seventeen, and another shot of the two of them, hard-muscled and lean on a beach with surfboards. Bobby told her they were roughly twenty-four in the shot—it had been right after he learned about his aneurysm. There were two other photos; a candlelight shot of her and AJ looking into each other's eyes the night they went to the Potter's Place, and a shot of the two of them right after they married, and were honeymooning on Little Palm Island.

He was cremated that afternoon, and the next day the funeral home presented the family with the ashes, evenly divided into two containers. She thanked his parents for their hospitality but said she needed to return home to Texas. She made plans with his parents for them to come down and stay with her for a little while when their granddaughter was born. And then she was ready to go.

Bobby had been quiet and kept to himself through the events, but Cass made it a point to stay by his side even though he didn't seem to notice her at times. Her heart broke over his pain. They had truly been like brothers, and it was even more apparent how deeply it grieved Bobby to lose someone he loved with a connection that went beyond friendship.

He had been there for AJ when his heart was in the deepest and darkest moments of his life, and she knew AJ would want her to be there for him. It wasn't an attempt to find something beyond the friendship they developed for each other. She knew her heart wasn't ready for anyone to take AJ's place, but she could be a friend, a friend who cares at all times, a friend who understands, a friend who helps heal a wounded spirit.

"You know I want you to come back to Texas with me," she said as she helped him pack his belongings.

He looked so dejected and empty. She knew the feeling only too well, but it had been AJ himself with his beautiful video who pulled her out of that pit of despair.

He shook his head no, "I was going to go online in a little while and book my flight back to Northampton."

"Why? You said yourself that your boss didn't expect you back anytime soon. Your belongings are already at your mom's house, and the flat is gone. Please, Bobby," she said, reaching out and resting her hand over the back of his, "I want you to see my company. AJ wanted you to see it, too. Fly back with me and my dad. Stay with me for a week or two so we can talk."

His eyes watered as he continued to place his clothes into the suitcase, "I—I don't know, Cass. You're doing well, and you don't need me bringing you down."

"Bobby, I do need you. I have some plans to make and you're a big part of those plans. I want to go to Texas, but I have to go back to the UK, and I'll need your help."

"For what?" he said, wiping his cheeks.

She pulled out the last note AJ had written to her and tried to put it in his hand.

"I can't, Cass," he said when he realized the personal nature, "that was for you, not me."

"He wrote you a note, too. Did he tell you he wanted you to help me put some of his ashes inside Kingdom Hill?"

A genuine look of surprise crossed his face, "He just told me he wanted me to watch over you and the baby, if you'd let me, but to be careful and not to push it."

His face grew red, and she knew it wasn't simple embarrassment, this was much more complex.

"Then you have to read at least the last part of my letter because you're in it. And he's right; I shouldn't try to do it alone."

With trembling hands he took the folded bottom half of the second page and read AJ's request to Cass. He did indeed want her to place some of his remains at the site where he said God answered his most needful prayer.

"I'll do it by myself if it makes you uncomfortable to be with me," her words weren't meant to be hurtful, just truthful.

He looked up at her and offered a tender smile, "Being around you doesn't make me uncomfortable, quite the opposite, actually. And—and, I'm feeling—well, guilty, I guess one could say."

"Over what? Being a good friend?"

"I started out wanting him to help me get close to you, and to be honest, I was upset with him when he told me he was falling for you. How," he said, choking back the tears, "could I have been jealous because he fell in love?" he shook his head and stopped, too emotional to continue.

"I'm flying out in two hours and I still need a good friend. Think it over, but it's okay if you decide to go home."

When her dad was putting their bags in the trunk of their rental car, Bobby came up beside her carrying his, "Have room in the boot for a friend's bags?"

She smiled.

Once in Texas, not only was he impressed with Cass's operation, but realized her dad could use a hand. Her father was good at motivating a team; Bobby was good at the business end of business. He accepted her offer of employment, but absolutely refused staying at the cabin, even though she told him there was an apartment over her hanger. They decided, together, that with Cass's expanding figure, she should wait to place his ashes until after the baby was born.

In her eighth month, she signed up for Lamaze classes. When she asked him to be her coach, she watched him turn a shade of red she hadn't seen since she came parading out of the motel bathroom in Moffat in a bath towel.

"Are you absolutely positive you want *me* to be your coach?"

"Would you like to be one of the first people to see AJ's daughter come into this world?"

The redness faded as he smiled, "More than anything."

But she had serious doubts about whether he'd make it through labor without passing out. He turned ghost-white as the teacher made sure all the male coaches knew *exactly* what to expect in the delivery room.

She didn't know why she worried. When the time came, and they found themselves in the hospital, with all modesty shot completely to hell, he was the most encouraging and supportive coach in the maternity ward.

March twenty-seventh, at two-seventeen in the morning, Aimee Jewel entered the world.

Once she had been cleaned and wrapped in a warm blanket, they placed her in Cass's arms as Bobby reached and put his finger in her tiny grasp. "She looks just like AJ," he whispered, trying to hold his emotions in check.

Cass sobbed her eyes out as she nodded in agreement, "She's the most beautiful thing I've ever seen."

When they ushered in all the proud grandparents, everyone agreed she did indeed look exactly like her daddy.

His parents stayed for two weeks before returning to Virginia, but Cass told them she would visit often, so they could watch their grandchild grow. And, when little Miss AJ reached six months old, she would get to spend a few days with her grandparents while Cass and Bobby took some of AJ's ashes to a special place.

EPILOGUE

The summer sun filtered down through the swaying trees as Cassandra watched AJ playing. She tiptoed around the tree trunks, trying her best to keep from giggling. At six years old, she was stunningly beautiful. Her blond hair was French braided on either side of her head, ending in two pony tails just below her ears. Her eye color and her hair were the only things that were Cass's, everything else belonged to the man Cass missed every day. Suddenly, a small reddish haired little boy came around one of the trunks and yelled, "Boo!"

The chase was on as AJ ran after the screaming toddler.

Cass leaned against Bobby's shoulder as she watched the children. She didn't say anything, but she had to wipe away an escaped tear. He kissed the side of her head, whispering in her ear for her to tell him what was wrong.

"Nothing is wrong," she said, finding her smile, "I was just thinking about when we were in the hospital right after AJ woke from surgery, and he was teasing you about getting his nurse pregnant. He said in a few years our kids would be old enough to play together. I had no idea how prophetic his statement would become."

Suddenly, the three year-old tumbled over a tree root and began to cry.

"I have it," Bobby started to say when they watched AJ reach down and lift her little brother up and brush him off.

"Are you okay?" came her sweet, slightly accented voice.

Bobby had been with her since she learned to talk, and some of his English accent rubbed off and blended with her Texas tone, giving her voice a unique, almost musical quality. "Come on," she continued, taking his hand, "we'll get a band aid from Mummy and Papa." She knew Bobby wasn't her true father, but he was the father who loved and cared about her before she was brought into this world. When she referred to AJ senior, she spoke of him as her daddy; and she spoke of him often. She would tell people she was lucky because she had two fathers, one who loved and watched over her here, and one who loved and watched over her from Heaven.

"Did you get a boo-boo?" Cass asked as she reached down and pulled Robert Adam onto her lap. She kissed his scraped elbow and wiped his teary cheeks.

"I'm leaking," he stated seriously as he looked at a small bloody spot on his knee.

Everyone laughed. AJ, of course, didn't have the same deep laugh as her father, but the cadence was identical as it seemed to roll up from somewhere down inside her and then bubble over.

"Do you want me to get something to stop the leak?" Bobby asked him. "You know we have to clean it up first."

His face puckered into a grimace. "No, Papa, don't clean it," he whined, "It'll burn."

"I promise it won't burn. Come with me inside and I'll fix it."

He looked up at Cass with his big blue eyes, "Can't kisses fix it?"

Cass gave him a gentle smile and a hug, "Kisses make it feel better. Papa's going to help it heal so it can get better."

He sighed as he slid from her lap and took his father's hand, toddling away he muttered, "I bet it's gonna burn."

Cass and AJ looked at each other and giggled quietly.

"Come here, pretty girl," Cass said, holding her arms open. She pulled the sun-warmed body against her own and kissed her temple. "Are you excited?" Cass whispered in her ear.

AJ nodded, "I like Scotland. Will we be back when school starts?"

"Oh, yes. You aren't going to miss first grade. Mrs. Beckley would be horribly disappointed if you weren't in her class."

AJ giggled, again. Mrs. Beckley had been her kindergarten teacher, and then decided to move up to first grade. AJ was thrilled o know she would have the same teacher. "Is the house finished?"

Cass nodded, "Every part, right down to a playhouse for you and your brother."

"Can we get some sheep?"

"I don't know. We'll have to see if Grandma Rose wants to take care of them. But, she told me on the phone she's planted a big garden, just like in your Peter Cottontail book."

"Yay!" she said, clapping her little hands together, "I hope we'll have bunnies just like in the story. I'm going to go tell Bobby." She kissed her mother's cheek, then slipped off Cass's lap and dashed into the house.

Cass closed her eyes and let the Texas sun beat down and saturate every pore. She had one week to finish up things here in the States before they flew to the UK. They started the plans for the house last year, and construction completed eight months later. They didn't want the house to be empty nine months out of the year, so when Bobby's mother recently sold her place in Northampton, she was willing and excited to accept their offer to move into their guest cottage.

This would be the first full summer they would spend at Kingdom Hill. It seemed like time was finally settling down in their lives, allowing them the opportunity to enjoy their families. After she lost AJ, Bobby stayed with her until Aimee Jewel was born and then, two months later he was gone. He said it was time to go back to his life and let her move forward with hers.

She was crushed at first. She had become dependent on him being there to confide in, someone to talk to when the ache of what she lost hit her, someone who stepped into her business and took all the pressure off of her, but then she realized she hadn't given him any reason to think she'd ever want to be anything more than his friend. He reminded her before he left that he would always be her friend and if she ever needed him, he'd return before a day could go by.

When her daughter was six months old, she left her with her grandparents in Virginia and met him in the UK. Together, they went to Kingdom Hill and scattered some of AJ's remains above and inside the hill. But it was still only good friendship between them; by this point she was certain she would never feel for another man what she felt for AJ. She flew home with the ache that hadn't eased since she lost the love of her life. She resigned herself to the fact that she would not be able to fulfill AJ's request to not be lonely.

She hadn't been home in Texas a month when her dad suffered a stroke. She had just put her fragile world back together, and now it was falling apart, again. She sat at his bedside, holding his hand, and praying for a miracle when she felt a warm and familiar touch. She didn't know who called him, or how he found out, she was just glad he was there for her and the baby. Bobby took over running her business once again.

Her father couldn't speak, but he would look at her and squeeze her hand in response to things she would ask him. He couldn't swallow which left a feeding tube as the only way to get nutrition in him. Some medical professionals gave her hope for his recovery, others weren't sure. She had to make the tough decision to place him in a nursing home and wait to see if he would improve. The days turned into weeks, and the weeks into a month, and then a month into two. He was stable, but he would never return to a normal life.

Then one evening, she asked Bobby to come out to the cabin, so she would have someone to talk to, but instead she simply broke down and fell into his embrace. She was crying in his arms, apologizing for ruining his life when she felt his fingers under her chin, tipping her eyes up to meet his—and then he said the most beautiful words.

"You didn't ruin it. I tried to step away because it was what I thought you wanted, but I'm not happy unless I'm around you. I love you, Cass."

And, for the first time, he brought his lips to hers. The kiss was sweet, tender, emotional, and straight from his heart. She found herself answering his kiss as the loneliness began to slip away. The hunger for him had been there for quite some time, she had simply been refusing to acknowledge it. AJ wanted her to be happy and loved, but she was so stubborn that she almost allowed the one person both of them trusted to slip through her fingers. For the second time in her life, she would fall in love.

"What is that big smile for?" came Bobby's voice.

She opened her eyes, squinting in the sunshine, "I was just remembering the first time you kissed me."

"Really?" he said, seating himself beside her on the lounger. He kissed her with obvious need, "The kids are playing tea party in AJ's room, and they're trying to get Charlie in a little dress. You know ıow long that can last. How about we rediscover the first time we id something else?"

"I miss the fact that you don't blush anymore."

"Cass, we need to make love with the lights turned up; you still ıke me blush."

She laughed as he offered her his hands, and pulled her up nto her feet. They hadn't traveled any farther than the bottom of he staircase when the doorbell rang.

"It can't be," she said, noticing the brown uniform through the door glass.

Bobby reached the door before she did, and opened it. The UPS man was standing there with a package, "Mrs. Rose? I need to get a signature."

Cass noticed the address label. This was something she had been hoping would arrive before they went on their trip. "Thank you," she said, signing and returning his board. She took the package and went to the kitchen counter and began opening it.

"Is that what I think it is?" Bobby asked.

She didn't answer; the box fell away and a hardcover novel was removed. There had been a million reasons why she hadn't finished it after AJ passed away: their daughter's birth, being a new mom, her father's illness, marrying Bobby, and then the birth of their son. But after Bobby Junior was born, she sat down and finished writing what had been too emotionally difficult before.

She had no writing credits, which would have made it challenging to get it published, but she didn't want any credit. She contacted AJ's former boss at National Geographic and told him AJ left more than family members and friends behind to remember him by; he'd left something very special. She was put in touch with an agent, who contacted a publisher, and the long process of publishing a book began. The publisher wanted it on the market by the time all the hot summer reads hit the shelves. She didn't think they'd make it in time.

She turned it over and looked at the picture of the handsome man staring back at her, and she felt his presence.

"You know he would have wanted you to take credit for writing part of it," Bobby reminded her, placing a kiss on the back of her neck and wrapping her in his arms.

"No, he was the writer and he deserved this. And," she said still holding it in her hands, "all the proceeds will go into an account for

Aimee."

"So are you going to have this first copy framed on the wall, or—"

"No. The publisher is sending me several copies to share, but told her I wanted the very first one off the press for something special."

"What are you going to do with it?"

"I'm going to wrap it up and place it inside the hill with all the scrolls. I think he'll like that," she said, her hand brushing over his image. She paused for a breath as her emotions caught midway in her throat.

"Cass, are you really happy being with me, or is it because he told you he wanted us to be together?"

She still held the book in her hand as she turned to look at him. "He may have paved the way, but my heart wasn't given to you by Adam. You earned what I feel for you the same way he did, don't ever doubt that. I'm happy with you because *I* love *you*—there isn't any other reason."

He cupped her face in his hands kissed and her lips tenderly, several times, "Open it," he whispered.

She opened the cover and turned to where the story began. Her hands were trembling because there was no stopping it now; it was already on its way to store shelves.

It was a place that didn't seem to fit into the surrounding landscape. There is a natural lay to land; certain features are expected to fall into place when you've studied it all of your life.

She closed it and laid it down gently on the countertop. She didn't have to go on; she knew it like she knew the rhythm of her own heart.

The story of an ancient kingdom destroyed by a woman who allowed her childhood nightmare to become her reason to lead a twisted life, and of a present-day woman who found that very kingdom and lived a similar marred life, would be revealed to the world. But the difference was that Emiline destroyed the man who, at one point, loved her so deeply he would have done anything to help her beyond her disfigured inner spirit. Cassandra chose to change, trusting the one who fought to help her beyond the distortion to discover the transforming power of love. One found her ending. The other found her beginning. Both happened in a breathtaking place called Kingdom Hill.

ABOUT THE AUTHOR

Lindsay is a Florida native and lives with her husband and two daughters in a quiet log cabin on the central west coast. Her son is currently serving in the United States Army. She is a network administrator for a local high school.

Novels: Heart of the Diamond
Untouchable (book I)
Unforgivable (book II)
Untraceable (book III)
Kingdom Hill
Erotic Novelette: The Substitute

Lindsay enjoys hearing from fans. You can contact her at: Delagair@gmail.com

You can also find her under Lindsay Delagair on Twitter and Facebook.

Made in the USA
Columbia, SC
05 September 2022

66668631R00205